MOONLIT SHADOWS
TAKEN

MOONLIT SHADOWS
TAKEN

SHAWNA GAUTIER

For my husband, Bobby.
I couldn't have done this without you.

For my children, Matthew, Alex, and Kayla.
Never give up on your dreams.

1

SAMANTHA DAVIS stared out her bedroom window into the depths of the moonlit forest bordering her backyard, unsettled by its eerie silence. In the two weeks since she and her mother had moved to Wolf Hill, not one bird had chirped, not one squirrel had chattered, nor had one deer grazed in the tall patches of grass. Aside from the overabundance of foliage, life did not seem to exist here.

She eyed the mighty pines towering high above her home. Their thick branches fanned out like arms with claws, ready to strike at any moment as they cast their sinister shadows across her bedroom walls. She felt as if something lurked within them and watched her as she slept.

Exhausted, she let out a weary yawn and decided to climb into bed, but a sudden rustling in the thicket of blackberries at the edge of the yard caught her attention. A chill ran down her spine. Ignoring her body's warning, she leaned forward to get a better glimpse, squinting through the darkness.

The bush moved again. Samantha held her breath, waiting and watching. Suddenly, an enormous wolf leapt from the brush. Its eyes were the color of blood, and its thick fur was outlined in silver by the moonlight. In one swift move, it darted into the middle of her backyard. Then, it sailed through the air and into her open bedroom window, knocking her to the floor.

Samantha screamed as the deadly beast hovered over her, its fangs mere inches from her face.

The wolf narrowed its sinister eyes, and a vicious growl tore from its throat.

"Nooo!" Samantha sat up in her bed, sticky with sweat, her long hair sprawled about her face. With a quick hand, she brushed her hair aside and scanned her room for any signs of the wolf. Sunshine poured through the window. Aside from her pounding heart, all was quiet. She let out a sigh of relief.

"Get a hold of yourself, Samantha. It was just another nightmare," she whispered. Ever since she'd moved to this creepy town, she'd suffered recurring dreams of being attacked by wolves. Most of the time, she would awaken before the wolf could rip her to shreds. But twice now, the wolf had gotten her, sinking its fangs into her left shoulder with a bone-crushing pain and jolting her awake.

Plopping back onto her pillow, she wished she'd never moved away from her dad's house in California. She felt safer there. More secure. The only animals she ever had to worry about there were the seagulls flying overhead.

She glanced at the alarm clock on the nightstand. It was nearly eleven o'clock. She'd slept away half the morning again—thanks to restless nights filled with nightmares. With a heavy sigh, she pushed back the security of her comforter and climbed out of bed to get ready for the day.

She quickly showered and dressed in a short-sleeve top, her favorite faded blue jeans, and hiking boots. After applying light eye makeup in natural shades of brown to match her hair and eyes, she jogged down the stairs and into the kitchen. She snatched an apple from the bowl on the counter and went outside to wait for Jason— her neighbor across the road.

Samantha perched on the bottom step of the front porch and took a bite of her apple, welcoming the sun's warmth on her bare arms as it shielded her from the cool morning breeze.

She was excited to finally get out of the house this morning, which surprised her after being nothing but a recluse since she'd moved to town. The culture shock of the move had left her moping about the house for the last two weeks.

Wearing a smile, she crossed one stretched leg over the other and inhaled in a deep breath of fresh air, feeling better than she had in a very long time.

Samantha considered today's date a casual encounter—nothing to do with intimacy. Just two neighbors getting to know each other and possibly becoming friends. She hoped Jason saw it the same way.

It had been a while since she'd been out with friends. Not since her senior year in high school. Since then, she'd realized how shallow friends could be. How easily they could turn their backs on you when your life was no longer as perfect as theirs. But, after spending the last year alone, she desperately needed one friend in her life.

Despite having no friends there, she missed her beachfront home in California. If she concentrated hard enough, she could almost feel the grains of damp sand squish between her toes, smell the freshness of the salty air, and hear the gulls squawking above the ocean waves crashing on the beach.

She missed her grandpa too. It was hard to imagine Harry Meyers being ill. She and her mom had moved up to Oregon to live with him, but he had been admitted into the hospital before they'd arrived.

He had always been a strong man—so healthy he didn't look a day over sixty. But he was eighty-something now. His life was nearly over. And soon, he'd be nothing but a memory.

Samantha frowned. *I wonder why Mom won't let me visit him in the hospital. Grandpa can't be that sick, can he?*

With a heavy sigh, she shook her head and pushed the painful thought aside. *Come on, Samantha, don't get all emotional now. Jason will be here any minute.*

She looked to her left, at the wall of towering pines bordering the side yard. Living so close to the forest gave her the creeps, especially since her home was the last one on a dead-end.

Samantha chomped on her apple again and glanced across the

road, hoping to see Jason. There was still no sign of him.

"Where are you?" she whispered, wondering how far back his driveway went. His house was hidden somewhere behind the thick wall of trees lining the whole opposite side of the road.

She let out a heavy breath and looked over her right shoulder. There was no sign of life at the neighboring house either—the only other house along the road, aside from hers and Jason's. It sat about a hundred feet away from her house, with no fence or border to show where the patchy grass of her grandpa's yard turned into the patchy grass of their yard. A few pine trees and a large oak were scattered about their front yard though—something her yard lacked to shield the house from the summer heat. On the other side of the neighbors' single-story home, a grove of pines hid the main road.

Samantha sank her teeth into the apple one last time before tossing the gnawed core into the empty moving box sitting by the front door. She hoped the neighbors next door would be as friendly as Jason. Sighing, she closed her eyes and pointed her nose toward the sky, basking in the sunshine.

"Beautiful day, isn't it, Samantha?" A deep voice broke the silence.

She flung open her eyes, startled to see Jason staring down at her. She was rattled by his being able to creep up so swiftly without her being aware of him.

"Jason, you scared me." She placed a shaky hand on her chest and exhaled.

He let out a light chuckle, showing off his charming grin. At least six feet tall, he towered over her, creating a large shadow angled perfectly to shield the sun from her eyes. His dark blond hair shone brightly in the sunlight.

"Sorry, didn't mean to scare you."

Samantha felt silly for being afraid. She stood on the bottom step to greet him at eye level. "It's okay. I don't know why I was scared. I knew you'd be here any minute. And you can just call me Sami. It's what my friends—" she paused at her near slip-up "—I mean, it's what everyone back home called me."

"Sami it is then." He looked down the length of her body. "I see you wore boots and jeans like I suggested."

She glanced down at her new boots. "Yep. Where are we going?"

"Right there." He pointed at where the road stopped—the end of the pavement marked by an old wooden barricade. "There's a trail there. Benefit of living on a dead-end road surrounded by wilderness."

She eyed the tiny break in the trees beyond the crumbling asphalt, wondering if the wolf of her nightmares actually did exist in there. "Is it dangerous?"

Jason furrowed his brow. "It's safe. I go hunting all the time. Unless you're afraid of deer or rabbits, you have nothing to worry about."

She smiled. Still feeling leery about entering the forest that had plagued her nightmares since she'd moved here, she decided to trust the handsome man her grandpa had often praised. "Are we going far? Maybe I should bring some water?"

"Already taken care of." He turned slightly and pointed to the black backpack he wore.

She hadn't noticed the backpack until then, thanks to his forest-green T-shirt. His shirt not only clung to every muscle of his broad chest, but also seemed to make his hazel eyes look like green gems, a distraction she couldn't seem to pull away from.

He eyed the porch under his boots and smiled. "Hey, the porch is gray now. It used to be white like the rest of the house. I hadn't even noticed."

"Yeah, my grandpa painted it recently, I guess."

"So, are you ready?" he asked.

"Sure, but I need to leave a note for my mom in case she gets back before I do."

Jason followed her inside and took a seat at the breakfast bar to the left of the door.

She stood in the kitchen, on the other side of the breakfast bar, and began writing on the notepad left lying there.

"It's been a long time since I was in here last." He grinned and rapped his knuckles on the black granite countertop. "No more faux-wood laminate and mustard yellow cupboards. This place is actually *awesome* now! There used to be a wall here." He pretended to place both palms on an invisible wall over the breakfast bar. "You couldn't even see the kitchen when you walked in the front door. Now, it's all open to the living room."

He gestured with his hand toward the living room, to the right of the front door. "And the wood flooring is *so* much better than the rust-colored shag and olive-green linoleum that used to be in here." He grimaced. "Mustard, olive green, and rust, all crammed into the same space. I swear I felt nauseous every time I was in here." His disgusted look melted into a grin. "But not today."

She giggled and set the pen down on the counter. "Good. I'm glad you don't feel nauseous. I'm sorry my grandparents' house used to make you sick."

He chuckled under his breath.

"And I'm glad I didn't see it."

"Lucky is more like it." His smile disappeared, and he let out an uneasy breath. "I'm sorry about your grandma passing," he said, his tone gentle. "She was almost like a grandma to me at times. She was always so nice." He gulped. "She and your grandpa both."

Sami nodded, trying to keep sadness from taking over. She'd thought about her grandma often over the past year. About the phone calls full of love and laughter, and the fun-filled summer visits at the beach. But no matter how hard she tried, she couldn't shake the haunting guilt of not attending her grandmother's funeral to say good-bye.

Tears brewed, but she managed to keep them in. "Yeah. I really miss her too." She thought of her grandpa's illness. *Mom won't tell me what's wrong with him, but maybe Jason will.* "Umm, I was wondering…do you know what happened to my grandpa?"

"Uhhh…" He shrugged, avoiding her eyes. "I was back east with my parents when he was admitted into the hospital."

"Oh."

"Your mom didn't tell you what was wrong with him?"

"No." She shook her head.

"Sorry."

"It's okay." Not wanting her problems to mar their day together, she smiled. "Are you ready?"

He stood and motioned outside. "After you."

They went outside and headed left, across the side yard toward the forest, along a slightly worn path in the grass that Sami hadn't noticed until now. The path had probably been worn by her grandpa when he'd set out to hunt or hike. She was suddenly eager to explore the same forest her grandpa had always spoken of.

Jason took the lead, and they entered the forest via the trail.

Sami slowed her pace, shocked by the eerie environment.

Evergreens towered above aggressively, uniting like ranks of soldiers, blocking the sunlight and creating dark shadows all around. Fallen logs lay dead and rotting, brought to life only by blankets of moss and burrowing insects, filling the air with the musty stench of damp soil. An overwhelming silence engulfed the air like a thick fog. Fortunately, some of the sun's rays had managed to break through the thick barrier of pine trees to create sporadic patches of serene light, allowing wildflowers to sprout here and there.

It certainly wasn't the bright and cheery forest she'd imagined as a child from her grandpa's stories. The forest of her imagination was airy, filled with wildflowers, butterflies, and birds chirping playfully. There were even squirrels and deer scurrying about. But not here. This forest seemed sinister and void of life.

She knelt in the damp grass to take in the sweet fragrance of a cluster of yellow flowers.

Jason turned around. "Buttercups. They sure brighten the forest, don't they?"

"Sure," Sami replied with an unsure tone, not quite seeing it in the same light he did. She stood and glanced at the surrounding shadows, expecting the wolf of her nightmares to jump out from behind a tree and rip her to shreds. Her eyes met Jason's again, but she smiled to hide her fear.

He winked. "So, how do you like living in Wolf Hill so far?" He continued along the path.

She wanted to lie and tell him everything was great here, but she couldn't. She needed to be reassured her life wasn't in danger. "Well, the forest is beautiful…but it's also a little creepy." She wrinkled her nose, dreading his reaction.

"Creepy?" He let out a disbelieving laugh and spun around but extinguished his grin as soon as his eyes met hers. "Don't worry. I know these woods like the back of my hand. We won't get lost or anything. I won't let anything happen to you. Okay?"

Her only options at this point were to trust him or turn around and run home without looking back. Not wanting to ruin her chances of having at least one friend in Wolf Hill, she chose the option that wouldn't make her look like a complete idiot.

"Okay." She forced a smile.

He stared at her for a moment before creasing his brow. "Are you sure you wanna keep going? If you're too scared, we can turn back and maybe do something else?"

She felt silly for being scared. Jason obviously wasn't. He seemed to know exactly what he was doing and where he was going. She took in a deep breath and tried to overlook her insecurities about the unfamiliar world. As long as it didn't include the wolf of her nightmares and the bears her grandfather had often mentioned, their walk was an adventure, just like the ones she'd had on the beach when she was a child.

"No, I'm fine. Really. This is pretty cool, actually. I've never been hiking in the forest before. Back home, it was always just along the beaches. If you can even call that hiking. Compared to all of *this*, I mean." She eyed the tall pines, their tops disappearing somewhere high above, and glanced back at Jason.

Jason grinned. "I'm glad. There's a really cool clearing about thirty minutes from here. I think you'll like it. As a matter of fact, I *know* you'll like it."

"I can't wait to see it," she replied eagerly.

"Good."

They continued their hike. Along the way, Sami stopped to admire the various wildflowers and foliage she'd never seen before.

She knelt to run her hand over the frond of a fern. Its smooth ridges tickled her palm.

"That's a fern," Jason said.

She snickered. "Ha, ha. I know what a fern is. I've just never seen one up close."

"Well, if plants in the forest impress you, get ready to be blown away when we reach the clearing." He smirked and continued on.

Because she periodically stopped to study her new surroundings, it took close to an hour to reach their destination. When they finally arrived, Sami couldn't believe her eyes. The clearing was actually a large grassy meadow, full of sunshine and flourishing with wildflowers in a multitude of vibrant colors.

She smiled, taken away by its beauty. "Wow! It's like something you only see on TV."

"If you think this is amazing, wait 'til I show you this," Jason said, his tone eager.

Sami followed him as he tromped across the meadow to the other side. Standing on the edge, they overlooked a very small, crystal-clear lake, surrounded by grassy edges, various sized boulders that looked as if they had been meticulously set in place, and more wildflowers sprouting here and there. A mountainous wall of rock, about twenty feet high, curved around the far-right corner of the lake. Next to the cliff, from nearly halfway up, a small waterfall cascaded into lake, emitting a miniature rainbow.

"It's beautiful," Sami said with awe. She closed her eyes and inhaled deeply, enjoying the sweet scent of flowers mixed with the woody pine of the forest and the freshness of the pure mountain air.

"Wolf Lake." He grinned. "I thought you'd like it. You should see it in the winter when it snows. It's pretty awesome then too."

A comfortable silence fell over them as they took in the view.

"Do you want some water?" He walked over to a couple of boulders along the meadow's edge and sat on the larger one.

"Sure, thanks." She took the bottle he offered and gulped down half of it. Then, she sat on the smaller boulder to admire the lake. "I should've brought my camera. It was a gift from my grandparents a couple of birthdays ago."

"I guess you'll have to bring it *next* time," he said with a hopeful voice, yet his expression remained cool and nonchalant.

She raised one corner of her mouth, knowing he was hoping for a yes as far as next time was concerned. "Right, I can bring it *next* time."

Jason flashed a grin.

"Until then…" She slid her cell phone from her back pocket and snapped a picture of the lake.

Her cheerful demeanor faded as her grandpa's stories filled her thoughts again. She decided the only way to get past her fear of a dangerous wild animal lurking nearby would be to simply ask.

"So...I was sort of wondering...are there any bears around here?"

Jason sighed as he pondered the thought. "I've been coming here with my dad since I was four and have never seen one. Not even a bear track. I guess there used to be bears around here, but for some reason the numbers have dwindled over the years. Now, they're gone."

He hesitated for a moment. "But there are stories of wolves being seen in the area. That was years ago though. I've never seen one myself," he added, his voice holding a hint of uneasiness. "They keep to themselves mostly."

Sami heard the uncertainty in his voice but questioning him seemed to be an invasion of his privacy. Instead, she pretended not to notice.

"Oh. Well, that's better than bears, right? So, is that why we haven't heard any animals in the forest today? Because the wolves ate them all?" She shook her head, realizing how ridiculous she sounded.

The corners of his mouth curled up. "No, there are plenty of animals still in the forest. They just get quiet when they sense danger."

Wide-eyed, Sami looked around, hoping there were no predators nearby.

Jason stared at her for a few seconds before he smiled and shook his head. "No, they think *we're* the danger."

"Oh, I get it now." Sami snickered, her cheeks hot with embarrassment. A sudden wave of nausea knotted her gut. *Uh oh! Please don't throw up!* She thought to herself as she clutched her grumbling stomach.

Jason glanced at her abdomen and flashed a half-smile. "Are you hungry? I brought peanut butter and jelly and cheese crackers." He reached into his backpack and pulled out a paper lunch bag.

"You heard that, huh?"

"I think it echoed across the lake, Sami," he teased and handed her the bag.

Her cheeks flushed with warmth again, but thankfully, the nausea dissipated. "Thank you. I didn't realize it was lunchtime already." She looked toward the sun, which was already making its descent westward.

"Yeah, time seems to go by pretty fast when you're out here."

Out of the corner of her eye, she noticed him watching her. She glanced over, mesmerized by the way the sunlight brightened his hazel eyes.

Their gazes locked for a brief moment before she looked away and took a bite of her sandwich. They continued to eat in silence for a few minutes, enjoying the food and beauty surrounding them.

"Good sandwich." She tilted her head back and dropped the last bit into her mouth.

Jason had already finished his lunch. "Ah, it was nothing. I couldn't very well drag you all the way out here and not feed you. Besides, bears like their meals with a little meat on their bones."

Her jaw hung open before she realized he was just teasing. "Ha, ha! Not funny!" She giggled.

Jason started to laugh. "Sorry, that was wrong of me. But you should've seen the look on your face."

"Too bad for you…." Her voice trailed off in a playful manner. "I was gonna offer to bring lunch next time, but now…." She shrugged.

"Okay, okay! I'll stop laughing!" He pressed his lips together, but a hint of a smile remained. "I promise," he finally added with a straight face.

Sami felt silly for actually believing he would feed her to the bears. She smiled and raised one eyebrow. "Well, as long as you promise."

Jason grew quiet as he stared at the lake. He shook his head, and regret filled his eyes. "Yeah, I don't know why I said that. It was stupid."

She furrowed her brow, wondering why he sounded so down all of a sudden. *Does he really think he offended me?* "No, Jason. It's all right. I know you were just joking."

Jason looked into her eyes and let out a deep sigh. "I get a little carried away with my joking sometimes, so don't take offense to anything I say."

"Okay, I won't." She smiled but suddenly wondered if there was more to the story. *Maybe it's not about offending me at all? Maybe something bad happened in his past? Or maybe I'm just reading into it too much and need to get a grip.*

Glancing at the shoreline, Jason's eyes lit up. "Hey, do you want to have a rock skipping contest?"

His sudden cheerful demeanor eased her worries. "Sure, but you'll probably win."

"You can't be that bad at skipping rocks. Come on." He stood and reached for her hand.

Sami's cheeks flushed as his warm hand encircled hers. She let him pull her to her feet and help her down the slope of hardened dirt and grass clumps.

"Actually, I've never skipped a rock before."

He looked at her as if she were crazy. "Ever?"

"Ever. But how hard can it be, right?"

When they reached the water's edge, he let go of her hand and began gathering smooth, flat rocks about the size of a dollar coin. He handed her a few and grinned. "Good thing you have the best rock skipper *ever* to teach you."

"Right," she agreed.

She watched and listened as he explained what to look for in the perfect rock. Then, he leaned to one side and flicked his wrist, demonstrating how to develop the perfect throwing technique. She tried and tried to glide her rocks across the water as smoothly as Jason's had, but each toss ended with the lake swallowing her rock on the first *kerplunk*. On the very last attempt, her rock skipped once.

"I did it!" she shouted and spun on one foot to smack Jason's raised palm with a high five. "It took over an hour, but I finally did it."

He grinned. "See, your lessons have paid off." His grin fell flat, and he shook his head. "You're terrible at rock skipping. I think you need more lessons."

"I know I am." She let out a hopeless sigh. "Maybe next time we should just have a rock *throwing* contest instead? Or rock collecting? I think that would be more up my alley."

"Rock collecting?" He scrunched his face as if put off by the idea. "No way! You will learn how to skip rocks, even if it kills me." He chuckled under his breath and looked up at the sky.

The sun was already threatening to disappear behind the tips of the evergreens.

"We have to head back soon," he said.

"Okay." She couldn't help feeling a little disappointed that their time together was almost over. She and Jason had gotten along better than she had expected. He was fun to be around, seeming to not have a care in the world. Her first friend in Wolf Hill. Giddiness filled her chest, but she kept a cool exterior.

"But—" Jason raised his eyebrows "—since it's warmer out than it was supposed to be, we could get our feet wet to cool down first."

"Sounds good to me." She slid her cell phone from her back pocket, set it on a nearby boulder, and bent to remove her boots.

Jason eagerly copied her until they were both barefooted with their jeans rolled up to their knees. Then, he marched right into the water.

Sami followed him into the lake, trying to ignore the frigid burn on her skin.

Together, they frolicked along the shoreline, laughing as they kicked water at one another. At one point, Jason picked her up and threatened to dunk her, but her persistent begging and puppy-dog eyes saved her. Jason wasn't as lucky. As soon as he set her back on her feet, she pushed him and ran toward the bank to ensure her safety. Behind her, she heard a loud splash. She spun around, shocked to see Jason rising from the water, soaking wet.

With huge eyes, he let out a throaty laugh. "Ohhh ho hooo, that was cooold!" He eyed the water dripping from his clothing.

Sami stared at him with her mouth wide open. "Jason, I'm so sorry."

His eyes narrowed into slits, but a grin slowly formed, reflecting playful revenge.

Afraid he would throw her in, she backed away with her hands in front of her. "Jason, I'm sorry. I didn't mean to," she pleaded through uncontrolled snickers. "Really, I swear!"

Ignoring her plea, he charged straight toward her.

She screamed and turned to run, but he quickly caught her from behind, wrapping his arms tightly about her waist and letting his freezing wet clothes soak into hers.

"It's cold, Jason!" she shouted, giggling and trying to wriggle free.

"I know it's cold," he said smoothly.

"Please! I'm sorry!" she screamed while laughing.

Jason let her go and she spun around to face him.

"Apology accepted." He smirked and winked.

She breathed a sigh of relief. "Thank you!"

"You're most welcome," he said smugly. He glanced at the sky again. "I guess we should start heading back."

"All right, I guess I'm ready."

They shimmied their socks over their wet feet, pulled on their boots, and collected their phones.

Jason extended his free hand to hers.

Sami took his hand and let him help her up the bank to the meadow, wishing her cheeks wouldn't flush every time he touched her and hoping it wasn't noticeable. With Jason leading the way, they followed the path through the trees.

2

I T WAS late afternoon by the time Jason guided Sami out of the forest and accompanied her up the porch steps. The darkness under Sami's eyes showed her exhaustion, which didn't give him much hope for her accepting a dinner invitation, but he thought he'd give it a shot anyway.

He stopped at the front door. "So, maybe we could hang out later?"

Sami paused and lowered her gaze to the bunch of wildflowers in her hand. "Actually, I'm pretty tired. After being a recluse for the last two weeks, I'm not used to the physical activity." She met his stare again with guilt in her eyes. "Maybe tomorrow?"

Disappointment filled him, but tomorrow was better than nothing. It wasn't a complete rejection—just a rain check. "Sure. I'll see you tomorrow. Maybe we can go swimming? I'll stop by in the morning and see if you're up for it."

"Okay." She gave him a warm smile that nearly melted his heart.

Jason turned and jogged down the steps. He stopped at the bottom and waved. "See you tomorrow."

"Thanks for today, Jason. I had fun."

"It was my pleasure." He bowed majestically before he headed across the yard to the road. Behind him, he heard the sound of her front door close.

He couldn't shake the huge grin off his face. His date with Sami had turned out great, and he couldn't wait to see her tomorrow. Instead of going home, he decided to head to the main road to a spot behind the mailboxes where he'd seen numerous flat rocks, perfect for skipping.

Hands in his pockets, he strolled along, sending pebbles skittering across the road with the tip of his boot. His thoughts settled on Sami and all her beauty—her full smile, soft brown eyes, silky strawberry-scented hair, and of course, her rockin' body.

When he reached the end of their road, he turned left, opposite the direction of town. No one lived out this way, except for Sheriff Briggs, but the sheriff's house was farther down the main road. It was peaceful here. Quiet. Just the way Jason liked it. No one bothered him, and no one reminded him of what had happened thirteen years ago.

He shook his head and sighed. "Let it go already, Jason," he muttered under his breath.

He passed the mailboxes and hopped over the ditch to the edge of the forest, to where the water gathered in a low spot during heavy rains and created a small creek that spilled into the ditch. It was dry at the moment, but that would soon change with upcoming storms.

Kneeling, he dug his fingers into the hardened mud to free the smooth rocks. When he had accumulated around two dozen, he filled his jean pockets to bulging.

The sound of a branch snapping echoed from the forest, startling him. He sprung to his feet and scanned the trees. Silence engulfed the air.

"Huh?" he said under his breath, wondering what type of animal was out there. The branch snapping hadn't been too far off. Thirty feet, maybe. And it had been a hefty snap—from a branch at least half an inch thick—nothing a small animal could break.

He picked up a rock the size of a baseball and chucked it in the direction of the noise. Pine needles swished, and branches thwacked as the rock buzzed past them. It bounced off the ground and tumbled across dead foliage, crunching loudly along the way before it cracked to a dead stop against a tree trunk somewhere out of sight.

Jason held his breath, waiting for the animal to sprint away, but nothing happened. Aside from a gentle breeze rustling the tops of the trees, the forest was as silent as ever.

Maybe a dead branch partially snapped from a tree? Or maybe an extremely large pine cone fell from the top? He peered into the maze of branches above him. *But I didn't hear it bounce. It would've bounced.* That left only one more possibility.

"Who's out there?" Jason called, deepening his voice, trying to sound as threatening as he could.

He waited for an answer or some movement but was met with stillness and silence.

"Probably just a branch getting ready to fall," he mumbled under his breath.

A hearty rumble broke the silence. Jason peered over the top of the mailboxes at the sleek '68 Charger owned by Sami's neighbors. The car stopped at the end of their road for a few seconds before it turned right on the main road, headed toward town.

"Assholes," Jason muttered under his breath and shook his head.

Sami quickly filled his thoughts again. Wearing a slight grin, he headed home.

SAMI COULDN'T help smiling as different thoughts of her day flashed through her mind. After bidding Jason farewell, she'd clomped upstairs. She had reached no farther than the top step when there was a knock at the front door.

Figuring Jason had forgotten something, she hurried back down the stairs and opened the door.

A strange young man stood before her. He appeared around the same age and height as Jason, with slightly tousled dark brown hair and a strong jawline turned irresistibly charming by the cleft in his chin.

Her eyes locked with his for a moment before she lowered her lashes.

Now, she found herself staring at the blue plaid shirt buttoned over his very broad chest. She let her gaze fall farther to the strong definition in his forearms. Everywhere she looked on this perfect man, she felt as if she were gawking, and that he could see it. Rather than continue to make a fool of herself, she decided to just face him again.

"Hi." His rich brown eyes lit up slightly as he eyed the length of her body. He cleared his throat. "Umm, I'm your neighbor." He pointed to the house next door. "I'm Billy. Billy Holden." He held out his hand.

"Hi." Sami shook the dumbfounded look off her face and grabbed his hand. Her heart fluttered unexpectedly when his warm, rough fingers wrapped around hers. "I'm Samantha…Davis. Actually, it's just Sami."

She didn't understand why she was so nervous. Sure, she had been a little nervous with Jason, but not like this. Almost all the stories her grandpa had ever told her as a child had had the Holden children and Jason McAllister in them. She felt like she practically knew this man standing before her, yet her heart pounded. She wondered if he could hear it.

"It's nice to finally meet you, Sami." He eyed her awkwardly.

"It's fine," she said, finding it hard to stop staring—he was more handsome than she had imagined from her grandpa's stories. She suddenly realized her reply made no sense, and her eyes widened. "Oh, no, I mean, it's nice to finally meet you too." She let out a nervous giggle, hoping her cheeks weren't as bright red as they felt.

Billy raised one corner of his mouth before he gulped. "Well, I better get going. I just wanted to stop by and say hi. You know, the *neighborly* thing to do. Sorry it took a couple of weeks. My brother and I were out of town visiting my sister in California. We just got back earlier today."

"Really? California?" She bit her lower lip. "That's where I'm from. Monterey."

"Yeah, I know. Harry used to talk about you all the time."

She raised her eyebrows, hoping her grandpa hadn't told him anything too personal. "Really? I didn't know that. I assumed, but I didn't know for sure. He used to talk about you too."

"Uh oh." Billy's eyes widened. "All good things, I hope?"

"All good things…mostly."

He flashed a sheepish grin.

The slamming of a screen door drew their attention to the house next door. A man rushed down the steps of Billy's front porch and hopped into the black car sitting in the driveway. The car horn suddenly wailed.

Billy shook his head. "Sorry. I have to get going. My brother's waiting on me. He can be a pain sometimes."

"Sure. Uh, thanks for stopping by. It was nice to meet you, Billy. I guess I'll see you later." She raised her hand, gesturing good-bye.

He backed up and stumbled into the potted bougainvillea on the front porch. "Uh—" he chuckled under his breath "—didn't see that there on the way up."

"Careful on the way down the steps," she teased.

He grinned. "I'll see you later, Sami. Oh, and tell your mom, uh, Carol, that I said hi."

"I will." Completely smitten, she watched the way his jeans hugged his butt as he hurried off across the yard and into his.

Billy climbed into the passenger seat of the older car before looking in her direction.

Afraid she'd been caught gawking *again*, she quickly took a step back and slammed the door. *Crap, I hope he didn't see me.* She rolled her eyes and shook her head, embarrassed. So far, Wolf Hill contained two of the friendliest, most handsome men she had ever seen, and she had just been befriended by them both.

"Maybe moving here wasn't so bad after all," she whispered. At that moment, she decided to stop feeling sorry for herself and stop pestering her mom about moving back to California.

BILLY HOPPED into the passenger seat of his car, more than irked. He glared at his brother sitting behind the wheel. "Honking? Seriously? What the hell?"

Mike grinned smugly. "You were taking too long. I'm hungry."

Billy shook his head, knowing it was pointless to try to talk to his older brother about respect. Mike said what he wanted and did what he wanted when he wanted. No matter what.

Billy glanced at Sami's house. She was standing in the doorway, watching him, but suddenly darted inside and shut the door.

He smirked. It felt good to know she was interested in him because he was definitely interested in her. For some reason, when she'd opened the door, he'd expected her to still be the little girl running wild on the beach he'd envisioned from Harry's stories. But she was a woman now, and more beautiful than he could ever have imagined.

He recalled the way her long brown hair had fallen loosely across her shoulders, framing her breasts. The way her soft brown eyes had held a certain innocence, like those of a doe. And how her cheerful smile had seemed to make all his worries fade away for the brief moment he had been with her.

"Was she hot?" Mike's gruff voice and the rumble of the engine interrupted the silence. He grinned devilishly and revved the engine before he threw the shifter into reverse. The tires crunched over the gravel as he backed out of the driveway.

Billy stared at his brother blankly. For some reason, he didn't want to tell Mike anything about Sami. He felt a need to protect her, yet he didn't know why. Maybe it was because she was Harry's granddaughter. Or maybe it was because, through all the stories he'd heard about her, he considered her a good friend—even though this was the first time he'd officially met her. Regardless, he knew he had to appease his annoying brother with some sort of an answer, or Mike would make him the target of ridicule for the rest of the evening.

"She's not bad," Billy replied casually.

"Not bad?" Mike looked at him as if he were crazy. "What in the hell kind of answer is *not bad*? What'd she look like?"

Billy grew irritated. "Dude, I don't know. She had long brown hair and brown eyes. What difference does it make?"

Mike halted at the stop sign at the end of their road and studied him curiously before the corners of his mouth curled into a huge grin. "You remember what color her eyes are? You like her!"

Billy rubbed his forehead as if he were rubbing away a headache. "Why are you so irritating, Mike?"

"Because you like a girl," Mike taunted. He turned right and headed toward town.

"Yeah, Sami seems nice. So what?"

"Sami?" Mike questioned. "Harry always called her Samantha. So why are you calling her *Sami*?"

Billy sighed heavily and rubbed his forehead again as the first pangs of an actual headache awakened. He knew the only way to get Mike off his back would be to give him some sort of a detailed response.

"I don't know. I guess Harry called her Samantha. She told me to call her Sami." The volume of his voice increased as he spoke. "Are you happy now? Are you happy that you're an irritating prick, and the older you get, the more irritating you get?"

Mike grinned with satisfaction. "You're usually not this easy to rile up, little brother. She must be hot. And I'm pretty sure you like her."

"Why can't you just shut your mouth? You're like a twelve-year-old." Billy shook his head and let out an exhausted sigh. He reached over and turned on the radio loud enough to drown out any more of Mike's mockery.

3

"**S**AMI." SHE tested her new name aloud in the privacy of her bedroom. A new name for a new start in life. She smiled as thoughts of her day with Jason and getting to meet Billy danced through her mind.

For the first time in a year, she felt somewhat happy again. It had been a bad year due to the breakup of her parents' marriage and the death of her grandmother. Sami had been so depressed, she'd decided to put off college for a while. She'd even cut ties with her friends as they prepared to leave for college. With all the gossiping that had been going on behind her back, they were hardly friends anyway.

But now, she felt good enough to spend the rest of the evening unpacking boxes and organizing her bedroom just the way she wanted it.

Hands on hips, she stood in the doorway, and studied her new bedroom, satisfied with the way it had turned out. Along the right wall, a brown wicker hamper stood next to her closet door. The wall in front of her encased a large window covered with sheer white curtains. Her bed—covered with a gray comforter, purple pillows, and lavender sheets—jutted to the middle of the room from the left wall. An enlarged picture of the sunny beach taken in front of her California home hung over it.

Next to her bed, near the window, an oak nightstand housed a lamp and a few seashells she and her grandpa had collected at the beach when she was a child. A matching computer desk sat on the other side of the bed with various family photos tacked to the wall, framing her computer monitor. To the left of her door, a square beveled mirror hung above her dresser.

"Welcome home, Samantha," she whispered with pride as the heavy burden of moving finally lifted.

A glimmer on her dresser caught her eye. She focused on the silver pocketknife—a birthday gift from her dad. At the time, she hadn't been too thrilled about receiving a pocketknife as a gift. But now, she was grateful. It was a token of his love and something to remember him by.

The front door opened and banged shut.

"Samantha, I'm home!" her mother called.

Sami hurried downstairs, anxious to share the details of her day. "Hey, Mom, what's up?"

"You left the door unlocked, that's *what's up*." Her mom raised her eyebrows.

Sami rolled her eyes. "Oh, Mom, come on. We live in the middle of nowhere. Nothing's gonna happen way out here."

For as long as she could remember, her mother, Carol Davis, had always lectured her on the fact that she took too many risks. Like the time when she had been fourteen and had climbed out to the end of the rocks with waves crashing over them to rescue her best friend's favorite kite. Or the day when she had been nine and had walked home from school along busy streets by herself because she had missed the bus. Or when she had been seven and had snuck out of her upstairs bedroom window and climbed down the trellis to camp out in the backyard under the light of the full moon to watch for shooting stars.

She sighed, wondering when her mother was going to accept the fact that she wasn't her little girl anymore.

"Crime happens everywhere, Samantha," Carol said. She pulled the band from her shoulder-length, sandy blonde hair. "Please keep the door locked. I worry about you enough being out here in the wilderness by yourself all day."

"Then maybe you should've brought me with you all those times you came to visit Grandma and Grandpa. Maybe I'd know more about how to live in the wilderness."

"Your grandparents came to visit you every summer and almost every Thanksgiving. Besides, I only visited here when something tragic happened. And I wasn't about to expose you to any of that. You were just a little girl."

Sami crossed her arms. "I was nineteen at the time of Grandma's funeral, and you still wouldn't let me come."

Carol sighed. "It was a tragic time. I didn't want you to see me so sad. I didn't want you to see your grandpa so sad. But let's not discuss this right now. Please. I'm exhausted."

"Well, you can stop sheltering me. I'm twenty. I'm not a child anymore."

"I know. I'm working on it. But you still have to keep the doors locked around here."

"Okay. But *you* have to stop worrying about me so much. Jason lives across the road, and Billy and his brother are next door. They were raised here. They're still alive and well after all these years of living here."

"Oh? I didn't know they were back." Ease replaced the worried tone in her mother's voice. "You're right. I just worry about you because I love you. You're just about all I have left."

"I know, Mom. I love you too." Sami noticed tears glistening in her mother's hazel eyes. She couldn't stand seeing her mom cry. It made her cry too.

Sami quickly changed the subject. "Guess what? I finally got out of the house today."

Carol's look of dismay turned into a huge smile. "I'm glad! I was worried you'd never give life in Wolf Hill a try. So, what'd you do?"

"I went hiking with Jason."

Carol's smile fell flat. "Hiking? Where?"

Sami rolled her eyes again and sighed. "Don't worry. It was safe.

We just followed the path right next to the house. We didn't go far. It was fun. He showed me where Wolf Lake was. It's pretty amazing up there."

"I don't know about you being in the forest like that. What about bears or…*other* wild animals?"

"Mom, Jason's been in and out of this forest for years. He knows it like the back of his hand. He said there haven't been any bears around here for over twenty years."

Carol sighed. "He's right. I guess there haven't been any—" She stopped mid-sentence.

"Any *what?*"

"Any…bear sightings. Just like Jason said." Carol shrugged her shoulders.

Sami didn't like the hesitation in her mother's voice—the same hesitation that had been in Jason's voice earlier. "It sounded like you were gonna say something else."

Carol pursed her lips and shook her head. "Mmm, nope. I was just trying to think back to the last bear sighting. But it was so long ago, I can't even remember. I'll stop worrying so much." She went to the refrigerator, pulled out a casserole, and stuck it in the microwave to heat up.

Sami watched her. Her mother was purposely avoiding making eye contact—something she had often done to cover up being untruthful. But trying to get any information from her mother was a lost cause. They'd only end up arguing. And from the tired look in her mom's eyes, now wasn't the time to push the issue. Her mom had been through too much lately.

When dinner had heated through, they both sat down at the breakfast bar to eat.

Carol glanced at the vase full of wildflowers on the table along the kitchen wall. "Those are pretty."

"They're for you." Sami took a bite of her cheesy meal.

"Aw, thank you, sweetheart."

"You're welcome." She smiled. As she continued to eat, Sami stared out the kitchen window into the growing darkness. She looked at the clock on the wall. "Eight o'clock? I didn't know it was that late already."

"That's the wonderful thing about living away from the hustle and bustle. The *way* you live becomes more important than how much *time* you have left to do it in."

Sami nodded, pretending to understand the full impact of the statement. "So, when do you think I'll be able to visit Grandpa?"

A guilty look crossed her mother's face. "He's too weak right now for visitors. They wouldn't let you in."

Sami grew worried. "Why is he so weak? What's the matter with him?" she asked, hoping to finally get a straight answer.

"To tell you the truth, I'm not exactly sure. When I know more, I'll tell you."

"Is he gonna be okay?"

After a short pause, Carol nodded. "It'll just take some time."

She could tell her mom was hiding something again. Frustrated, Sami wanted to give her mom a piece of her mind, but she didn't want to upset her. All she could do was wait for a time when her mom could no longer avoid a truthful explanation.

"Promise you'll let me know as soon as you find out anything?"

Carol's sadness gave way to a feeble smile. "I promise," she said. "So, you went hiking with Jason today? How is he doing?"

"Good, I guess. He wants to take me swimming at the lake tomorrow."

"Oh, can you maybe go the following day instead? I need you to go to the grocery store. We're running low on a few things. And if you could run a couple more errands for me, you'd be helping out so much. I won't have time between work and taking care of your grandpa."

"Work? You got a job?"

"Yep. At the hospital where your grandpa is. I couldn't let my nursing skills go to waste."

"Oh, that's cool, I guess. Maybe I should get a job too?"

"Your dad and I really want you to take the summer off and enjoy life a little before you start college in the fall. You are still planning to take classes at the community college, aren't you? Besides, your tuition money is already set aside, and your dad sent you some spending money so that you wouldn't have to work this summer. We want you to get an education. It's important. And we know what a rough time you've had lately with our separation and the move and all. We want you to enjoy life a little before school starts."

Sami began to regret her decision to move here with her mom. She was a woman, yet still being treated like a child. Still having her life led for her. Even so, moving back to California and leaving her mom here alone was inconceivable. She decided to wait a little longer before announcing she was putting off college for another semester or two.

"I know, Mom. Thanks. I'll thank Dad too," she replied casually to hide her guilt.

"You're welcome. Just don't spend all your money at once. Make it last through the summer, please. I have to start work early. Orientation day." She flashed a strained smile—something she often did to show how nervous she was. "I'll leave the money on the counter and a list of what needs to be done."

"Okay. And don't worry, Mom, you'll do great tomorrow." She gave her mother a reassuring smile.

"Thanks, sweetheart."

After they finished their dinner, Sami said good night and disappeared to the comfort of her bedroom. The hike combined with lack of sleep due to recurring nightmares had nearly pushed her to the point of exhaustion.

She changed into a tank top and shorts and sent a quick email to her dad to thank him.

As soon as she snuggled comfortably between the cool lavender sheets, the curtains fluttered.

"Great, I left the window open," she whispered and climbed out of bed. Eyeing the window, she was suddenly afraid to go near it. With cautious steps, she crossed the room. When she reached the window, she yanked it shut and latched it. Not being able to help herself, she peered into the dark shadows of the forest—just as she had done in her nightmares.

Red eyes appeared at the edge of the yard.

Sami froze and her breath caught in her throat. *Holy crap! What is that? Am I in danger?* She peered harder through the window, trying to visualize a shape.

The eyes disappeared.

Seconds later, a melancholy howl filled the forest.

The eerie cry sent goose bumps down her limbs. *Did I just see a wolf?* Wolf or not, she was terrified. She thought of running downstairs to her mother's room, but the hum of water being pushed through the pipes meant her mom was in the shower.

Anxious for night to be over, Sami darted across her room, jumped into bed, and pulled the covers to her chin. Another howl bellowed in the distance, much farther than the first. Relieved the wolf was travelling away from her home, she relaxed her weary muscles and closed her eyes.

4

SAMI FLUTTERED her eyes open and stretched, glad she hadn't suffered another nightmare. Seeing a wild animal, a wolf, or *something* in the forest last night had been nightmare enough. She yawned and forced herself to climb out of bed to face the day.

After her shower, she went to her closet and chose a loose-fitting red tank top adorned with a sequin heart. From her dresser, she pulled out a pair of faded denim cutoffs. Temperatures were supposed to reach the nineties today, which was unusual for this early in the summer.

She dressed, slid her feet into white flip-flops, and inspected her appearance in the mirror over the dresser. On top of the dresser, her white-gold locket lay in a heap next to her pocketknife. The locket had been a birthday gift from her mom, but Sami's chest grew heavy at the sight of it. She opened the tiny heart and stared at the picture of the three of them as a family taken at her high school graduation just last year. Back then, she'd thought her parents were a happy couple.

Tears burned her eyes, but she blinked them back. She had shed enough tears over the last few weeks and was determined to be happy again. With a heavy sigh, she snapped the locket shut and clasped it around her neck. Then, she ran downstairs to the kitchen and placed a couple of frozen waffles in the toaster. As soon as they popped up, a loud knock rattled the door. Sami's heart skipped a beat at the unexpected boom. She shook her head, feeling silly for being frightened, and went to the door and opened it.

"I was wondering if you felt up for swimming today? It's gonna be hot out." Jason grinned, showing off his teeth.

"Sorry," she replied, feeling bad for rejecting him again. "I have some errands to do for my mom today."

His enthusiasm faded. "Oh, that's too bad." A cunning smile crossed his face. "Maybe I could come with you? I could show you around town."

If it had been any other time, she wouldn't have minded, but feminine items were included on the list, and she didn't want Jason to know. "Well…" She hesitated, thinking of a way to let him down gently without divulging the details. "I don't think it would be a good idea. I have some personal things to take care of."

"Oh." His eyes filled with disappointment. "Well, that's okay. Maybe we can go swimming tomorrow?"

She was relieved he hadn't given up on her altogether. "Sure, tomorrow sounds good. Let me give you my number, you know, to make it easier to get hold of me."

Jason grinned. He reached into the pocket of his khaki shorts and pulled out his cell phone. "Here. I'll let you type it in."

She took his phone and entered her number. "Here you go." She handed it back to him. "I'll let you enter my name."

"Cool. I'll text you my number later. See you tomorrow." He winked.

"Bye." Sami watched him walk away and went back inside.

She snatched her purse from the counter, along with the money her mom had left, and headed out the front door.

Standing on the porch, she stared with some hesitation at the 1957 Chevy Bel Air sitting in the gravel driveway alongside the house. She was sure her grandpa was the original owner. Now that he was too ill to drive, it was hers, though she hadn't driven it yet.

From the layer of dust covering the red and white paint, the car looked as if it hadn't moved for quite some time.

"Okay, let's get this over with." She jogged down the steps to the driveway. Her flip-flops slid across the loose gravel, but she quickly regained her footing.

When she safely reached the driver door, she pulled it open and plopped onto the seat, wrinkling her nose at the faint smell of cigars looming in stuffy the air. She yanked the door shut and cranked the window handle until the window rolled all the way down.

The seats were a little worn, but there were no visible cracks or tears. She ran a finger over the smooth, yet dusty, red paint of the dashboard. *How cool—a metal dashboard! And a push button radio?* She smiled, awed by the nostalgic technology. Unable to help herself, she pushed one of the buttons, watching as the red line clicked to a different channel.

"Okay, let's see what this baby's got." She shoved the key into the ignition and turned it. The engine tried to turn over. *Rur, rur, ruurrr, ruuurrrr…* It stopped. She tried again. *Ruurrr, ruuurrr…* Nothing.

"Need a jump?" a deep voice asked.

Sami screamed and jerked to face the intruder leaning in the driver window.

"Sorry." Billy laughed a little. "I didn't mean to scare you."

Relieved to see it was just her next-door neighbor, she placed a shaky hand over her heart, trying to calm its erratic beating. She smiled, feeling silly. "It's okay."

"Sorry. I was just leaving when I heard you trying to start your car. It sounds like the battery again. I can jump-start it if you have jumper cables."

"Okay, but I don't know if I have any."

"I'm pretty sure you do. I lent my cables to Harry, uh, your grandpa, a few months back. He must've just forgotten. I figured he needed them more than I did. And now, I guess *you* need them more than I do." He grinned. "They're probably in the trunk."

She got out of the car and handed him the keys.

As he took the keys, he glanced down at her tank top.

She looked down to see what had caught his attention. The sequins shimmered in the sunshine.

"Nice shirt." He smiled and went around to the back of the car.

"Thanks." Sami watched as he opened the trunk.

He wore a gray T-shirt today, its sleeves hugging his ample biceps. The sight of his manly strength sparked a sudden energy in her chest. She shook her head and cleared her throat, forcing herself to divert her attention to the task at hand. She peered in the trunk, disappointed to see only a spare tire, a jack, and a first aid kit.

"Hmmm." She bit her lower lip, deep in thought. "I remember my mom saying he had a bunch of tools in the basement. Maybe they're down there?"

"Okay, I'll wait here while you go look." He leaned against the car and held out the keys, letting them dangle in front of her.

"Um, are you serious?" She took the keys and scrambled for a reason to have him accompany her without revealing her fear of going to the basement alone—thanks to late night horror movies. She'd dreaded it when her mother had sent her into the wine cellar at their home in California. A disturbing bump or creak of some kind always made her heart thump. She was sure the wine cellar was haunted.

"I'm not going down into the basement by *myself*. I mean, I, uh, I can, but I'm sure it'd be faster if you helped. The basement is probably big and unorganized. I'm sure it might take a while. But if you helped…" She paused, hoping he finally understood without her having to admit her fear.

He grinned sheepishly. "Just kidding, Sami. I'll come with you. I wouldn't really make you go down there by yourself. Your grandpa told me you're afraid of basements."

She wasn't amused by Billy's lack of compassion. "Ha, ha. Very funny. And I was just a little kid at the time. I'm not afraid of basements *now*." It wasn't a lie exactly. She only feared what might be lurking *in* the basement. Not of the basement itself.

He pressed his lips together to suppress his smile. "Sorry, didn't mean to offend you. Come on." He motioned with his head toward the backyard.

Still humiliated, Sami decided to drop the subject. She followed him around the side of the house to the backyard, and down the worn concrete steps to the metal basement door. Deep scratches had been gouged into the slate colored metal—some reaching as high as the top of Billy's head.

Sami eyed the intimidating damage, glad she hadn't come alone. "What could've done that? A raccoon?" She knew she was wrong.

Deep lines creased Billy's brow. "I don't know. Definitely something bigger than a raccoon. It could've been a wolf, maybe, standing on its hind legs. Maybe it chased an animal down here or something. But don't worry, they're usually afraid of humans. Of course, if you see one, don't try to pet it or anything."

"Thanks," she replied with dull enthusiasm, offended Billy actually thought she might be naïve enough to pet a wolf. "I'll try to restrain myself."

So far, Billy seemed to be the exact opposite of Jason. Though he was friendly, he wasn't *overly* friendly. Going out of his way to make a good first impression seemed the furthest thing from his mind. And he wasn't afraid to express his thoughts, no matter how arrogant he sounded.

Billy's expression softened, and his eyes held a hint of regret. "These look pretty old anyway." He ran his finger down one of the scratches. "See how rusty they are?"

"Okay then…shall we?" She jiggled the knob. "Great, it's locked."

"Do you have a key?" Billy asked.

"No. My mom couldn't find it." Sami was relieved. She would rather disappoint her mother with no groceries than go into the basement. The door's appearance was horrifying enough. Of course, it was a little less horrifying with Billy at her side.

"Shoot." She pretended to sound disappointed. "I guess I'll just have to wait until my mom gets home."

"Okay then." Billy shrugged and motioned with a hand up the stairs. "After you."

An awkward silence filled the air as they headed up the steps and back to her car.

Billy cleared his throat, finally breaking the tension. "Actually, you should probably think about getting a new battery. I think the old one is original to the car." He let out a nervous sounding chuckle.

"You don't wanna get stranded anywhere."

She nodded. "Yeah, I guess that would be the smart thing to do. I would hate to get stranded. Especially at night. Especially *here*." She gestured toward the looming forest with the swoop of a hand.

Billy eyed the forest uneasily before meeting her gaze. "I can take you into town to get one. I'm going to the auto shop anyway to pick up a part for my brother's motorcycle."

"Really?" She hesitated, wondering if trying to converse with him all the way into town and back would end up being a mistake. He sure didn't seem like the Billy her grandpa used to talk about.

Then again, five minutes of conversation was hardly enough time to get to know someone. And just because she didn't like him teasing her about the basement, it didn't make him a bad guy. It just meant he accidentally found her sore spot.

What she couldn't get past was the way he'd just eyed the forest. There seemed to be something he wasn't telling her. Something he was afraid of. She wondered if it was the same thing her mother and Jason were hiding.

Regardless, she really needed a battery. She finally gave him a slight smile.

"Thanks. That would be great."

"Good. Do you have everything?"

She reached through the driver's window and grabbed her purse. "Yep, all ready." They started across the driveway toward Billy's house. She stumbled over a loose rock, and her flip-flop slid across the gravel, throwing her off balance. Her arms flew up in an unsuccessful attempt to regain her footing. A gasp escaped her lips as she fell backward.

In one swift move, Billy caught her around the waist and pulled her to his chest.

Eyes wide, Sami stared at him with a shocked look, not sure if her heart pounded from the near fall or from their bodies being pressed together.

"Are you all right?" Billy let go of her and took a step back.

"I-I think so." She let out a shaky breath. "It's a good thing you were right next to me. Thanks. That probably would've been pretty painful…and embarrassing."

"Anytime," he replied, sounding casual.

"I guess my shoes don't have much traction." She took another step, and her other foot slid across the uneven ground. She tensed and stopped mid-step.

"Just be careful," Billy ordered, his hands hovering around her sides as if he were ready to catch her again. "Here—" he wrapped his hand around hers, interlocking their fingers "—just don't almost fall again." He winked and led the way to his car.

"I couldn't fall right now if I wanted to." She spread her fingers to show him how tight he held them.

"Sorry, but I'm not letting go until we're on steady ground."

"That's okay. I don't really want to almost fall again anyways." *And I don't really want you to let go of my hand either,* she added silently, enjoying his touch.

They walked across the yards until they reached his car.

Sami was glad he hadn't let go of her hand yet—his driveway was also gravel. "What kind of car is this?" She ran her free hand across the smooth black paint, impressed with the car's beauty.

"A '68 Charger," he replied with a proud grin.

"Well, you work fast." A ruggedly handsome man—in his early thirties and around the same height as Billy—stepped off the front porch. He had dark brown eyes, almost black, with the same color hair. A few days' worth of stubble covered half of his face.

Pulling Sami with him, Billy stepped into the yard to greet his brother.

"Sami, this is my brother, Mike," Billy announced and narrowed his eyes at Mike as if he were giving him a warning.

"Nice to meet you, Sami," Mike said. The corners of his mouth curled up slightly. He glanced down at her tank top and then back to her face.

Sami smiled, nodded, and managed to mumble a nervous-sounding, "Hi."

"So, little brother, are you two an *item* now?" Mike grinned and gestured toward their interlocked hands with a smooth nod of his head.

Billy straightened, yanked his hand from Sami's, and stepped away from her. He cleared his throat. "Uh, she almost fell."

Feeling just as awkward, Sami cut in to explain. "Yeah, my shoes…"

She made a weak attempt to laugh through the embarrassment as she slid her flip-flop across the ground in an effort to show Mike what had happened. Her shoe caught on a grass clump and shot off her foot. Feeling like a complete idiot, she let out a nervous snicker and wriggled her toes back around the strap of her flip-flop.

Mike eyed them before he spoke. "If you say so…. You two have fun. And don't forget my part, Billy. I wanna get my bike running before nightfall." He hopped up the steps, strutted across the porch, and disappeared into the house. The flimsy screen door banged shut behind him.

Billy looked down at Sami with an apologetic half-smile. "Sorry about that. He can be a pain sometimes."

"Oh, you don't have to apologize. He seems pretty cool." She was trying to be optimistic, though she finally understood where Billy's sense of humor came from.

"Right." He crinkled his forehead and gave her an uncertain look. "Anyway, are you ready to go?"

"Sure," she replied, hoping to get out of there before Mike returned to humiliate them further.

Billy opened the passenger door for her before getting into the driver's seat. The engine rumbled to life, and they headed toward town.

MIKE STEPPED out onto the front porch, beer in hand, just in time to catch the last glimpse of Billy's car before it disappeared around the corner.

He sat on the edge of the porch and leaned against the railing. After cracking open his beer, he took a long swig, enjoying the bitter crispness.

Staring at the swaying treetops across the road, his thoughts drifted back to when he'd stood at the living room window and watched as

Billy had caught Sami mid-fall. Billy had even held her hand as they made their way back to the house.

It wasn't like his little brother to be so damn hung up on woman, rushing over to play the hero. Billy's interest in Sami was different. A spark flickered in his brother's eyes again, one Mike hadn't seen since the bullshit that had taken place thirteen years ago.

He shook the thought from his head and guzzled the rest of his beer.

A loud *snap* erupted from one of the towering pines across the road. He eyed the tree, shocked to see one of the limbs broken and dangling. It tore free and plummeted to the ground with a heavy thud.

"What the fuck?" He crossed the road to inspect the fallen branch. It was about an inch in diameter and green for the most part, though the center was rotted. Even with the decay in the middle, the branch couldn't have fallen by itself.

Moving only his eyes, he scanned the branches above him, knowing damn well the only thing capable of creating damage like that was a human who'd stepped on a branch too small to carry his weight or a good-sized animal. But he didn't hear anything scurry off. Of course, with the wind blowing, something could've scurried off without being heard.

Holding his breath, he glanced around the forest and listened for any sound that stood apart from the rustling of branches. Hearing nothing unordinary, he picked up a handful of small rocks and flung them out into the trees. They thwacked their way against and between tree trunks before thudding to the ground. He waited for any signs of heavy movement, but there wasn't any.

Not satisfied, he tromped through the ferns and brush at the base of the pines, looking for tracks from any animal that could've created the damage. After a couple of minutes of searching the ground, he looked up again, straining to see through the maze of branches above. He saw nothing.

He sighed. "Probably just a fat raccoon or possum living up there somewhere. Oh well, time for another beer." He headed back to the house.

SAMI STARED out the car window into the dense forest as Billy drove along the winding road toward town. An uncomfortable silence filled the air. Sami wanted to spark an interesting conversation to break the awkward tension, but all that came to mind was how stupid she must've looked by almost falling and the lame explanation she'd given to Mike as to why she and Billy had been holding hands. Rather than embarrass herself further, she kept her mouth shut and enjoyed the peaceful drive.

Thankfully, they reached town within a few minutes. Wolf Hill seemed to be a quiet, quaint town, but more on the side of being too quiet and too quaint. Almost to the point of being creepy.

Sami stared at the one-story and two-story businesses in need of a makeover. The paint was peeling on most of them. Some of the old buildings even looked abandoned. And signs were either faded, missing letters, or had burned-out bulbs.

She furrowed her brow, realizing there were no people out enjoying the day, like there always had been in Monterey. There were no happy couples strolling the sidewalks hand in hand. No children bouncing along as they ate their ice cream. If it hadn't been for a guy in a baseball hat crossing the street and few cars parked in front of some of the businesses, Sami would've mistaken Wolf Hill for a ghost town.

She felt as if she were in one of those horror flicks where a group of teenagers stop for gas in a deserted out-of-the-way town and the viewers yell, *No! Don't stop! Keep going, you idiot!*

Deep down, she wished she could just keep going and have Billy drive her straight out of this eerie town. But, for now, she was trapped there. She sighed and suppressed the thought.

When they finally reached the auto shop, Billy parked, and they went inside. Luckily, they both found the exact parts they needed. However, the unwelcoming glare that the gangly, beady-eyed mechanic gave her quickly dissolved her smile. She looked at Billy to see if he noticed, but he was busy inspecting Mike's part. She suddenly had to get out of the shop.

"I'm gonna go wait outside." She handed Billy enough money for the battery and hurried out the front door.

She headed straight for Billy's car and leaned against the passenger door, wondering what she'd done to wrong the man standing behind the counter. *Does he have me mixed up with someone else? Maybe Grandpa has something to do with it. Or Billy. Or maybe it's because I'm not from around here.*

In such a small town, Sami was sure the rumor that she and her mother had become permanent residents had spread to everyone.

I hope the rest of the townspeople are friendlier.

Billy exited the store, toting a battery and a small paper bag, his warm smile easing her worries.

"That was fast." Sami beamed.

"Yes, it was." Billy put the items in his trunk before unlocking her door.

When Billy backed out of the parking lot, the swaying motion sent a wave of nausea through Sami's stomach and straight to the back of her throat. She swallowed hard, clamping one hand over her mouth and the other over her abdomen.

Billy slammed on the brake pedal, stopping the car with a sudden jerk. "Are you all right?"

She lowered her hand from her mouth. "Uh, I'm feeling a little sick." She flashed a wary half-smile and humiliation crept into her cheeks.

His eyes widened. "Are you gonna throw up?"

"No. I don't think so. Just feeling a little carsick. I probably just need to eat something. I got distracted and forgot to eat breakfast this morning." She rolled down the window and took a deep breath of fresh air. "Maybe if you could just drive a little slower around corners it might help. And if there's a drive-through around here?"

"Sorry. There aren't any drive-throughs in this town. But there is a diner up the road." He headed toward the diner before she could reply.

"I don't wanna make your brother wait for his part," she protested, yet silently hoped he wouldn't give in.

"Ah, don't worry about Mike. It's not even noon yet. He still has all day. Besides, I'm getting hungry myself." He glanced her way, his eyes full of worry.

Relieved, she laid her head back on the seat, still clutching her stomach.

"Are you sure you don't need me to pull over?"

"I'm sure," she said, trying to ease his worry.

But she wasn't sure at all. She tried her hardest to concentrate on the road in front of her and on the fresh air rushing in on her face. Her stomach churned and cramped. Just when she thought she was going to have to ask him to pull over, the engine stopped.

"We're here." Billy jumped out, raced around the car, and opened her door. Looking down at her, he furrowed his brow. "You don't look so good. You're really pale." He held his hand out.

"I'll be fine. I just need to get out of the car," she replied, her voice strained. Taking his hand, she slid off the seat and stood on shaky legs.

With her hand tightly in his, Billy walked her into the diner.

The smell of greasy bacon blasted Sami's senses, causing her stomach to churn again. With the steady chatter of conversation buzzing in her ears, she scanned her new surroundings, hoping to find the bathroom nearby. To her left, she spotted restroom signs posted on the paneled walls at the entrance of the hallway.

Various pictures and newspaper clippings of the town's history also hung on the walls. The back of the diner housed a long yellow-laminated counter lined with blue padded stools. In the middle of the room sat tables of the same yellow hue, surrounded by either blue or green padded chairs. Along the windows lining the front and adjacent walls were matching booths.

Suddenly, the entire room grew silent.

Sami looked around the half-filled room, realizing all eyes were on her. She gulped, feeling more uncomfortable than she ever had in her life. Though their stares weren't as searing as the auto shop man's had been, they were still disturbing.

Why are they all looking at me? Do they even know who I am? Do they hate me, or are they just curious?

Some of them stared at her tank top, and then back at her face again. Sami nonchalantly folded her arms across her chest to hide the shimmering heart, wishing she'd chosen something else to wear. She looked at Billy.

Billy shook his head and gave the onlookers a disapproving glare before he turned his attention back to Sami.

Slowly, the heavy silence filled with the clanking of flatware on porcelain and the hum of voices, though the tones were softer and more cautious than they had been when she and Billy had first walked in.

"Don't worry about it," Billy reassured. "They're just curious about the new girl in town."

She nodded, not convinced that her being the new girl was the only reason everyone had stopped mid-conversation to blatantly stare at her. And they hadn't been friendly, welcoming stares either. She felt as if, for some reason, everyone loathed her—everyone except Billy, Mike, and Jason. Something was going on, but so far, no one was divulging any details.

"Right. I'm the new girl in town. Lucky me," she replied in a flat tone.

Billy flashed an apologetic smile. "Come on. Let's find a place to sit." Without waiting to be seated, they went to the booth in the back corner, away from prying eyes and ears.

Sami slid onto the seat facing the back wall. That way, even if people were still staring, she couldn't see them. But now that she was no longer distracted, the urge to vomit was noticeable again.

She looked at Billy. "Can you order me a lemon-lime soda? I'm going to the restroom."

"Sure," he replied. "Are you okay?"

"I will be." She slid out of the booth and headed toward the restroom, praying she didn't vomit in the middle of the diner. To avoid prying eyes, she kept her focus averted to the white vinyl flooring dotted with blue and green specks.

By the time she reached the restroom, her sickness had eased. She splashed some cool water on her face, took a few deep relaxing breaths, and headed back to their booth, remembering to keep her head down.

When she returned, a woman was sitting across from Billy. The stranger's black hair fell in curls around her shoulders, and her amber eyes were seductively enhanced with lavender shimmer. Sami noticed the woman's mounded breasts pouring out of her purple tank top, and quickly looked away, suddenly feeling like a plain Jane compared to this goddess.

Jealousy nipped at Sami's heart to see this stranger sitting with Billy.

Billy smiled at Sami as if he were relieved to see her again. "Here she is. Jessica, this is Sami. Sami, Jessica." He gestured toward each of them.

Jessica smirked. Standing slowly, she eyed the length of Sami's body. Her eyes narrowed. "Hello, *Sami*," she said hotly through her smile.

Sami was offended by Jessica's rude behavior. There was no way she was going to let someone so unfriendly call her Sami. That name was reserved for Billy. She smiled flatly.

"It's Samantha. And it's nice to meet you, *Jessica*."

Jessica glared at her before she turned. "Well, I guess I'll see you later, Billy." Her eyes were softer now, as was her tone.

"See ya," Billy replied casually and looked at his menu.

Jessica paused at the end of the booth for a moment, glared at Sami again, and strutted away—her cutoffs barely covering her rear.

Billy flashed another apologetic smile, which seemed to be a thing now—him silently apologizing for the rude townspeople. She hoped the newness of being an outsider would wear off soon.

"Sorry about that. She's not the friendliest person in town," he said.

"I can tell." Sami took her seat and glanced at the lunch menu, wondering if all the women in this town were just as mean.

"Oh, here." He slid two packets of saltines in front of her, along with a glass filled with lemon-lime soda. "So, how do you feel? Any better?"

She took a sip of her soda. "A little. I'll feel better once I eat. Thanks for the crackers."

He nodded.

The waitress arrived to take their order.

Sami held her breath, wondering if the woman would be as unfriendly as the customers.

"Hello, there. Are you two ready to order?" The woman smiled.

Sami smiled back at her, relieved to be greeted with something other than a glare. "I'll have the toasted turkey sandwich and fries, please."

The server looked at Billy.

"I'll have the same."

"All right then." The woman gathered up the menus. "Your order will be out in a jiff."

"Thank you," Sami and Billy replied at the exact same time.

"Jinx, you owe me a Coke," Billy belted out.

The waitress smiled and left to turn in their order.

"You already have one." Sami grinned smugly. She opened the crackers and took a bite.

"All right then, you owe me one later."

She finished swallowing her cracker. "Okay, I owe you. As soon as you're done with that one, I'll buy you another one."

"Nice try. They give free refills here."

"Well, there aren't any rules saying I have to pay for the drink I owe you."

"I suppose there isn't." He grinned.

Sami smirked and glanced out the window. An old red car drove by on the street, reminding her of her grandpa's car and her grandpa. "Can I ask you something?"

"Sure," Billy said.

"Do you know what's wrong with my grandpa?"

He stared at her with a blank expression, clearly taken off guard. "Uh, well…I'm not sure." He furrowed his brows. "Your mom didn't tell you?"

Sami shook her head. "She said she doesn't know exactly what's wrong with him. Just that he's ill and too weak for visitors. I was just wondering, since you live right next door, if you knew anything?"

Billy stared at his glass before looking her in the eyes again. "Sorry."

She sensed Billy knew more than he let on, but maybe she was wrong. All she knew for sure was that she was disappointed to have to rely on her mom for information.

The waitress arrived with their food.

"That was fast," Sami said.

The woman set Sami's food on the table and then Billy's. "It's today's special. The cooks prepare them ahead of time because people around here usually order the special for lunch. These were fresh off the grill as I turned in your order. Just holler if you need anything else." She smiled and went to another table across the room.

Sami picked up her turkey sandwich and took a bite.

"You must've been really hungry. I think you ate half of it in one bite." Billy raised one corner of his mouth before chomping on his sandwich.

"Ha, ha," she retorted playfully. "And, yes, I am really hungry. And I'm not used to fast service. Back home, it seemed like everything took forever."

"See, it's not so bad living here."

"No, I guess not."

She smiled, pleased to finally find a bright side to Wolf Hill—aside from Billy and Jason, that is. She suddenly thought of the stillness of the forest and how it seemed to be void of all living creatures. Not convinced Jason had been honest with her, she decided to ask Billy.

"I was wondering…I haven't seen any wild animals or heard birds chirping since I've been here. Is that normal?"

Billy shrugged. "It has been a little quiet lately, but I've heard birds chirping, and Mike and I still hunt. There are animals. I know they grow quiet when they sense danger, and they stay away from it. Maybe they know we're the danger." He grinned and raised his eyebrows. "Maybe they don't wanna end up on our dinner plates."

Sami giggled. "Maybe I should stay away from you too, so I don't end up being your next meal."

"Maybe you should." He smirked.

They continued their silly banter while they finished their lunches.

"Well, what do we have here?" A familiar voice interrupted.

Billy's smile faded when he focused on Jason.

"Hi, Jason." Sami beamed, happy to see him.

"So…" Jason took a few more steps until he stood right next to the booth. Looking at Sami, he smiled. "Is this the personal business you had to take care of today?"

Noticing his pulsating temples, Sami saw right through Jason's fake smile. He was offended to see her with Billy, especially after she'd told him that he couldn't accompany her today because of personal reasons. She felt terrible.

"I'm sorry, Jason. My car wouldn't start. It needed a new battery. Billy was nice enough to bring me into town to get another one."

Billy didn't say a word. He just stared at Jason as if he wanted to rip his head off.

"Oh, well, that was *nice* of you, Billy," Jason said snidely and glanced Billy's way before turning back to Sami. "Are we still on for tomorrow?"

Sami was relieved that Jason wasn't upset with her. "Yes, we're still on for tomorrow."

"Good. Let me know if you need help with your car, Sami." He smirked in Billy's direction.

"It's already taken care of," Billy said, his tone as cold as his glare.

With fury in his eyes, Jason met Billy's challenging stare, but after a few seconds his gaze softened, and he gulped before turning back to Sami. "Don't forget, it's your turn to bring lunch tomorrow. I'll be over in the morning at around ten o'clock. If that's good for you?"

"Sure, that sounds good." Sami smiled uneasily. The tension between Billy and Jason was so thick she could hardly breathe. She didn't understand the animosity between them but was curious to know what had caused it.

"I'll see you tomorrow then." Jason winked and walked away.

Sami eyed Billy cautiously, wondering if he were still angry. "I take it you two don't get along?"

Billy grinned through tightly closed lips. "So, where are you two going tomorrow?"

She decided not to pry. "To Wolf Lake. He took me hiking up there yesterday. He came by this morning wanting to go swimming today, but I had to come into town for my mom. So, we're going tomorrow. You should come with us. It'll be fun." She was hoping for a yes, but the bitter look in his eyes dissolved her hopes.

There was an uncomfortable silence before he cleared his throat. "No, you have fun. I have some things to do tomorrow."

She hid her disappointment with a smile. "Oh, well. Maybe, if you get done early, you can make it?"

"Maybe. Are you ready to go?"

"Sure." A *maybe* was definitely better than a *no*. She reached for her purse to get her money.

"No, let me." He fished his wallet from his back pocket and pulled out a twenty.

"Um, you don't have to."

"It's the least I could do after making you carsick." His eyes softened, and he set the money on the table.

Relief settled over her when his smile returned. She didn't want to be caught in the middle of his and Jason's rift, nor did she want to be the reason for making things worse between them.

"Okay, I'll pay next time. I owe you a soda anyway. And you didn't make me carsick. It's just something I've been flawed with recently. But it's getting better. I think."

"Good. I mean about the 'it's getting better' part. So, do you need a doggy bag in case you get sick again?"

"Ha, ha! No, I'll just throw up on your floorboard if I need to." She laughed, starting to feel more at ease with his sarcastic sense of humor. She felt silly for having been offended by it before.

"I was afraid you were going to earlier. You had me pretty worried there for a minute." Billy chuckled under his breath.

Smiling, they both got up and headed outside to his car.

On the way home, instead of heavy silence filling the air, they shared some of her grandpa's stories of each others' childhood adventures and misadventures. Within fifteen minutes, they were home.

Billy replaced Sami's old car battery with the new one and checked the tire pressure, spark plugs, and fluid levels. "I think you're good to go." He snatched the red rag from his back pocket and wiped the grime from his hands before he closed the hood.

Sami eyed his flexed biceps and the definition in his forearms, trying to ignore the sudden energy running through her.

Billy dusted his hands together and turned to her.

Sami lifted her lashes to meet his stare, hoping he didn't catch her gawking.

One corner of his mouth rose before he spoke. "I'll take the old battery back to the parts store to recycle it, if you want."

She bit her lower lip, wondering if his slight smile meant he'd noticed her staring. She pushed the embarrassing thought from her head and forced a confident smile. "Sure. And thank you so much for everything."

"It was no problem." He picked up the old battery from the ground and cradled it in one arm.

"Don't forget your brother's motorcycle part." Sami snatched the small paper bag from the roof of her car and set it on top of the battery. "So, maybe I'll see you at the lake tomorrow?" She remained hopeful despite the reluctance in his eyes.

After a few seconds, his eyes softened, and he sighed. "Maybe. I have some work to do. But I'll try."

"Okay. Thanks again for your help today." Anxious to get the shopping done before her mom returned home, she got into her car. The engine rumbled to life with the first turn of the key.

Billy stood at the edge of his yard, watching her.

She leaned her head out the window. "It sounds really good. Thank you so much!"

He smiled with closed lips and nodded.

A sudden ache filled her chest. For some odd reason, she didn't want to leave his company. *Are you that pathetically lonely, Sami?* She shook her head and backed out of the driveway, watching as Billy walked across his yard toward his house. She waved as she drove past him.

A SUDDEN heaviness filled Billy as he watched Sami drive away. Stopping in the middle of his yard, he shook his head, disgusted with himself. *Why in the hell am I bummed that she's leaving? Get a hold of yourself, dumbass! You're acting like a whupped dog! She's Harry's*

granddaughter for crying out loud. The same man who's been like a dad to you all these years. What would he say if he knew you had the hots for his granddaughter?

He recalled the way Sami had eyed his muscles while he'd worked on her car. And how red she'd turned when he'd finally made eye contact with her. A slight smile crossed his face at how good it made him feel to watch her desire him. About how good *she* made him feel when they were together.

"Ah, Billy...," he whispered and let out a heavy sigh. "What in the hell are you getting yourself into? You've been a mess for the last decade. She deserves better." He shook his head and eyed the driveway leading to Jason's house.

"Talking to yourself again?" Mike approached from behind.

Without looking away from the heavily wooded driveway, Billy handed his brother the package containing his motorcycle part. "Guess who's back."

Mike sighed. "Yeah, I know. I saw Jason drive by earlier." He put a firm hand on Billy's shoulder. "Maybe things will get better this summer, little bro."

"Don't hold your breath," Billy replied cynically. "Jason's already trying to sink his fangs into Sami."

Mike narrowed his eyes. "How?"

Billy turned and headed toward the house with Mike at his side.

"Apparently, he took her hiking up to the lake yesterday, and he's taking her swimming tomorrow."

"So, what are you gonna do about it?" Mike asked.

Billy shrugged and gave him a puzzled look. "Why is it up to me to do anything about it? Sami's a grown woman. She can see who she wants."

"Because you like her, and it would piss you the hell off to see her with Jason. And I'm tired of seeing you pissed off all the time."

Billy sighed, irritated that his brother was being a pain in the ass again. Sure, he was attracted to Sami, but if Mike found out, he'd never hear the end of it. Besides, for now, they were just friends.

"I don't like her. I mean, she's a nice person and all, and I think of her as a friend, but I don't *like* her." He stepped up onto the porch and set the battery down against the railing.

Mike walked past Billy and pulled the screen door open. "Just a minute ago you were pissed that Jason was trying to 'sink his fangs' into her. And last night, you said she was hot. And now, you're acting like you're not even interested?"

Billy gritted his teeth. "Dude, I never said she was hot. *You* did! And I'm just pissed about Jason because— You know why! Anyway, she's *Harry's* granddaughter. Jason's not good enough for her! *I'm* not good enough for her!"

Mike stared at Billy with a blank expression before his eyes filled with disappointment. "Billy, you had no control over what happened all those years ago. It wasn't your fault. It's time to get over the anger and self-doubt and start living again. And you're right, I don't think Jason's good enough for her. But as for you, you're wrong." He turned and went into the house.

Billy stood dumbfounded, unable to recall the last time his brother had said anything caring. Mike was only capable of being the hard-ass everyone was afraid of or the arrogant pain in the ass who couldn't take anything seriously. It didn't matter though, Mike was right, it was time to stop being so angry. Billy didn't know how in the hell he was going to accomplish the feat. Anger had just become a part of him over the years, even though happiness was something he desperately needed.

Still frustrated and baffled by his brother's new personality, he stormed across the porch and went inside, letting the screen door slam shut behind him.

5

I SLOWLY descend the worn cement steps until I reach the door covered with scratches. My heart races with fear as I reach for the knob. Turning it, I push the door open and step inside the cold, dark room. A thin cord dangles above me, and I give it a gentle tug. The light is dim. Metal shelves overflowing with clutter surround the room. A door on the opposite wall captures my attention. Fear consumes me as I cross the room. With a trembling hand, I reach for the knob and turn it, but the door won't open.

Sami tensed and opened her eyes. She sat up, staring at the sunshine streaming through her window. "Huhhh, it was just another nightmare." She shook her head and ran her fingers through her hair. *Why do I keep having these dreams? Am I really that freaked about wolves and basements?*

She glanced at the alarm clock on the nightstand. It was already nine fifteen. She jumped out of bed to get ready for her trip to the lake with Jason. When she'd finished, she ran downstairs to the kitchen to prepare ham and cheese sandwiches for lunch. She made a couple of extra sandwiches in case Billy decided to show. She placed the lunches in brown paper bags, and then into her backpack, along with some colas, water, and chips. She added sun block, a towel, and her camera.

She set the backpack down by the front door and eyed her sneakers, cutoffs, and blue tank top, wondering if she should change into more appropriate clothes for the hike. She tucked her dangling locket under her tank top to keep it out of the way.

Footsteps clomping across the porch caught her attention.

Right on time. I guess what I'm wearing is fine. She opened the door.

Jason stood before her, wearing a charming grin. "Sun's shining, and it's already warm out. It doesn't get any better than this."

"Hi, Jason!" Returning the smile, she eyed his attire of cross-trainers, blue swim trunks, and gray T-shirt, feeling more at ease with her choice of clothing.

She gave a casual glance toward Billy's house to see if he had changed his mind, but there was no sign of him or his car. She kept smiling to hide her disappointment and reached for the backpack.

"Here, let me." Jason hoisted up the backpack and worked his arms through the straps. "Wow! What do you have in here? Rocks?" He chuckled. "Aw, crap!" He squished his eyes shut and shook his head. "I forgot the rocks."

"You were gonna bring rocks?" She crinkled her forehead.

"Skipping rocks." He shrugged. "I guess that means you didn't bring any, huh?"

She pressed her lips together and shook her head. "Sorry, no. I did pack some extra food and drinks. Just in case. Billy said he might show up."

Jason clenched his jaw and smiled. "Sorry to disappoint you, but it looks like he's not coming." With a quick nod he gestured towards Billy's empty driveway. "I saw him and his brother loading up their tools early this morning. They're sort of the town's handymen."

"Oh. I guess that means there's more for us then." She shrugged, deciding it was best to keep hiding her disappointment. She could already tell from Jason's tight-lipped and fake-looking smile that he didn't like where the conversation had gone.

This definitely wasn't the way she'd imagined making friends here. She'd had no idea her only two friends would end up being enemies.

Maybe somehow, someday, they could get past their differences and finally get along. Billy and Jason used to be friends at one point. After all, they had lived across the road from one another all their lives. Besides, her grandpa's stories proved it.

Sami followed Jason to the trail, where they began their hike through the forest. It was nice walking under the protection of the trees where the air stayed cool. When they reached the clearing, the air turned hot and humid.

"You're right. It is hot out today," Sami said, fluttering her shirt to dry the perspiration dampening her torso.

"Yeah, but that's a good thing because the water's gonna feel good." Jason led the way across the meadow and down the slope to the lake.

They spread their towels out across the grass and plopped down to drink some water and rest.

Jason wiped the sweat from his brow with the back of his forearm and stood. "So, are you ready to get wet?" He peeled off his shirt and kicked off his shoes.

"Um…" She was caught off guard by his toned physique. *Wow! What is it with all the guys around here? It's like they're all superhuman.* She bit her lower lip.

A smug grin crossed his face.

Embarrassed, she averted her gaze and reached for the sun block. "Sure, but I burn pretty fast." She stood to discard her clothing but hesitated when he didn't look away.

He smirked and focused his attention on the waterfall.

Sami kicked off her sneakers and shimmied out of her shorts. She sat back down and pulled her tank top over her head, exposing her royal blue bikini. She suddenly felt naked. To hide her embarrassment, she concentrated on rubbing sun block across her exposed skin.

Jason knelt beside her. "Here, allow me." He took the bottle and gestured toward her back.

Though she felt uncomfortable, she smiled and turned. Gathering her hair, she held it up out of the way.

Jason squirted the sun block into his palm and began rubbing the cream over her bare back. He took his time, covering every inch of flesh.

When he was done, he cleared his throat. "There, all done."

Without warning, he jumped up, ran to the water, and dove in.

"Whoa!" he yelled when he resurfaced. "The water's great! Jump in!"

Hoping the higher temperatures had warmed up the lake since the last time they'd been there, she went to the water's edge and dipped her toes in. Its iciness cut through them like a knife. "It's still cold!" she shouted, crossing her arms across her chest.

"Only at first, but you can't inch your way in. You have to just jump in like I did."

Against his advice, she waded in slowly until the frigid water reached her knees. The burn was almost unbearable. It wasn't as noticeable when they were here last, running and splashing one another. But now that she was expected to immerse her entire body, the coldness consumed her.

"Come on! Just dive in! It only takes a second to get used to it."

"You mean it only takes a second before I go numb and can't feel anything anymore," she replied playfully.

He laughed and splashed water at her.

She screamed and jumped back before the icy droplets touched her skin.

"You better get in before I come and get you," he warned as he waded toward her.

"No, wait!" she pleaded and backed up until her feet were back on the shoreline. "Okay, okay! I'll get in!"

To calm her nerves, she formed her lips into a circle and let out a long breath. Before she could talk herself out of it, and before Jason decided to come and get her, she ran into the water and dove into its icy depths.

She'd originally intended to dive under the water as far as she could toward the waterfall before she broke for air. But the shock of the frigid temperatures cut her dive short. She scrambled to the surface and gasped.

"It's freezing!" she shrieked.

Her teeth had already begun to chatter and goose bumps covered her flesh, turning so hard they hurt. She crossed her arms to shield them from the cold, while attempting to tread water using only her legs. Struggling to stay afloat, her head bobbed in the water.

Jason swam to her, laughing. "Maybe I'm just a little more warm-blooded than you are." He wrapped his arm around her and pulled her to his chest.

"I c-can swimmm," she tried to protest through chattering teeth while secretly relishing his warmth.

"It looks like you're about to drown," he teased. "I'm not letting go 'til you're safe." He swam toward the shore on his back using one arm, while he held her tightly against his chest with the other.

Jason's skin was so warm that she didn't protest. She laid her head on his chest and closed her eyes.

When they reached the shore, Jason helped her out of the water, holding her hand to keep her steady. He grabbed her towel, gave it a good whip to ensure its cleanliness, and wrapped it around her.

Her teeth chattered uncontrollably. She was sure her lips were blue.

"Are you gonna be all right?" he asked with a look of concern.

"Y-yeesss," she stuttered. It was all she could manage to say.

In jerky movements, she spread her towel on the grass and lay down on her back. She closed her eyes and welcomed the warmth of the sun's rays. It didn't take long for her lips to stop quivering and for her muscles to relax.

"The goose bumps are gone. That's a good sign," Jason said.

She opened her eyes to answer him and tensed, startled to see him propped on one elbow, lying next to her. Right next to her. Almost too close.

Jason gazed into her eyes and pressed his lips to hers.

Stunned, Sami turned her head to the side and pushed him away. "What are you doing?"

Jason furrowed his brow, confused. "I-I thought you liked me."

She closed her eyes and sighed as she thought of a way to let him down gently. "I do like you, Jason…." She opened her eyes just as his lips touched hers again.

Her breath caught in her throat, and she pushed him away. "Jason! What are you *doing*?" she shouted and sat up, trying to control her trembling hands and shaky voice. "I *do* like you! But only as *friends*!"

"I think that means if you try to kiss her again I'll break your jaw!" Billy's voice boomed from behind them. He stood at the edge of the meadow glaring down at them with his rifle slung over his shoulder.

Jason's eyes filled with fury. "What the hell, Billy? Spying on us?"

"I came to make sure Sami was okay. Looks like I got here just in time!" he snapped.

Jason quickly pulled his shoes on and glared at Sami. "I thought we were more than friends, *Sami*."

"Jason, I... I..." She shook her head and sighed. There was nothing she could say to better the situation. The damage was done. She felt awful.

Jason snatched up his belongings and stormed up the slope. He stopped just long enough at the top for him and Billy to glare at each other before he stormed off.

Sami could've sworn she heard one of them growl. With tears burning her eyes, she shook the ridiculous notion from her thoughts and gathered her clothes, anxious to hide her vulnerability.

STANDING AT the edge of the meadow, Billy watched helplessly as Sami dressed and gathered her things, wishing he could run after Jason and kick his ass. He didn't have a clue about how to make Sami feel better, but from the distraught look on her face, he knew he had to try.

He let out a heavy sigh and made his way down the bank to where she stood. "Are you okay?"

"I just wanted to be friends. Apparently, he wanted more," she said with a shaky voice.

"I'm sorry he did that to you. Girls around here practically throw themselves at him. He doesn't take rejection well. As a matter of fact, I don't think he's ever *been* rejected before."

Sami snapped her head around to face him. Her eyes reflected both hurt and anger. "Well, he's got me all wrong! I don't *throw* myself at anyone!"

"I know. I think he knows that now too."

She nodded and lowered her gaze to the rifle. "Why'd you bring a gun? To scare Jason?"

Taken by surprise, he restrained the urge to laugh. Sure, he wanted to teach Jason a lesson, but not by threatening to shoot him. "No, it's for protection. You know, wolves, bears."

A look of concern replaced her anger. "What? Bears? Jason said there haven't been any bears around here for years."

"Yeah, well, there's not exactly a fence keeping them out either."

"And," she said, her voice louder, "you both said wolves are *afraid* of humans."

"They are, but they're also wild, unpredictable animals. They do what they have to in order to survive."

"Why would Jason put me in danger like that? Why didn't *he* bring a gun?"

Billy wondered the same thing. Jason knew how dangerous being in the wild could be. "Wolves usually aren't seen in the day, but you can never tell."

"I can't believe I trusted him to keep me safe from wild animals without a gun."

"Jason can be arrogant. Almost like—" he held his breath, trying to find the right word "—like he thinks he's indestructible."

"I wish I would've known that sooner," she said with a bitter look.

So do I, he replied silently. "Come on. I'll take you home." He picked up the backpack and worked his arms through it before leading the way up the bank, across the meadow, and to the mouth of the trail.

As they entered the forest, he noticed Sami being overly cautious. She walked along, eyeing every large tree and shadow as if a wild animal might lunge at any moment.

Billy stopped and watched her, suppressing a smile. "I'm sorry, Sami. I didn't tell you about the wild animals to scare you. I just told you, so you'd be more careful. Aware. We'll be okay. That's why I brought my rifle."

She smiled sheepishly. "Okay. I'll try to relax a little."

"Good. Ladies first?" he asked, motioning toward the trail in front of him.

"No, that's okay. I'm not gonna relax *that* much. I'll follow you."

He nodded and continued along the path.

They walked quietly for a few minutes, through the dense forest, both lost in their own thoughts. Every time the wind kicked up, Billy caught a whiff of the intoxicating coconut scent of the sun block Sami wore, and it was driving him crazy. It seemed each time they were together his desire for her grew. So how in the hell was he supposed to just be friends with her?

The sound of Sami's footsteps ceased behind him. He turned around to see what she was doing. Using one hand to brace herself against a tree, she waved the other hand at her flushed cheeks as if she were trying to cool herself down.

"Ummm." She swallowed hard. "I don't feel so good. I haven't eaten anything."

"Okay, let's rest a minute so you can eat. Did you bring anything?"

The color drained from her face. She threw both hands over her mouth and darted from the trail. She braced herself against a tree, dropped to her hands and knees, and vomited.

Billy rushed to help her but stopped when he realized there was nothing he could do to help. "Are you okay?"

Facing toward the tree as she heaved, she shook her head and held a hand up, motioning for him to stay put. Locks of hair fell from her shoulders and hung in front of her.

Ignoring her silent plea for privacy, Billy gathered her hair and held it back.

When the sickness finally subsided, she sat back.

Billy pulled the towel and a bottle of water from the backpack. He wet the towel and handed her the rest of the bottle.

With a shaky hand, Sami took the bottle and managed a slight thank-you of a smile. She rinsed her mouth out thoroughly and spat the tainted water before she gulped what was left.

Billy felt bad for her. She had already been through a lot lately with her parents separating and her grandfather's illness. And, to top things off, the townspeople had been rude to her. Even her first friend here had ended up being an arrogant ass.

Don't worry. Things will get better. I promise, he vowed silently. He handed her the towel. "Feel better?"

"Yeah, I think so," she replied, her voice raspy. She buried her face in the wet towel and slid it down her face, wiping her eyes, cheeks, and mouth in one swipe.

"We can sit on that log over there, so you can eat." He grabbed her arm and helped her up.

She let out a shaky breath and followed him to the log. "I guess you've noticed that I get sick if I don't eat."

"Yeah, I seem to have caught on to that. Here—" he handed her the backpack and they both sat down "—take as much time as you need."

"Thank you." Sami rummaged through the bag and pulled out two sandwiches. She handed one to him.

He really wasn't hungry, but he figured she'd feel more comfortable if he ate with her. "Thanks." He wriggled it from the clear plastic bag and took a bite.

It irked Billy to be eating something that was meant for Jason. But being polite was more important at the moment. Even so, he couldn't completely hide his resentment. It ran too deep.

"I guess this was meant for Jason?" he said, holding up the last bit of the sandwich before popping it into his mouth.

"Actually, it was meant for you. I was hoping you'd make it, so I made some for you too."

"Really? Thanks." It felt good to know she'd been thinking of him, but he didn't let on. Thoughts of Jason trying to kiss her popped into his head again.

"I'm sorry I didn't come sooner."

"It's okay. I'm just glad you did come. Otherwise, I'd probably be walking home by myself right now, scared to death." Her eyes scanned the forest again.

"Ah, I don't think Jason would leave you out here by yourself." He was disgusted with himself for defending the arrogant prick, but he knew Jason wasn't the type of guy who would purposely put anyone in harm's way. Especially not a woman.

She looked at him curiously. "You hate him, but you're protecting his honor?"

"No. I'm not protecting anything of his. I just know he wouldn't leave you out here alone. It's too dangerous and easy to get lost.

Anyway, do you feel better?"

"Yes. I feel much better. Except for being completely humiliated about getting sick in front of you."

"Don't worry about it. It's nothing I haven't seen before. You should see Mike when he's hung over." Billy let out a throaty chuckle.

"Maybe I'll pass on that." She laughed.

"Are you sure you're okay? You still look a little pale, and your eyes are dark."

"Yeah. I'm just feeling kind of tired now. Maybe I need a nap? I haven't been getting much sleep lately."

"You're right. We should get going. You'd probably feel better if you were at home." He stood and reached his hand out to help her up.

She placed one hand in his and grabbed the backpack with the other.

"Give me that." Billy shook his head as he took the backpack from her.

"I don't wanna burden you any more than I already have."

"Sami, you haven't burdened me in the least bit. I'm just glad I was here to help."

"Thank you for helping me today, Billy. And yesterday."

"Ah, you don't have to thank me."

She turned her attention to the forest and looked around.

"Don't worry, you're safe. Are you ready?"

"Yeah." She nodded.

"Okay then, let's go." He gave her a reassuring smile and continued along the trail.

JASON REACHED his front porch and collapsed on the top step to catch his breath. The daunting sprint home from the lake seemed to have soothed his anger. But after being rejected by the woman who'd held a piece of his heart since he was a child, it didn't ease the hurt.

He yanked off his T-shirt and wiped the sweat dripping from his brow before tossing the shirt aside. *Why in the hell was I so quick to make a move? I should've just waited.* He ran a hand through his hair. *Sami's not like all the other girls around here. She's sweet, innocent, and genuine-hearted. And dammit if all those traits don't make me want her more!*

He leaned against the railing and stared into the forest, wondering if Billy was more her type. The quiet brooding guy who didn't let himself get close to anyone or let anyone get close to him. When he'd seen Sami and Billy at the diner yesterday, they'd looked pretty comfortable together—talking, laughing, and getting to know each other.

Jason clenched his jaw at the seething thought. *I'm the friendly, charming, go-out-of-my-way-to-help-people kind of guy. Not Billy! But it doesn't matter now. I blew my chances with her the minute I tried to kiss her.*

It was too soon. Way *too soon. I should've just waited.*

And now, I have to sit back and watch her fall for Billy. Not that Billy's a bad guy. Just one who's had a hard time in life ever since—

No! Don't frickin' go there again! Just because Billy can't let go, it doesn't mean you have to do the same.

He let out a heavy sigh, snatched up his shirt, and went in the house to take a long, cold shower.

6

FOR BILLY, the hike back hadn't seemed as long as usual. Probably because of his and Sami's conversation about how it was to live at the beach or in the middle of a forest. He usually hiked the trail by himself when he set out to hunt or to just be alone. He preferred it that way—privacy to reflect on the past and how life would've turned out if he could change what had happened.

He shook his head, trying to keep the disturbing memories from entering his thoughts, something that seemed much easier to do when Sami was around. Despite what she'd been through just this morning, she retained a cheerful demeanor, which eased his broken soul.

"Are you sure you're all right?" Billy asked as they trudged up Sami's porch steps.

"Yeah, I feel much better since I ate." She smiled and patted her stomach.

His expression turned serious. "No. I mean about what happened before that. With Jason."

Her smile faded. "I'll be okay. I just hope I don't run into him anytime soon. That would be a little awkward." She glanced at the driveway across the road.

"I know that I live right next door, but let me give you my phone number. You know, just in case you need anything."

"Okay, sure." She opened the door and went inside.

Billy followed her into the house. He stood in the entryway and looked around the room. "Did you know Mike and I helped Harry with the remodeling?"

"I didn't know that. So, what did you do in here?" she asked, letting her eyes sweep the living room and kitchen.

"Let's see…. I painted the walls. Helped install the cabinets. Laid the flooring in the living room. And helped set the granite in place."

Sami smiled. "You did a really great job. It's all beautiful." She went to the kitchen and spotted a note on the counter.

"Ah, it's just work," Billy said, watching Sami as she read the note.

"Great." Sami crumpled the note and tossed it into the garbage.

"Is everything all right?"

"Yes," she replied with uncertainty before letting out a hopeless sigh. "Well, sort of. My mom has to work tonight. I haven't quite gotten used to the forest and complete darkness yet. It's a little creepy." She grabbed the notepad and pen off the counter and handed them to him.

Billy had a sudden urge to protect her. To keep her from being afraid. "I'll give you my home *and* cell number." He jotted them down and handed the notepad and pen back to her. "I can stay if you want me to. Or you can come over to my house until your mom gets back." He held his breath, hoping she'd take him up on his offer.

Sami's eyes filled with reluctance. "I'll be fine. I have to get used to living in the forest sometime."

"Are you sure? Because it wouldn't be a problem." He had never tried this hard to change anyone's mind about anything. He and Mike had learned long ago to not get too close to people. But, for some reason, he hadn't been able to get Sami out of his thoughts since she'd moved here.

She paused and captured her bottom lip with her teeth. "Yes, I'm sure. Besides, you live right next door. It's not like I live out here totally alone. It's just until midnight. I'll be fine."

His hopes fell flat, but he shrugged to appear casual. "Okay then. If you need anything, just call me. I'll be right over. *Anything*. Even if it's just to borrow an egg or something."

"I will." She snickered and walked him out to the porch.

"Anything," he called over his shoulder as he jogged down the porch steps. He gave her one last reassuring smile before he walked across her yard and into his.

SAMI'S INSECURITIES were eased by Billy's presence. Now that he was walking away, she felt vulnerable again. She wanted to take him up on his offer, but she also didn't want to appear like a child needing a babysitter. She was sure he had something better to do than to sit around and keep her company for the day.

After he was out of sight, she glanced at the shadowed forest, growing wary of the way it seemed to dominate over her like a bully does its victim.

She closed the door and locked the deadbolt. Then, she ran upstairs to take a shower.

When she finished her shower, she put on her cozy navy sweat pants and gray tank top before she went back downstairs and turned on the TV. She hadn't realized how exhausted she was until she snuggled into the corner of the couch and pulled the plush purple throw over her cool skin. A yawn escaped, and she decided to close her eyes for just a minute.

I reach up with a trembling hand and open the front door. Standing in the doorway, I stare into the dark forest. I sense something out there, watching me, though I can't see it. Heavy breathing cuts through the silence, followed by a deep growl.

A loud banging jarred Sami from her sleep. She jumped up from the couch and eyed the room. Aside from the dim light emitting from the TV, the entire house was dark.

The pounding echoed through the room again. She breathed a sigh of relief when she realized someone was knocking on the front door.

With a hand over her chest to calm her thudding heart, she flipped the light switches on the wall—illuminating the living room and front porch—and opened the door.

Billy stood there, grinning with one hand behind his back. He studied her for a moment and his grin faded. "Sorry, did I wake you?"

"Yeah, I guess I fell asleep watching TV." She ran her fingers through her hair to smooth out any unruliness.

"I'm sorry. I just wanted to come by and see if you were okay. I didn't mean to wake you. I heard the TV on."

"Oh no, it's fine. I've been asleep for too long as it is. I didn't know it was almost dark out. I don't wanna be wide awake all night. What time is it anyway?"

"Around eight or so. I can stay for a while. I mean, if you want."

Her heart soared. Not wanting to seem too eager, she hid her smile between pursed lips. "I don't wanna burden you. I'm sure you have better things to do than babysit me."

Billy smiled and crinkled his forehead. "Sami, trust me, you're *not* burdening me. Is that why you didn't wanna hang out earlier?"

She smiled halfway and shrugged. "A little. That and I was tired."

"I'm glad. To tell you the truth, I thought it was because you didn't like me," he said.

"What?" She furrowed her brow. "Of course, I like you, Billy."

She paused and bit her lower lip, wondering if she should've worded it differently and hoping he didn't think she had a crush on him now. Sure, she was attracted to him. He'd traipsed all the way through the forest and rescued her, in a sense. And he seemed to be coming to her aid a lot lately. How could a woman *not* like a man like him? A hero, so to speak. But she certainly wasn't ready for him to know that. What if he didn't feel the same way about her?

Billy grinned. "Good. I like hanging out with you. It's cool having a friend right next door."

Her heart sank from the word *friend*. His feelings for her couldn't have been clearer. *Maybe he already has a girlfriend? Or a boyfriend? I hadn't thought about that.* She swallowed her hurt and forced a slight smile.

"Besides," he said, pulling a large paper bag out from behind his back, "I brought dinner from the diner. You know, in case you forgot to eat. I didn't want you to get sick again or anything."

Billy's thoughtful gesture put a smile back on her face. She stepped aside to let him in. "I can't very well pass up something to eat."

"No, you can't." He grinned and closed the door.

Sami went to the refrigerator and grabbed two colas.

Billy sat on a barstool at the breakfast bar. He fished two cheeseburgers from the bag and set them on the counter, along with two containers of fries.

She took a seat next to him and handed him his drink.

"Thanks," he said.

They looked at each other and their gazes locked. A nervous flutter filled Sami's chest, and she turned her focus to the food. *That was intense. Maybe he does like me more than I thought? Or maybe I just made a fool of myself. Just try to act normal, Sami.*

Billy cleared his throat and took a bite of his cheeseburger.

"You're welcome," Sami said before chomping on a fry.

Billy gave her a puzzled look. "For what?"

"The soda." She smirked, glad she wasn't the only one whose mind was muddled by their intense gaze.

"Oh, right." He smiled modestly, raising only one corner of his mouth.

"And thank *you* for dinner," she added.

"Anytime." He pointed to her burger. "It's better if you eat it while it's warm."

"Right." She picked it up and took a bite. "Mmm. This is delicious!" she said with a hand clamped over her mouth to hide the food.

"The best cheeseburger you'll ever taste," Billy said with satisfaction and took another bite.

"So, how'd you know I forgot to eat anyway?"

"Really, after what happened yesterday and today, are you seriously expecting an answer?"

She smiled and nibbled on another fry.

"Hey, did you know it's supposed to storm tomorrow?" Billy said.

"Really? I did *not* know that. It's all right though, I don't have plans anyway." She shrugged and continued to eat.

"You should get some candles or flashlights ready. The power usually goes out during storms."

"Great. Thanks for the warning," she grumbled, already dreading the thought.

"I have to work in the morning, but maybe we could hang out tomorrow afternoon if you want?" His voice sounded hopeful.

"Sure, that would be cool." She tried to sound nonchalant, but on the inside, she was soaring.

They finished their dinner and then sat on the couch to watch TV. Though she had been anxious for her mother to get home earlier in the evening, Sami was now thankful to have more time with Billy.

She suddenly realized she hadn't seen Billy's parents around. They were often included in her grandpa's stories when she was a child, but not for a long time. Not for years.

"Billy, can I ask you something?"

"Sure."

"Where are your parents?"

Billy's expression turned serious, and his eyes grew dim. "They died when I was twelve."

Sami's jaw dropped open. She felt awful for asking. "I'm so sorry. I just remembered my grandpa talking about them before—when I was little—when he would come to visit. I didn't realize... I didn't know."

"It was a long time ago. Don't worry about it."

Though he sounded casual, the thick tension in the air proved otherwise. She shook her head. "I'm sorry, Billy. I didn't mean to upset you."

He let out a heavy sigh, as if he'd been holding his breath. "You didn't. It's just, everyone around here already knows about it. So, I've never actually had to tell anyone before. You just shocked me is all." He gave her an unsure smile. "So, are there any good movies on tonight?"

Though he'd changed the subject, she could still sense his pain. She wanted to hug him, or at least pat his arm. But they were still getting to know each other. It would be awkward. Especially since he seemed strong-willed and proud.

Thankful he had changed the subject, she grabbed the TV remote off the coffee table and flipped through the few available channels. The only movie playing was about werewolves.

"We don't have to watch it if you're too scared. We can do something else," Billy said.

"No, it's fine. I actually like scary movies. Ironic, huh?" She smiled.

"Very," he replied with a surprised look. "I would never have guessed."

Feeling brave since Billy was with her, she turned off the lights to improve the visual effects of the movie. A couple of times, during the scary parts, she screamed and almost jumped into his lap.

"Are you sure you don't want me to hold your hand?" Billy teased.

Though she laughed with him, she didn't make any effort to scoot back over to her side of the couch. She sat as close to him as possible without actually touching him. So close she could feel the heat radiating off his body, and she relished the feel.

It was after eleven o'clock when the movie finally ended.

Billy stretched and yawned. Exhaustion darkened his eyes.

"You don't have to stay until my mom gets home. I'll be okay. I know you have to work in the morning." She tried to be brave again, but only for his sake.

"Are you sure?" His mouth opened wide, releasing another yawn.

"Yes, I'm sure. You look tired. You should go home and get some sleep."

"Okay, I think I will." He rose from the couch and stretched his arms over his head before he went to the door.

Sami followed him.

Billy turned and his eyes locked on hers. "I had fun tonight," he said, his tone soft.

Sami's heart rate sped up. From the look in his eyes, she was sure Billy wanted to kiss her. And the thought scared her. "Yeah, me too." She gulped.

He lowered his eyes to her lips, staring at them briefly before he looked at her again. "So...tomorrow then?"

"Tomorrow," she whispered back.

"Good night, Sami." He paused for a moment longer as if he wanted to say something more or *do* something more before he finally turned and opened the door.

"Good night, Billy."

Feeling a mixture of both desire and disappointment, she stood in the doorway and watched as he made his way across her driveway before disappearing into the moonlit shadows of the trees in his front yard. Then, she shut the door and locked it.

7

SAMI AWOKE by nine o'clock the next morning and hopped out of bed to get ready for the day. With her head soaring in the clouds as she thought of her time with Billy the previous night, she threw on a gray tank top, covered it with a lavender plaid flannel to keep cozy during the rain, and pulled on a pair of jeans. Then, she hurried to the kitchen and made bacon, eggs, and toast for breakfast, along with a fresh pot of coffee.

Carol entered the kitchen wearing her bathrobe. "Wow! You made breakfast and coffee? Is it Mother's Day?" she teased.

"No, Mom. I just thought since you've been working so hard that I'd help out. You know, do more around the house and all." Sami sat at the kitchen table and took a bite of her toast.

Beaming with pride, Carol joined her. "Well, thank you. It looks delicious!" She shoved a forkful of scrambled eggs in her mouth and her eyes lit up. "Mmm. Very good. It's been awhile since I've had a hot breakfast."

"Thanks, Mom. Did you know it's gonna storm today?"

"I know. Early this afternoon, I think," Carol said. "And it's much colder out today than it has been. What crazy weather. Hot one day and cold the next. I sure miss the mild weather in Monterey." She shook her head and let out a dismal sigh. "Anyway, I'm leaving early today to visit your grandpa before my shift starts. And to beat the rain. It really downpours here. I don't like driving in it."

"What? You have to work tonight?" Though last night had technically been her first night alone, it had only lasted for an hour. Yet, every creak and moan had frightened her. She swore the house was haunted. Now, she would have to spend the entire day and night alone, by mere candlelight if the weather decided, and she wasn't looking forward to it.

"Sorry, sweetheart. It looks like I'll be working night shifts from now on. I know you're afraid of the dark, but they're short-handed at night. It's the only full-time position open right now. Plus, it pays better. Maybe you'd feel better if you quit watching all of those scary movies."

Sami wanted to defend herself and pretend she wasn't affected by the horror flicks, but her mom was right. They did scare the crap out of her, though she'd never admit it.

She decided not to make her mom worry any more than needed. Not only was she being childish—thinking the house was haunted and being afraid of the dark—she was also being selfish. Her mom had lost everything she'd ever known and had moved back to a place she loathed to care for her ill father. And lately, all Sami had done was think about herself.

"It's okay, Mom. I understand. Don't worry about me. I'll be fine. And I'm not afraid of the dark. It just took a little time for me to get used to living in the wilderness, but it's not so bad now."

"Okay." She smiled. "Oh, I almost forgot. I don't want you to worry, but the power goes out sometimes when it storms."

"I know. Billy already warned me."

"Oh? So, how is Billy?"

"He's good. He came over last night and hung out with me," she replied, keeping a casual tone.

Carol raised a curious eyebrow. "Oh, really?"

Sami pressed her lips together, trying to hide her bashful smile. "No, Mom. It's not like that. We're just friends. We might hang out again later today."

"I see." Carol's face held a knowing grin. "What about Jason?"

The humiliating events of yesterday crossed Sami's mind. If she told her mom what had happened, she would never hear the end of it. Neither would Jason. And she certainly didn't wish the wrath of her mother's lectures on anyone. After all, Jason wasn't a *bad* guy. He'd just thought she was interested in him.

Sami shrugged. "We're just friends too."

"Right." Carol stared at her, wearing a disbelieving smile before she ceased her playful tone. "I'm glad you have friends around to keep you company while I'm at work. I won't have to worry so much now. Oh, and don't let me forget to leave you the candles and flashlights I bought the other day. They're out in the car."

"Okay."

Her mom could be overwhelming at times, treating her as if she were still a child. But, thankfully, the overbearing parenting was lessening. *Maybe mom's been so overprotective because of all the hardships she's been through lately. Sort of like an outlet for her stress—something she doesn't even realize she's doing. Or maybe she's trying to hold on too tightly to the only thing in her life that's still hers—me.*

She watched as her mother's gaze settled somewhere outside the kitchen window. She studied her mother's features, noticing the dark circles under her eyes. How could she have not noticed how exhausted her mom appeared before now? Fine lines had even settled in around her hazel eyes and full forehead. And her once-vibrant complexion had paled and dulled.

"Are you feeling okay, Mom?"

Carol yawned. "Yes. Why?"

"No reason. You just look a little tired is all."

"Oh." Carol smiled, lips closed. "That would be from lack of sleep, sweetheart. Working as a nurse can do that to you sometimes. Speaking of which—" she stood and gave Sami a couple of soft pats on the back "—I have to get ready for work. Thank you for breakfast."

While her mother disappeared into her room to get ready, Sami gathered the dirty dishes and put them in the sink to rinse them. A cup slipped from her hand and landed in a bowl of soapy water, splashing suds across her neck. She wiped it away with her hand and realized her locket was missing.

"Oh no!" *Where is it? I have to find it!*

Sami plunged her hand into the sudsy water, running her fingers over and under the silverware sitting at the bottom. She dried her hands on a dish towel and scanned the counters and floor in the kitchen before making her way into the living room. Not seeing it anywhere on the floor, she slid her fingers into the crevices of the couch and pulled out the TV remote and a quarter.

"Dammit!" She set the items on the coffee table and rushed upstairs to the bathroom. Nothing. She searched her bedroom. Still nothing.

"Nooo. Where is it?" The previous day's events flashed through her thoughts.

She remembered tucking it under her tank top just before Jason had knocked on the door yesterday. But she hadn't noticed it dangling in front of her while she'd vomited in the forest.

Please don't let it be in the lake.

Not wanting to lose it forever under a layer of silt, she decided to try to beat the rain and head to the lake. She shoved her feet into her hiking boots and grabbed her cell phone and pocketknife off the dresser. On her way to her mother's room downstairs, she worked the knife into the front pocket of her jeans and slid her phone into the back pocket.

"Mom!" she shouted, pounding on the bedroom door.

Carol opened the door, her face full of worry. "What is it? What's wrong?"

"Nothing," Sami managed rather calmly. She had to let her mom know where she was headed, in case something went wrong, but couldn't let her know she'd lost the locket. She blurted the only excuse that came to mind. "I forgot my camera at the lake yesterday. I need to go get it before it starts to rain. I don't want it ruined."

Carol's look of worry deepened. "Oh, Samantha, I don't know. You shouldn't go up there alone."

"It'll be fine, Mom. Billy and Jason go up there all the time. Besides, I have my cell phone. If I don't get back before you leave, have a good night at work." She hurried toward the front door, trying to avoid any more protest.

"Don't go up there alone," Carol called out. "Maybe Billy or Jason can go with you?"

"All right. I'll go ask them now." Sami opened the front door, not bothering to look back. If she made eye contact now, her mom would know she wasn't being truthful. She hated lying, but there wasn't any way around it this time.

"Good. But promise me you won't go up there if they can't go. It's not safe!"

"I know. Bye, Mom!" She rushed out the door and slammed it shut, anxious to get away.

Thick dark clouds loomed overhead, and the air was cooler than it had been yesterday. Thankfully, it wasn't raining yet.

Should I go back and grab a jacket? No, Mom will just try to stop me from going. I'll be fine if I hurry.

Sami threw a quick glance toward Billy's driveway, hoping to see his car, but it wasn't there. She eyed Jason's driveway, but quickly shook the notion from her thoughts.

Don't be a wuss. You can do this by yourself.

She took a deep breath and ran into the forest alone.

BILLY HOPPED up the steps of the front porch just as Carol stepped outside. She was dressed in blue scrubs with her hair pulled back into a bun.

"Hello, Billy. How are you doing?" She smiled.

"I'm doing all right, Carol. And you?"

"Fine. Just headed to work."

"How's Harry doing?"

Carol hesitated. "He's still the same, but Samantha doesn't know about what happened yet. I'm hoping to avoid her knowing anything at all. If it comes down to it, I'll tell her when the time is right."

Billy didn't agree with keeping Harry's condition from Sami, but he had to respect Carol's wishes and continue to keep his mouth shut. He nodded.

"Is Sami here?"

"No. She left her camera at the lake yesterday," Carol replied, looking apprehensively at the darkening sky. "She went to get it."

Billy tensed. *What? Sami went into the forest alone? What was she thinking?*

"She should be home soon."

"Okay," he said as if it were no big deal, trying to keep calm for Carol's sake. "Maybe I'll just head up there and meet up with her."

"Oh, that would be great! I think Jason's up there too. I told her not to go alone. Hopefully, she didn't." She shook her head. "But you know Samantha. She can be stubbornly independent sometimes, going against all better judgment."

"Oh, I'm sure." Billy nodded and hid the dread pounding through his veins with a smile. He knew Sami went into the forest alone. He'd seen Jason's car parked in front of the diner on his way home. But, after yesterday, he was sure she wouldn't have swallowed her pride and asked the jackass to go with her.

The angry sky rumbled, and raindrops spattered on the roof.

"I have to get going before it starts raining too hard. You two have fun tonight." Carol hurried to her car and climbed in. She waved through the windshield and the engine awakened.

Billy waved back and watched Carol drive away. As soon as she was out of sight, he ran home and grabbed his rifle. Then, he raced into the forest, heading for the lake.

SAMI CRAWLED on her hands and knees, combing through the grass with her fingers. "Where is it?"

The clouds rumbled above, and the lake began to dance with tiny ripples.

If it's not in the grass... She eyed the lake, unable to see the bottom with the rain disturbing its surface. She shook her head and sighed.

I guess I have to go in. I have to find it.

Feeling awkward about stripping outside, she reluctantly undressed down to her black bra and underwear. The air was cold, but tolerable.

She eyed the forest, which seemed eerier under the darkness of the clouds. An uneasiness swept over her, and she felt as if she were being watched.

A sudden wind kicked up, cooling the air dramatically. She shivered and crossed her arms over her chest. "Okay, here it goes." She took in a deep breath and exhaled. A cloud of white mist escaped her lips. Before she could talk herself out of it, she trudged forward in the exact same spot she had jumped in yesterday.

The frigid burn on her legs sent an instant wave of rock-hard goose bumps over every inch of flesh. Summoning all her inner strength, Sami took another deep breath and immersed herself into the icy depths of the lake.

The searing pain engulfed her entire body. Even her eyes hurt. She thought for sure they'd freeze open. Air bubbles escape her lips as she sank, and she searched the pebbles lining the bottom of the lake.

She was just about to go back up for air when the water illuminated briefly, and a silver shimmer on the lake floor caught her eye. Taking a closer look, she focused on the delicate features of the locket.

Yes! She quickly snatched it up with a handful of dirt and tiny rocks. Nearly out of breath, she planted her feet on the bottom of the lake and sprang up through the water's surface, gasping for air.

Lightning flashed and thunder pounded the sky.

Startled by the boom, Sami's breath caught in her throat and she sucked in raindrops. She hacked and sputtered, trying to clear her lungs, until the urge to cough subsided.

She suddenly realized the danger of the situation. *Please God, don't let me drown out here.*

Anxious to get to shore, she flailed her arms forward and kicked vigorously until her hand hit the smooth pebbles of the shoreline.

Teeth chattering, Sami propped on her hands in the shallow water and took a quick moment to catch her breath. She pulled herself to her feet and crouched forward, hugging herself to shield the biting wind as it chilled her to the bone. Her body trembled violently, and she thought for sure she'd soon be covered with a layer of frost.

She picked up her jeans and shoved each foot into a pant leg, but her wet skin caught on the fabric, making the simple task of dressing difficult. Frustrated, Sami hopped up and down until both feet pushed through the bottom holes of the jeans. She continued her struggle with the rest of her clothing. Yanking. Pulling. Unrolling each item to lay flat against her damp skin. For some odd reason, she thought when she had finally accomplished dressing she'd be warmer, but she'd forgotten to factor in the rain soaking her clothes.

This was a stupid idea!

Freezing inside and out and trembling from head to toe, she shoved the necklace into the front pocket of her jeans and began to climb up the bank. Hunched over and using both her hands and feet so she wouldn't slip back down, she pulled herself up the muddy slope using clumps of grass as leverage. When she finally made it to the top, she tried to run across the meadow, but her legs were weak and heavy. She couldn't run. She could barely even walk.

A flash of light and a loud *crack* filled the menacing forest.

She screamed and jumped back, staring at the angry clouds.

A sudden growl erupted from somewhere close by.

Afraid, Sami spun around, eyeing nearby bushes and trees. She couldn't see any wild animal, but she knew it was out there somewhere. A desperate will to live sent a rush of adrenaline through her veins, and she darted toward the path.

The icy rain fell harder, and thunder boomed.

Why did I have to be so stupid? Why did I come out here alone?

Sami eyed the forest as she neared it. The animal belonging to the growl could be in there. But she had no choice. It was the only way home.

She stumbled onto the muddy path. Though the trees sheltered her from some of the rain, they also blocked out most of the light. Shadows loomed everywhere.

Her body continued to tremble. It even felt as if her lungs were quivering, making it difficult to suck in a full breath of air. She crossed her arms, trying to steady the shaking and shield herself from the cold, but it didn't help.

Another growl rumbled behind her.

Sami came to a sudden halt and spun around, expecting the viscous wolf of her nightmares to lunge at her. But there was nothing there.

Whatever had made such a deep growl had to be dangerous enough to kill her. But she wasn't ready to die. Not today.

Hot tears burned her eyes and left warm trails down her cheeks. With a trembling hand, she reached into her pocket and pulled out her knife. She opened it, wincing as the sharp blade sliced through the forefinger of her right hand.

Blood oozed from the wound and streamed down her palm, fanning out like watercolors on a canvas.

Light flashed again, along with another loud *crack*.

Sami jumped and let out an ear-piercing shriek. Wasting no more time, she bolted along the trail.

Heavy raindrops broke through the tops of the trees and began to pound down all around her as thunder and lightning dominated the angry sky. The booming was so loud, she barely heard herself cry. And if she couldn't even hear herself, she wouldn't be able to hear her stalker.

Out of breath, lungs burning, she continued to run—terrified of what wild animal might be out there and hoping it was scared off by the commotion of the storm.

Holding onto the only shred of hope she had, Sami forced herself forward until her legs grew too heavy with exhaustion. She tripped and fell onto the muddy path.

She tried to scramble to her feet, but had no energy left.

I'll just rest for a minute.

Looking around, she spotted the fallen tree she and Billy had sat on yesterday. She crawled to the log and leaned her back against it, trying to calm down enough to catch her breath.

I should call Billy. Maybe he's home now. She wriggled her wet fingers into her jeans pocket and yanked out her cell phone.

No Service illuminated across the screen. "No!" She let out a hopeless sigh. In a last paltry attempt to find warmth until she regained the energy to press on, she bent her knees to her chest and pulled her flannel shut around them.

BILLY SPRINTED along the muddy path as the rain poured down, anxious to find Sami and trying not to think about the horror that had taken place in this very forest thirteen years ago. Dread filled him, making his legs feel heavy. The suctioned squish of the mud under his boots didn't help either. But he pounded his way over the mud, somehow managing the strength to run faster than he ever had before.

After what seemed to be the longest minutes of his life, he rounded a bend and spotted her in the distance, leaning against a fallen log and looking the opposite way up the trail. She gripped a pocketknife in one hand and blood dripped down the other.

"Holy shit, she's hurt," he whispered and rushed to her side.

She snapped her head around and her eyes locked with his.

"Billy?" She frowned and her chin started to quiver.

"Sami, what happened? Is this your blood?" He grabbed her hand and flipped it over, spotting a cut on her forefinger. "It looks okay. It's not too deep, but it's bleeding pretty good." He gripped her waist and hoisted her from the ground before easing her onto the log.

"Shit, you're frozen." He slid the rifle from his shoulder and leaned it against the log. Then, he shrugged his heavy work jacket off and draped it around her shoulders.

"I-I'm so glad to s-see you," she cried.

Billy peeled off his T-shirt and wrapped it around her hand to stop the bleeding, ignoring the rush of cold air on his skin.

She stared at his bare chest and shook her head. "Y-you n-need your shirt."

"It'll be soaked soon enough. I don't need it. And I'll take that," he said and carefully slid the four-inch blade from her trembling hand. "Are you hurt anywhere else?"

"It's j-just my f-finger." She bit her lip to steady it. "I accidentally c-cut it."

He focused on the shiny metal of the blade. "Silver? Nice knife." He folded it and slid it into his front pocket. Though still worried, the fact she'd nearly lost her life over something so meaningless angered him.

"What are you doing out here, Sami? It's just a stupid camera. You could've gotten lost or come across a wild animal. Or froze to death. What were you thinking?"

"I lost the locket my mom gave me for my birthday," she croaked. "It was in the lake."

"What? You went in the lake? Are you *crazy*?" he snapped. "You could've drowned! It's too cold! You're probably suffering from hypothermia." He sat next to her and pulled her into his arms, attempting to warm her faster.

"I can't...breathe, Billy."

He loosened his grip. "I'm sorry. It's just the forest is dangerous, Sami. You can't come out here alone."

"I know that *now*. I was so scared. I didn't think I was gonna make it home. And I heard something growling."

"You did?" He eyed the shadows. Not wanting to scare her any further, he kept calm. "Whatever it was, it's probably long gone by now. Especially with all the lightning and thunder." He let out a long, relieving breath and stood. "Let's get you home."

From the way Sami rose to her feet with careful movements and kept her shoulders slouched, Billy knew she was exhausted.

He slung his rifle over his shoulder and scooped her into his arms.

"I can walk," she protested as he clomped along the trail.

"You can barely stand, Sami. I need to get you home fast, so I can warm you up."

"Okay. Maybe just for a little bit. Until you get too tired," she said, her voice weak. She laid her head against his chest and closed her eyes.

Hurrying along the trail, Billy carried her cold, limp frame as she slept. He'd only met this sleeping beauty three days ago, but in just a short time, she'd stirred something deep inside he just couldn't shake. No woman had ever had this kind of power over him before.

He'd learned years ago to not trust or get too close to anyone. Yet, here he was, trusting her *and* falling for her—falling hard. And there was nothing he could do to stop it. He didn't know how in the hell it had happened, but one look at her, and he'd lost all control.

Come on, Billy. Get a grip! You can't drag her into your fucked-up mess of a life. She deserves better!

He stopped briefly to ensure her chest still moved with life. Satisfied with its steady rise and fall, he continued forward.

SAMI FLUNG open her eyes and looked around as lightning flashed across the walls. She was on the couch in her living room, covered with her purple throw. She gasped and sat up as memories of the lake and the growling in the forest flooded her thoughts.

"Do you feel better?" Billy exited the kitchen and sat next to her.

She let out a sigh of relief when she saw him. "Yeah, I do. Just a little groggy and sore." She yawned and stretched her aching muscles. "How long was I asleep?"

"About four hours. You were exhausted."

"*Four* hours? And you carried me all the way home?" She felt awful for putting him through such an ordeal.

"Yeah, it was nothing."

"I'm sorry. I didn't mean to cause all this. I should've just waited until the storm passed. I was so stupid!"

"Don't worry about it. It's over now. You're safe, and you found your locket," he reassured, his eyes filled with compassion.

"Thank you for saving me," she said. She looked down and noticed the bandage on her finger. "And for saving my finger. I owe you my life."

"Any time," he replied. "And all you owe me is the same courtesy if I ever do anything just as stupid."

This time, she didn't take offense to his blunt honesty. She knew she deserved it. "Deal." She smiled.

"As long as I don't have to carry you home," she added, trying to make light of the matter.

"Well, that's not fair." He grinned. "Oh, and I put your pocketknife on your dresser."

"Thanks. It was a birthday present from my dad."

"My dad gave me one for my birthday too when I was a kid. A Buck Folding Hunter knife. But I lost it." He sighed, his eyes holding a hint of sadness. "I understand why you had to find your locket."

"I'm sorry, Billy."

He cleared his throat, and the sadness in his eyes vanished. "Don't be. It was a long time ago."

She nodded, deciding it best to respect his privacy and change the subject. "I know I'm a heavy sleeper, but I can't believe that I slept through everything."

"Probably from the effects of hypothermia. I'm glad you're feeling better. Are you hungry? Mike brought over some stew he made earlier. And some biscuits. I kept it warm on the stove for you."

"Wow! That was nice of him. It sounds really good. And smells good too. I'm starving." She stood and tossed the blanket aside but stopped when she realized she was wearing a dry pink sweatshirt and gray sweatpants. Shocked, her hands flew to her chest. Her bra was missing, and she was sure she wasn't wearing panties either.

"Uh!" she gasped and turned to Billy, wide-eyed. "These are different clothes. Where are my clothes? My…" She was too ashamed to say underwear in front of him.

Billy jumped to his feet. He stared at her hands covering her breasts, and then looked away. "Uh…." He grimaced. "Well, you were frozen…and dead asleep. I had to get your wet clothes off." As he spoke, he grew increasingly defensive. "I had to get you dry and warm. I pulled your sweatshirt down over your, you know—" he motioned toward her breasts "—before I took your bra off. And then I covered you with a blanket before I changed you out of your wet pants."

She eyed him warily.

"Well, you would've done the same thing for me, *right*?" he asked, his face strained with frustration and guilt.

The possibility of Billy having seen her naked was humiliating, but she kept composed. After all, he had only done what he thought was best for her.

"Well…you had to get me dry, I suppose." An awkward silence filled the room before she spoke again. "As long as you didn't see anything, right?"

"I promise I didn't!" he blurted. "I couldn't just leave your wet things on. You were so cold, it felt like you were *dead*!" He ran his fingers through his hair. "I'm not some pervert, you know. I completely respect you."

"I understand, Billy. I'm just grateful you found me and helped me. It's fine, *really*. So, let's just forget about it, okay? And thank you *again* for saving me. You are my true hero."

Billy stared at her with a puzzled look, obviously not expecting her to relent so quickly. He nodded cautiously.

Another uncomfortable silence plagued the moment before she finally rummaged around for something else to say. "And please don't tell my mom about any of this. I'd never hear the end of it. She'd probably ship me back to California. And ask Mike not to say— Wait a minute!" Her eyes grew wide and her voice wary. "Did your brother happen to be here while you were putting me in dry clothes?"

"No. He wasn't here. It was just me." Billy's voice was calm and softer now. "I'm sorry. I didn't mean to invade your privacy. You were just ice cold. I was worried. I almost took you to the hospital, but Mike said you'd be okay if I just got you dry and warm. So, I changed your clothes and—" he looked down at his boots "—I sort of laid on the couch with you to warm you up faster. Until I got too hot." He gulped and looked at her with uncertainty as if he were about to get in trouble.

"Oh." She was too uncomfortable to look him in the eyes yet was secretly thrilled at the thought of his body against hers. She eyed the blue plaid shirt he wore over a gray T-shirt, wondering if he had been clothed when he'd warmed her up.

As if he could read her mind, he quickly added, "I had all of my clothes on. Honest."

"Well, thank you. I was just a little embarrassed at first, but it's okay. If it wasn't for you, I'd probably still be out there, lost and frozen in the forest. Or dead." She shrugged and shook the thought from her head. "I don't know."

A deep rumble and a loud *crack* rattled the living room window.

Sami screamed, startled by the explosion. The lights went out, engulfing the room in darkness.

"Great, power's out," Billy said.

Afraid, Sami rushed to Billy's side, accidentally bumping into him.

"Whoa." He put both hands on her waist to steady her. "It's okay. I take it you don't like storms?"

"There aren't really any storms like this where I lived. Just a drizzling rain and fog mostly." Feeling silly, she stepped back from his grasp, glad the darkness kept him from seeing the fear in her eyes. She remembered the candles. "Oh no! I forgot to get the candles from my mom before she left."

"Actually, she left them on the counter." Billy groped his way to the breakfast bar. On his way there, he ran into the wooden barstool, its legs screeching across the floor. "Ow!" He chuckled under his breath.

"Are you all right?" She couldn't help but giggle.

"Yeah." He fumbled with the candles and matches.

Afraid to be in the dark living room alone, Sami tiptoed to the kitchen and waited behind him.

A soft glow illuminated the room.

Billy turned and tensed. "Geez, Sami, you scared the crap out of me!" He grinned. "I didn't know you were right behind me."

"Sorry," she snickered.

"It's okay. We should eat before the stew gets cold."

Sami pulled two bowls from the cupboard and filled them with the steaming stew, while Billy poured two glasses of milk. They sat at the breakfast bar to eat.

She hadn't realized how hungry she was until she took her first bite of the warm and hearty stew—just what she needed after nearly freezing to death. Within minutes, her bowl was empty. She washed down the last bite with a gulp of milk.

"That was delicious! Your brother is a pretty good cook." She smiled with satisfaction while patting her full stomach. She set her glass of milk on the counter with a clank. Some of the liquid splashed up over the rim and splattered onto Billy's T-shirt.

He eyed the wet mess. "Look what you did to my favorite shirt." He frowned, though the glimmer in his eyes reflected play.

"Oops," she said with a guilty smile.

Billy slid his buttoned shirt off his shoulders, and then yanked his T-shirt over his head. "Good thing I wore two shirts today."

"Mmm hmm." Sami bit her lower lip and watched as the

candlelight reflected off the contours of his biceps and muscular chest, highlighting each cut magnificently. She gulped and looked away. Not being able to resist, she watched him from the corner of her eye.

Billy tossed the T-shirt on the counter and slipped the blue plaid shirt back on.

Watching his bare chest slowly disappear as he buttoned his shirt from the bottom up, Sami suddenly remembered that she had no underwear on. Feeling uncomfortable, she flashed an uneasy smile, dreading having to ask him to accompany her upstairs, so she could finish dressing.

He eyed her curiously and smiled halfway. "What?"

Sami stared at the darkened staircase. "Uh…I was just wondering if maybe you could come upstairs with me while I put more clothes on?" Her cheeks grew warm.

Billy glanced down at her clothing with a puzzled look and his eyes widened. "Oh…sure." He snatched the flashlight from the counter and fumbled with it, trying to turn it on.

Sami pushed the rubber button at the base of the flashlight and smirked.

"Right." He let out a heavy breath as if he were trying to get his nerves under control. With a smooth nod of the head, he motioned to the stairs. "Come on."

Sami went first but stopped at the bottom. She stared up the staircase and into the eerie shadows of the hallway that led to her bedroom. "Ummm, maybe you could go first, since you have the light."

"Sure." He led the way up the stairs. "Which one is your room?"

"The door at the end of the hall." Though she wasn't thrilled about having her room at the end of the hall, it was the largest room—big enough to fit her dresser and desk without feeling cramped.

Billy led the way down the hall and opened the door. He handed her the flashlight. "Here you go. I'll be downstairs."

Fear crept over her at the thought of being alone. "What? No. I mean—"

Billy started to laugh but tried his hardest to suppress it by pressing his lips together. "I'm just teasing, Sami. I'll be right here."

"Ha, ha! You're not very funny sometimes, Billy Holden." She smiled and set the flashlight on the dresser.

"I thought it was funny," he said with a smug grin. He grabbed the doorknob and proceeded to close the door.

"No!" she belted out. "Just leave it open. You can just turn around and look the other way." If he hadn't caught on earlier that she was afraid of the dark, he certainly knew now.

"Okay, okay." He turned and faced the hall. "You know, after what you went through in the forest today, you should feel safe in your own bedroom."

Humiliated, she retaliated with only part of the truth. "It's the storm. I'm not used to it." Wasting no more time, she began to undress.

"It is a pretty vicious storm. And maybe it would help if you stopped watching all those scary movies," he teased.

"Yeah, well, would you rather I make you watch mushy love stories with me?" she retorted playfully while digging through her underwear drawer.

"You make a good point."

Sami dressed quickly and ran a hand through her hair to smooth it. "Okay. All done."

Billy turned around and entered her room. "So, this is your room, huh?"

"Yeah. Boring," she replied flatly, wondering what his room looked like.

"No, it's cool." He shoved his hands into his pockets.

She crossed the room to the window and watched as lightning flashed across the forest, illuminating it with a strobe-light effect. A deep rumble rattled the window.

Billy's footsteps approached from behind. "You shouldn't stand too close."

Her eyes grew wide and she turned around to face him. "Really?"

"Really," he whispered, and his eyes locked on hers. He grabbed her wrists and took a couple of steps back, pulling her with him. He gulped and wrapped his arms around her waist.

His intense gaze and soft touch sent a flutter through her heart, quickening its pace.

This is it—he's really going to kiss me this time. She placed her hands on his chest, anticipating what was to come.

He slowly leaned down and pressed his soft lips to hers, and suddenly, nothing else mattered. She closed her eyes and relaxed against him, welcoming his kiss and the instant euphoria that came with it. He pulled away, their heavy breaths colliding, and then he molded his mouth to hers again. As they kissed, tiny hints of his silky tongue brushed against hers, clouding her mind in a sensual fog. She couldn't think clearly anymore. All she knew in that moment of time was being in his arms as he gave her the most magical kiss she'd ever experienced.

Slowly, he pulled away. They gazed into each other's eyes, taking a moment to gather their senses and to catch their breaths. Sami never wanted this moment of newly discovered feelings to end.

Lightning flashed, drawing Billy's attention to the window. He tensed, his face full of worry. "What the hell?" He released his hold on her and rushed to the window.

An immediate chill ran down her spine, devouring the euphoria within seconds. "What's the matter?" She peered over his shoulder, shocked to see red eyes staring at them from the forest. "What is it? Is it dangerous?"

Billy remained silent, squinting to see through the darkness and the fury of the storm.

Lightning flashed across the sky again, briefly exposing a large, hairy figure hidden amongst the trees. The forest darkened and lit up again, but the figure was gone.

"I think it's a wolf, but I don't see it anymore," he said.

"Really? I've seen it before. I was hoping it was just a raccoon or a deer or something."

"What? You saw it before? Why didn't you tell me?" He sounded angry. "It could be dangerous."

Sami shrugged. "I don't know. I thought it was just a normal thing to see in the wilderness. Is it something I should be scared of?"

Billy hesitated, before his eyes softened. "I'm sure it's just a wolf.

It's okay. Just be careful. Don't go into the woods alone again, *please*! And you probably shouldn't go outside at night for a while either."

"A wolf?" He'd made it sound harmless, but after her nightmares, she was sure he was just trying to ease her fear.

"As soon as the storm passes, Mike and I'll see if we can track it."

"Are you gonna kill it?"

"Yeah, if it's been coming this close. It's not like it just wandered into town for a few days. It's obviously been here before with the way your basement door looks."

Sami wanted the wolf gone, but killing it seemed wrong. "You can't just kill a wolf, can you?"

"I haven't actually *seen* a wolf around here before. I know they have been seen in the area, but not for a long time. Not for years." He shook his head and took a deep breath. "But for some reason, there's one hanging around your house. It's not as afraid of humans as it should be. It's not safe, Sami."

Her nightmares of the wolf came to mind, along with the scratches on the basement door. It was hard enough trying to feel safe here at night, and now, there was a dangerous wild animal to contend with. It seemed with every step forward in her new life, she suffered a giant step back.

"So, what now?" she asked. "Can it get in the house? Can it just come right into our front yards and attack us?"

"I'm pretty sure it can't get into your house. But you need to be more careful outside. And your mom too."

"Oh! My mom! What time is it? She might be home soon." She looked at the alarm clock, but it was blank from the power outage. "Did you find my cell phone in my jeans?"

"Yeah. It's on the kitchen counter. Come on." He snatched the flashlight from the dresser, grabbed her hand, and led the way down the hall.

On the way to the kitchen, all Sami could think about was their kiss. Their *first* kiss. It had left a feeling inside she'd never known existed. Sure, she'd been kissed before, but only a couple of times in high school, and they had been awkward at best. No other had left her feeling so giddy inside. So alive. Billy had awakened a brand-new desire in her—one she didn't quite know how to react to yet. All she knew, was that she wanted to be in his arms again, with his lips on hers.

Maybe I should kiss him again? She smiled at the thought, but it quickly faded. *Unless he didn't enjoy it as much as I did. I'm still new at this and he's older than me.*

She remembered her grandpa mentioning over the phone a few months back that Billy and Jason were the same age—twenty-five. Which meant Billy definitely had more experience than her and probably with experienced women.

Maybe my kiss wasn't good enough. But he's holding my hand. If he didn't want to kiss me again, he wouldn't be holding my hand, right? Or maybe he's only holding it because it's dark and he doesn't want me to trip and fall down the stairs.

Rather than risk being rejected and humiliated, Sami decided to wait for Billy to initiate the next kiss.

When they reached the kitchen, Sami looked at the time on her phone. "Nine o'clock. I thought it was later than that."

"Yeah, it's been a long day."

As soon as she set her phone back on the counter, it rang. They both jumped at the unexpected disturbance.

Sami answered with a hand over her heart. "Hi, Mom…. What…? Why…? When…? Tomorrow…? No, it's okay. I don't want you to drive home in the storm either, and he's here now. I'm sure he wouldn't mind…. Okay. I'll see you tomorrow…. Bye." She hung up and set the phone back on the counter.

"What was that all about?" Billy asked.

"My mom's not coming home tonight. She doesn't wanna drive home in the storm. She asked if you could stay here with me. Or if maybe I could stay at your house."

"Sure. No problem. I could stay here, I guess. On the couch."

"Good, there's no way I'm staying here by myself tonight."

"There's no way I'd let you," he said with a deep voice and wrapped his arms around her waist.

Sami's breath caught in her throat, and all of her previous doubts disappeared.

Billy leaned his head toward hers, but this time, she met his lips halfway. Their kiss was soft at first, making her insides flutter. When Billy pushed his tongue past her lips, their kiss intensified, consuming her in passion. His lips devoured hers, taking control and guiding each mouthful this way and that while their tongues swirled together. This kiss was very different from the first one. It ignited an energy which seemed to excite every inch of her body, making her want more.

Billy slid his hands up her back and entangled his fingers in her hair, kissing her so powerfully she was sure her heart was near exploding. Slowly, he loosened his fingers and slid his hands back down to her waist before pulling his lips from hers.

Breathing raggedly, they gazed into each other's eyes, still smoldering with desire. Billy released a long, controlled sigh. He placed both hands on either side of her face and kissed her gently, lips closed. Then, he rested his forehead against hers.

"Uhhh, I guess I got a little carried away," he whispered breathlessly.

She swallowed hard and gave a slight nod, still trying to control her labored breathing and pounding heart. Still trying to make her mushy insides feel normal again. "Yeah, me too," she said, her tone soft.

A thunderous *boom* shook the window.

Sami jumped back at the unexpected blast.

"It's okay." Billy pulled her into his arms again and gazed into her eyes. "This is gonna be a long night," he admitted, his voice husky.

"Yeah…it is," she whispered.

8

"**N**O, MOM, we didn't do anything like that. We just sat on the couch and talked about stories from when we were kids, and then we fell asleep," Sami argued from the couch, arms crossed.

Carol sat in the recliner across from her. "Well, what was I supposed to think, coming home and finding you two on the couch together, wrapped under a blanket?"

"I *am* twenty, Mom. But, no, we were just talking. Anyway, you're the one who wanted him to stay the night!" she snapped.

"I know. It just surprised me. That's all," Carol said, her tone softer now. "I thought he'd be on the couch and you'd be upstairs. I just want you to be careful. I was your age when I got pregnant with you." She paused, deep in thought. "I remember being so sick for the first few months. I even fainted a few times. And the lack of sleep and constant care." She shook her head and sighed. "Don't get me wrong, having you was the best part of my life and I wouldn't change that for anything. But it's not easy being pregnant and raising a baby when you're so young. And it's expensive."

"Mom, we're *not* having a baby! We *didn't* have sex! Don't worry.

When I'm ready, I'll be careful." Her first sex lecture had been given to her at the age of thirteen, which was expected.

But now? At age twenty? Sami rolled her eyes, praying for the conversation to be over.

"I know, sweetheart. I'm sorry. I just worry about you is all. Just last month, you were still a teenager."

Sighing at the thought, Sami recalled her recent uneventful birthday at her home in Monterey. After she and her mother had spent all day packing up half of the house, her father had returned home from work that night with a simple round chocolate cake. She had been able to tell from their darkened eyes that her parents were emotionally depleted. Yet, they'd pressed on with the quaint tribute, wearing false smiles as if they were happy again.

Sami knew the charade had been for her sake. For the sake of her special day. So, she had partaken in the faux celebration by smiling as she'd opened her gifts—the locket from her mom and the pocketknife from her dad. It was the last time they had all sat at the dinner table together. And, because he'd gotten called back into work that night, it was the last time she'd seen her father.

Carol let out a heavy sigh, an indicator she was finally easing up. "So, did you make it home yesterday before it started to pour?"

Sami had forgotten about almost freezing to death in the storm. She smiled uneasily. "Uh, yeah. Found my camera."

"Good." Carol's gaze shifted to Sami's bandaged finger. "What happened?"

"I cut it trying to open my pocketknife. It's not bad."

Her mom frowned and opened her mouth to speak, but Sami didn't want to hear another lecture, so she beat her to the punch.

"Oh, and I think we saw a wolf last night."

Carol's jaw dropped. "What? A wolf? Where?"

"Out back. In the forest. Billy and his brother are gonna see if they can track it. He said we need to be more careful when we're outside."

Carol sighed and her gaze settled somewhere out the window, her eyes reflecting sorrow. Suddenly, as if snapping back to the present, she turned back to Sami. "They usually don't come close to humans. But they are wild animals. I don't want you going into the forest anymore. You could've crossed paths with it yesterday."

Thoughts of the previous day's events crossed Sami's mind. The growling she'd heard had probably been the wolf. If her mother found out she *had* crossed paths with it, and that she had been alone while it had happened, her mom would drive her right back to California this very minute.

"Billy had his rifle," Sami said.

"What about Jason?"

Sami grew uncomfortable, wondering how to proceed. She didn't like lying, but easing her mom's worries was of utmost importance, so she gave the only answer she could. "Jason did too."

"Good." She stood and yawned. "I'm exhausted. It was a long night, and I didn't sleep very well in the hospital bed. I need to take a nap before work today."

"All right, Mom."

"I'll see you in a few hours." Carol went to down the hall to her room.

Sami decided to run upstairs to shower. When she was finished, she went to her room and put on a pair of cutoffs, a pale purple top, and a pair of sneakers. Thoughts of Billy's lips on hers kept her head in the clouds most of the morning. She couldn't wait to see him again. With a slight smile on her face, she pranced down the stairs and into the kitchen to make some breakfast.

After she ate her cereal, she kept herself preoccupied by doing the dishes, tidying nearly every room in the house, and sweeping the front porch. But no matter what she did to make the time pass more swiftly, the day seemed to drag by.

Satisfied the porch was well-swept, she leaned the broom against the house and took a seat in the white wicker loveseat, wondering how long it would take Billy and Mike to track the wolf. She stared up at the deep blue sky, dotted with white billowy clouds, glad to see the sun shining today. She took in a deep breath of the crisp air. Everything smelled fresh and clean.

The front door opened, and Carol stepped out onto the porch, dressed in blue scrubs.

"Off to work already, Mom?"

"Yes. The morning flew by." Carol shook her head and sighed.

Sami stood and gave her a hug. "Have a good day at work."

"Thanks, sweetheart." Carol headed down the steps to her year-old Audi sedan. "And stay out of the forest, please," she added over her shoulder as she climbed into the car.

"I will." Sami stood in the driveway and waved as her mother pulled away. She glanced next door. Billy's car was in the driveway, along with Mike's motorcycle.

I wonder if they're back yet? Or are they still out there? She eyed the forest, listening for their voices, but didn't hear or see anything. She wanted to find out if Billy was home—to knock on his door. But with the possibility of a hungry wolf nearby, she decided to call him first.

Sami went back inside and grabbed her cell phone from the counter. She pressed Billy's name on the screen. The call went straight to his voicemail.

Huh, now what am I gonna do? She frowned.

The rumble of a car engine drew her attention to the living room window. A new yellow Mustang with black racing stripes turned onto Jason's driveway. She caught a glimpse of Jason's face before he drove away.

What is it with guys and their cars around here? She shrugged, figuring they needed something to keep them busy in this isolated place.

The mishap with Jason crossed her mind. The more time passed, the worse she felt. They were neighbors and friends, and she wanted their relationship to be amicable, especially since they were bound to run into each other often.

Besides, it really wasn't his fault. Jason had thought she'd shared the same feelings as he had. He was probably just as humiliated about the whole incident. If not more so.

Maybe I should go talk to him? She stepped out onto the porch and stared at the dark wooded driveway across the road. *I'm sure it'll be okay if I hurry. Should I take my car? No, that would be silly to just drive right across the road. I'll run. I might even be able to catch him before he gets into the house.*

Before she could talk herself out of it, she yanked the front door closed and darted across the yard. When she reached Jason's driveway she didn't slow down.

It was dark and eerie under the trees' thick branches, but she kept her mind off the daunting sprint by focusing on the road ahead of her.

A pain shot through her side and she stopped to catch her breath.

Where in the hell is his house? I thought it was on the other side of these trees.

Up ahead, to the left, the driveway disappeared around a bend. *His house has to be close now. Probably just around the corner.*

Sami picked up her pace again, keeping a slow steady jog to avoid another cramp. She turned the corner, but up ahead was another bend—this time to the right. *What the hell?*

A surge of fear crept over her. Here she was, in the middle of the forest with a wild wolf roaming about, and she could be attacked and eaten at any moment.

She eyed the trees and bushes lining the driveway, wondering if the wolf was lurking nearby. *Should I keep going, or turn back?* At this point, she was sure Jason's house was closer than her own, so she decided to keep going.

A loud *snap* stopped her dead in her tracks. She held her breath, listening and waiting for whatever was out there to reveal itself.

Another *snap* pierced the silence, closer than before.

Sami scanned the forest, but still couldn't see anything through the trees' dense growth.

An overwhelming silence filled the air, followed by heavy breathing and another loud *snap*.

Terror enveloped her as she began to fear for her life. As she turned to run, she tripped and stumbled forward, but quickly regained her footing. She sprinted around the next bend, relieved to see Jason's house at the end of a long, dark tunnel of trees. She wanted nothing more than to be able to scream out for Jason, but for some reason, she couldn't. All she could do was run. She didn't slow or look back. She kept running until she finally broke through the shadows and into the sunlight. Her sprint continued across the paved parking area, along the walkway, and up the porch steps. On the last step, she tripped and stumbled forward.

JASON SET his groceries on the kitchen counter and headed back down the hall. As he neared the front door he heard the faint sound of a woman crying.

"What the…" He hurried to the door and yanked it open, shocked to see Sami flying straight toward him. With quick reflexes, he planted his feet firmly and caught her, but force of the impact sent him stumbling back against the closet door.

"What the hell? Sami? What's the matter?"

"Something's out there! It was chasing me!" she shrieked through heavy breaths.

Her shrill voice sent a chill down his spine. "What's out there?" he demanded.

She pushed away from him, slammed the door shut, and locked the dead bolt.

He looked out the narrow window but didn't see anything unusual.

"I don't know! But I heard something in the forest! I could hear it breathing! It was getting closer, but I couldn't see it! Then I just ran!" Sinking to her knees, she sucked in a ragged breath and wiped away her tears with the back of her hands.

Jason peered out the window again before turning back to her. "I don't see anything now." Another tear rolled down her cheek and a sudden urge to comfort her tugged at his heart. He knelt beside her and pulled her into his arms. "It's gonna be okay. You're safe now." He pulled away and with a gentle touch, placed an index finger under her chin and guided her gaze to meet his. "Okay? You're safe now. It's probably just an animal. It can't get in here."

He plucked some tissues from the table next to the door and handed them to her.

With a trembling hand she took the tissues and dried her cheeks and nose. "Billy and I saw a wolf in the forest last night behind my house," she said with a shaky voice.

Dread filled him, but he kept calm for her sake. "What? A wolf?

Are you sure?"

"Yeah, I think so. A really big one. Tall. I saw it a couple of other times too, from my bedroom window." Her distraught expression suddenly turned to an angry one. "I thought they were afraid of people, Jason! That they stayed *away* from us!"

"They usually do." He sighed and swiped a hand over his mouth. "I've never actually *seen* a wolf here. Not deep in the forest and especially not in anyone's backyard." He opened the closet and pulled out a double-barreled shotgun. "Stay here. I'll be right back."

"No! Please don't go out there! Don't leave me here!" she pleaded, grabbing the back of his shirt.

Jason stumbled back but quickly regained his balance. He turned and looked at her in disbelief. "Hey, heyyy," he said in a soothing voice and wrapped an arm around her.

"Please, *please* don't go out there!"

"I'll be okay. *You'll* be okay. I *have* to go out there, Sami. I'll just be right on the porch. You can stand in the doorway, okay?" He gazed into her eyes, waiting for a sign of trust.

She nodded, but her eyes filled with reluctance.

Jason released his hold on her and opened the front door. He eyed both ends of the long porch and stepped outside without making a sound.

Sami stood in the doorway.

A light breeze kicked up, sending a large maple leaf scratching its way across the driveway into the grass of the front yard.

Jason cautiously made his way down the steps and scanned across the lawn to the blackberries at the edge of the yard, and then past the brush into the forest, waiting for any sign of movement. He saw and heard nothing out of the ordinary. To his left, the forest lining the driveway and parking area also remained quiet.

He picked up a few small rocks from the flower bed lining the base of the porch and chucked one into the trees to the right of where he stood. There was no sound of an animal scurrying off. Throwing harder, he sent another sailing over the front lawn. It disappeared into the trees and was followed by silence. He threw the last rock into the forest just past the paved parking area to his left. The rock came to a crunching halt and then all remained silent.

Jason sighed and trudged up the steps. "There isn't anything out here, Sami. Maybe it was just a deer or something. Or possibly a wolf, but there's nothing out there now." He motioned with a hand toward the foyer.

Her brow creased with uncertainty, and she stepped back into the house.

As soon as Jason entered, Sami shut the door and locked it again, her face puckered with worry. "There was something out there in the forest. It was after me, Jason. I *heard* it!"

"You didn't see it, though. Maybe it was just as scared of you?"

"But I heard it get *closer.*"

"Did you actually hear it chasing you? You would've heard it running across the pavement."

"No," she admitted with a frown.

"It probably didn't even come out of the woods. It was probably scared of you too." He smiled, trying to ease her fear.

She let out a shaky breath. "Maybe you're right. Maybe I just freaked out after seeing a wolf last night and thought… I don't know. Maybe you're right."

"What were you doing, anyway?"

She lowered her gaze and bit her bottom lip. "Coming to see you. I feel bad about what happened the other day, and I just wanna make things right somehow. I still want us to be friends." Her hope filled eyes met his again.

Jason's expression softened. He felt like a fool for kissing her, but for some reason, he always protected his damaged ego with anger. It was hard enough for him to apologize to people for even the slightest of reasons, let alone for damage *he* caused. But he was determined to change that now, starting with the woman he desperately wanted to kiss again, yet he knew he had probably lost his only chance.

He sighed. "Yeah, I'm sorry, Sami. I shouldn't have tried to kiss you. It was wrong. And I'm definitely sorry for getting mad at you over it. You didn't deserve that. I just thought we were on the same page, you know?"

"I know. And I'm sorry I'm on a *different page,* but I don't wanna lose you as a friend."

"It's all right. I'm over it. Besties?" he teased with a smirk.

She snickered and nodded. "Sure." Her smile faded, and she bit her lip. "Uhhh, there's just one more thing I need to talk to you about."

"Sure. Shoot!" He grinned.

Sami opened her mouth to speak, but a knock on the door stopped her.

Jason unlocked the deadbolt and opened the door.

Jessica walked right in, wrapped her arms around his neck, and crushed her lips to his.

Jason pulled away and cleared his throat. "I have company."

He stepped free from Jessica's arm-lock and motioned to Sami with a quick nod while giving Jessica a once-over. Her hot pink tank top barely contained her breasts, and her white cutoffs were the shortest he'd ever seen them. It was on days like these he wished he'd never broken up with her.

"What's *she* doing here?" Jessica snapped.

"Uh, she's my neighbor," Jason replied with his brow furrowed. He didn't like Jessica's haughty tone, a constant flaw of hers, which was one of the reasons he'd told her they should just remain friends. The other was the fact that she was too clingy. She'd already hinted about moving in with him after their first night in bed.

"Yeah. I know. I met her at the diner the other day when she was with Billy." Jessica's voice was cold. "But what is she *doing* here?"

Jason narrowed his eyes. "We're *friends*, Jessica. You know, like me and you! She can be here if she wants to be."

"Hi, Jessica," Sami said in a soft tone.

When Jessica didn't reply, Sami gave Jason a puzzled look and shrugged. "I was just leaving anyway. I guess I'll see you later, Jason." She headed out the door.

"Wait!" Jason grabbed her arm. "You're not walking home. I'll drive you."

"*What?*" Jessica fumed.

Sami put her hands up as if to stop him and shook her head. "Uh, no that's—"

"I'm taking you home, Sami. I'll carry you if I have to." Jason took her by the hand and led her across front porch and down the steps. He turned to Jessica, who stood in the doorway twirling a lock of hair around her finger, and said, "I'll be back in a minute."

Jessica stomped across the porch and parked her rear on the top step.

As he and Sami climbed into his car, Jason released a burdened sigh, wondering how he was going to get rid of Jessica for the day.

"Sorry about that," Jason said. He started the car, revved the engine, and sped along the driveway. "Apparently, she has a hard time letting go."

"To tell you the truth, I'm glad you're not together. I was trying to figure out why you kissed me if you already had a girlfriend."

"Come on now." He raised one corner of his mouth. "You have to give me more credit than that. I know I'm a ladies' man, but it doesn't mean I'm a man of many ladies at once."

Sami smiled. "I suppose it doesn't."

"Thank you." He grinned. "And besides, what happened between me and Jessica ended before you moved here."

"Oh." Sami nodded. "Sooo, Jessica seems…*possessive*. And she definitely doesn't like me."

"Jessica's just had a hard time in life. Her parents died awhile back, so she moved here to live with her uncle. You know, the sheriff. He just lets her do what she wants to keep her happy. Plus, she's jealous of you. She's never had competition like you before. A hot chick from sunny California."

Sami furrowed her brow "I think I'm pretty average. Jessica's the one who's beautiful. On the outside anyway."

Jason let out a surprised chuckle. "You've got to be kidding me. You're one of the most beautiful women in town. You shouldn't underestimate yourself."

Sami's cheeks turned pink. She looked away and let out a heavy breath. "So, doesn't anyone have a normal life around here?"

"Depends on what you mean by normal." He winked and pulled up in front of her house.

"Well, thanks for giving me a ride."

"No problem," he replied. "See you later, Sami."

"Bye, Jason." She hopped out of the car and walked to her front porch.

Jason turned his car around and sped away.

BILLY HAD just pulled a fresh T-shirt over his head when he glanced out the living room window and saw Jason's car pull up next door. The passenger door opened, and Sami climbed out.

That's where you were? With Jason?

Jealousy heated his blood. He rushed out the front door and across his yard into hers. "Sami, I looked all over for you. Mike and I were about to go up to the lake and see if you were there. You were with Jason?"

She descended the porch steps, her movements slow and cautious. "I'm sorry. I just wanted to apologize to him for the other day. To make things right again."

Billy fumed on the inside. It took all his self-control to keep from exploding. "*He's* the one who should be apologizing!"

"I know. And he did." Her lip started to tremble. She swallowed hard. "I just felt so bad, Billy. I didn't wanna lose him as a friend. He just thought I liked him back is all. The same way I like you." Tears glistened in her eyes. She looked toward the sky and shook her head, obviously trying to keep them from falling.

Billy suddenly felt like a jackass. He wrapped his arms around her and hugged her tightly, lifting her off the ground. After he set her back down, he swiped a gentle thumb across her cheek, wiping away a lone tear.

"I'm sorry I got mad, Sami. I know he's your friend too. I was just worried about you. And then, when I saw you with him…" He shook the bitter thought away.

"I know. I understand. Just please don't be angry with me. It seems either I hurt you by being his friend, or I hurt Jason by being yours. I don't want to be caught in the middle of the rift between you."

"I'm not angry with you. And you're right, it's not fair to you. I'm sorry. I'll deal with it somehow. Okay? I promise."

"Okay," she agreed with a smile and threw her arms around his neck.

Billy gave her a tight squeeze and lifted her again. He didn't know how in the hell he was going to keep his promise. Just the sight of Jason made his blood boil. But he was willing to do anything for Sami. He set her back down and released her from the bear hug.

"So, did you find the wolf?" she asked.

"No, we found some tracks here and there, but no solid lead. The rain washed most of them away."

"I thought I heard it while I was walking to Jason's house."

"What? You *walked* over there?"

Guilt filled her eyes. "Actually, I ran. Jason had just pulled up, and I thought his house was just behind the trees. I didn't know how far it was."

"Samiii," Billy said, his voice heavy with disappointment. "I thought I made it clear that it wasn't safe out here. Not until we find the thing. *Really*, it's not safe."

"I know. I didn't think his house was so far. Anyway, I heard something. It was in the forest behind me, getting closer. I heard branches breaking, and I could hear it *breathing*. Then, I ran as fast as I could to Jason's house. He looked around but didn't see anything. I could've sworn it was chasing me. Jason said if it had been, I would've heard it running across the driveway, but I didn't. I *know* that it was behind me though, Billy. I *know* it!"

Billy eyed the mouth of Jason's driveway. He knew they had to check the forest there, but he dreaded the thought of having to ask Jason's permission. He turned to Sami again, imagining the dreadful outcome if whatever had been chasing her had actually gotten her. "Maybe I'll call Jason and ask if Mike and I can look around his property. Come on." He grabbed her hand and led her toward his house.

Mike was sitting on the front porch, drinking a beer.

Billy explained the details to his brother, and then, called Jason.

Jason wasn't too thrilled to have Billy and Mike poking around his house, but he also didn't want the wolf or wild animal to be a danger to anyone. Jason agreed on one condition. He would search with them.

After Billy walked Sami back to her house, he instructed her to stay put, *inside*, where she'd be safe. She wanted to accompany them, but finally agreed to stay home.

Then the two brothers headed on foot to Jason's with their rifles slung over their shoulders. They had just crossed the road when Jessica emerged from the mouth of Jason's driveway in her black convertible. She blew them a kiss and sped away.

Billy grimaced and glanced at Sami's house.

Sami stared at him from the doorway, arms crossed, with a dissatisfied look.

He flashed an apologetic smile and continued on.

"Looks like Jessica has the hots for me," Mike said with a smug grin. "Probably because you're ugly."

"Whatever makes you feel better about yourself, Mike," Billy replied in a flat tone.

Up ahead, Jason rounded the corner and strutted toward them, carrying a shotgun.

Billy clenched his teeth and gave a quick nod, trying to keep calm.

"We don't have to pretend to be best buds," Jason said dryly. "Let's just get this over with." He flashed a taunting smile. "For *Sami's* sake."

Billy shot him an evil glare. He wanted nothing more than to rip Jason's head off at that moment, but his brother's firm hand on his shoulder stopped him.

"Save it for later, guys!" Mike scolded as if dealing with unruly children. "I wanna catch this bastard already. I have a hot date tonight."

"With *Jessica*?" Billy asked, shocked.

"Wait, what?" Jason glared at Mike.

"No!" Mike's tone was defensive. "Not with *Jessica*! What in the *hell's* the matter with you guys?"

Billy turned his focus back to Jason. Just the sight of him pissed him off.

Jason narrowed his eyes at Billy before he finally lifted a hand toward the trees. "After you," he said with a devious smile.

Billy eyed Jason's shotgun, smiling back with as much animosity.

"No. After *you*. I insist!"

Jason eyed Billy's rifle. "No. *You* go ahead. You're the one with his panties all in a bunch these days!"

"I wonder why!" Billy shouted, taking a step toward Jason.

"I'll go!" Mike boomed. "Jason, you search to my left, Billy, the right. And quit it with the bullshit! You guys are giving me a frickin' headache."

They headed into the forest and found broken branches on the ground, along with huge prints in the mud—only a few feet away from the pavement. For a wolf, the prints were not only unusually large, they appeared to be mutated—having an almost human-like heel, only stretched to a longer length. Nearly two inches in front of the prints were holes gouged in the mud from abnormally large claws. The prints led straight to the driveway where Sami had been earlier.

"What the hell?" Billy's gut knotted. The thought of how close it had come to Sami scared the hell out of him.

"Son of a bitch!" Jason said, his face wracked with worry. "It *did* come after her."

"What the fuck kind of prints are those?" Mike said. "It looks like some kind of deformed wolf. And why are there only two prints? It's like the thing got up on its hind legs and ran after her."

"I heard her crying as she came up to the house, but there was nothing there when I opened the door. Except for Sami that is," Jason said.

"She was crying?" Billy asked angrily as if it were Jason's fault.

"Yeah, *idiot*! She was being chased by the frickin' mother of all wolves." He pointed to the large prints.

Billy clenched his teeth. "Don't make me have to threaten to break your jaw again!"

"Let's go!" Jason challenged, motioning for Billy to come at him.

Mike stepped between them. "Enough already! Dammit! Let's just concentrate on finding this fucker for now!"

After one last icy glare, they finally agreed, and separated to scour the edges of the driveway for prints that might have led off into the forest. They found nothing.

"It's like the asshole just walked away down the middle of the frickin' driveway." Mike had a puzzled look on his face.

"I looked around our houses before we came over," Billy said. "There was nothing there either. Just some washed-out prints from last night."

"Great!" Jason sighed and threw his hand into the air. "It's a good thing my parents aren't here. My mom would've freaked and sold the house for sure." He shook his head with a disgusted look on his face. "Okay guys, this was fun and all, but I'm going home. And," he added dryly, "I'll let you know if I kill the son of a bitch, and you let me know if you kill the son of a bitch." He turned and stormed away.

"Wait a minute?" Mike stopped him. "Your parents aren't here?"

Jason spun around with an irritated look. "No. They're not coming back. They've decided to stay on the East Coast. They like it there. Me? Not so much." He continued to walk away.

Billy's phone rang. He pulled it from his pocket and answered it. "Hello? Hi, Mrs. Roberts…. What…? Now…? No, it sounds like an emergency, and that's really generous of you…. Yeah, I'll be there in about thirty minutes…. Sure. Bye." Not wanting to leave Sami alone, Billy pleaded with his eyes for Mike to take the job for him.

Mike shook his head. "No, man, I can't. I have a date. You don't know how long I've been waiting for this woman to finally say yes."

"We can't just leave Sami home alone. She was chased by some mutant wolf today. She's scared to death."

"What?" Jason's voice echoed toward them. "Did I hear that *Sami* needs someone to keep her company tonight?" He smiled wryly and strutted back toward them.

"No!" Billy snapped, glaring at Jason.

"Come on, Billy," Mike said in his *let's be reasonable* tone. "You might not be home until after dark. You can't just leave her here alone. *I'd* be scared to be home alone at this point. Well, I mean, if I were a chick."

"Yeah, come on, *Billy*," Jason taunted. "I'll keep her *safe*. I won't leave her side all night." He smirked.

Infuriated, Billy lunged toward Jason, but Mike caught him by the arm. "Cool it, little brother!" Mike shouted. He turned to Jason, his expression full of warning. "Enough, Jason! This isn't helping Sami out at all! Can't you guys just be cool for a couple of frickin' hours, for Sami's sake?"

"Whatever!" Jason said, glaring at Billy. "Obviously, you have some damn claim on her. So, do you want me to babysit or not?"

Billy scowled, still wanting to kick Jason's ass but trying his damnedest to restrain himself.

Mike punched Billy in the arm.

"What the hell?" Billy glared at his brother.

"Sami's waiting!" Mike reminded.

Billy shook his head. "Whatever!"

Mike pointed to Jason. "You behave. She means a lot to him."

"Yeah, whatever." Jason sounded more subdued. "We're just friends. She's already made that loud and clear." He stormed off toward Sami's house.

Without another word, Billy and Mike followed.

9

J ASON SAT back on Sami's couch. "So, it appears that you and Billy…" He shook his head with an irritated look in his eyes.

Sami eased onto the recliner. Unable to look him in the eyes, she lowered her gaze to his black T-shirt and then to his worn jeans, fixating on a hole just above his knee. "Did Billy tell you?"

"No. He didn't have to. I could tell by the way he wanted to bash my face in every time I said your name."

"Oh…sorry," she replied, her eyes still averted to hide her guilt. "I tried to tell you at your house earlier. But Jessica interrupted."

"I guess you prefer the silent, brooding type?"

Sami snapped her head up and faced him again, feeling awful for leading Jason to believe he wasn't good enough for her. "No, Jason. You're a great guy. But…I don't know. It just sort of happened. I don't know why. I'm sorry." They had barely made up and there was already another wedge between them. She had to make him understand.

"So, is that why…at the lake…?"

"No. Billy and I weren't together then. It just happened last night." She studied his face, but his annoyed expression offered no comfort.

She couldn't lose him as a friend again. "Please, Jason, don't be mad at me. I want us to be friends."

Jason was quiet as he stared into her pleading eyes. Suddenly, he slapped the top of his thighs and stood. "Oh well, I'll deal. So, what do you wanna do?" He sounded almost like himself again.

She smiled, glad he hadn't given up on their friendship. "I don't know. It's so nice outside. Maybe we could just hang out on the porch. It'd be better than being locked up in here for the rest of the day." She sighed and peered out the window at the bright blue sky.

"I don't think hanging out outside would be the smartest thing to do. But we could go into town and get something to eat. I'm starving." He patted his stomach and grinned.

Sami smiled. "Okay, let's go." She bounced up from the couch and snatched her purse off the counter before they headed outside.

When they reached her car, Jason frowned. "You know, if you gave her a bath she'd turn all shiny and pretty again."

"Ha, ha." Sami smiled and hopped in. She turned the key, and the engine rumbled to life.

Jason plopped onto the passenger seat and shut the door. "Can you drive this thing?" He smirked.

She squinted and backed out of the driveway. Then, she threw the shifter into drive and stomped on the gas pedal. The tires spun, sending gravel flying behind them, and they thrust forward toward the main road.

Jason rubbed his hands together and chuckled through an eager grin. "Yeah! That's what I'm talking about!"

Giggling, she shook her head. "Boys."

She took a right toward town, listening as Jason bragged about his car along the way—to the speeds to which he'd tested its limits, and that he used to roast the tires down their road until Harry had put a stop to it.

When they reached the diner, they walked in and sat at a booth. After the waitress took their order, they exchanged stories from their past and teased each other until their food arrived. Starving, they both dug into their burgers.

"Well, well, well." Jessica was suddenly standing next to their table, glaring at Sami. "You move fast, don't you? First, it was Billy. Then, Jason. Now, Jason *again*? Is Billy next again? You just can't make up your mind, can you?"

"We're just friends," Sami replied, trying not to let Jessica's hostility rattle her.

"Come on now, Jessica. Play nice," Jason warned.

Sami thought being polite might help to smooth the tension between them. "Would you like to join us, Jessica?"

Jason stared at Sami with his mouth open and his eyes shifted to Jessica.

A look of disgust crossed Jessica's face. "What? *Me*? Sit with *you*? Have you lost your mind, *Samantha*?" she scoffed.

Sami didn't understand why she was being so spiteful. "No, I—"

"I don't care what you thought!" Jessica continued sharply. "Why don't you just ask your *lunatic grandfather* to join us while you're at it?"

Jason squished his eyes shut as if Jessica had divulged something she wasn't supposed to. He opened them again and glared at Jessica. "That's enough!"

Sami grew wary. "I-I don't know what you mean."

Jessica looked at Jason, and her lips curled into a cunning smile. "She doesn't know, does she?"

"Come on, Jessica!" Jason pleaded with an angry tone. "Don't do this. Especially not here."

A surge of adrenaline pumped through Sami's veins, and her heart rate increased. She dreaded what she was about to hear but calmly waited for Jessica to finish.

Jessica's smile faded into a vengeful sneer. She lowered her head, leaning close to Sami's ear. "Your crazy grandfather kidnapped me and locked me in his basement because he thought that I was a *monster*!"

Sami's jaw dropped. Jessica had to be lying. "What? Why are you saying this to me? Why are you being so hateful?"

"Jessica, you *are* a monster! Just leave!" Jason demanded.

Jessica ignored him. "Everyone knows. Jason, Billy, your mother, the whole town. Everyone, except *you*!"

Shock took over Sami's thoughts, and she couldn't speak. All she could manage was to shake her head in denial. *It can't be true. It can't be. She has to be lying. Grandpa could never commit such a monstrous act.*

Sami looked at Jason, waiting for him to deny the accusation.

Guilt filled Jason's eyes and he looked down at the table.

Feeling betrayed and foolish, Sami slid from the booth, eager to leave.

"Dammit, Jessica!" Jason stood and threw money on the table. "Come on, Sami," he grabbed her hand.

With tears blurring her vision, Sami let Jason lead the way out. She kept her head down to avoid the prying eyes of nosy customers.

As soon as they reached the car, Jason placed his hands on her shoulders and tilted his head down to look directly into her eyes. "I'm so sorry, Sami. You weren't supposed to find out like this. I'm sorry."

His apology was meaningless. Jason had known all along, and he'd purposely kept it from her. Everyone had.

She knocked his arms from her shoulders and stepped back. "So, it's true? It's all true?"

His eyes filled with remorse. "Your mom didn't want anyone to say anything. She wanted to tell you herself when she thought you were ready. When *she* was ready."

"My *mom*? That just figures!" Sami threw her hands in the air. She wanted to be angry, but a sudden heaviness filled her chest. She was humiliated and heartbroken. "I wanna go home, Jason," she said in a dismal tone. With a shaky hand, she handed him her car keys and climbed into the passenger seat.

It was quiet on the way back. Sami stared out the passenger window, not really seeing any one thing—except a blur of green rush by.

How could Grandpa kidnap someone? How? And why did Mom keep it from me? Did she really think I wouldn't find out? She felt like a complete fool. Like the laughingstock of the town. *Haven't I been through enough already? Can things get any worse in this creepy place? Maybe I should go back to California, where life is normal.*

Deep in thought, Sami hadn't realized the drive was over until they pulled into her driveway. Her gaze flicked to the darkened forest—

dusk had even settled in.

Jason turned the car off and sat back. "Are you all right?"

She shook her head. "No."

The rumbling of an engine and headlights drew their attention to the approaching '68 Charger as it pulled up next door. Billy climbed out and headed their way. When he focused on Jason behind the wheel, his brows came together in question.

Billy made his way around the front of the car to Sami's window. He leaned down and peered in.

"Hey, what are you guys up to?" he asked lightheartedly, but his clenched jaw gave away his fake enthusiasm.

Sami wanted to throw her arms around Billy and tell him the awful details, but he already knew everything. Her heart ached with betrayal, and she felt like an idiot for trusting everyone. Tears stung her eyes again, but this time, she couldn't keep them contained. They slipped over her lower lashes and roll down her cheeks.

"What the hell happened?" Billy glared at Jason. "What'd you do?"

Needing privacy, Sami opened the door and headed for the house, but Billy grabbed her arm.

"Sami, what's the matter?" Billy asked, his eyes full of worry.

She sucked in an unsteady breath and wiped a hand across her wet cheeks.

"It wasn't me, Billy," Jason said over the roof of the car. "It was Jessica." He looked carefully into Billy's eyes and nodded as if Billy could read his mind.

"Nooo. She didn't. That *bitch!*" Billy's nostrils flared, and he cocked his jaw to one side.

"I tried to stop her," Jason said. "But she didn't care. She made a big scene in the middle of the frickin' diner!"

"I'm so sorry, Sami," Billy said with desperate eyes. "I wanted to tell you, but I had to respect your mom's wishes. She didn't want us to be the ones to break it to you."

Sami wanted to be mad at him, but he was right. They were innocent parties to her mother's lying game.

"It's okay," she said calmly as the hurt turned to frustration. "I understand why you didn't tell me. I just can't believe this is happening. I can't believe my grandpa could *do* such a thing. And I can't believe my own *mom* didn't tell me—" her voice grew louder as the frustration turned to anger "—that she's been *lying* to me all this time! I feel like a complete *fool*! And I can't believe all the bad things that have happened lately! I mean, are things *ever* gonna be *normal* around here? It's bad enough I've been having nightmares all the time. Now, it feels like I'm *living* in one!"

Billy and Jason stared at her with shocked expressions. They glanced at each other, back to Sami, and then, behind her.

Sami spun around to see what they were looking at.

Mike stood there with a surprised look on his face. "It sounds like you could use a drink," he said smoothly.

"What?" Billy belted out. "Dude, she's only twenty!"

"So? I think all of us have had a few drinks a time or two, or more, when we were younger than that. Am I right?" Mike challenged both men.

Sami contemplated Mike's offer. As she had unleashed her rant only moments ago, she had been sure it had meant only one thing— she'd finally snapped. Surprisingly, now that she'd released her stress, she felt emotionally stronger than ever. With renewed determination, she sucked in a deep breath and exhaled.

"You know, you're right. I could use a drink."

Sami marched across the yards with her chin held high. She didn't have to look back to know the guys were right behind her—the thudding of multiple boots and continuous crunching of grass gave them away. When she reached the front door, she stopped.

With an unsure look on his face, Billy opened the door and motioned with a hand for Sami to enter. He held it open for Jason too, but Jason was oblivious to Billy's seething glare. Either that, or Jason didn't care. Billy glanced back at his brother and shook his head, clearly irritated by Jason's presence.

Mike put his hands in front of him, silently motioning for Billy to keep calm.

Standing alongside the wall, just inside the front door, Sami and Jason waited for the brothers to enter.

Mike brushed past Billy and flicked the switches on the wall, brightening dining room straight ahead and the living room to the right of the front door. He made a beeline straight past the dining table and into the open kitchen.

Sami rested her hands on the back of the black leather sofa near the front door and admired the various rifles stored in the gun cabinet on the opposite wall. In the far right corner, next to the front window, was a large flat-screen TV. To the left of the sofa, sat a matching leather recliner. The worn oak coffee table in the middle of the room was cluttered with magazines and various remote controls.

"We can sit at the table." Billy went to the dining table and sat down.

Sami followed and took a seat adjacent to him. She admired the quaint, U-shaped kitchen with white cupboards, yellow laminate countertops, and black appliances. Light gray linoleum lined the floor. She looked closely at the yellow, diner-style table, running her fingers along the smooth surface of the shiny metal wrapped around the outer edge of it. The padded chairs were black.

"Is this from the diner?" she asked.

Jason pulled out a chair and sat adjacent to Sami.

"That it is," Mike replied matter-of-factly as he went to the fridge along the back wall and pulled out a wine cooler. "There were some left over when we did the remodel." He twisted the cap off and set it on the table in front of her. "And since Billy demolished the last table we had…" He shot Billy a dissatisfied look.

Billy rolled his eyes. "You're the one who left your work boots in the middle of the floor. And, dude, when'd you get wine coolers?" He scrunched his face in disgust.

"You should've turned the light on, so you could see," Mike spouted back. "And they were for my date. She said they were her favorite. But I cancelled."

"What? Why?" Billy asked.

"I figured I wouldn't be much company worrying about that damned wild animal running around here all night, chasing Sami or you." He eyed Jason. "Or you either, I guess."

Jason smirked. "Bummer. But how sweet," he taunted.

"Yeah, bro, you didn't have to do that," Billy said.

"I know." Mike let out a long, forlorn sigh as he pulled three beers from the fridge. He handed one to Jason and Billy before sitting in the empty chair across from Sami.

"Sorry, Mike," Sami said. The last thing she wanted was to be a burden to anyone.

"Don't worry about it," Mike replied, his voice kinder than usual. "None of this is your fault."

Sami nodded and took a sip of the sweet, red cooler. Not only did it quench her thirst, it tasted like fruit punch with a fizzy twinge to it. "Mmm, it's good."

She took another sip—a longer one—before she tipped her head back and gulped it down. She stopped to take a breath.

Without moving or blinking, the guys stared at her as if she might have another meltdown at any moment.

Sami smiled, trying to keep from laughing at their frozen faces. "Guys, I'm okay."

Their unsure expressions remained unchanged.

"Really, I'm okay now. I just needed to vent. You know, get it all off my chest." She finished the rest of the wine cooler and set the empty bottle on the table with a clank. A warm fuzziness invaded her thoughts.

"Good! She's okay," Jason said with assurance as he slapped his hands on the table. "That's all I needed to know." He stood and held up his beer. "Guys, Sami, it's been fun, but I have to go." He headed for the door, taking the beer with him.

"Need a lift?" Mike called out to him.

"Thanks, but no thanks. I'll just grab my shotgun from Sami's house and—" he opened the closet to the right of the front door and pulled out a flashlight "—borrow this flashlight." He disappeared out the front door without looking back.

"Bye, Jason!" Sami shouted. Her head felt like it was swimming, and her entire body was relaxed. She looked at Billy. "Can I have another one?"

Billy hesitated as he studied her. "Maybe that's not such a good idea."

"Come on! Just one more," she pleaded with the saddest puppy-dog eyes she could muster.

As soon as Billy's unsure expression turned into a look of defeat, Mike let out a devious chuckle.

Sami jumped up and went to the fridge. She grabbed one more wine cooler and two beers. On the way back to her seat, she set a beer down in front of each of the men.

Billy grinned halfway. "I'm glad you're finally having a little fun, Sami. I'm sorry you've had such a rough time here so far."

She smiled back at him. "Me too, Billy. Me too…. But let's not think about any of that other stuff 'til tomorrow, 'kay?" She took another sip. Followed by a few more. "Come on. What are you guys waiting for? Am I the only one drinking tonight?"

"I've got your back, Sami." Mike raised his beer and chugged it.

"And *you*, Billy…?" She smiled, admiring his handsomeness. She rose from her chair and plopped into his lap. Feeling dizzy, she sank against his chest and nuzzled her face into his neck while enjoying the feel of his arms around her. "Do you have my back?"

"You know I have your back, Sami," Billy replied, his voice full of compassion. "But I don't feel much like drinking tonight. I think I'll just sit here and enjoy you instead."

"Awww, isn't that sweet," Mike teased.

"Shut up!" Billy threw a wine cooler cap at him.

It bounced off his taut chest and rolled across the floor.

Mike grinned. "Since you won't be needing *these* anymore…" He took Billy's untouched beers and cracked one open.

Sami suddenly had an idea. "Hey, I know. Let's play cards!"

Mike reached over to the buffet against the wall and pulled a deck of cards from the top drawer. "I'll deal," he said and began to shuffle them.

Over the next couple of hours, they played various games of poker. New to the game, Sami lost every time. But it didn't matter. For the first time since she'd moved here, she didn't have a care in the world. She decided to sit the next hand out as she finished her last drink.

She set the empty bottle aside and yawned. The dizzying effect of the alcohol seemed to have lessened, but the force of gravity felt stronger now, almost as if it were sucking her into her chair. She crossed her arms, propped them on the table, and rested her weary head on them as if they were a pillow. Another yawn escaped and she closed her eyes.

Mike and Billy's voices faded into the background.

BILLY SMILED as he gazed at the sleeping beauty sitting next to him.

"Looks like your girlfriend has had enough," Mike said.

"I guess she has." Billy pondered Mike's words for a moment before he replied, "Girlfriend? I haven't actually asked her to be my *girlfriend* or anything. I mean, I know we like each other and that we're sort of together...."

Mike stared at him blankly before his face puckered in disgust. "Dude, knock it off. You sound like a chick. You guys nuzzle, hold hands, sit in each other's laps, hold each other's hair back while you hurl. She's your girlfriend."

Sami snickered. "I can hear you, you know," she mumbled. "And—" she opened her eyes and looked at Mike "—why do you know that I hurled?" Her eyes shifted to Billy.

"Well, you know, he's my brother. I sort of told him that you hurled?" He shrugged his shoulders and flashed an uneasy smile, hoping she wasn't angry with him.

"Well, *boyfriend*, did you also tell him that you're a good kisser? You know, since you're telling him private stuff and all." She got up from her chair and sat in his lap. Then, she puckered the sides of his mouth together with her fingers, talking to him as if he were a baby. "Well, did you?"

Mike guffawed. "Oh, little brother, you are gonna have to kick my ass before I ever let you live this one down!"

Billy was amused by her silly behavior. But he knew she'd had enough to drink. He lowered her hand, kissed her on the forehead, and gazed into her eyes. "I promise I'll keep my mouth shut from now on. Now, let's get you home." He flung another bottle cap at Mike, but this time harder.

"Ow." Mike laughed, rubbing the middle of his chest. "That wasn't cool!"

A loud ringing filled the air. They all looked at each other for a moment before they simultaneously reached into their pockets and pulled out their phones.

"I win!" Sami shouted and held up her phone while it continued to ring. "It's my mom."

"Uh, I think I should answer that for you." Billy reached for her phone. He looked at Sami and held one finger to his lips. "Shhh."

Sami grinned. "Okay."

"Uh…let me show you where the bathroom is, Sami." Mike jumped up and led her down the hallway.

Sami was completely perplexed. "How'd you know I had to use the bathroom?"

"Lucky guess." Mike smirked.

"Hello?" Billy answered the phone. He listened to Carol speak but didn't reply until he heard the bathroom door shut. "Yeah, this is Billy. Sami's in the bathroom…. I'm so sorry, Carol…. I'll take care of her. And, if there's anything Mike and I can do, just let us know…. Sure…. Bye."

Mike sat back down. "What was that all about?"

Billy set the cell phone on the table and let out a forlorn sigh. "It's Harry. He had a heart attack. He might have a few days left at most."

"Oh man…that's…" Mike shook his head and gulped.

"Yeah, tell me about it." Billy sighed.

They had known Harry all their lives. He and their father had often hunted together or worked together remolding homes.

Harry Meyers and his wife had been there for him, Mike, and their sister, Megan, after their parents had died. The Meyers had always checked in on them to see if they had needed anything and had often surprised them with groceries or clothes to help Mike out with the expenses. Harry had even supplied Mike with work and had taught him how to build homes from the ground up. On weekends, and later, after high school, Billy had accompanied them to learn the trade.

When Harry's wife had fallen ill, Billy and Mike had returned the kindness. They'd dropped off groceries or pre-cooked meals and had maintained their yard. They had even donated their own supplies and time to help fix Harry's deteriorating home.

Tears burned Billy's eyes, but he didn't let them fall. "I know he lost it there at the end with Jessica and all, but he's still a good man."

"Yeah, it's too bad," Mike replied, his voice glum. Sitting back, he ran his fingers through his hair.

"I never thought I'd hunt again after Dad died," Billy said quietly. "But Harry wouldn't have it. He's the one who finally got me out there again."

Imagining the day as if it were happening all over again, Billy's thoughts drifted back to nine years ago, to the morning Harry had come to the front door for him and wouldn't take no for an answer.

"You up for hunting today?" Harry stood there grinning, wearing a camouflage baseball hat and shirt, with a rifle slung over his shoulder.

Billy had been aching to go hunting again, but he just couldn't bring himself to step one foot in the forest since his dad's death. He let out a long sigh. "I don't know."

"Aw, come on!" Harry urged. "It'll do you some good. Anyway, I could use the extra set of eyes. My eyesight isn't as good as it used to be. Get your things together. I'll wait."

He finally relented, feeling he owed Harry the help. "Okay." He went to the gun cabinet and reached for his rifle, but his father's old .22 Ruger caught his eye. He ran his hand over the smooth wooden stock, wondering whether to use it.

Unable to resist, Billy carefully removed the rifle from the cabinet—his dad's prized, lucky rifle.

Mike will kick my ass if he finds out, but for some reason, I just can't leave you behind, Billy thought silently, admiring the rifle. He peered down the hall to make sure Mike wasn't coming and snatched a box of ammo from the drawer.

"Don't forget your vest," Harry shouted through the screen door.

Billy grimaced and listened for movement coming from Mike's bedroom, but all remained silent. He picked up the bright orange vest from the bottom of the cabinet and went out to the porch, easing the front door shut behind him.

"I'm gonna scare the animals away wearing this thing," Billy complained, working his arms through it.

"It's for your own safety. Now, I can see you." Harry winked before eyeing the rifle in Billy's hand. "Nice choice."

Billy shoved the box of ammo into his vest pocket and they headed across the yards and into the forest. As soon as he entered the barrier of trees, Billy grew anxious. He'd never hunted without his dad, and he just didn't have the courage to do so yet.

"I change my mind. I can't do this." He clenched his jaw to keep the tears in, suddenly feeling haunted by his dad's absence.

Harry sighed and motioned with a nod of the head for Billy to sit on a nearby log with him.

Billy complied, carefully leaning the rifle against the log.

After a brief silence, Harry leaned forward and rested his elbows on his knees. He scratched his gray-and-brown whiskers before he clasped his dried-out hands together. "I know how hard it was for you to come here today. You're very brave. Your dad would've been proud."

Resentment filled Billy and he shook his head. "My dad doesn't even know I'm here or that I even exist anymore."

"Maybe not, son, but do you see that rifle sitting there next to you?"

Billy briefly glanced at his dad's rifle. He leaned forward, resting his elbows on his knees like Harry, and stared at a cluster of yellow flowers at his boots.

"Ever since your dad got it, he never went hunting without it. It was his lucky rifle. He never missed a shot with it. Not one." He sighed and scratched his whiskers again. "We were out hunting one day, and he told me that he was going to give it to you on your sixteenth birthday, when you were old enough to respect it. That way, he could always be at your side when you hunted, even when he wasn't around anymore."

Tears stung Billy's eyes as his dad filled his thoughts, blurring the flowers into a yellow smudge. He quickly wiped them away. "Today's my sixteenth birthday," he said with a shaky voice.

Harry nodded. "I know. Happy birthday, son."

Though Billy's heart could never be whole again, at the moment, it soared. He threw his arms around Harry, trying to keep more tears from falling. "Thanks, Harry."

Harry gave him a quick hug and a couple of firm pats on the back before he stood. "Now, come on," he said with a nod toward the trail. "Let's go round you up a nice slice of birthday venison to go with the cake my wife is baking for you."

Billy had wiped his eyes dry on his sleeve. Then, he'd picked up his rifle and had followed Harry into the forest with his dad at his side.

"You okay, little bro?" Mike's voice snapped Billy from his thoughts.

Billy glanced across the table at his brother, and then picked up a wine cooler cap and began fidgeting with it. "Yeah, I'll be okay."

SAMI SMILED as she exited the hallway and sat back down. Her head was still foggy from the alcohol but slowly becoming clearer. Gulping down as much water as she could from the bathroom faucet seemed to have helped.

She stared at Billy as he fidgeted with a bottle cap, waiting for an answer. "What'd my mom say?"

Mike and Billy stared at each other for a moment.

Sensing something wrong, her smile faded. "Well?"

Billy continued to play with the cap. "Oh, uh, your mom has to stay at work longer, so she wants you to stay here tonight. She doesn't want you to be home alone all night."

Sami was relieved, but at the same time, didn't like how childish her mother's request made her look. "I can stay home by myself. I'm not a little girl."

Billy placed his hand over hers. "I know, but with the wolf prowling so close, she doesn't want you to be alone. Anyway, I was looking forward to spending more time with you tonight."

Sami pressed a bashful smile between her lips. "In that case, I guess I'll have to obey her wishes, just this once." She stood. Feeling a bit off balance, she gripped the edges of the table.

Drinking suddenly seemed like a bad idea. Her thoughts were still a little foggy, and now, nausea swept through her stomach. She couldn't wait to feel like herself again.

"I'll be right back. I'm gonna go change into something more comfortable and grab my pillow." Without another thought, she went to the front door and opened it.

"Sami, wait!" Mike and Billy called out to her.

"I'll only be a minute," she answered without looking back. As she pushed through the screen door, she shut the front door behind her. Guided by the pale glow emitted from the porch light, she headed home.

She was halfway across their yard when Billy and Mike caught up with her. Both were armed with shotguns.

"What are you doing?" Billy sounded irritated. "You can't just walk home by yourself. It's not safe!"

"Oh, yeah. I forgot." She covered her mouth with her hand as if she were in trouble. "Sorry."

Billy sighed and grabbed her hand. "It's all right. But the next thing you drink is a bottle of water."

"Okay." She grabbed him by the shirt, yanking him close to her. Standing on her tiptoes, she crushed her lips to his.

Billy wrapped his arm around her and indulgently honored her request until Mike cleared his throat. Then, Billy pulled away, took her hand in his, and led her to the house.

"Awww, Jason left the porch light on for me." She smiled.

"Yeah, that was real nice of him," Billy said with a hint of animosity.

Mike followed them inside and sat on the couch.

"I'll be right back." Sami gave Billy a quick peck on the lips and ran up the stairs. Halfway up she stumbled and gripped the railing to steady herself.

"Are you okay?" Billy asked.

"Yes, I'm okay." She flashed him an uneasy smile. Careful with each step, she ascended the rest of the stairs and went into her bedroom. She threw on a pair of blue sweatpants and a white T-shirt. Before heading back downstairs, she grabbed an extra blanket from the hallway closet.

"Shoot, I forgot my pillow." She hurried back to her room.

The bedroom window caught her attention. For some strange

reason, she was drawn to it. She *had* to look. To see if *it* was out there, watching her. She decided it best to turn off the light first. With the help of the alcohol to dull the fear, she proceeded to the window and peered out into the darkness.

Standing in the middle of her backyard, looking directly at her, was a large creature with blood-red eyes, its hairy silhouette and pointed ears highlighted in silver by the moonlight.

A horrific scream tore from Sami's throat. She turned to run but tripped and crashed to the floor.

"Sami!" Billy yelled, barreling into her bedroom before she could pull herself up from the floor. He helped her to her feet. "Are you okay? What happened?"

Mike bolted in behind him.

"It's out there!" she yelled, pointing to the window, her hand trembling. "In the backyard!"

Billy and Mike rushed to the window.

"There's nothing there." Billy turned back to her.

She pointed out the window to the exact spot where she had just seen the creature. "It was standing right there, *staring* at me. It was *watching* me. With *red* eyes." She was sure, now, that she was being hunted by some monster.

"Sami, you stay here," Mike ordered. "Billy and I will go look around."

"What? No! I'm not staying here by myself!" She wasn't sure what she had seen, but she was certain it had been standing. And if it stood, then it was possible the beast could walk right through her front door and tear her to pieces.

Mike stopped in the doorway and turned around. He sighed, his face full of uncertainty. "Sami…maybe it's the alcohol talking?"

She clenched her teeth, angered by Mike's insult. Sure, she'd never had alcohol before, but she knew she was in her right state of mind. She was *not* imagining things, and she'd be damned if she let him make her look like an idiot. Desperate to make him understand, she gripped his broad shoulders to get his attention.

"It's not the alcohol, Mike! It was *real!*"

Mike glanced at each of her hands on his shoulders before he raised his eyebrows. "All right. Anyone brave enough to handle me this way at least deserves my attention."

She released her hold on him, her anger lessening now that he was actually going to listen. When she spoke again, her voice was more subdued. "Some furry creature, man, or *something* was standing there, staring at me with red eyes."

"I'm sure it was just a wolf," Mike replied. "Billy and I will go kill it."

"No, Mike! *No!* It's *not* a wolf! It was *huge!* And it was *standing* there, on *two* feet, *watching* me! And since when do wolves have red eyes?"

"It was probably just the way the porch light was reflecting in its eyes," Mike suggested.

Pursing her lips to keep her anger under control, she crossed her arms and shook her head.

Mike sighed and looked at Billy.

"Something's not right, Mike. Sami's always trusted our word that it was just an animal or a wolf. That she was still safe. But not this time. She's scared to death. She clearly saw something else. Hell, I'm a little freaked now. I think it's time we call the sheriff."

S AMI, BILLY, and Mike stood in the middle of the road with red-and-blue lights flashing all around. Nearly the entire sheriff's department surrounded them.

"Wow," Sami said, clutching Billy's hand. "Is all this really necessary?"

"It's a small town," Billy reminded. "They don't get much action around here. Come on." He motioned with his head toward her house. "Let's go wait up on the porch."

He led her across the yard and up the porch steps.

Mike followed them.

Sami leaned against the railing and watched the commotion, trying to keep her tattered nerves under control.

One of the men wearing a brown uniform and hat made his way toward them.

"Here comes Gordon Briggs," Billy said. "He's the sheriff."

Sami tensed, nervous about speaking to the man, but his jovial smile immediately lessened her worry. He marched right up the porch steps to greet them.

"Mike, Billy." The man reached out to shake each of their hands.

"Sheriff Briggs." Billy and Mike each returned the greeting.

"You must be Samantha." The sheriff took his hat off, exposing his captivating amber eyes and black hair mixed with gray. He extended his hand.

"Nice to meet you," Sami said politely and shook his hand.

"So, you're the one everyone's been talking about for the last couple of weeks." Sheriff Briggs put his hat back on and adjusted it with a quick tug of the brim. "You moving to town has caused quite a stir, with you being Harry's granddaughter. Plus, we don't get very many new faces around here." He grinned.

Sami nodded and hid her humiliation behind a weak smile. Jessica was right—everyone knew about what her grandpa had done, and they were all talking about her behind her back because of it. For the first time since she'd moved here, she was glad to be living out of town, in the middle of the forest, and away from prying eyes and ears—even with a wild beast running around.

Sami, Billy, and Mike took turns filling Sheriff Briggs in on the details. With the aid of dogs and flashlights, deputies scoured the areas around both homes. They took pictures, measured prints leading into the forest, and were in and out of the houses. One of the dogs dashed down the basement stairs, whining and sniffing around. One of the deputies tried to open the door, but it was locked.

Sami and Billy searched the entire house for the basement key. Mike even helped, but they came up empty-handed. They all went back out onto the porch.

"Did you find the key to the basement, Samantha?" Sheriff Briggs asked as he approached them.

"No, we couldn't find it," Sami replied.

"I'm sorry," he said, "but we're going to have to kick the door in. We have to get in there. You said earlier that you saw the animal standing. If that's the case, then it could very well be a man in a costume trying to scare you. We need to make sure no one's hiding in your basement."

Sami nodded her approval.

Sheriff Briggs headed around the side of the house. "All right, kick it in," he shouted toward the backyard.

"My mom's gonna freak," Sami grumbled as she plopped onto the wicker loveseat.

"Sorry." Billy sat down and wrapped an arm around her.

Mike took the seat on the other side of Billy and let out a long sigh.

Sami's only solace at the moment, besides being with Billy, was staring across the road at Jason's driveway and watching the flashlight beams move this way and that, crossing each other like playful swords of light. One flashlight in particular stood out from the others as it came directly toward her. The light grew closer, and she recognized Jason's silhouette.

"One hell of a day, huh?" Jason trudged up the steps and sat on the porch railing to face the three of them. "I take it they didn't catch the big bad wolf yet?" He turned off the flashlight and tossed it to Mike.

Mike caught the light and set it down on the porch. "Nope. They followed its tracks into the forest, but then they lost it."

"You mean they lost *him*," Billy corrected.

"What? You mean like a male wolf? Or do you mean it was a *him*, like a *guy*, him?"

Billy glared at Jason. "Sami saw him standing on two feet in the backyard. So, yeah, a guy."

"Well, excuse me," Jason grumbled.

Sami yawned and rested her head against Billy's chest, staring at the faint light of morning illuminating the horizon. She began a pointless battle with her heavy eyelids, trying to keep them open. Unable to fight the exhaustion any longer, she closed her eyes.

BILLY SCOOPED Sami up, carried her into the house, and gently laid her on the couch. He didn't dare put her upstairs, knowing she'd be terrified if she woke up alone. He covered her with the soft purple blanket that lay draped across the arm of the couch and kissed her forehead, wishing he could join her. He yawned and went back outside.

"We didn't find anything," Sheriff Briggs said, standing at the bottom of the steps. "Aside from the tracks he left behind, that is.

Strange too. Samantha said she saw it standing like a man, but the tracks appear to be that of a wolf. A very large wolf. There'll be a car posted out here for the next few days, just in case. And we'll continuously patrol the area. I know you're not the best of friends, but I suggest that you three—" he gave Jason, Mike, and Billy a warning glance "—band together and be on the lookout. If it is some crazed lunatic, everyone could be in danger here, not just Samantha. Oh, and we'd call someone to fix the basement door, except you two are already here," he said, motioning to Billy and Mike.

"I've got it, little brother. You stay here in case Sami wakes up." Mike jogged down the steps. "See ya around, Sheriff." He gave a quick nod to Sheriff Briggs and headed around the side of the house.

"Thanks, Sheriff." Billy clomped down the stairs and shook Gordon Briggs's hand again.

"Holler if you see anything unusual." Sheriff Briggs headed away but stopped abruptly and turned back to face them. "Oh, and tell Samantha and Carol that I'm truly sorry about Harry."

Billy had forgotten all about Harry. Exhausted in every way possible now, he ran his fingers through his hair and nodded. "I will."

"What? He died?" Jason asked with a shocked look.

"No," Sheriff Briggs replied. "But he's taken a turn for the worse, I'm afraid." Without another word, he walked away to round up his deputies. Within minutes, they had cleared out of the entire area, with the exception of the one patrol car that remained.

SAMI OPENED her eyes and focused on Jason sprawled on the recliner, his mouth wide open as he snored. Billy was asleep at her feet, curled in the corner of the couch. She glanced at the clock on the wall—it was already a little after two in the afternoon.

She crept off the couch and tiptoed to the kitchen window. Her mom's car sat in the driveway. Assuming her mother was sleeping, Sami decided to talk to her later. She tiptoed upstairs to take a shower. Afterward, she threw on a loose-fitting purple tank and gray shorts before she hurried back downstairs.

Billy stood at the bottom of the staircase, waiting for her with a warm smile.

Jason was still snoring.

"Hey." Billy's tone was gentle. "I was hoping I'd make it back before you were done."

Puzzled, Sami stopped at the bottom of the steps. Billy wore different clothing now—a brown T-shirt and a darker pair of jeans.

"You mean, you left?" she asked.

"Just for a few minutes. You know, to shower and change."

"Oh."

"So, it was quite a night, huh?" he said.

She recalled the dreadful events, disappointed they hadn't found the predator. She wouldn't be able to rest easy until they did. "Yeah, I'm not looking forward to another one."

"Don't worry. There's a deputy posted outside, and they'll be searching the area for a few more days. I think you can rest easy now."

"I hope so. I just can't stop thinking about it."

"Maybe this will help...." Billy cupped her cheeks and guided her lips to his, easing her worries with an indulgent kiss.

"I suppose this means you won't want to go back to California," Carol said calmly as she walked past them and into the kitchen.

Billy and Sami jumped out of each other's grasp.

Sami turned and faced her mom, hoping the shame in her eyes wasn't obvious. "Uh, I didn't hear you get up."

"I should go," Billy said. "I'm sure you two have a lot to talk about."

"Billy," Carol said in a soft tone, "does she know?"

Guilt filled his eyes and he shook his head. "No. I thought it'd be best if she heard it from you."

Sami grew wary. "What's going on?"

"We should go." Billy walked over to Jason and pushed the lever back on the recliner, making it spring into the upright position.

Startled, Jason jumped up and scanned the room. He focused on everyone and smiled. "Morning."

Billy clenched his jaw. "It's already almost three, you—" He stopped and took a deep breath. "It's almost three in the afternoon, Jason," he said calmly. "We have to get going. Carol and Sami have some things to discuss."

"Oh, okay, right." He grabbed his rifle and headed for the door. When he reached the porch, he stopped and turned around. "Oh, and I'm very sorry about Harry. If there's anything either of you need...."

"What?" Sami's chest grew heavy.

Billy glared at Jason and hit him in the arm.

Jason narrowed his eyes and made a fist, ready to hit Billy back.

"What do you mean you're sorry about my grandpa, Jason? What happened to him?"

Jason's eyes widened and he lowered his fist. "Uhhh..." He shook his head. "I'm sorry. I'll see you later." He hurried away without looking back.

Billy gulped. "I'm sorry, Sami. I'll be right next door if you need me."

"Wait a minute, Billy." She turned to her mother. "Will you please tell me what in the hell is going on for once? I'm tired of all these secrets! I'm tired of being the laughingstock of town! What's wrong with Grandpa, and why did he lock Jessica up?"

Billy turned to leave.

"No! Please don't go! Stay!" Sami pleaded. His caring and comfort had been the only thing that had gotten her through all the madness over the last few days.

Carol glanced at Billy and nodded.

"Okay." Billy grabbed Sami's hand and gave it a reassuring squeeze. "I'll just be right here on the porch. I won't leave." He went outside and closed the door.

Sami spun around to face her mother. "Please just be honest with me for once, Mom."

Carol's eyes filled with tears. "Your grandpa suffered a heart attack last night. He doesn't have much longer."

Sami's chin trembled and she started to cry. "When, Mom?"

"He's really weak, but he won't give up. He keeps fighting. He has a few more days, at most. I'm so sorry, sweetheart."

"Can I see him?"

Carol rubbed her forehead and sighed. "Your grandpa...he's not in his right mind and never will be again. He's in a psychiatric hospital. He doesn't stop talking about that night. About Jessica being a monster. He thinks almost everyone he talks to or sees is a monster, including me sometimes. He's really confused, sweetheart. That's why I haven't let you visit him. I'm just trying to protect you from him. From him calling you a monster. I want you to remember him for the kind, loving man he was. Not for the confused lost soul he's become."

Chin quivering and tears flowing, Sami released her pent-up pain. "So, you don't want me to see him? I don't even get to say good-bye? You did the same thing with Grandma. You wouldn't let me to go to her funeral to say good-bye. And I regret it, Mom! I feel guilty every time I think about her, but the only one who's at fault here is you! You can't take this from me! Not again! You can't take away my only chance to say good-bye to Grandpa!"

"I just feel it's for the best." Carol stepped toward her.

"No!" Sami shouted with her hands up. She was tired of tiptoeing around her heartbroken mother. And she was tired of not challenging her mother's dishonesty like she should've in the first place.

"Why'd you lie to me, Mom? Why'd you keep so many secrets? Everyone around here knows more about my life than *I* do! It's so *humiliating*! Everywhere I go, people stare at me. Some even glare like they *hate* me!"

"Samantha, I'm so sorry." With pain in her eyes and arms extended, Carol took another step toward Sami.

"Just stay away from me! You've done enough!"

Sami snatched her purse from the counter, jerked the door open, and headed straight to her car, shielding her swollen eyes from the blaring afternoon sun. She had to get away from her mom. She needed time to sort things out and to find out exactly where her grandpa was.

"Sami, wait!" Billy called out as he headed toward her.

She stopped at her car door and gave into her pain, covering her face with her hands to hide her tears.

Billy pulled her into his arms. "I'm sorry, Sami." His voice shook with sadness. "I'm so sorry."

"I can't believe my mom!" Sami cried. "She doesn't want me to see my grandpa. But I have to say good-bye, Billy," she said, smearing the tears away with the back of her hands. "I've never forgiven myself for not being able to say bye to my grandma."

Billy glanced at the deputy's car and motioned with a nod of his head toward his house. "Let's go inside and talk."

Sami nodded. Before they reached Billy's yard, the deputy stepped out of her car. "Everything okay?" she asked.

"As good as can be expected, Brenda," Billy replied, and they continued to his house.

Billy opened the front door and motioned for Sami to enter. "Are you sure you don't wanna sort things out with your mom?"

"I don't wanna see her right now," Sami said glumly and went inside.

Billy went to the dining table and pulled out a chair for her before sitting down. He snatched a napkin from the buffet behind him and handed it to her.

"Thank you." Sami took the napkin and plopped down. She dried her eyes and rubbed the napkin across her nose.

"Are you okay?"

"No, I'm not. I'm so mad at my mom right now." She gritted her teeth to keep the tears from coming back.

"I don't think your mom meant for things to turn out this way. She just did what she thought was best for you."

"She kept important things from me. Things everyone around me knew. Things *I* should've known before I even stepped foot in this creepy un-private town. Now, my grandpa's dying, and I don't get to say good-bye? How is all that best for me? I'm *twenty*, not *ten*."

She looked at Billy, noticing the pain in his eyes, and she suddenly felt terrible for being so selfish.

"I'm sorry, Billy. I know you're just trying to help. And I know this is hard for you too. You lived right next door to my grandpa your whole life. You're probably closer to him than I've ever been."

"Don't worry about me." Billy stood and pulled her into a tight embrace. "I just wish I could make *you* feel better."

There was a knock at the door. Billy answered it. "Brenda? Is something wrong?"

Wondering if the deputy had any news about the stalker, Sami approached the door and stood next to Billy.

Brenda shook her head. "No, just making sure Samantha's okay."

Sami studied the middle-aged deputy who stood no taller than herself, wondering if she was being genuine or just doing her job. Her brown eyes reflected sincerity, and her soft smile was warm and caring.

Brenda tilted her hat back and a lock of black hair fell against her cheek. She tucked it behind her ear and cleared her throat. "I guess we haven't officially met." She stuck her hand out. "I'm Brenda Cruz. As you can see, I'm one of the local deputies."

Sami shook the woman's hand. She was expecting a firm grip from Brenda but was met with a grip that matched her own—gentle and friendly. Deciding Brenda's motives were sincere, Sami gave way to a subtle smile.

"It's nice to meet you, Brenda. I guess you already know who I am."

Brenda nodded. "I do. And I know your grandpa. I have to say, it's been an honor knowing him. What he did to Jessica, it's just the illness. That's why he's in a hospital and not in jail. He is still a great man with a genuine heart. Don't forget that."

The deputy's words brought comfort to Sami's soul. Her grandpa wasn't the monster Jessica had made him out to be. He was still the same man Sami looked up to and loved, and he always would be. She swallowed hard to hold back tears.

"I won't forget," Sami said in a quiet tone.

Billy placed a gentle hand on Sami's back and rubbed it in a soothing manner. "Thanks, Brenda," he said.

"Sure. I'll leave you two alone. Let me know if there's anything else I can do." Brenda headed back to her squad car.

Billy closed the door and turned to Sami. "I wish I could help take your pain away."

A sudden idea popped into Sami's head. "I know how you can help."

"How?"

"You can take me to see him."

His forehead wrinkled with concern. "They probably won't let us in. I think your mom has made sure of that already."

"We could try."

Billy looked into her eyes, pondering the thought. Finally, his gaze softened. "Okay, we'll try."

A huge smile crossed her face and she gave him a big squeeze.

He let out a light chuckle and opened the door. "After you."

Sami's eyes widened. "Are we going now?"

"The sooner the better."

"Thank you!" She planted a big kiss on his lips and hurried to his car. Before she knew it, they were on the road, headed for their destination.

Sami stared out the window at the blur of the forest whizzing by, trying to imagine how her grandpa might look now. But she wasn't able to envision him any other way than the robust, strong-minded, and physically fit man she'd always known.

She recalled a time when she was twelve, when she and her grandpa had been walking along the beach, and she'd finally talked him into hiking along a trail they had discovered. The trail was situated about halfway up a twenty-foot tall cliff. When they'd stood at the shoreline and peered around the rocks, they could see another beach just past it.

She'd always wanted to go there, to the other beach, but her grandpa had never allowed her the liberty. He had been afraid she'd get hurt. But, this time, she'd convinced him she wasn't a baby anymore, and that she'd be careful.

A soft smile formed and Sami envisioned the day with her grandpa as if it were happening all over again.

"This is gonna be so great, Grandpa!" she smiled.

He gripped her hand and chuckled. "Yes, it is. But be careful."

"I will." With her grandpa's hand wrapped tightly around hers, they stepped onto the trail. From the ground, it didn't look so high up. But, now that she was hiking up it, her heart stopped every time she looked down at the ocean smashing against the jagged rocks below.

She squeezed her grandpa's hand tighter as he led her along the cliff, trying to keep her focus on the path ahead.

When they made it safely to the other side, she breathed a sigh of relief.

"Yay! We finally made it!" She smiled.

"We sure did!" He winked.

Standing at the end of the trail, they stared at the small beach surrounded by rocky cliffs. Not one footprint marred the sand. By its firm appearance, the tide swallowed it up nightly.

Her grandpa scratched his whiskers and sighed. "We can't stay, pumpkin. The tide will be in soon."

She was disappointed. They'd finally made it to the other side of the rocky mountain she'd been yearning to conquer, and they couldn't even make their mark on it. Tears threatened to spill, but she held them back.

He stared at her with hesitance before his blue eyes softened. "But we can take our sandals off and walk on it for a quick minute."

Excited, she used her big toes to slip her sandal strap from each heel and wriggled her feet out of them. "Okay, I'm ready."

Her grandpa used the same technique to remove his sandals. "Ladies first," he said with a gentlemanly bow and a gesture of a hand toward the beach.

She shook her head and wrapped her hand around his rough fingers. "Let's take the first step together." She waited for him to nod and said, "One, two, three, step!" And, together, they made their mark on the untouched land.

The warm sand squishing between her toes felt even better on their new beach than it had on the other beach. It was softer for some reason. Or maybe she just thought it was. Maybe she was just overjoyed to have finally set foot on the unknown.

After their footprints and their names marked up the beach from one side to the other, they put their sandals back on and started back along the cliff-side trail.

Avoiding looking down, she tripped on a loose rock. Her foot slipped off the path and toward the jagged rocks below, scaring the breath out of her. In an instant, her grandpa tightened his grip on her hand and grabbed her other hand, lifting her effortlessly through the air. Before she knew it, she was facing him—her feet planted firmly on the trail.

"Are you okay, pumpkin?" He hugged her tight. So tight, she heard his heart thudding in his chest.

She pulled away and looked up at him. "I almost fell, Grandpa," she admitted, still shaken.

He shook his head, and with a warm smile said, "No, you didn't. I had you the whole time."

She finally gave way to a light smile. "I love you, Grandpa. You're my hero."

He gave her another reassuring hug and a kiss on top of the head. "I love you too, and I will always find a way to keep you safe. Now, let's get back before your mother starts to worry. And it's best if you don't mention anything about this little adventure to her."

She nodded, knowing her mom would never allow her back to the beach with her grandpa if she found out.

He took her hand in his again, and they continued along the trail toward home....

The cessation of the engine snapped Sami from her memories, and she glanced at Billy.

"You've been awfully quiet. Are you okay?" Billy asked.

"I will be," she said, her tone glum, and peered through the windshield at the century-old hospital towering in front of them. Cracked steps led up to the entrance. The green hedges on either side didn't soften the sinister appearance of the red-brick building.

"It looks a little creepy," she admitted warily.

"It's just old," Billy reassured. "So, are you sure you wanna go through with this?"

She suddenly wasn't so sure. It had been over a year since she'd last seen her grandpa, and now that he'd lost his mind, it was almost as if she were saying good-bye to a stranger. *Will he even know who I am? Will I even know him?*

Regardless, she knew she'd never forgive herself if she passed up this opportunity.

"Yeah," she said, trying to ignore the nerves wracking her gut. "I'm ready."

They climbed out of the car. A cold gust of wind blew past them, and the sky darkened with clouds.

"Great," Sami whispered under her breath. She felt as if she were about to enter the mouth of something evil.

Billy grabbed her hand, and they proceeded up the steps. When they reached the door, he pulled it open and waited for her to enter. Afraid, she bit her lower lip and shook her head.

"You first."

He nodded and went inside.

Sami stayed right on his heels. The inside of the hospital wasn't as creepy looking as the outside. The pale blue walls and light gray flooring were much more inviting.

They headed to the desk in front of them.

"Can I help you?" a plump, gray-haired woman said flatly, eyeing them through her horn-rimmed glasses.

"Uh, we're here to see Harry Meyers," Sami answered, her voice unsteady.

The woman typed his name into the computer and narrowed her eyes. "Are you family?"

"Yes. I'm his granddaughter."

The woman continued to eye them suspiciously. "How old are you?"

"I-I'm twenty."

She looked at Billy. "And you?"

"I'm twenty-five. I'm her husband," Billy said calmly.

Sami's body stiffened, and without realizing it, she tightened her grip on his hand.

Billy clenched his jaw. He looked at Sami and lifted one corner of his mouth.

The woman smirked.

Sami held her breath, afraid the woman knew they were lying.

"He's on the third floor. Room three thirteen."

"Thank you." Billy gave a quick nod.

"Mmm hmm," she replied as she continued with her paperwork. "Just go on through the door and to the elevator. I'll buzz you in."

Still holding hands, they followed the woman's instructions. As soon as they were in the elevator, Billy wriggled his fingers from Sami's tight grip and shook his hand.

"Ow, Sami." His laugh was low and throaty. "Do you have some hidden powers I should know about?"

"Oh, sorry! I didn't realize. I was just nervous."

The elevator doors opened and they both sighed as reality sank back in.

Billy wrapped his hand around Sami's again and led the way to her grandpa's room.

A tall, burly security guard stood at the door, staring at them. "Family members only."

Sami gulped, intimidated by the man's unwavering gaze.

"This is his granddaughter." Billy looked straight into the guard's eyes. "And I'm her husband."

The man looked down at their interlocked hands and back to Billy's eyes.

"We…" Sami bit her lower lip, trying desperately to hold back her forming tears. "We came to say good-bye." She clenched her teeth to steady her trembling chin.

The guard's expression softened. He looked at Billy and nodded.

Sami and Billy entered the dimly lit room and walked around the blue curtain. Machines were everywhere, beeping and monitoring. Her grandpa lay in his bed, connected to tubes but sleeping peacefully.

Tears slipped down Sami's cheeks as she made her way to her grandpa's bedside. She placed a shaky hand over his. The proud, strong man she had known was but a memory. Now, his face was carved into deep lines, and his near-translucent skin merely draped over bulging veins and protruding bone structures. The frail man before her, whom she loved beyond words, was dying.

Harry fluttered open his tired eyes and a slight smile crossed his thin lips. "Samantha…" He croaked. "I knew you'd come. You've gotten so big…. You've gotten sooo biiig…."

"Hi, Grandpa." She smiled and took a deep breath to steady the tremble in her voice.

Harry chuckled weakly. "You watch out for those evil werewolves now, you hear? They're out there, and they'll get you! They almost got me. They almooost diiid…." He closed his eyes and drifted back to sleep.

Goose bumps covered Sami's flesh. She had been prepared for her grandpa's crazed utterances, but actually hearing them scared the crap out of her.

"I won't ever forget the times we shared together." Her voice cracked. The moment she'd been dreading had finally come. She cleared her throat and continued. "And I won't ever forget your stories. You'll always be my hero. Good-bye, Grandpa. I love you." She kissed him on the cheek.

Billy put a hand on Harry's shoulder. "Good-bye, Harry," he said, his voice deep. "You've been like a father to me, Mike, and Megan. And we'll always be thankful for everything you've done for us. We love you." He pulled his hand away and gulped.

The monitors began to beep faster and louder. Harry clamped his bony fingers around Billy's wrist and narrowed his eyes. "I know what happened! You take care of my granddaughter!" he ordered sharply.

Sami gasped.

"Promise me you'll protect her!" Harry shouted.

"I'll protect her," Billy said, his eyes wide.

A nurse rushed into the room. "You'll have to leave now. He needs his rest." She hurried to the bedside and pried Harry's fingers from Billy's wrist. Another nurse came in and injected something into his intravenous drip.

Billy put a protective arm around Sami and led her toward the door.

Crying uncontrollably, Sami looked back at her grandpa one last time. He was sleeping peacefully again.

With her head against chest, and one hand over her eyes to hide her sorrow, Sami relied on Billy's guidance to lead her out of the hospital and back to his car.

11

DARKNESS ENGULFED the forest by the time Billy and Sami pulled into the driveway. The porch light flicked on, and Mike came out to meet them with his shotgun in tow. They all decided to go to Sami's house so she could rest.

Billy led the way up the porch steps and unlocked the front door for her.

Sami went inside and into the kitchen. The thought of never seeing her grandpa again was unimaginable but hauntingly real. Through the blur of tears, a note on the breakfast bar caught her attention. She picked it up.

Samantha,

I'm so sorry about everything. I hope you find it in your heart to forgive me one day. I know you went to see your grandpa. I let them know you were coming. I'll call you

*if there are any changes in his condition.
I left a chicken casserole in the fridge for
you and your friends. See you tomorrow.*

Love, Mom

Sami let out a shaky breath and set the note back down. She pulled the casserole from the fridge and put it in the oven. She wanted to stay mad at her mom, but she couldn't. Her mom was hurting too, probably even more so since it was her father who lay dying.

Billy sat on the couch next to Mike and began telling him about what had happened at the hospital.

"I'm going upstairs for a minute. I'll be right back," Sami said glumly and headed up the stairs.

"Do you want me to come with you?" Billy asked.

"No, I'll be okay. I'll just be a minute." With her grandpa's last words haunting her thoughts, Sami went into her bedroom and straight to the window, not bothering to turn on the lights. Thankfully, there was nothing outside watching her.

What was staring at me last night? A mutant wolf standing on its hind legs? A deranged serial killer? Or are there really such creatures as werewolves out there?

She shook her head at the ridiculous notion. "There are no such things as monsters, Samantha," she whispered. Not feeling safe by herself in her dark room, she rushed out of the bedroom and down the hall. She went to the bathroom and splashed cool water on her face before heading back downstairs.

Jason was sitting on the couch next to Billy. It almost appeared as if they were amicable again.

A smile crossed her face. *Maybe there's hope for them after all.*

"There she is." Jason stood, wearing his charming grin. "We were beginning to wonder if we needed to come up there and check on you."

"No, she'd let us know if anything was wrong. Her scream is shrill enough to make the hair on your head stand on end," Mike teased.

"Ha, ha," Sami replied playfully and finished descending the stairs.

Jason crossed the room and gave her a big bear hug. "I just wanted to make sure you were okay." He set her back on her feet and shoved his hands in his pockets.

"I'll be okay...*eventually*," she said.

She glanced at Billy. By the way he stared icily at Jason, he was angry about the hug. Luckily, Jason didn't notice. When Billy's gaze met hers, his eyes softened and a slight smile formed.

"Um, my mom made enough casserole for everyone. Do you guys wanna stay for dinner?"

"I was hoping you'd ask. It smells delicious!" Jason rubbed his hands together. "I'm starving!"

Billy's expression fell flat. He noticed Sami staring at him and his smile returned. "You know I'm not going anywhere."

Mike winked. "Count me in."

"Oh, and if you don't mind," Jason said eagerly, his eyes full of hope, "there's a baseball game on tonight. The Yankees are playing."

Sami was amused by his childlike excitement. "Who are they playing?"

"The Giants," Jason replied.

"Cool. *Go Giants!*" she cheered.

Jason frowned. "Aw, come on. That's not funny! You're gonna jinx my team!"

"Yeah, you take that back, or we'll ship you back to California," Mike said.

Everyone laughed.

"Don't worry, Sami." Billy winked. "I've got your back."

"Suck-up," Mike teased.

"Yeah! What a kiss-ass!" Jason agreed.

Sami smiled at their wholehearted attempt to ease her sorrow. But Billy and Jason being around one another was a bomb waiting to explode. She hoped they'd become friends again before it happened.

When she went to the kitchen to pull the casserole from the oven, Billy jumped up to help her, followed by Mike and Jason.

They all sat in the living room to eat their cheesy meals while they watched the game. Billy and Sami sat together on the couch, along with Mike, and Jason sat in the recliner. With all the recent misfortunes they'd endured, they all needed this one night to relax and enjoy themselves.

"SEE, I told you you'd jinx my team," Jason teased after the game.

"Aww, don't be mad," Sami teased back.

They were the only ones talking. Billy and Mike were silent. Too silent. They were sitting on the couch with their eyes closed and mouths open, their breathing steady.

"Do you want some chocolate chip ice cream?" Sami whispered to Jason.

"Definitely," he whispered back.

They went to the kitchen, prepared their late-night snack, and sat at the round oak table along the back-kitchen wall to enjoy it.

Sami couldn't help wondering why Jason and Billy hated one another.

"Jason, can I ask you something?" She spoke quietly so she wouldn't wake the sleeping brothers.

"Sure, I think," he replied, his tone wary.

She bit her lip, contemplating whether to ask and knowing Billy might get mad if he found out.

"Well?" he urged.

Not able to stand not knowing any longer, she gave in to her curiosity. "What happened between you and Billy?"

Jason sighed and lowered his head. A few seconds passed before he looked her in the eyes again. "I figured Billy would've told you already."

She shook her head, seeing a sorrow in Jason's eyes she'd never seen before. She suddenly felt horrible for prying. "Never mind," she blurted. "I'm asking too much of you, and it's definitely none of my business."

Jason lowered his gaze to the table again. He rubbed his forehead and a heavy sigh escaped his lips. "You know, Sami...I've never talked about this before with anyone. But, now that you ask..." He gulped. "…I realize I've needed to talk about it with someone for a very long time."

He inhaled deeply and exhaled. "I'm sure you already know from your grandpa that uh…me and Billy, we didn't always hate each other." He grew quiet again and swiped a hand across his lips. "I'm sorry. This is just really hard to talk about."

"I know. If you can't talk about it, I understand. It's okay."

"No, I'm sure you'll hear about it sooner or later. Especially living in the same town as Jessica. Probably better to hear about it from a friend, right?"

"Only if this is what you need, Jason," she said softly.

"Okay…here it goes…. When we were twelve, and for as long as I can remember before then, Billy and I were the best of friends." He cleared his throat. "But then, one day, I wandered into the forest alone…and before I knew it, I was lost." Jason looked down at the table. He picked up his spoon and began fidgeting with it.

"My dad and Billy's dad, Rick, came looking for me. They brought their guns, you know, in case they ran into any wild animals. Somehow, they separated, and my dad thought…"

He shook his head and clenched his jaw. "There was a terrible accident," Jason continued with a shaky voice. "Somehow, my dad got confused and accidentally shot Rick." He paused and let out an unsteady breath. "He was hurt really bad, but my dad had to leave him alone to get help." Jason looked at Sami with tears in his eyes. He quickly looked back at his spoon.

"When he finally returned with help, Rick was almost unrecognizable because…" He gulped, and tears spilled from his eyes. "Because a wolf had gotten to him before they did. He was beyond saving."

"Oh my God!" Sami said, horrified. "That's terrible!"

Jason nodded, still unable to look her in the eyes. "His mother, Ann, was devastated. She died shortly after that from flu complications… but we all know she had a broken heart."

He tossed the bent spoon back onto the table and used his shirt to dry his face. He quickly regained his composure and looked her in the eyes again. "So, there you have it. His parents are dead, and it's all my fault. We've been enemies ever since. End of story."

Sami sat dumbfounded, trying to overcome the shock of Jason's tragic story. She wiped away her tears with the back of her hands.

"No, Jason. It's not your fault. It was just a terrible accident. It was never your fault."

"Yeah, well that doesn't change what happened." He looked over at Billy and Mike sleeping peacefully on the couch. "They've had such a rough time since then. Mike dropped out of college to raise Billy and his sister. They were all so sad and angry for a long time. And, as time passed, my mom and dad just couldn't bear to see it anymore.

"So, even though they loved living here, as soon as I graduated, we moved to the East Coast and only came back to visit during the summers. But they didn't come back with me this summer. And that's it." He shrugged and looked over at Billy again before turning his attention back to her. "Billy still blames me, and so do I."

"I'm so sorry for everything that happened, Jason. But you can't blame yourself. You were only twelve years old. *Billy* was only twelve. Why do you think Mike doesn't hate you? Because he was older. He *knows* it wasn't your fault. You and Billy were too young to see that. You didn't even know how to deal with loss.

"Billy lost his parents and so did you. *You* lost them too. And then, you lost Billy. How does a twelve-year-old know how to handle that? It was just easier for him to put the blame on someone and hate them rather than to face what it really was. A tragic accident."

"Well, try convincing *him* of that." He looked over his shoulder again.

"I think he'll eventually come around. I think he's already starting to."

"I'm sure that's only for your sake, Sami. Not for mine. Anyway, it's late. I have to get going."

Sami couldn't stand the thought of him being alone after having to relive the tragedy of his childhood. One that had changed the course of his life forever.

"Please stay, Jason. You're in that big house all alone. Just for tonight. You can sleep in the guest room upstairs."

"Don't worry about me. I'll be fine. I have guns. I'll come back tomorrow, okay?" He gathered their empty bowls and took them to the sink.

As she watched him rinse the dishes, the need to comfort him tugged at her heart. "Can I drive you home?"

He turned around with a baffled look on his face. "And then, what? I drive you right back home so I know you're safe?" He shook his head and smiled. "Thanks anyway, but my car is out front. And I brought my shotgun. If I see anything suspicious, I'll let a shot out to alert the deputy."

"Okay." She walked him to the door and gave him a hug. She couldn't help it. With all the pain he'd gone through all these years and thinking everything had been his fault, her heart went out to him.

"Good night, Sami," Jason said as he headed for his car.

"Good night, Jason," she called out to him. When he was safely in his car, she closed the door and rested her forehead against it, her thoughts on the tragedy of Billy's parents and the hard life he'd endured since. Tears filled her eyes again. She turned around and gasped, shocked to see Billy staring at her.

"Oh, Billy! I didn't know you were standing behind me." She tried to sound lighthearted as she wiped away her tears.

"What was that about?" he asked, his eyes filled with uncertainty.

"Oh, I just said good night to Jason." She smiled in an attempt to hide her guilt.

Billy stepped closer to her, reached the back of his forefinger to her cheek, and wiped away a tear. "What was *that* about?"

She was afraid to tell him—afraid he'd be angry with her for prying. But she knew he deserved the truth.

"I… He…" She lowered her head and bit her lip. "I asked him what happened between you guys. Why you hate each other so much."

He let out a sigh. "Oh."

Confused, she snapped her head up. "What do you mean, '*oh*?' What'd you think happened?"

"It's nothing."

"What? Tell me."

"Uh…I just thought…he tried to kiss you again," he said, his voice heavy with guilt.

She smirked. "He'll never do that again, Billy. I'd never let him." She wrapped her arms around his neck and gazed into his eyes. "I only want *you* to kiss me."

Billy grinned. Granting her wish, he pulled her close and planted his lips on hers.

"Don't you two ever get enough?" Mike's groggy voice interrupted.

Sami jumped out of Billy's embrace.

"Mike, what a surprise," Billy replied with dull enthusiasm.

Mike stretched out on the couch. He grabbed the purple throw draped over the back of it and pulled the blanket over himself. "Can you two keep it down? I need my beauty sleep."

Sami grabbed Billy's hand, flipped the switch on the wall next to the front door to darken the room, and led him up the stairs—guided by the faint light streaming through the window from the front porch. When they reached her bedroom, she turned on the light and sat on her bed.

Billy sat next to her.

"Are you mad at me for talking to Jason?" she asked, afraid of his answer.

"No. I'm not mad at you. I would've told you myself, but you never asked."

"I was afraid to. When we were at the diner a few days ago, I mentioned you two not getting along, but you changed the subject. And, the other night, when you told me about your parents passing away when you were younger, you changed the subject then, too. I didn't wanna pry."

"Well, we'd just met. I didn't wanna scare you off with my problems." He shifted closer until their shoulders touched. "So, he told you everything?"

"Yeah...he told me about getting lost." She let out a dismal sigh. "About the accident with your dad...and about your mom. I'm so sorry, Billy. I'm sorry you had to go through all that. I've been so selfish, going on about my meager problems since I've moved here. I don't know what I'd do if I had to go through what you've had to endure. I'm so sorry." She took his hand in hers, entwining her fingers between his.

Billy welcomed her comforting gesture with a gentle grip. "Your parents separating and your grandpa dying aren't meager problems, Sami. It was hard growing up without my parents. But I still had Mike and Megan. We stuck together and got through it. Plus, your grandparents were always checking in on us." He smiled. "You know, for a while after my parents passed away, do you wanna know what the *only* thing that made me smile was?"

Sami looked into his eyes.

"It was stories that Harry told me about *you*. He told me about how adventurous you were." He grinned smugly. "That's right, I know all about you walking along the dangerous cliff to the new beach, among other things."

Sami's mouth hung open. "You do?"

"Yep. Did you know your grandpa actually saw you trying to walk the trail by yourself a few days before he took you?"

She sucked in a quick breath. "Noooo." Her voice trailed off.

"He was going to stop you but said you'd had a change of heart and turned back after you'd only taken a few steps. So, he hid behind some beach grass until you passed by, and he followed you home to make sure you made it back safe."

She smiled sheepishly. "I got scared. It was more dangerous than it looked from a distance. But I remember him scolding me for sneaking out of the house when I got back. I didn't even know he'd followed me." She snickered. "That's probably why he ended up taking me to the other beach before he left—to satisfy my curiosity so I wouldn't try to go by myself again."

"Probably." Billy chuckled under his breath. "You know, your grandpa also said you were the most beautiful and caring girl in the world. That if anyone cried, it made you cry too. And you were always the first one there with a bandage and a kiss if anyone got hurt." His lips curled into a soft smile. "I always thought of you as some beautiful, adventurous Supergirl, cape and all."

"I had no idea you knew me so well before we'd even met." She smiled as her thoughts drifted. "My grandpa would tell me stories about you guys too. About how you and Jason would play baseball at the dead-end until the baseball went through my grandpa's living room window one day."

Billy laughed. "I remember that. We were so scared, we ran off and hid in the forest. He never did mention it to us. He just fixed the window." He sighed at the memory.

"And he said you, Jason, and your sister would go traipsing off into the forest to explore. But, he was afraid you'd run into a wild animal, so he would keep an eye on you guys. He loved you all very much."

"He's a good man," Billy said.

Sami sighed, dreading the days to come.

Billy cleared his throat. "You know, I always wanted to meet you when I was a kid."

"Me too," Sami said. "I always wished I could come here. I'd imagine you were my knight in shining armor, and you'd come and whisk me away into the forest on some wild adventure. For some reason, you were the only one that stuck out in my mind. Sure, I wanted to be friends with everyone, but I wanted *you* to rescue me." She smiled. "I guess we've actually known each other for a long time."

He nodded. "Yeah, we have. I even know your favorite song."

"Really? My grandpa told you my favorite song? What is it?"

"The Hawaiian version of "Somewhere Over the Rainbow"." He grinned smugly. "I heard him whistling it all the time, so I asked him why that song was so special to him."

Sami hid a bashful smile between pinched lips. "Silly, huh?"

"Nothing about you is silly." His smile faded. "And you are *not* selfish, Sami. Don't ever believe for a second that you are."

His comforting words put her guilt at ease. She nodded.

"And, as for me, my brother, and my sister, we're doing okay now. We've put it all behind us."

A thought occurred to her. "Billy?"

"Yeah?" He gazed down at her.

"Please don't get mad at me for asking, but if everything is all in the past now—" she mentally braced herself for his reaction "—then why haven't you forgiven Jason?"

Billy grew quiet for a moment before he released her hand and rose from the bed. He sat on the desk chair and faced her. "I don't know.

All these years of hating him and blaming him, I guess it eventually just became a part of life." He shrugged and glanced at the alarm clock. "It's already after midnight. Maybe we should get some sleep?"

"Okay," she agreed, deciding not to push the Jason issue any further.

Billy stood. "So, are you gonna be okay up here by yourself?"

"What? Stay please! Stay with me." She was afraid to be alone. Afraid to face *death* alone. She kicked off her shoes, climbed underneath the covers fully clothed, and patted the bed next to her. "There's enough room."

She could see in his eyes that he was silently struggling with the notion.

"What about your mom? What if she comes home?"

"She won't be home until later in the morning."

Billy finally gave in and smiled. He slipped off his shoes and turned out the light. Then, he climbed next to her and placed his arm under her head.

She snuggled against him, staring at the claw-like shadows on the ceiling created by the trees.

Billy looked up at the ceiling. "What the hell? I think I found the source of your nightmares."

"Yeah, but I'm used to them now."

"If you say so." He kissed her on the forehead. "Good night, Sami."

"Good night, Billy." For the first time since she'd moved in, Sami felt safe sleeping in her own bedroom. Content and in the arms of the man who'd held a piece of her heart since she was a little girl, she closed her eyes and gave into exhaustion.

12

SAMI JOLTED awake from the ringing of her cell phone. She snatched it off the nightstand and answered. "Hi, Mom." She rolled over to face Billy for support, but he was gone. All alone, she listened quietly as her mother explained how her grandpa had reached his final hours of life and that she would stay with him until he had passed. Sitting in bed with her knees to her chest, Sami buried her face in her hands and cried. She didn't even hear the door open when Billy walked back in.

"Was that your mom?"

She nodded.

"Is it Harry?"

Sami nodded again. "He only…has a few more…hours." She barely managed through sobs.

Tears rolled down his cheeks, and he pulled her into a tight embrace. They sat quietly for a minute, before he pulled away and dried his face on the sleeves of his blue T-shirt.

"I'm so sorry. Are you gonna be okay?"

She nodded and sniffled, trying to control her tears. "Yeah, I'll be okay. I'm just gonna miss him."

He grabbed some tissues from the desk and handed them to her. "I know. I'm gonna miss him too."

After she dried her eyes, Billy kissed her forehead and pulled her back into his arms.

Glancing at her dresser, Sami focused on the picture of her grandparents, realizing they'd soon be together again. The thought brought a sense of peace to her heart.

Her gaze shifted to the small mirror sitting on her desk, and her disheveled face came into focus. Her eyes were red and swollen, and her hair puffed this way and that. She was a mess.

"If you don't mind, I need to take a shower and change," she said, pulling away from him.

"Okay. I'll be downstairs. I'll let Mike know."

"Okay." She watched him leave before she finally climbed out of bed. Forlorn, she went to the picture on her dresser. "Good-bye, Grandpa…. I love you."

Head down and heavy-hearted, she made her way to the bathroom.

BILLY HAD just sat at the kitchen table when Sami entered. Showered and refreshed, wearing a loose-fitting white tank top and jeans, she looked like she was feeling much better. The ache in his heart eased a little.

Inhaling deeply, Sami smiled at Mike, who was standing at the stove. "Mmm, pancakes? Smells delicious."

Mike nodded and pressed his lips together, his expression reflecting his sorrow. "I'm sorry about Harry. He'll be missed." His voice was gentler than usual.

Sami forced a smile and captured her lower lip with her front teeth.

Billy could see she was near tears again. He went to her and took her into his arms.

"I'll be okay," she said with a quavering voice.

"Okay," Billy said in a soft tone, trying hard to keep his own tears from forming again. They both sat at the table to keep Mike company while he cooked.

"Maybe I should call Jason and tell him?" Sami suggested.

The front door opened and Jason walked in.

"I already did," Mike said. "I hope that's okay."

"It's fine. I'm glad you did," she replied.

Given the circumstances, Billy didn't mind either. Until Jason walked right up to Sami and gave her a big hug, lifting her from the chair.

"I'm sorry, Sami," Jason said, his voice glum.

Billy clenched his jaw but restrained his anger.

"I know," Sami said, hugging Jason.

Jason set her back down in her chair. He looked at Billy and gave a quick nod.

For Sami's sake, and out of respect for Harry, Billy unclenched his jaw and acknowledged Jason with the same gesture.

"Okay, let's eat," Mike announced as he set a platter of pancakes and a bottle of syrup in the middle of the table, along with enough plates and silverware for all.

Not knowing quite what to say under the circumstances, everyone ate in silence. The mood was completely solemn. Soon after, the phone rang, and the news came that Harry Meyers had passed.

Though they all wanted to mourn together, they also wanted to be alone. Mike went home to take care of some business. Jason sat on the front porch, staring out into the forest. And Billy sat on the couch with Sami in his arms.

Carol arrived home within the hour. Brenda had been nice enough to give her a ride home while another deputy drove her car back for her.

Sami met her mother at the door and threw her arms around her. "I'm sorry, Mom. I'm so sorry."

"I know, sweetheart. Me too," Carol replied.

It was all they could manage as they cried together.

"Carol." Billy cleared his throat, trying his damndest to be strong. "I'm very sorry about Harry. If there's anything I can do to help...."

"Thank you, Billy," Carol said, her face scrunched with pain.

He gave Sami a gentle pat on the back. "I'm gonna go outside to give you and your mom some time. Okay?"

"Okay." Sami nodded and sniffed.

Billy's chest grew heavy at the sight and sound of her sadness—hers and Carol's both. He escaped through the front door before he lost the battle with his own tears.

Mike had returned and was sitting on the wicker loveseat. Jason was on the matching chair on the other side of him.

Not wanting the guys to see his tears, Billy turned away and pulled the neck of his T-shirt over his eyes, drying the wetness. Then, he sat next to Mike.

All three of them sat quietly for a few minutes, staring into the forest, listening helplessly to the uncontrolled sorrow coming from inside the house, while contrarily trying to keep their own sorrow under control.

A few minutes passed before Jason cleared his throat and broke the silence. "Uh, Billy? I just wanted you to know…I'm sorry, man."

Billy grew irritated. "Don't be sorry for me. You knew Harry as well as I did."

"No, I mean—" an uneasy silence filled the air and he let out a heavy sigh "—for getting lost that day."

Billy tensed, taken off guard. He wasn't ready to dredge up the past. He gulped and looked at his brother for help.

"I'm gonna check on Carol and Sami." Mike stood and went into the house.

Jason rose from his chair and sat on the porch railing, facing Billy. "I didn't mean for anything to happen."

Billy fell silent as memories of the tragedy flashed through his mind. The way Harry had desperately pounded on the front door and had broken the news of his father's death. The sound of his mother's blood curdling scream right before she'd collapsed. The last breath his mother had ever taken. And the unbearable sorrow that had spread through the house and had never really gone away, no matter how much time had passed.

Suddenly, all the hatred Billy had harbored boiled to the surface, and his eyes bore into Jason's. "What were you doing out there *alone* anyways? You've *always* been arrogant! *Always!* It's *always* been about *you!*"

Fury raged through Billy's blood. He lunged at Jason and grabbed him by the shirt with clenched fists. "You knew you weren't supposed to go out there by yourself! You *knew* it! What the *hell* were you thinking!"

He released Jason and stepped back, sucking in heavy breaths and trying to gain control of his rage.

Jason shoved a hand into his jeans pocket. "I was looking for this," he said with a husky voice. He pulled his hand from his pocket and opened it, revealing a Buck Folding Hunter knife.

Mouth wide open, Billy stared at the familiar knife before he slowly reached out and took it. With trembling hands, he unfolded the blade to read the inscription.

FOR MY SON, BILLY. LOVE, DAD

Billy's heart grew heavy as recalled the day his dad had given him the knife—his twelfth birthday. He'd been frantic when he'd lost it in the forest one day while he and Jason had been hiking with Mike.

"I remember you were so upset about losing it that you cried." Jason gulped. "I'd never seen you cry before, so I went to look for it…. I was so frickin' happy when I finally found it. I started running back along the trail, but somewhere…somehow, I got turned around." He ran a quick hand through his hair. "I tried to give it to you after the funeral, but you wouldn't even look at me. You *hated* me." He shook his head. "I know I should've given it to you sooner, but I didn't even know how to approach you. I was afraid to."

Billy clenched his teeth, trying to hold back the tears that stung his eyes, but he was powerless to stop them. He cleared his throat. "I can't believe you found it. I thought it was gone for good."

"Yeah, well, I had to find it—you were my best friend." Tears dripped down Jason's cheeks and soaked into his shirt.

Billy felt awful for treating his best friend so badly all these years. Hating him. Blaming him. He cleared his throat again and pressed his lips together to steady the quiver.

"I'm sorry, Jason." Billy shook his head. "I'm sorry. I know it wasn't your fault. I was just so pissed at the world. I just—" He was at a sudden loss for words.

"It's okay, man. I would've hated me too. As a matter of fact, I did for a long time." Jason stood and gave Billy a couple of firm pats on the shoulder.

That wasn't enough for Billy. He grabbed Jason by the shoulder and yanked him into a strong embrace. "I'm sorry! I'm so *frickin'* sorry!" He cried away the guilt weighing heavily on his soul.

Jason gave Billy sturdy pats on the back. "Me too, bro! Me too!"

The front door opened.

Billy and Jason quickly separated and wiped their eyes dry on the sleeves of their shirts.

"Now that's more like it!" Mike belted out, grinning proudly. "I was beginning to think you two would *never* kiss and make up."

13

THE DAYS following her grandpa's passing rushed by like a blur. The phone rang nonstop. Close friends of her grandparents, and those who still respected her grandpa, came to visit off and on throughout the daylight hours to offer their condolences. Homemade dinners began to overflow the refrigerator so much that Sami and her mother started sending food home with Mike, Billy, and Jason. And vases filled with flowers congested the house and the front porch.

Sami dreaded the morning of the funeral. The mood downstairs was solemn. Melancholy, she stayed in her room for as long as she could. She slipped into a sleeveless summer dress—the only black dress she owned—and tied her hair back into a simple ponytail.

Staring at herself in the mirror, she traced her finger along the delicate locket hanging around her neck, wishing her father could be there too. She needed his strength and comfort.

"Samantha!" Her mother's voice echoed from the bottom of the stairs. "It's time!"

Reluctantly, Sami left the sanctity of her bedroom and slowly descended the stairs. Deputy Brenda Cruz, Mike, Jason, and Billy had been over all morning, helping to prepare for the gathering that was to take place after the funeral. A gathering she was dreading. If it were up to her, she'd rather come home and flee to her room where it felt safe, quiet, and private.

Billy stood from the couch and greeted Sami with a smile as she descended the steps.

"There you are." He met her at the bottom and wrapped his arms around her waist. "You look beautiful today. Are you ready?"

She hugged him tightly, not wanting to let go. "I guess so." She stepped back and smoothed out the lapel of his suit. "You look very handsome."

"Good morning." Her mother's voice came from behind.

Sami spun around to face her mom, welcoming her quick, but whole-hearted, hug.

"You look nice, sweetheart." Carol tucked loose wisps of hair behind Sami's ears.

Sami eyed her mother's mid-sleeve black dress and a soft smile formed. "You look nice too, Mom."

"Thank you. I'm going to ride with Brenda. You can ride with us also, but I'm sure you'd be happier with Billy. I understand."

"Thanks, Mom."

"We'll see you there, Carol." Billy held Sami's hand, guiding her out the front door and to his car.

As she and Billy pulled out of Billy's driveway, Mike and Jason exited her house, followed by her mom and Brenda—all heading to their cars parked out front. Like Billy, Jason and Mike wore black suits. And Brenda, a gray top and black pants. The mourners all wore black, a color reminding Sami of the dark, menacing forest surrounding her. Her instincts told her to flee Wolf Hill—bury it deep within the past and never look back.

Maybe she could get her mother to move back home to California now that she no longer had to care for her grandpa. But, even if her mother agreed, the mere thought of leaving Billy made Sami's heart ache.

She glanced at Billy as he drove along the winding road through the forest. He flashed a tender smile, extinguishing the ache and making her heart flip-flop again. At that moment, she realized she couldn't leave him. That this menacing, dark forest *was* her home now. And it scared the hell out of her.

"Are you okay?" Billy broke the heavy silence.

"I'll be okay," she replied in a dismal tone. She looked up just as Billy slowed and pulled onto the long drive leading to the top of Cemetery Hill. It too, was surrounded by the same dreadful forest.

As they neared the top of the hill, the forest seemed to back away, bowing respectfully to a large and open grassy field scattered with headstones and tombs. Some were near crumbling. Others appeared new and polished.

Like the sanctity of a church against evil, the graveyard felt like the only safe place in the forest—its fated residents having already paid the ultimate sacrifice with nothing left to fear and nothing left to give.

Billy pulled off onto the gravel shoulder and parked. Mike and Jason pulled up behind them in Jason's car, followed by Carol and Brenda in the squad car.

Billy and Sami climbed out of the car and walked through the grass, to the rows of chairs facing her grandpa's mahogany casket. They took their seats in the front row. Mike and Jason sat in the empty chairs next to Billy. Though they were aware of the commotion of the arriving guests behind them, they sat silently—facing forward, and taking a moment to remember.

Sami didn't move, nor did she look up, when she heard footsteps approach and take the empty seat next to her. Deep in thought, she stared at the cascade of white roses draping her grandfather's casket, remembering their sunny days at the beach together. She did, however, sense the stares of the three handsome men sitting next to her.

She glanced over at Billy, Mike, and Jason, wondering why they were all staring at her with warm smiles on their faces. Without warning, the person who had just sat next to her wrapped his strong, familiar hand around hers.

Sami's heart stopped. She turned to face the unseen guest. "Dad!" She threw her arms around his neck and started to cry, finding comfort in his familiar sporty scent and the rough stubble against her cheek.

He hugged her tightly and patted her back. "Hi, Samantha."

"I thought you weren't coming?" She pulled away to see him clearly. His black wavy hair was streaked with silver, more so than the last time she'd seen him, and his brown eyes appeared darker.

"I made it happen. I wanted to be here for you and your mother." He leaned forward. "Billy, Mike, Jason." He gave a quick nod. "It's good to see you again. Not under these circumstances, of course, but it's still good to see you."

"Greg." Mike returned the nod.

Smiling, Billy and Jason also greeted him with a nod.

Carol took her seat on the other side of Greg, and soon after, the funeral proceeded.

Everyone fell silent as the minister spoke, guiding them all in saying farewell to Harry Meyers, as well as blessing him and guiding him into his afterlife journey.

When Billy and Sami returned home, guests were already gathered throughout the house, on the front porch, and around the folding tables set up in the front yard. Sniffles could be heard, as well as stories of her grandpa's past, and even laughter now and then. Trays of food were spread about the kitchen, along with bottles of beer and wine. Nearly half the town had come together to remember Harry Meyers and to say farewell.

DUSK SETTLED in before the last of the guests had finally said good-bye. Billy left also, to give Sami time alone with her parents.

"So, how long are you staying, Dad?" Sami asked as the three of them sat comfortably in the living room.

He let out a long breath, his eyes filled with guilt. "I have to leave tonight. I'm catching an early morning flight out of Portland. I couldn't find anyone to cover my flight tomorrow night."

"What? Can't you stay longer? Can't someone else take over for you?" she pleaded. It had been weeks since she'd seen him last, and she missed him. She missed being a family. What she didn't miss was having a pilot for a father.

"I'm sorry. I have to get back. If I could stay, I would."

Sami nodded. Back home it had always been the same story. He had a flight to catch, traveling hundreds—sometimes thousands—of miles away, leaving her and her mother to figure out life alone. But he was here, at this moment, and maybe, just maybe, he and her mother could work things out.

They sat and talked for an hour more before he bid his farewell.

Sami was crushed. It felt as if she had lost two men in her life today.

Her mom was also upset. She said good night, but before she walked away, Sami stopped her.

"Mom?"

"Yes?"

Sami wanted to ask if there was any hope of saving their marriage, but after seeing the darkened corners of her mother's eyes, she decided to ask about it later.

"Good night."

"Good night, sweetheart." Carol disappeared down the hallway.

Needing comfort, Sami decided to see Billy. Not wanting to worry her mother, she didn't tell her. She grabbed the keys hanging on the wall above the breakfast bar and turned off the lights, leaving only the porch light on. Then, she tiptoed out the front door and locked it as quietly as she could.

The porch light popped, and everything went black. "Great!" She squinted through the darkness, trying to focus on her surroundings. There was no moon out tonight, which made seeing anything nearly impossible.

Her heart started to race. She glanced at Billy's house, but there were no lights on. In the dark it looked as if his house wasn't even there. "Shoot, they must be sleeping already."

A cool wind awakened and howled its way through the forest. She shuddered, wondering if her stalker was out there, waiting for the perfect moment to strike—the perfect moment being now.

Sami scanned the road, looking for the squad car, but it was too dark to see. She fumbled with the keys, struggling to match the right one to the slot and using her fingertip as a guide to find it as if she were reading Braille.

"Come on, dammit!" she urged herself, frustrated and scared.

The wind died, filling the air with absolute silence again. The soft crunching of debris and the snapping of twigs stirred in the forest across the road.

Fear ran down Sami's spine. Hands shaking, she tried the last key and shimmied it into the slot. The knob turned, and the door opened. Relieved, she hurried inside and shut the door, locking the dead bolt.

Then, she rushed upstairs to the safety of her bedroom.

14

NOT WANTING to get out of bed and face the day, Sami slept in the next morning. She did, however, want to see Billy. So, she eventually dragged herself out of bed, choosing to wear her favorite lavender blouse, cutoffs, and a pair of flip-flops. She trudged downstairs to the kitchen. Her mother was at the table, sipping her coffee and still wearing her bathrobe.

"Good morning." Carol smiled.

"Morning." Sami returned the smile. She made herself a bowl of fruity rings and sat at the table. As she ate her cereal, she studied her mother's features, shocked to see how dark and swollen her eyes were. It looked as if she'd been up crying half the night.

"So, do you have any plans for today?" Carol's tone held only a hint of melancholy.

Sami knew her mom was trying to be strong. She decided to put off seeing Billy until tomorrow.

"I was thinking of maybe just staying home today and spending time with you."

Her mother's sad eyes filled with warmth. "Aw, sweetheart, you don't have to do that. I'm sure you want to see Billy. I'll be okay. I need some time to myself anyway."

Sami frowned. "Are you sure, Mom? I can stay and keep you company. I *want* to."

"Thank you, but no. You go hang out with your friends today. I just need to rest. I was up half the night. I'll probably sleep most of the day."

She sighed, knowing there was no changing her mother's mind. "Okay, I guess I'll see if Billy's home."

"Oh, sorry, I completely forgot. He came by earlier, but you were still sleeping. He and Mike had some work to do, but he said it'd only take a few hours."

"Oh, okay," Sami said as if it were no big deal, trying to hide her disappointment.

"Jason stopped by to see how you were doing, though. He said to call if you need anything." Carol took another sip of her coffee. "Maybe you should see what he's doing today? It'd be good for you to get out and get your mind off of things."

"Yeah, maybe you're right. I'll call him."

After breakfast, Sami put her bowl in the sink and glanced out the window. The patrol car was missing. Her heart skipped a beat.

"Where's the deputy?"

"They stopped coming the day before the funeral. There haven't been any sightings since that night. They think the wolf migrated somewhere else."

Sami grew upset. Without the deputy out front, she felt vulnerable again. "But it looked more like a *man*, Mom. He was *standing*."

"The sheriff said they found four prints in the forest. They think maybe it's just some freakishly oversized wolf. The backyard is full of shadows when the moon is out. Maybe it wasn't standing at all."

"But I *know* what I *saw*!" Anger replaced her worry. She was tired of everyone telling her what she *thought* she'd seen that night instead of believing what she really *had* seen.

"There's no sign of anything or anyone. Whatever it was, it's gone now." Carol let out a relieving breath. "We can finally rest easy. Now, maybe things can get back to normal around here."

Sami was disappointed they'd called off the search, but glad they hadn't seen any signs of the man, wolf, or whatever it was. She recalled the sounds she'd heard in the forest last night. It wasn't the usual loud *snap*. The disturbance was lighter, like a deer traveling along or possibly a raccoon.

Maybe what I heard last night was nothing to fear at all. Billy, Mike, and Jason go hunting, so there have to be harmless wild animals out there somewhere.

"Okay. I won't worry then. I'm going to Jason's." She headed for the door, more than ready to put everything behind her.

"Wait, don't you want to call him first?" Carol scrunched her brows together.

"No, but don't worry, I'll drive across the road. Okay?" Sami shook her head. "I thought you said we could finally rest easy. And now, you're gonna turn right around and be worried about me going outside again?"

Carol sighed. "You're right. Just be careful."

"I will."

Sami pulled the door closed and pranced down the porch steps, enjoying the warmth of the sun kissing her skin. She tilted her head back, inhaling the fresh air as a gentle breeze wafted through her hair.

Squawking drew her attention to a cluster of birds soaring overhead. *Wait, birds are chirping!* She grinned, trying to recall whether she'd seen any birds lately. But, she'd been so wrapped up in whatever danger might be out there, she'd forgotten to pay attention.

She eyed the forest. It was still as dark and creepy as ever. Not wanting to take any chances, she hurried to her car, climbed in, and locked the door. Then, she drove across the road and along the wooded driveway.

Jason was outside washing his car when she pulled up. She parked and hopped out to greet him.

He met her with a huge grin. "You're just in time." He pulled an oversized, soapy sponge from the blue bucket at his feet and tossed it to her.

Sami screamed and jumped back as the sponge splattered at her feet, splashing cold, sudsy water on her bare legs. "Not funny, Jason!" She giggled.

"It was *very* funny, Sami. You should've seen the look on your face."

She picked up the sponge and threw it back at him. "You're crazy if you think I'm gonna help you now."

Jason picked up the hose and grinned devilishly. "I beg to differ."

"You wouldn't dare!" Her eyes widened, and she backed away.

He took a step closer and aimed the spray nozzle at her.

She held her hands above her head. "Okay, okay, I'll help. Just don't shoot!"

He laughed and handed her the hose. "Here, you can rinse."

Sami took the hose and flashed a playful grin. "Oh, you shouldn't have done that." She pointed it straight at him and pulled the trigger, dousing him with water.

"Hey!" he shouted, laughing and trying to shield himself with his hands. He gave up and went after her instead.

Sami hadn't expected him to chase her. She screamed and threw the hose as far away as possible before she ducked behind the car.

Jason picked up the hose and sprayed it into the air, releasing a steady shower all over Sami and his car.

She screamed as the frigid water shocked her senses. The hose water was just as cold as the lake. "Okay, okay, I'm sorry!" She laughed, stepping out from behind his car. "Please! I'm sorry! I'll be good!"

Jason released the trigger and pointed it right at her. "Are you sure?"

"Yes, I'm sure! I promise!" She held her hands up in front of her, waiting for the water to strike again.

"Truce?"

"Truce!" she begged.

"I'm glad you're feeling better today, Sami." Jason winked and pointed the hose at his car.

She walked over to the porch steps and sat down to watch him rinse his car. "Yeah, I do feel better today, Jason. My mom said there hasn't been any sign of the wolf or whatever it was for days now. They think it migrated somewhere else."

"Really?" He turned off the water and sat next to her. "That's good. Now, maybe we can go swimming at the lake again. It's supposed to reach the nineties later this week."

"That sounds like fun. But, this time, I think I'll just sit on the bank and watch. That water is way too cold for me."

"Mike used to take me and Billy camping up there when we were younger. Maybe we can arrange something like that again soon."

"Yeah, that'd be cool. I've never been camping before."

Jason furrowed his brow. "What? You've *never* been camping?"

"Nope. Not once."

"Wow, we're definitely gonna have to plan a trip then." He stood and held his hand out. "Come on. I'll get you a towel and a dry shirt."

Sami let him help her up and followed him inside. She wandered down the short hall to the right of the foyer which opened up to a large living area on her left. It was nicely furnished with a black leather couch and loveseat, and solid mahogany trimmed the doorways and made up the bottom half of the walls. The top half of the walls were painted deep beige and hung with oil paintings of various landscapes—the forest, the grassy meadow sprinkled with wildflowers, and even a large painting of Wolf Lake.

A large picture window and French doors made up the opposite wall of the living room, with an amazing view of the forest and a humongous grassy hill dotted with a few trees in the distance. To the right of the hallway, eight chairs padded with black leather surrounded a large dining table. Straight ahead, past the hallway, was a large kitchen island with a black granite countertop and four barstools in front of it. Beyond the island, along the back wall, the rest of the kitchen matched the mahogany and black granite theme, with stainless steel appliances.

Sami admired the large open space. Even with the dark colors, the recessed lighting, along with the sun shining through the large living room window, brightened and warmed the place.

"Nice house."

"You've been here before," he said as he led the way back down the hall, past the front door, to the stairway.

"Yeah, but the first time I was being chased by a wolf. I didn't notice anything except for the near heart attack I was having," she reminded as she followed him upstairs, admiring the same decorative theme along the way.

"Oh, that's right. Good thing that's over now." At the top of the stairs, he pulled a towel from the closet.

"Thanks." Sami took the towel and followed him down the hallway to his bedroom. A queen-sized bed draped in black and gray bedding lay under the oversized window. She turned around, surprised to see the biggest flat-screen TV she'd ever seen mounted to the wall.

"Are you sure you can see the TV all the way from your bed?" she teased.

He grinned. "The bigger the better. As soon as they come out with a bigger screen, this one's coming down."

She giggled under her breath and shook her head. Another painting of Wolf Lake, hanging over his desk, caught her eye. "That looks just like the one downstairs."

"Yeah, my mom likes to paint." Jason went to the closet door next to the desk. "Here, I think this'll work." He held up a blue T-shirt, waiting for her approval.

"I really don't need it," Sami said. "I'm sure I'll dry soon."

"Trust me, Sami, you need it." He grinned and handed her the shirt. "I'll be downstairs." He left and shut the door.

Sami didn't understand what he had meant. She went to the dresser and looked in the mirror. Her lavender shirt was completely see-through, revealing the paleness of her skin, her belly button, and every detail of her lacy lavender bra.

She felt the heat rise in her cheeks as her face turned beet red, wondering how she was going to go back downstairs and face him again. She remembered he had already seen her in her bikini at the lake. Maybe this wasn't as bad as it seemed. Either way, there wasn't anything she could do about it now—except to simply change her shirt and hold her head high.

She peeled off her wet blouse, changed into the T-shirt, and went back downstairs.

"I'll put it in the dryer for you." Jason took the wet shirt from her and disappeared through a frosted glass door along the back-kitchen wall.

He returned with a smug smile and headed to the couch. "Feel better?"

"Umm, no!" she replied in a snarky tone and sat next to him. "A little humiliated is more like it," she added with a smile.

Jason laughed. "I've already seen your beautiful, half-naked body before. And you had less clothes on at the time. It's no big deal."

"Right," she replied, still not seeing the situation in the same light he did.

"You wanna play some video games?" He went to the flat-screen TV in the corner of the room, next to the window. The TV was about the same size as the one in his bedroom. He turned it on, along with the gaming system, and grabbed two controllers off the entertainment center.

"Sure, sounds like fun. But I have to warn you—"

"Let me guess, you've never played video games before?" he teased.

"No, dummy. I just wanna let you know that I'm gonna kick your ass in racing."

"Oh, yeah?" He plopped onto the couch and handed her a controller. "We'll see about that!"

They sat and played video games for a couple of hours. When Jason finally gave up on trying to come in first place, they made turkey sandwiches and ate lunch together. Though Sami was having a great time with Jason, she couldn't wait to see Billy again.

"Well, I should get going, Jason. Thank you for lunch and all." She gave him a hug.

"It was my pleasure. Hey, maybe I'll come over later and talk to Mike and Billy about camping or at least swimming." He walked her out to her car.

As soon as Sami settled on the driver's seat Jason shut the door for her.

Sami rolled down the window.

"See you later, Sami. Roll your window back up and lock your door."

She smiled and shook her head at his protectiveness. "Bye, Jason. Thanks for letting me kick your ass in racing."

"Whatever! I get to be Mario next time. Then we'll see who wins."

Sami giggled and drove away.

BILLY OPENED the front door, wearing a huge grin, glad to finally see the one person he'd been thinking about all night and morning. He wrapped his arms around Sami and lifted her off the ground.

Beaming, Sami welcomed his big bear hug with a tight squeeze around his neck. "How long have you been home?"

"We just got back half an hour ago. You gave me just enough time to shower and shave." Billy couldn't wait any longer. He set her back on her feet and kissed her.

"Well, are you gonna just stand there and suck her face off all day, or are you gonna invite her in?" Mike asked.

"Dude, shut up!" Billy turned around and backhanded his brother in the gut.

Mike grunted and clutched his abdomen. "I'll let that one slide since your girlfriend's here."

Sami grinned. "I wish I had a brother or sister to bicker with."

"No, you don't!" they warned in unison.

"But you guys are so cute together," she teased.

"Whatever!" Billy poked her sides, trying to tickle her.

"Okay, okay!" She laughed, trying to dodge each poke. "I take it back! You guys are *not* cute together."

Billy took her by the hand and led her to the couch.

"How's your mom doing?" Mike dropped onto the recliner.

"She's still sad but seemed to be in better spirits this morning. She's looking forward to things getting back to normal around here."

"She'll feel better with time," he replied. "What about you?"

She shrugged, and her eyes glistened with moisture.

Billy put an arm around her and gave her a reassuring squeeze. "Us too," he said in a gentle tone. "It'll get a little easier each day."

She nodded, her face showing her effort not to cry.

Billy knew she was trying to be strong. He and Mike handled loss in a similar manner. They kept their minds focused on something else to dull the pain, rather than taking the time to dwell and suffer further. He glared at Mike, silently warning him to stop with the personal questions.

Mike cleared his throat. "We were thinking about barbecuing tonight. Are you up for it?"

Sami smiled. "Sure, that sounds really good. I am *sooo* tired of casseroles and lasagnas."

"Yeah, me too," Billy agreed.

Mike hopped to his feet and snatched his wallet from the coffee table. "I guess I'll go into town and pick up some steaks. Keys, little bro." He held out his hand.

Billy reluctantly handed his brother the keys, remembering the way Mike had ripped out of the driveway and squealed down the road the last time he'd taken his car.

"Be *easy* on her," he warned.

Mike winked, and a devious grin formed. "Any *other* requests?" he asked Sami in particular.

"No, anything's fine," she said.

"See you in a bit." He headed out the front door.

Billy turned his attention back to Sami, wondering if Carol dealt with loss the same way. "Do you think maybe your mom would like to come over?"

"I'm pretty sure she won't. She likes to be alone when she's sad. But I'll ask her. I need to go home and change my shirt anyway." She scrunched her face, as if she'd accidentally said the wrong thing.

Billy glanced at the over-sized shirt she wore. He gave her a puzzled look.

"Um, I went to Jason's today, and he was washing his car. Then I sort of got wet. So, he lent me a dry shirt."

Though they were friends again, Billy still didn't like the idea of Sami being alone with Jason or of her wearing his shirt. Flashes of Jason trying to kiss her at the lake filled his thoughts. He forced a half-smile and nodded.

"Oh? So, what'd you two do?" he asked, trying to sound casual.

"We just hung out. Played some video games. Ate lunch." She shrugged. "But I couldn't stop thinking about you, so I came home to see if you were back yet."

Billy suddenly felt like a jackass for being jealous. He trusted Sami.

And though it seemed weird to admit it, he trusted Jason.

"I missed you," he said, his voice turning husky.

The corners of her mouth curled into a subtle smile. "You did?"

"Very much." He leaned over and kissed her.

Sami wrapped her arms around his neck, welcoming his kiss.

He pulled away just far enough to whisper, "Did you miss me too?"

"Very much," she whispered through a heavy breath.

Pleased with the effect he had on her, Billy crushed his lips to hers, deepening their kiss. She kissed him back eagerly and pressed her soft body against him, an act which nearly drove him crazy. With his lips still on hers, he laid her back on the couch and covered her body with his.

He pulled away briefly, their heavy breaths mingling into one, before he molded his lips back to hers. He left the sweetness of her mouth to taste more of her, letting his lips trail down the front of her neck. Then, he slowly kissed his way back to her lips and slid his tongue into her mouth. She gave him what he was seeking, reaching her sweet tongue out to play with his.

He slid his hand from her waist to her plush buttocks, while leaving a trail of wet, hot kisses down the side of her neck to her nape. There, he gently caressed the sensitive area with his tongue, leaving her writhing with pleasure.

Sami reached up under his shirt and glided her fingertips across his back, sending goose bumps down his limbs. He shuddered and slid his hand back to her waist, and his lips found their way back to hers. They kissed hungrily until he slowly pulled away and gazed into her passion-filled eyes.

"Sami..." he whispered through a ragged breath. He was ready to fill her body with pleasure, but he knew now wasn't the right time. And because of that, it was dangerous to keep going. He wanted their first time together to not only mean more, but to be more private and not rushed. More importantly, he wanted to wait for the perfect moment to tell her he was falling in love with her. Reluctantly, he sat up and pulled her with him.

Sami let out a heavy sigh and bit her lower lip. The disappointment in her eyes was evident.

Without another thought, he leaned down and kissed her again in an attempt to make her feel better. He meant to kiss her softly—a kiss they could both pull away from before it got out of hand. But the desire to feel every part of her molded to him again was too strong, dissolving all his sense. Together, they traveled back down the same road of passion he had just tried to rescue them from. Kissing, caressing, and knowing they were dangerously close to giving in to their escalating desires, and neither of them had the will power to stop it this time.

A loud knock on the door halted their passion.

They both froze, afraid to move. As reality sank back in, they pulled away from one another, taking in deep breaths to slow their breathing and dilute the euphoria.

Sami sat up, straightened her shirt, and ran her fingers through her hair before placing a shaky hand over her chest.

"You okay?" Billy smiled a half-smile, still seeing the look of passion in her eyes.

She exhaled and nodded.

There was another knock, this time louder.

"I'm coming! I'm coming!" Billy managed to say clearly now that his breathing was under control. He went to the door and opened it.

Jason stood there grinning, holding up Sami's shirt. "Thought I'd come over and see what's up." He walked past Billy and into the house. "You forgot this." He handed Sami the shirt over the back of the couch. In one swift move, he hopped over the couch and plopped next to her. "So, what's going on?" He looked back at Billy, then to Sami.

Sami's cheeks flushed pink. "I think I'll go put this back on now." She got up and hurried to the bathroom, keeping her eyes glued to the floor.

"Not much." Billy sat on the recliner, trying to get his emotions in check.

Jason suddenly shot him a disgusted look. "Dude! Did I interrupt something?" He jumped off the couch, looking back as if it had just bitten him.

Billy laughed under his breath. "No, no. You didn't interrupt anything. We're actually having a barbecue tonight. You in?"

"Cool, I'm in," Jason replied as he eyed the couch again before cautiously sitting back down.

SAMI SHUT the door and changed her shirt. Staring into the mirror, she traced her finger over her lips, still swollen and red from Billy's love. A tingling sensation awakened deep within and an ache filled her heart. Not a bad ache, a good one, which could only mean one thing. She was falling in love. Giddiness replaced the ache, and she couldn't help grinning.

"Get a hold of yourself, Sami," she whispered and bit her lip to contain her excitement.

She folded Jason's shirt, replaced her smile with a casual look, and went back into the living room. She handed Jason his shirt as she sat back down. "Thanks for lending it to me."

"No problem." He draped the shirt over the arm of the couch.

Billy eyed the thin fabric of her lavender blouse. "That's the shirt you were wearing when you got all wet?"

She smiled sheepishly. "Yeah."

"Yeah, I like that shirt!" Jason grinned, taunting Billy. "I think it's my *favorite* now."

"Dude, I am *so* gonna kick your ass!" Billy threw a couch pillow at him.

"Anyway—" Sami was desperate to change the subject.

"Yeah, *anyway*." Jason grinned. "Where's Mike?"

"He went to the store to get food for the barbecue," Billy replied. "We're all tired of casserole."

"You've got that right," Jason said. "So, Sami and I were talking today, and I found out she's never been camping before." He looked at Billy with a bewildered expression. "Have you ever heard of such a thing?"

Playing along, Billy crinkled his brow. "What? Never been camping? You've gotta be kidding me?"

"All right, all right," she pleaded through her smile. "Enough already! I'm sure there are lots of people who've never been camping before."

Jason raised his eyebrows. "If you can find one person in this town who's never been camping, I'll wash that dust-bucket you call a car every day for two weeks."

"You're on." She flashed a mischievous grin.

"And if you lose," Jason added, "you have to wash *my* car every day for two weeks, wearing *that* shirt!"

"No way! I'm not wearing this shirt!" Embarrassed, she crossed her arms over her chest in an attempt to cover herself from Jason's thoughts.

"Dude, knock it off." Billy threw another couch pillow at Jason, aiming for his head.

Jason smirked and caught the pillow.

They continued with their banter for a while longer, tossing the pillow back and forth while laughing until the front door opened. Mike walked in with his hands full. Jason and Billy jumped up to help.

"There's a case of beer and soda in the car," Mike said over his shoulder as he entered the kitchen.

Sami followed them outside. "I'm gonna go home and ask my mom if she wants to join us. I'll be back in a minute."

"Okay," Billy replied.

Traipsing across the front yards, a smile crossed Sami's face as thoughts of the day's events flashed through her mind—her bonding with Jason and her intimacy with Billy. Aside from missing her grandpa dearly, life in Wolf Hill finally seemed to be getting better. She ran up the porch steps and opened the front door.

"Hi, sweetheart," Carol said, her tone dismal. She was lying on the couch, watching TV. An empty bottle of merlot and a full wine glass stood on the coffee table.

Sami's heart grew heavy. "Hey, Mom." She tried to sound lighthearted. "Billy and Mike are having a barbecue. They were wondering if you wanted come over."

"Oh? Thanks, but no. I'm not feeling up to it." She forced a slight smile.

"Are you sure? It'll be fun. Or I could stay with you." She couldn't bear to see her mom so sad.

"I'll be fine here. You go have fun. There have been so many people over this week, I haven't had time to myself. I *need* time to myself."

"Okay." Sami gave her a hug. "I love you, Mom."

"I love you too, Samantha." She pulled away and smiled. "Now, go have some fun."

"Okay." Sami went to the door and paused. "Mom?"

"Hmm?"

"Have you ever been camping before?"

"No. You know I'm not the outdoorsy type. Why do you ask?"

Sami shrugged. "Just wondering. I'll see you later."

"Bye, sweetheart."

Sami shut the door and hurried back to Billy's. When she arrived, Billy, Jason, and Mike were in the backyard—just outside the kitchen door—lighting the mound of briquettes stacked in the middle of the barbecue grill. They all took a step back as the flames whooshed high into the air. They seemed to delight in the glory of it, grinning and nodding their heads, similar to the way cavemen would've reacted, she was sure.

She shook her head and smiled. "Can I do anything to help?"

All three of them turned and grinned.

"No, just enjoy yourself," Mike said. "Is Carol coming?"

"No. She's not feeling up to it. She just wants to be by herself for a while."

"Maybe next time." He went back into the house.

A picnic table sat in the middle of the yard. Sami moseyed to it and took a seat. Unlike their front yard, there were no trees in the backyard—just grass extending to the forest. Across the way, she had a clear view of the back of her house—her bedroom window, the sliding door to her mom's room, and the walkway leading down to the basement.

Billy and Jason left the grill and headed toward her. Billy sat next to her, and Jason across from them.

Sami couldn't contain her smugness. She looked at Jason and raised an eyebrow. "Guess what?"

He smiled. "What?"

"My mom…has never been camping before!" she taunted.

Jason's grin faded. "What is it with you people? Never skipped rocks before, never been hiking before, never been camping before," he grumbled in a childish voice. "Is that some California thing or something? Hell, I'm surprised you even know how to play video games." He shook his head.

Billy laughed. "Dude, quit your bitching and grab your bucket and sponge!"

Mike came out with a plate of raw steaks in one hand and a pan of foil-wrapped potatoes and corn on the cob in the other. "What'd I miss?"

Billy smirked. "They made a bet about whether Sami was the only person in town who'd never been camping. Jason's already lost. Carol's never been camping. Now Jason's throwing a fit."

"You should've known, Jason," Mike teased. "Like mother like daughter."

"Yeah, yeah, whatever. It's a good thing I like washing cars," Jason said.

Billy raised his eyebrows. "Good. You can wash mine while you're at it."

"Only if she helps." Jason gave a quick nod toward Sami. "But you have to wear that shirt."

Billy reached over the table and punched him in the arm.

Jason winced, holding his shoulder. "All right, man. All right. Geez!"

"Are you sure you don't need help, Mike?" Sami asked, feeling guilty about Mike having done all the shopping and now all the cooking.

"Nope, I got it." Mike slapped the steaks on the grill.

"Careful, Sami," Billy said. "Mike is very possessive over his grill. He might bite you."

"Kind of the way you are over your girl?" Jason said.

"Kind of the way you are over your car?" Billy retorted.

They all laughed.

"Hey, so is everyone up for a camping trip?" Jason asked.

"I'm in," Mike said as he situated the potatoes and corn on the grill. He joined them at the picnic table, sitting next to Jason.

"Me too," Sami said. "But only if Billy goes."

Billy wrapped an arm around her. "I can't very well disappoint you now, can I?"

Jason slammed his hands down on the table. "Good, then it's settled. Let's say, what? This weekend?"

"That's not good for us," Mike said. "We have some work over the next couple of weeks. But we're free after that."

Billy's eyes lit up. "Yeah, that'll be cool! There's a full moon then."

"Good," Sami replied. "There was no moon last night, and I couldn't see a thing outside when—" She stopped, realizing her mistake.

The excitement of the moment dissipated.

Jason furrowed his brow. "What do you mean? Were you outside last night? Alone?"

"Uhhhh." Sami bit her lip and shrugged. "Only for a minute."

"Why?" Mike asked.

"I thought you weren't going outside by yourself at night anymore?" Billy spoke before she could answer.

"Well," she added quickly before another word was said, "my mom said they called off the search because whatever or whoever I saw hasn't been seen. There are no traces of him. Or *it*. They think it migrated somewhere else."

"You still need to be careful," said Mike.

"Yeah, you can't be out at night by yourself," Jason scolded.

Sami grew irritated. "Guys, stop. I can't be accompanied everywhere I go like a child. I just stepped out on the porch to see if Billy was still up—" she looked at him "—and you weren't, so I went back inside."

She decided not to divulge the other details. Particularly hearing something roaming in the forest. Besides, whatever had been out there had been a smaller animal, she was sure of it.

Billy rubbed the small of her back. "I know you can't have someone with you every second. I'm sorry. But *please* don't go outside by yourself at night around here. And call me if you need anything. I'll come right over."

"All of what he said." Mike nodded toward Billy.

Billy glared at him. "You mean that you're *sorry*, and that she can call you if I'm not around?"

Mike grinned and winked at Sami.

"Ditto from me on all of what he said." Jason motioned toward Mike and flashed Sami a charming smile. His smile faded. "Now, back to our camping trip."

Sami snickered. "Thank you, guys. And I'm so excited about going camping!" She beamed as eagerness consumed her. She had been waiting for this moment—for all of them to hang out together as friends and to not feel caught between a burning hatred that should never have ignited in the first place.

Billy reached under the table and wrapped his hand around hers.

"Oh, wait a minute," Sami said, realizing she didn't know the first thing about camping. "What do I need to bring?"

"Don't worry about it, Sami. We've got it covered," Mike said. He stood and headed back to the grill.

"I have an extra sleeping bag you can borrow. Or you can share mine with me." Jason smirked and glanced at Billy.

Billy grinned.

Jason suddenly tensed and reached under the table. "Ow! Dude, I think you broke my shin." He chuckled under his breath.

Billy squeezed Sami's hand. "Just bring yourself and some extra clothes."

They continued to talk about the camping trip, and the three men reminisced about camping at the lake when they were kids. It wasn't long before the hearty aroma of seasoned steaks filled the air.

Sami took in a deep breath. "Mmm. Those smell delicious, Mike!"

"Yes, they do!" Mike agreed. He jumped up to check on them. "And they'll taste even better. Let's eat."

"Cool. I'll go get some plates and toppings for the potatoes." Billy hopped up and headed for the back door.

"I'll help." Sami followed him and returned with drinks for everyone while Billy carried the condiments. She and Billy had decided to stick with sodas while Mike and Jason enjoyed their beers. They all loaded their plates and savored every morsel as they continued to talk, laugh, and tease each other throughout the night. For the first time in over two years for Sami, and thirteen years for Billy, Mike, and Jason, life seemed full of purpose and hope again.

WEARING A white top, a pair of shorts, and sneakers, Sami trudged down the stairs, yawning.

"Good morning." Her mother smiled.

"Morning," Sami mumbled and yawned again. She took a seat at the breakfast bar.

"You came in late last night." Carol set a plate of pancakes in front of her.

"Thanks, Mom. Yeah, we had fun." A slight smile crossed her lips as she recalled last night. It was exactly what they had all needed—a little bit of fun.

"Good. I've decided to go back to work tonight."

"What? So soon?" She had been sure that her mother would take at least the week off. Something wasn't right.

"Yes. I've been expecting your grandfather's passing for a long time. I'm okay. I can't just sit around here dwelling on everything for days on end. I've had my time. Now, I have to move on with life."

"So, you'll be home late?"

"They need me to come in at three."

Sami frowned. Even with the danger long gone, she didn't look forward to being alone at night.

"You'll be okay. That thing is long gone," her mother reassured. "Besides, I'm sure Billy will keep you company."

Sami gave way to a smile and nodded, finally relaxing. She slathered her pancakes in syrup, cut off a hunk with her fork, and shoved it into her mouth.

"It won't be for much longer. They have a day shift opening up in a couple of months." Carol grew quiet and let out a long sigh. "There's something else I need to talk to you about. It's about me and your dad."

Sami's eyes twinkled. She expected great news until she focused on her mother's serious expression. She swallowed the mush in her mouth with a big gulp.

Her mother sat on the other barstool. "We're getting a divorce. I'm sorry."

Sami's chest grew heavy. She felt betrayed and abandoned by her dad. And, if she felt this awful, she knew her mom felt worse.

"Are you okay, Mom?"

Carol nodded. "I knew this was coming. Of course, I was hoping he'd change his mind when he was here, but I knew it was a long shot." She frowned and shrugged. "He just fell out of love with me somewhere along the way."

"I'm sorry, Mom." She gave her mother a hug. Tears threatened to fall, but Sami kept them in.

"I'll be okay, sweetheart. Right now, I'm just worried about you."

"I'm fine." Sami pulled away and pressed her lips together to keep her chin from trembling. She wanted to release her sadness, but she knew her mother had enough to worry about. And ever since her parents' fighting had crushed their happy home, she'd learned to deal with her troubles on her own—with the help of the ocean, of course.

On the verge of breaking down, Sami stood and headed for the front door. "I just remembered, I was supposed to meet Billy. I'll be back later."

She opened the door and hurried outside before her mother could see her tears. Without a second thought, she headed for the trail. With the wolf long gone and the ocean too far away, she needed the serenity of the lake. She ran, at first, to relieve the pain and frustration. As the anger and tears subsided, she slowed to a leisurely walk. For the first time since she'd moved here, Sami felt more at ease in the forest, finally able to appreciate its rugged beauty.

It only took thirty minutes to reach the lake. The air was warm and sticky today, with puffy clouds dotting the deep blue sky. She tromped through the meadow and sat on one of the boulders overlooking the lake, enjoying the beauty surrounding her.

As Sami stared at the shimmering ripples dancing across the water, her mind drifted to all the terrible events that had brought her to Wolf Hill, along with those that had followed. She thought about her grandpa's illness and death and how much she missed him. About her parents fighting, the separation, and now the divorce. Though she didn't want to admit it to her mother, deep down, she'd expected the divorce too. She just hadn't expected it to hurt so much or to be so soon after her grandpa's passing.

She also thought about her nightmares of being attacked by a humongous wolf, and about her red-eyed stalker—which everyone kept passing off as a mutant wolf, even though she wasn't so sure. What she did know was she couldn't hide out in her home for the rest of her life. Everyone else, including the sheriff's department, was positive whatever she had seen was long gone. Which meant she could finally feel comfortable in her own home—including the forest surrounding it.

A smile crossed her lips as she thought of Billy, and the way her heart fluttered every time she saw him, held his hand, or kissed him. A sudden ache awakened deep inside as she recalled their intimate moment on Billy's couch yesterday. She bit her lip to stifle her bashful smile.

Am I ready to take the next step with him? To give myself to him completely?

Bushes rustling at the far side of the meadow jolted Sami from her thoughts. She jumped up, holding her breath and praying it was just the wind.

The brush shook again, followed by a dreadful familiar *snap*.

"Oh no!" Panic shot through her. Whatever was out there could probably outrun her, but she had to try to get to safety. With fear coursing through her veins, she sprinted across the clearing toward the path.

"Sami, stop!" Billy's voice boomed from the other side of the meadow.

She came to an abrupt halt and saw Billy step clear of the bushes. Elated he wasn't a hungry wolf, she darted across the meadow and jumped into his arms, wrapping her legs around his waist.

Billy hugged her tight. "Sami, what in the hell are you doing up here? *Alone*?"

"I just came up here to think. To get away for a while." She hugged him tighter, happy to be alive.

"I thought you weren't gonna come out here by yourself anymore?" He pulled away just far enough to look her in the eyes.

"There haven't been any wolf sightings anywhere. And it's the middle of the day. I thought it'd be okay."

She unwrapped her legs from his waist, and he set her on the ground.

"What are *you* doing here?" she asked.

Mike appeared from where Billy had emerged.

"We were checking the area for wolf tracks," Billy said. "We wanna make sure it's safe before we camp up here." He cupped his hand to her cheek. "You can't come out here alone. If anything ever happened to you…" He shook his head, unable to finish.

She raised one corner of her mouth, awed by his display of emotion. But she couldn't ignore the worry in his eyes and decided to put his mind at rest.

"Well, I'm okay." She noticed a twig clinging to the hem of his gray T-shirt and brushed it away. "Lucky for me, it wasn't a hungry wolf chasing after me. It was just you and Mike."

Sami glanced over Billy's shoulder. Mike was making his way toward them, carrying a rifle and a shotgun.

She looked at Billy again. "So, did you find any tracks?"

"No, it's all clear," Billy said.

"Good. That just confirms whatever was lurking out there is really gone now," Sami said.

"Yeah, but it could always come back. You can't let your guard down. Not in the wilderness."

"If it could come back, isn't it a little too soon to be checking for tracks? Camping is still two weeks off. And why are we even camping if it could come back?" she asked.

"Don't worry, we'll check again before our trip. A few more times," Billy reassured. "And the mutant wolf probably is long gone, but we'll have our guns just in case. We wouldn't come out here without being armed, Sami, and you shouldn't either. After what happened, Jason even carries a gun around the houses again."

She sighed, feeling defeated. "Okay."

His warning glare softened. "So, why were you up here alone anyway? What's the matter?"

Sami's heart grew heavy again. She walked a couple of paces away to stare at the lake and to hide the moisture blurring her vision. "My mom and dad are getting a divorce."

"Oh, that really sucks. I'm sorry." Standing behind her, Billy wrapped his arms around her waist and rested his chin on her shoulder. "You sure have had a rough time lately. I wish I could make everything better for you."

His compassion put some of her pain at ease. She turned and gazed into his eyes. "Just you being here with me makes me feel better, Billy."

"Good." He leaned down and kissed her.

"Hu-um." Mike cleared his throat.

Billy pulled away and sighed. "I forgot you were here."

"Yeah, Sami seems to have that effect on you," Mike said and let out a big yawn. "You forgot this too." He handed Billy a rifle.

Billy smirked. "Dude, you look like hell."

"Fuck you," Mike said in a flat tone. He rubbed his eyes, which were dark with exhaustion.

Billy glanced at Sami. "So, are you ready to head back?"

"It's not like she has a choice," Mike said bluntly.

Sami nodded. "Yes, I am." She eyed their rifles. "Hey, maybe *I* should get a gun? Then I *can* come out here by myself."

Mike looked at her as if she were crazy. "Let's go. I need a nap." He tromped off toward the trail.

Billy smirked and motioned toward his brother with a nod of the head. "Hangover."

Sami giggled.

"Anyway—" Billy wrapped his hand around hers and followed his brother's lead "—do you really think a gun is a good idea after what happened with your pocketknife?"

"Ha, ha!" she retorted playfully. "But maybe you're right. I don't need a gun. I have you."

"That's true." Billy raised one corner of his mouth.

When they arrived back at Sami's house, Jason had just finished rinsing her car.

They stopped a safe distance away, trying to keep from laughing.

Jason pointed the hose sprayer at them. "Don't even think about saying anything. Just let me finish with a little dignity."

"Thank you, Jason. My car looks beautiful." Sami smiled.

"No problem, Sami. Anything for you." He winked and went to the water spigot, pulling the hose with him.

A squad car turned onto their road. As it drove toward them, Sami recognized Sheriff Briggs. The driver's window lowered and he leaned out. "Hey, Mike, Billy. I'm not sure if Jessica is home yet, so I thought I'd drop my key off so you two can fix those switches for me. Jessica said the damn things shocked her again last night."

Mike took the key from him. "All right. We'll head over there now."

"Good. If Jessica isn't home yet, she should be there soon. She's got the check. Thanks again, boys. Jason, Samantha—" he tipped his hat "—I'll be seeing you around." He turned the car around and drove away.

Sami was seething on the inside, but she kept quiet. She didn't want Billy to have to fix anything for Jessica. Just the thought of the woman made her blood hot, let alone Billy being with her all day. She shook the thought from her head, not realizing Billy had been studying her face until she looked at him.

"Are you gonna be okay?" Billy asked.

She nodded and forced a smile.

"Don't you worry about your girlfriend." Jason slapped Billy on the back. "She won't even know you're gone."

Billy ignored Jason and gave Sami a kiss. "I'll see you soon."

His kiss extinguished her jealousy. And, even though she loathed Jessica, she trusted Billy. "Okay."

"Huhhh, let's get this show on the road." Mike rubbed his temples.

Billy grinned at his brother. "I don't know why you drank so much last night."

"Don't even go there," Mike warned as he walked off.

"Hey, Billy? I'll miss you too," Jason teased.

"Yeah, yeah," Billy replied in a dull tone. He looked into Sami's eyes. "You sure you're okay? I'm sure Mike can handle it by himself."

She nodded. "I'm sure. You should help your brother. He doesn't look so hot today."

"Okay." He took a few steps backward. "I'll be back before you know it." Then, he turned and followed Mike.

"So, Sami—" Jason rubbed his hands together, drawing her attention from Billy "—you up for lunch at the diner?"

"Sure, sounds good. But I think I should drive so I don't get carsick. I didn't finish my breakfast this morning."

He raised his eyebrows. "You get sick if you don't eat?"

"Just lately, since I've moved here." She shrugged.

"Huh. Maybe from all the stress? Let's get going then, before you get sick." He hurried around to the passenger door of her car and hopped in.

Sami climbed into the driver's seat, started the engine, and headed down the road. She stopped in front of Billy's driveway just as he finished loading tools into the trunk of his car.

"Where are you guys headed?" Billy asked, peering through Jason's window.

"To the diner," Jason answered. "You snooze you lose, dude."

Billy walked around the front of her car to Sami's window, leaned his head in, and planted his mouth on hers.

"Gross! Come on! I'm gonna lose my appetite," Jason grumbled.

Billy pulled away and winked. "Shouldn't be too long. Maybe we'll see you at the diner."

She gave him a coy smile. "Okay."

After one last peck on the lips, Billy took a step back, watching as she drove away.

BILLY PARKED the car and stared out the windshield, eyeing the old two-story farmhouse which stood by itself at the end of a private road. The siding looked as if it had been painted white at some point of its life, but most of the paint had peeled off and the house now held a haunted aura.

"I hate coming here," Billy complained as he stared at the creepy house. He expected to see a ghost appear in a window at any moment. "Do you think the place is haunted?"

"I have no idea, but it gives me the frickin' creeps too," Mike said, staring with him. "Well, let's get this show over with, little brother."

They fished their tools from the trunk, headed across the patchy grass yard, and up the squeaky steps to the front porch.

"Maybe we should drive a couple of nails in those while we're here, so we don't have to come back anytime soon," Billy said, pointing to the steps.

"I like the way you think." Mike unlocked and opened the front door. He pulled his head back and grimaced. "Smells like ass in here." He pushed the door open all the way to allow fresh air in.

Billy peered over his brother's shoulder. The drawn curtains and wood paneling on the walls made the space too dark to see clearly in, even with the door open.

Mike reached his hand in and flipped the light switch. "Shit!" He jerked his hand back.

Billy let out a mischievous chuckle. "Hey, you found the switch."

"Yeah. Ha, ha, fucker!" Mike glared at him.

Billy went to the living room window and tugged back the curtain. A cloud of dust exploded into the air, whooshing into his face. He sputtered to keep the particles from entering his mouth. "Ugh!" He rushed to the front door for some fresh air while frantically dusting his hair and face.

Mike returned the mischievous laughter. "Karma's a bitch!"

"Asshole!" Billy said, yanking his shirt over his head. He went straight to the hose alongside the porch steps and turned it on, letting the water pour over his hair and face as he leaned forward. He shook the excess water from his hair and shut the water off. Then, he stormed to his car, threw his T-shirt on the floorboard, and grabbed a blue T-shirt he'd left in the back seat. On his way back across the yard, he pulled the shirt over his head and shoved his arms through the sleeves.

"Better?" Mike asked, grinning.

"Fuck you," Billy spat as he trudged up the steps.

Standing just inside the doorway, they glanced around the stale, dusty room. An old, brown plaid couch and a matching chair sat against the walls. The coffee table was littered with empty beer cans and crumpled bags from the diner. Dust and crumbs covered the old wooden flooring.

Mike scrunched his face in disgust. "Now I see why the sheriff isn't married." He shook his head and turned his attention to the switch.

"Yeah, it's frickin' gross in here." Billy stepped inside. "I don't think there's a single person in town crazy enough to wanna live here. Except for the sheriff and Jessica apparently."

"What about me?" Jessica demanded as she walked through the front door.

They both jumped. Mike's tool box slipped from his fingers and crashed on the floor.

"Jessica, you scared the crap out of us!" Billy snapped. He bent down and threw the lost tools back into the box.

"We didn't know you were home," Mike said.

Billy stood and dusted his hands together.

Jessica smiled. "I'm sorry. I just got back from a little walk." She strolled up to Billy and put her hands on his chest. "Is there anything I can do to make up for it, *Billy*?"

Billy grabbed her wrists and lowered her arms. "Not interested," he said dryly.

Jessica shrugged and sauntered up the stairs. "Suit yourself."

As soon as she disappeared, Billy whispered, "Let's just hurry and get the hell outta here."

Mike nodded and unscrewed the switch plate.

"Do you want me to turn off the breaker?" Billy asked, unable to pull his eyes from the mess surrounding him.

"Nah, it's a minor problem. But I need some wire nuts out of the car."

"Good," Billy replied in disgust. "I need some fresh air."

He went out to the car, opened the trunk, and began sifting through a bucket of odds and ends. When he found what he was looking for, he slammed the trunk shut and turned around, startled to see Jessica standing there, staring at him.

"Dammit, Jessica! Don't sneak up on me like that! You nearly gave me a heart attack."

"Did I?" she asked with innocent eyes. "I'm sorry, Billy. I wouldn't want to do that. What would poor Sami do?"

"Leave Sami out of this," he warned.

"Of course. I'd rather this just be between me and you anyway." A cunning smile crossed her face. She circled around him and grabbed his ass.

Billy stiffened. Angered, he clenched his jaw and spun around to face her.

"That's all right, Billy. I'd rather caress the front anyway." Jessica swiftly reached down and grabbed his genitals.

"What in the hell's the matter with you!" Billy roared and pushed her away. He felt guilty for allowing anyone but Sami to get close enough to touch him there. "You are such a bitch!" he snapped. He'd never hit a woman before, but he wanted to punch Jessica in the face.

Jessica laughed. "Oh, I think Sami's going to be mad at you," she taunted with a wicked grin. "Just imagine what she'll do when she finds out you let me touch you like that."

"Jessica!" Mike's voice blasted from the doorway. "Don't you have anything better to do?"

She glared at Billy. "Well, I guess I could go pay a visit to *Sami!*"

Billy narrowed his eyes. "You stay away from her!"

"My, my, my, don't tell me you're in *love* with her?" she scoffed.

"That's none of your fucking business! Just stay away from her! You've already done enough damage!" Without another word, he stormed away and into the house to assist his brother. The sooner they finished the better. Within a few minutes they were done.

"Okay, that'll do it." Mike finished tightening the last screw into the switch plate. "Let's get the fuck outta here!"

Billy gathered the tools and the toolbox, and they wasted no time heading out the door.

"Thank you, Mike." Jessica stood at the bottom of the porch. She handed him a check and smiled impishly at them. "And thank you too, Billy. You were great."

As they passed by her, Mike snatched the payment from her fingertips. Without a word, they jumped in the car and sped off down the road, leaving Jessica standing in a cloud of dust.

SAMI AND Jason had just finished their bacon burgers when Mike and Billy entered the diner.

Sami beamed when Billy approached. "You're done already? That was fast." She scooted over in the booth to make room for him.

Mike plopped next to Jason.

"Yeah, we finished as fast as we could." Billy's voice held a hint of uncertainty. He glanced at Mike, his eyes filled with a subtle warning.

Sami sensed something was wrong, and suspected Jessica had something to do with it. "Was Jessica there?" she asked, trying to sound casual.

Billy grabbed a menu. "Yep."

"Oh," she replied and waited for more details, but not one word was said.

The waitress arrived at the table to take Billy's and Mike's orders. She looked at Jason and Sami. "I'm sure you two don't want to eat *again*. Can I get you some dessert?"

"Sure, that sounds good." Sami smiled. "I'll take a chocolate shake."

"I'll have what she's having," Jason said.

While they were waiting for their order to arrive, Jason brought up the camping trip. They discussed what items each of them would bring and when they'd be leaving. Sami was disappointed with where the conversation had gone. She wanted to find out what had happened at Sheriff Briggs's house.

"Camping?" a familiar voice cut in.

They all focused on Jessica as she stood over them.

"Not you again," Mike said dryly.

"Well, count me in." Jessica smiled and twirled a long lock of her black hair around her finger.

"You're not invited, Jessica." Mike's tone was harsh.

She looked at Sami. "I'm sure *she* wouldn't mind if I came along, would you, *Sami*?"

Sami glared at her, remembering the pain and humiliation Jessica had caused in this very booth. "You're not invited, Jessica."

"Well," Jessica said with a smirk, "maybe Billy wouldn't mind. He didn't seem to mind today when I caressed his firm ass and fondled his package."

Shocked, Sami turned to Billy, waiting for him to tell Jessica to stop with her lies.

Billy grimaced and rubbed a hand across his forehead.

Sami knew from the guilty look in Billy's eyes that Jessica wasn't lying. "So, it's true?" She held her breath, waiting for Billy to answer.

Jessica looked down and pointed between Billy's legs. "Let's just say *wow*. He is hung like a horse. You are a very lucky girl, Samantha."

Billy shot Jessica an evil glare and turned back to Sami, his face full of regret. "Sami, yes, but it wasn't like that, okay."

His confirmation pierced Sami's heart like a knife. Her entire body shook as humiliation and heartbreak sank in.

"Get out of here now!" Mike ordered, glaring at Jessica.

"What the hell?" Jason looked at Billy, narrowing his eyes. "You mean it's really true?"

"No. Look, I can explain. It wasn't like that," Billy said with desperation in his voice.

"*Ta, taa!*" Jessica laughed as she sauntered away.

"Excuse me, Billy." Sami blinked to hold the tears in. "I need to get out."

Billy didn't budge. "No, Sami, please. It wasn't like that. You should've seen her, she just… She…" He shook his head and looked at Mike.

"Billy's right, Sami." Mike said. "It wasn't his fault. She just reached out and…" His voice trailed off, and he shook his head with an exasperated look.

Or a disgusted look. Sami couldn't quite figure out which it was. At this point, she didn't really care. The tears had finally found their way down her face and everyone was staring at her. All she wanted was to go home.

"I don't wanna hear anymore." She shook her head and ran her hands across her cheeks as visions of Jessica touching Billy haunted her thoughts. "I just wanna get out of this booth. I just wanna leave."

Billy finally stood and let her pass. "Wait. I'll drive you."

"No, just leave me alone." She hurried out of the diner and into the parking lot.

Billy followed her outside. "Sami, please listen to me," he pleaded, blocking her from opening her car door. With gentle hands he grabbed her shoulders. "*Please!* Just listen!"

Sami let out a heavy sigh and crossed her arms, waiting for him to finish. But it didn't matter what he had to say. He'd let Jessica touch him intimately, and he'd probably enjoyed it. What man wouldn't enjoy being fondled and caressed by a woman? Sami swiped at the tears staining her cheeks.

"I didn't want her to do *anything*! She just grabbed me without warning. I pushed her away from me. I got *mad* at her! I even called her a *bitch*! You *have* to believe me. I would *never* do *anything* to hurt you, Sami. *Never*. I *love* you."

Sami gasped as three simple words suddenly washed away the anger and pain and filled her heart with awe.

Billy leaned down and gave her a long, tender kiss. Then, he pulled away—just far enough to gaze into her eyes, waiting for her reply.

"I do believe you, Billy," she whispered. "I just got mad because I thought you should've done something to prevent her from…" She shook the disturbing thought from her head. "But I trust what you've told me. And I trust *you*. I was just hurt because…" She took a deep breath to steady her nerves as a sudden realization sank in. "…because…I love you too," she admitted softly.

Billy grinned. He wrapped his arms around her and lifted from the ground. "I was hoping you felt the same way."

Sami giggled and gave him a big kiss.

"Now that that's settled—" Mike's gruff voice interrupted their reunion.

Billy set Sami down, and they turned their attention to the two men leaning against Billy's car.

"Isn't that sweet?" Jason glanced at Mike, grinning.

"Nauseatingly sweet," Mike added with a sour look on his face.

Billy shook his head and smiled. "Jackasses."

Mike grinned and grabbed the takeout bag and Styrofoam cup from the hood of the car. He handed Billy the bag and Sami the chocolate shake.

Embarrassed, Sami bit her lower lip as she took the shake. "Thank you, Mike."

Billy opened the passenger door of Sami's car and shut it once she was in. He hurried around to the driver's side and tossed his keys to his brother.

"Be easy on my car, asshole!" Billy said. He hopped behind the wheel of Sami's car and started it.

Mike and Jason jumped into Billy's car.

"My little brother is a glutton for punishment!" Mike said to Jason, loud enough for his brother to hear over the revving of the engine. He leaned forward and winked at Billy.

"Let's see what this baby's got!" Jason shouted, rubbing his hands together.

Billy let out a heavy sigh before he drove out of the parking lot and down the road. "I hate it when he drives my car." He glanced at the rear-view mirror.

"Sorry." Sami frowned. She peered out the back window.

Mike and Jason were quickly closing in on them.

"Dammit, Mike!" Billy muttered under his breath.

Jason blew them a kiss as he and Mike sped past them, leaving them far behind within a matter of seconds.

Billy shook his head as he watched his car disappear around a corner in the distance.

When they arrived back home, Billy's car was nowhere in sight.

"Mike's probably showing Jason what my car is made of," he said with an irritated voice.

"I'm sure he'll bring your car back in one piece, right?"

He let out an irritated sounding sigh and shrugged.

"It looks like my mom already left for work. Do you wanna go inside?"

"Sure."

They climbed out of the car and went into the house. Billy kicked the front door shut with a smooth swipe of his boot and locked it. Then, he took Sami into his arms and kissed her as if they hadn't seen each other for days.

Sami closed her eyes, enjoying the dizzying effect he created through her entire body. His mouth left hers to leave a trail of soft kisses down her neck, sending goose bumps down her arms while his hand slid down her back to caress her buttocks. His mouth found its way back to hers again, and she moaned under his lips from the sensuality ignited by his loving touch.

Billy scooped her into his arms, carried her up the stairs, and to her room, where he laid her on the bed and nestled himself next to her.

His mouth met hers again, causing her mind to reel with drunken pleasure and leaving her body aching to be touched.

Billy lifted his head and gazed into her eyes. "Sami," he said, his voice husky. "I wanna show you how much how much I love you. I don't wanna stop this time."

Sami relished his declaration of love, but she was scared. They were about to cross that intimate threshold together, a step she had never taken before. But she was so filled with sensual pleasure and love for the man in her arms that she wanted more.

"Then…," she whispered with a shaky voice as her heart pounded with both anticipation and fear, "…maybe we shouldn't stop."

He let out a deep breath and brushed his nose against hers.

"But—" she added quickly before he kissed her again "—it's my first time." Afraid of his reaction, she averted her eyes to the cleft in his chin. When he didn't speak right away, she met his gaze again.

The passion in his eyes softened, and he gulped. "Then maybe we shouldn't—"

She placed her finger to his lips before he had a chance to end their passion. "I want to, Billy," she whispered. "Please…make love to me." She bit her lower lip, waiting for his response.

Billy lowered his head back to hers and gave her a long, tender kiss. He pulled away and slid his wallet from his back pocket. With one hand, he flipped it open and pulled out a condom. He set both items on the nightstand and enveloped her lips with his again. Reaching between them, he unbuttoned her shirt and eased it from her shoulders. Gently, he worked his hand under her back and unhooked her bra. It slipped from her shoulders, and he set it aside.

"You're so beautiful," he whispered and captured her lips with his, gliding his fingertips over her bare flesh.

Sami sucked in a ragged breath, shaken by his sensual touch. Suddenly desiring to feel his bare skin on hers, she pulled his T-shirt over his head and tossed it to the floor. Her eyes and hands roamed over his chiseled torso and broad shoulders before she slid her fingers to the back of his neck.

Billy let out a shaky breath and crushed his mouth to hers. He slid his hand across her abdomen and up her back, making her shudder.

Unable to wait any longer, they discarded the rest of their clothing and completely gave into their escalating desires, combining their bodies, hearts, and souls as one.

16

THE NEXT two weeks seemed to drag by. Carol was hardly ever home. She was either busy with work or running errands. And, when she was home, she slept.

Billy worked long hours with Mike, leaving Sami mulling around the house for most of the day. She was so bored, she decided to find a job just as soon as they returned from their camping trip—despite her parents wanting her to take the summer off.

Though completely exhausted after work, Billy, and sometimes Mike, would come over to keep her company through dinner. Jason, on the other hand, was over every afternoon to wash her car before joining them for dinner as well. Though she wanted nothing more than to be able to spend her days with Billy, she was grateful for Jason's company.

On the eighth day, she tried to let Jason off the hook, insisting her car was shiny enough. But Jason wouldn't have it. A bet was a bet to him, and he was determined to honor it. After the two weeks were up, and he had finished washing her car for the last time, Sami insisted on buying him lunch at the diner.

"Thank, God!" Jason said as he flopped next to Sami on her couch.

"I never thought I'd say this, but I actually *hate* washing cars now!"

Sami giggled. "Maybe next time we make a bet, I'll lose and have to wash *your* car for two weeks." She straightened the hem of her lavender summer dress, eyeing the details of the tiny, blue flower print.

"I hope so. It's the only way my car's gonna get washed for a very long time."

She glanced at his khaki shorts and white T-shirt, both wet in spots. "Do you wanna go home and change first?"

He shook his head. "Naw, it's hot enough outside. I'll dry soon."

"Are you ready to go?" she asked.

There was a knock on the door. Sami jumped up and went to the door, hoping to see Billy. When she opened it, a middle-aged stranger stood before her. He had black hair streaked with gray and stern eyes almost as dark as his hair. Although he was physically fit and handsome, he had an unsettling presence. She glanced at the blue full-size truck parked in front of the house.

"Hello. You must be Samantha." His voice was deep but kind.

"Yes," Sami replied in a soft tone, feeling intimidated.

Jason came to the door. As soon as he set eyes on the visitor, he grabbed Sami's arm and pulled her aside.

Before she could speak, Jason stepped in front of the stranger and narrowed his eyes. "Steve. Haven't seen you around lately. I was hoping you'd left for good."

"I heard you were back for the summer, Jason. Your parents decided not to join you this time around, huh?" Steve smiled.

"It's just me!" Jason snapped.

Sami tensed at Jason's outburst. She suddenly feared the stranger standing in her doorway.

"That's a shame." Steve diverted his attention back to Sami. "If you haven't already guessed, I'm Steve Garrison." He extended his hand past Jason.

Using caution, she shook his hand. "It's nice to meet you."

Jason clenched his jaw and stepped directly in front of her, breaking their grip. "Why are you here, Steve?"

"Carol invited me. I'm taking her to dinner," he replied casually.

Sami's jaw dropped, and anger replaced her fear. *How could she do this? She's barely separated from Dad, and she's already going out on dates?* She stormed straight to her mother's room and pounded on the door. Not bothering to wait, she opened it and stepped inside, closing the door behind her.

Her mother stood in front of the mirror hanging above the dresser, checking her make-up.

"When were you gonna tell me about Steve?" Sami tried to cover the hurt in her voice with anger.

"Oh. I'm sorry. He's a little early. I meant to talk to you before he got here. I know this is hard for you, but I have to move on in life too. Steve is a very nice man."

"Well, I don't like him." Sami crossed her arms. In twenty years, she had never seen her mom with any man other than her dad, and the thought twisted her insides.

"It's okay. You have a right to be upset. The divorce is affecting you too. And don't worry, he won't ever replace your father." Her expression softened. "But I deserve to be happy too, Samantha."

Still angered and hurt, Sami simply nodded.

Carol opened the door. "I can't keep him waiting." Without another word, she went into the living room.

Sami reluctantly followed.

"Hello, Carol." Steve nudged past Jason. He took her hand and kissed the top of it. "You look beautiful."

Sami rolled her eyes, disgusted by Steve's cheesy display.

Jason shook his head and cocked his jaw to one side.

"Thank you, Steve." Carol blushed, smoothing out her black cocktail dress.

Sami eyed her mother's mounded bosom and gritted her teeth. Seeing her mom with another man made her entire life before Wolf Hill seem as if it had all been a waste of time. She couldn't wait to get out of there.

"We have to get going." Sami hurried to the door, wriggled her feet into her white flip-flops, and made a beeline for her car.

Jason followed her.

"I'll see you two later," Carol shouted from the doorway.

Sami had the car running and in reverse before Jason had even opened the passenger door.

"Hey, wait up. Don't leave me behind." The car was slowly rolling back when Jason jumped in and shut the door.

Sami was so angry, she couldn't speak. She just sped away.

"Are you all right?" Jason asked with a worried look on his face and fastened his seatbelt. "I can drive if you want me to."

Sami took a deep breath and slowed down. "Sorry. I just can't believe my mom is with that *creep!*"

"Yeah, he's a creep all right. Among other things," he said with underlying cynicism.

"What do you mean?"

"Ah, it's nothing." He shook his head, staring out the window.

Sami pulled over on the side of the road, kicking a cloud of dust into the air all around them. She narrowed her eyes. "We're not leaving until you tell me, Jason! My mom is *with* that guy!"

Jason stared at her blankly for a moment before a pleased smile crossed his face. "You know, the more time I spend with you, the more I see the stubborn Sami your grandpa always talked about."

"Jason!" she snapped, her patience running thin.

He raised his eyebrows and sighed. "You don't wanna know."

"I do! Please, tell me," she pleaded, her voice softer now.

After a few seconds of silence, Jason sucked in a deep breath and exhaled, as if preparing himself. "My mom and dad didn't decide to stay on the East Coast because of what happened with Billy's parents years ago. That's the reason they *moved* to the East Coast, but they always came back during the summer for vacation, hoping things had settled down enough to be able to move back. But you know how the damn townspeople are around here." He shook his head. "Anyway, last year things changed.

"My dad and I were out hunting, and my mom was home alone. Steve had stopped by to see my dad, and since my mom knew we'd be back any minute, she invited him in. She didn't realize until after he was in the house that he was drunk. When we got home, Steve was hugging her and trying to kiss her."

Jason's jaw tightened. "She was struggling to push him away when my dad came in and pulled him off her. They got into a fight, but Steve overpowered my dad. So, I came up behind him and hit him in the head with a vase, but I got a solid punch to the jaw. I fell back and hit my head and lights out. When I came to, the sheriff had Steve in cuffs, and he hauled him off. My mom and dad got a restraining order against him, but this is such a small town, they couldn't completely avoid him. And the rest is history."

"Jason, that's terrible! We have to go home and tell my mom before—"

"She already knows," Jason cut in. "My mom told her last year when she was here for your grandma's funeral."

"If she knows, how can she be with a man like that?"

"Believe it or not, Steve is actually *liked* by everyone in town. They just passed it off as him having *one too many* that day. Then, he pleased everyone by quitting drinking because of it." He shook his head with a disgusted look on his face. "He hurts an entire family and ends up being a frickin' saint!"

Sami was disappointed with her mother. "How can she be so lonely she'd settle for such a scumbag? Isn't there any other single man in this town she can date?"

"I don't know, but there isn't anything we can do about it. So, can we go eat now?" He grinned.

She was irritated at how quickly he could push problems behind him and look forward to something else. She stared at him blankly before she gave in to his charming smile, realizing he was right—there wasn't anything they could do about it.

"Okay, let's go." She put the gearshift into drive and headed for the diner.

They spent an hour eating lunch and enjoying chocolate shakes before they headed back home.

When they returned, Billy was there to greet her. As soon as she parked the car, she got out and threw her arms around him.

Billy caught her and lifted her off the ground. "I missed you too."

"You're home early. Does that mean you're finished with the job?" she asked with eagerness.

He grinned. "Yes! That means we're finished with the job." He set her back on her feet and eyed the length of her body, his eyes filling with desire. "You look beautiful in that dress." He leaned down and stole a kiss. Then, he glanced at her mom's car in the driveway. "Your mom doesn't work tonight?"

"No, she's on a date." She frowned.

"Oh, bummer. I'm sorry."

She shrugged. "I'll be okay."

"I know what would make you feel better." He leaned down and gave her another kiss, melting her worries away.

"Dude, where's my kiss?" Jason interrupted, holding his arms out to Billy.

Billy glared at him. "How's about I give you that ass kicking I owe you instead?"

Mike stepped out onto the front porch of his house. "Game's on!" he shouted.

Jason smirked. "Sorry, dude, maybe I'll let you kick my ass later." He hurried across the yard and into the house.

Sami couldn't bear to sit through a baseball game right now. It had been two weeks since their first lovemaking, and with Billy having been so busy and exhausted, it had been their last. She missed being intimate with him. "So…there's another game on tonight, huh?"

Billy rubbed his palms together. "Yes, there is!"

"Oh, okay then." She was beginning to wonder if she had been so terrible at making love that he didn't want her in that way anymore. Head down and shoulders slumped, she headed for his front door.

Billy ran up behind her and scooped her into his arms. "There's a game on tonight, but I don't care because I want to spend time with *you!*" He carried her across the yard, up the porch steps, through the front door of her house, and kicked it shut behind them.

She beamed, feeling silly for doubting his love for her. She decided to make light of the matter. "I was beginning to think you didn't want me anymore."

He raised one corner of his mouth. "Are you crazy, woman? Loving you again was all I could think about these past two weeks. And then seeing you in this dress…" His eyes filled with desire and kissed her hungrily.

She tightened her grip around his neck and savored every moment of his lips caressing hers. But kissing him wasn't enough. She ached for more.

With his lips on hers, he ascended the stairs, not stopping until they reached the comfort of her bed. He pulled away long enough to lay her down and cover her body with his, before he crushed his lips to hers again. As their mouths and hands roamed each other's bodies, they discarded their clothing along the way....

SAMI OPENED her eyes and looked around her dimly lit bedroom, the only light coming from the setting sun as is spread its orange hues across the walls. She reached over and stroked the silky hairs of Billy's bare chest. His eyes were closed, and his supple lips taunted her with their sensual power. Not being able to resist them, she pressed her lips to his.

He pulled her on top of him and planted a kiss on the tip of her nose. "I love you too."

"I thought you were sleeping." She traced a finger over his mouth.

"I don't wanna waste my time sleeping. I was just resting for later."

"For later?" She eyed him curiously.

Billy grinned, and in one swift move, rolled on top of her.

Sami giggled. "Does your *later* mean right now?"

"Uh huh," he answered huskily and lowered his lips to hers....

"OH NO!" Sami jumped out of bed and ran across the dark room to the light switch.

Billy sat up, trying to adjust his eyes to the sudden bright light. "What's the matter?"

"Billy, we fell asleep! It's nine o'clock! My mom might be home any minute if she's not home already," she said, frantically gathering clothes from the floor and fumbling to get dressed.

His eyes filled with hunger. "Do you know how beautiful you look running around *naked*?"

She gathered his clothes and threw them at him. "There's no time, Billy!"

"Okay," he said in a dismal tone, yet he was smiling. Starting with his jeans, he put his clothes back on.

Sami straightened out her hair and slowly opened the door. Everything was quiet. They tiptoed down the stairs, straining to see through the darkness. Not even the porch light was on.

"I don't think she's here," Billy said, turning on the lights.

"Good!" Sami placed a hand over her pounding heart. "I can only imagine the lecture I would've had to suffer through for the rest of the night."

"Yeah, that would've been tough," he agreed. "So, do you want to order a pizza? I'm starving." He grinned and patted his stomach. "You've depleted my energy."

Sami's mouth watered at the thought. "Mmm, that sounds good. But do they deliver this late?"

"Yeah, 'til ten."

"Okay, but can we have it delivered to your house? I don't wanna be here when my mom gets back from her date."

"Let's go eat then." He wrapped his hand around hers, led her out the front door, through the darkness of their yards, and into his house.

Jason grinned at them from the kitchen, while holding two beers. "It's about time you two showed up!" He headed back to the couch, handing a beer to Mike as he passed by.

Mike shot them a quick grin from his seat on the recliner before he turned his attention back to the TV.

Afraid they knew she and Billy had been making love all night, Sami kept her head down as she made her way around the back of the couch and to the front of it. She decided to sit at the far end, away from the two men and closest to the front door. Keeping her focus on the TV, she pretended to be interested in the baseball game.

Billy went to the phone on the kitchen counter and ordered the pizzas. After he hung up, he sat on the couch between Jason and Sami.

Jason glanced at Billy. "So, what have you two been up to?"

Billy crossed his arms and leaned back casually. "Nothing. Just hanging out."

Sami watched the movement on the screen, trying to look nonchalant and hoping they wouldn't guess. Out of the corner of her eye, she noticed Jason and Mike give Billy an inquisitive look. After a few seconds, they both grinned wryly at him.

She cringed on the inside, trying to suppress the humiliation creeping into her cheeks.

Billy narrowed his eyes at them and shook his head with the slightest of movements.

Jason diverted his attention back to the game. "Pizza, huh? Sounds good."

Mike clasped his hands behind his head and sprawled back in the recliner. "There better not be any olives on the pizza, little brother, or I'll kick your ass!"

Billy put his arm around Sami.

His love automatically eased her tension. She snuggled closer to him and focused on the game. But her attention span didn't last long. At some point, her mind drifted back to their lovemaking.

"Sami? Did you hear me?" Jason asked, wearing a slight smirk.

Sami tensed, jolting back to reality. "What?"

"You were just spacing out over there," Jason said.

Mike grinned. He looked at Billy and pressed his lips together, stifling his amusement.

Sami was completely humiliated. *Do they know what I was thinking about? Did I say something out loud? God, I hope not!*

"Sorry. I'm just tired and hungry," she said.

"I'll bet you are," Jason replied.

Billy glared at him.

A knock on the door saved her from further embarrassment.

She jumped up and rushed to the door, desperate to get away from their knowing glances. Behind her, there was a rustling on the couch, but she paid no attention. She heard Jason laugh, but it was muffled as if he were trying to keep quiet.

"Ow, dude. What the hell?" Jason said, still laughing.

Sami imagined Billy punching Jason in the arm and smiled. She opened the door and handed the delivery man the money Billy had set on the entryway table.

Billy jumped up to help. He took the boxes and set them on the dining table.

The atmosphere changed to a less embarrassing one as they all sat around the table and enjoyed their meal. They made more plans for the camping trip, which was quickly approaching. Jason and Mike opted to scour the area for new tracks while Billy and Sami were going to head into town for food and supplies. If all went well, they were going to leave on Friday—the day after tomorrow.

Jason left after they ate, and shortly after, Billy walked Sami home. They stopped short when they saw Steve's truck parked in front of the house.

"What?" Sami said. She couldn't stand the thought of Steve being in her house with her mom, and she couldn't stand the thought of being in the house while he was in it. "Why is he here? I don't wanna go home, Billy. It's already after midnight. What if he isn't leaving tonight?" The thought of Steve in her mom's bed made her nauseous. "I can't stay here with…with that *man* in my house with my *mom*. I—"

"Shhh…" Billy cupped her cheeks with his hands. "It's okay, Sami. You can stay with me tonight."

She took a deep breath to calm her nerves and nodded.

"Come on." He grabbed her hand, and they headed back to his house.

Thankfully, Mike had already gone to bed. Billy led her to his bedroom and locked the door.

Sami eased onto the bed with her head down, thinking about what Jason had said about Steve.

Billy pulled a T-shirt from his drawer and handed it to her. "Hey," he said, keeping his voice low. "It'll be okay." After a short silence he said, "So, I take it your mom was on a date with Steve Garrison tonight?"

"Yeah," Sami whispered, unable to control the bitterness. She set the T-shirt aside. "And Jason already told me *all* about him."

"I'm sorry, Sami, but your mom's known Steve for a long time, you know. I'm sure she knows what she's doing."

"But how can she be with someone who attacked Jason's mom like that?"

"Did Jason also tell you that his mom and Steve have a history together, before Jason's dad came into the picture? And that his mom actually broke up with Steve to be with his dad?"

"No, he didn't tell me that part." She shook her head, wondering why Jason had left out the details.

"Maybe Jason doesn't know about that part. I heard it from Mike after the incident between Jason's mom and Steve had spread around town last year." He sat down and put an arm around her. "Don't get me wrong, though, Steve had no right to do what he did. But I don't think we know the whole story."

"Even so, I just get this weird creepy vibe from him. And now, he's in my house."

"Besides that one time, he's been pretty harmless. And your mom seems like a pretty reasonable person. I'm sure if he's weird or creepy in any way, she'll toss him to the wolves." He raised one corner of his mouth.

Sami smiled at the thought. "You're right. My mom can take care of herself. I should stop worrying."

"Yes," Billy agreed as he lifted her chin so that his lips could reach hers. He gave her a generous mouthful before he pulled away. "There," he whispered, "that should make you feel better."

"Not yet." She pulled his head back to hers.

Billy chuckled huskily under her lips and lowered her back on the bed. Then, he reached over and turned out the light.

17

SAMI WOKE the next morning, alone in Billy's bed and completely naked. Feeling vulnerable, she scanned the room for her clothes. A wide dresser sat against the opposite wall with Billy's clothes strewn on top. She eyed the desk next to the bedroom door, spotting her dress draped over the chair in front of it.

After she dressed, she went to the bathroom to freshen up before she went to look for Billy. When she found the house empty, she went outside. Billy was in the front yard with Mike and Jason.

They all turned their heads and smiled. "Good morning," they greeted her in unison.

Not expecting the attention, Sami's cheeks flushed with warmth. If there ever was a doubt in Mike and Jason's heads about her and Billy's sexual relationship, there certainly wasn't now.

Not able to make eye contact with anyone but Billy, she managed a pathetic-sounding "Morning."

Billy gave her a light peck on the lips. "We can go into town whenever you're ready. Mike and numbnuts were just about to head into the forest."

"Okay, I'm just gonna go home and shower first," she replied. She couldn't wait to be alone with Billy for the afternoon, away from all the knowing smirks.

"I'll be waiting." Billy smiled.

Jason winked at her. "Do you need help, Sami? I can wash your back for you."

Mike reached out and punched Jason in the arm.

"Ow, man." Jason winced through a weak laugh. "Not that arm again."

"Aw, poor numbnuts," Sami teased, patting Jason's arm as she passed by him.

"Not you too," Jason called out to her. "You're supposed to have my back, Sami."

Sami turned, blew Jason a sympathetic kiss, and continued on her way. To her relief, Steve's truck was gone. But her mother's car wasn't. She took a deep breath, mentally bracing herself for a lecture, and opened the front door.

Carol sat at the kitchen table drinking her coffee. "You're home late," she said casually.

Sami closed the door and stepped into the kitchen. "Yeah, I was at Billy's. I would've come home last night, but I saw that Steve was here…after midnight. So…"

She didn't want her mother to know she and Billy were intimate now. She didn't know why exactly. After all, she was twenty years old. But, over the years, she'd learned to avoid any topic with her mother that might result in a long, educational chiding.

"Yes, Steve stayed the night," her mom said in a quiet tone.

Sami shook her head to escape the mental image. "I'm gonna take a shower."

"Samantha…"

Sami let out an impatient sigh and waited for her mother to continue.

"I really like Steve, and I wish you would respect that." Her tone was sincere.

There was nothing left for Sami to say. She was nowhere near ready to accept another man in the place where her father had always been. But her mom wasn't giving her a vote in the matter.

"I'm running late. Can I take my shower now?"

"What plans do you two have for today?" Carol asked, obviously trying to keep their conversation amicable to avoid conflict.

"We're going shopping for our camping trip tomorrow."

"Oh, that sounds nice. Have fun."

"Thanks." Sami jogged up the stairs before she was questioned further and tried to concentrate solely on getting ready, pushing anything Steve-related from her thoughts.

After her shower, she went to her bedroom to dress. She stared into her closet, wondering what to wear. Since it was going to be hot out that day, she chose a white tank top and a pale blue skirt which rested mid-thigh.

When she looked in the mirror to admire her outfit, she noticed the locket still hanging around her neck. The sight of it both saddened and angered her. It was a long-lost memory of what would never be again. She seriously doubted her parents were happy during the time the picture had been taken. She was sure it had all been a ruse for her sake.

With a heavy sigh, she took it off and placed it back into her jewelry box where it would remain for good. She grabbed her purse and tiptoed downstairs, hoping to avoid her mom and a possible lecture. Seeing no sign of her mother anywhere, Sami hurried out the front door.

Billy was sitting on his front porch, holding a small paper bag, when Sami ran up to him.

His eyes lit up. "You look nice today!"

"Thank you." She grabbed his hand and pulled him toward his car. "Are you ready to go?"

"What's the hurry?" he asked, his brows scrunched together in confusion.

"I just wanna get out of here before my mom tries to question me about anything else." Sami hopped into his car and shut the door.

Billy shook his head and smiled. He climbed in and set a paper bag on the seat next to her. His eyes widened, and he looked past Sami toward her house.

She was sure it could only mean one thing. "No! Is my mom

coming over here?" She couldn't bear to look.

His lips curled into a sheepish grin. "No, I'm just kidding."

"That's not funny!" She pushed his shoulder.

"Actually, it was. You should've seen the look on your face." He laughed.

Wearing a slight smirk, she sat with her arms crossed, staring at him and failing to see the same humor in it he did.

"Okay, I'm sorry. I guess it wasn't that funny." He leaned over and kissed her, wrapping one arm around her shoulders and placing the other hand on her thigh. Slowly, he slid his hand higher up and under her skirt.

She giggled and pushed his hand away. "Billy, there's no time. We have to go."

"I know, I know." He sounded disappointed. "It's just that skirt you're wearing is driving me crazy."

"I can run upstairs and change into a pair of jeans if that'll make things easier on you."

"Not a chance." He settled back into his seat, started the car, and pulled out of the driveway.

"So, what's in the bag?" she asked.

"Breakfast for you. I figured you didn't take the time to eat, and that you got sidetracked somehow."

"Aw, Billy, thank you." She opened the bag and pulled out a large blueberry muffin and a bottle of water. She set the water in the cup holder of the center console. "How'd you know these were my favorite?" She took a bite out of the muffin, savoring its sweetness.

He grinned and winked.

She decided to share it with him and held it to his lips.

He took a huge bite. "Thank you," he mumbled through a mouthful.

She dusted the crumbs from his lips and his blue plaid shirt before brushing them from the crotch of his shorts.

A devious smile crossed his face. "Am I gonna have to find some deserted road to pull over on so I can have my way with you?"

She smirked and took another bite of the muffin.

Billy slowed through town but kept driving until the town was behind them. He sped up again and continued down the road to the highway.

Sami was confused. "Wow, this skirt must be really driving you crazy because you totally passed up Wolf Hill."

"We're going to the next town up the road. I need to get some more ammo and everything's cheaper there."

Giddiness filled her chest. "You mean we're going to a *real* town with stoplights, fast-food, and strange people who don't know *anything* about our lives?"

He chuckled. "Yep. So, since all you've known is the diner since you've moved here, I'll let you choose where to eat."

"I want the first fast-food restaurant you see, but we *have* to go through the drive-through."

"You're easy to please." He grinned. "Okay, we'll go through the drive-through, but we have to eat by the river. There's a cool place my dad used to take Mike and me fishing that I've been wanting to see again."

"Okay," she said with a hint of sorrow in her voice.

It saddened her that Billy had to live half his childhood, and now, the rest of his life without his parents. She wished things had been different for him. That he was actually going to the river to fish with his dad today, instead of merely reliving a distant memory. She glanced over at him and held his hand. But he didn't look sad at all. He was smiling and singing to the rock song on the radio. She smiled as her heart went out to him.

WITH A stressed look on his face, Mike scoured the shoreline of the lake for a third time, assuring nothing had been missed.

Jason let out an impatient breath. "Dude, I think it's all clear."

"Seems to be, but I just don't know if this is such a good idea." Mike eyed the dark pines towering above the back side of the lake. Even though the sheriff had given the all clear on Sami's stalker, wolf, or whatever the hell it was, he just couldn't shake the uneasy feeling in his gut. The forest just didn't seem right lately—not since he and Billy had returned from their California trip.

"It's fine. We'll be heavily armed. No mutant wolf has a chance against us!" Jason stuck his chest out and beat his fists against it as if he were king of the jungle. "Besides, we can't hide out in our houses and live in fear for the rest of our lives." He gestured toward the trees with a swoop of a hand. "This is our home. Let's take it back."

"Yeah, I guess you're right," Mike reluctantly agreed.

Jason grinned. "Hey, why don't we come up here tonight instead? We don't have anything better to do."

Mike pondered the idea. Wondering what time it was, he pulled his phone from his pocket and crinkled his forehead. "There's no service here?"

Jason looked at him as if he were stupid. "You just now figured that out?"

"I've never had to use my phone out here, dumbass."

Jason smirked. "I get service in the meadow sometimes. If I'm lucky. But we don't need our phones. We have guns, remember?"

Mike let out a long sigh, finally giving in. "Tonight sounds good. I already have what I need set out."

Jason grinned. "Cool! Let's see if Billy and Sami are back yet."

"After," Mike replied flatly. With a nod of the head, he motioned toward the dark pines on the other side of the lake, towering over the rocky hill housing the waterfall. "We're checking over there first. Up around the creek."

A frown replaced Jason's smile. "Aww, come on! It's all rocky and steep over there."

"You're right," Mike said with a smirk, making it sound as if he were changing his mind. "Which is why you're going first." He gave Jason a shove in the right direction.

"Okay, okay. Geez!" Jason grumbled before he trudged around the lake.

On the other side, they made their way up the cliff-side, their task made difficult by the slippery footholds created by old, brittle pine needles.

"Is this really necessary?" Jason complained. Nearing the top, he glanced down at Mike.

Mike stopped climbing and repositioned his hand on the crevice he'd just let go of. He peered up at Jason. "Don't stop! If I fall into the lake because of you, I'm kicking your ass!"

Jason continued his ascent. All of a sudden, a piece of rock broke free, and he lost his foothold.

Mike jerked his fingers from the rock before Jason's boot could smash them and quickly planted his palm under Jason's boot, creating a temporary foothold for him by using all the upper body strength he could muster.

"Holy shit!" Jason looked down at Mike, wide-eyed. He quickly repositioned his boot into the crevice. "Thanks, man. We probably should've just went around."

"This way's quicker." Mike noticed blood trickling from a wound on Jason's shin. "Adrenaline pumping, is it?"

"Yeah, how'd you guess?"

"From the gash on your leg that you're not complaining about yet."

Jason hoisted himself to the top and sat on a nearby boulder to inspect his wound.

Using the same foothold, Mike swiftly maneuvered himself over the last rock and pulled himself to his feet.

"Ouch. Kind of hurts now." Jason flashed an uneasy grin.

Mike eyed Jason's khaki shorts. "That's why Billy and I wear jeans out here."

"Blah, blah, blah. You sound like my mom." Jason shook his head.

Mike knelt in front of Jason to inspect his wound. There was a good-sized gouge, but nothing needing stitches. "It's superficial. You'll live."

He glanced down at Jason's old shoes, ready to rip into him about the worn tread when he noticed a partial print in the hardened dirt. He brushed away the dead pine needles, exposing a print similar to the one they'd seen in the forest near Jason's driveway.

"Damn." Mike traced the large paw print with his forefinger.

"Shit." Jason knelt to get a better view. He brushed away debris next to the print, exposing another. "These don't look fresh."

"They're old. What's left of these were smoothed over from the last rain we had."

Jason stood and began to kick away debris with his boot, looking for more tracks. They wandered the area and found some here and there, in the same condition as the first set. None were fresh.

"Are we done here?" Jason asked, sitting back down on the boulder.

Mike gazed out over the lake and meadow to make sure they hadn't overlooked any grounds. Satisfied they'd covered all areas in the vicinity, he let out an exhausted sigh. "We're done."

"Good. Hold these for a second." Jason handed him his wallet and cell phone.

"What the fuck are you doing?" Mike took the items and noticed Jason's bare feet.

Jason picked up his boots and tossed them to the bank below. Without warning, he jumped off the cliff.

Mike peered over the edge just in time to see Jason plunge into the water.

He resurfaced seconds later. "Woohoooo! That was great!" he hollered.

"Idiot." Mike shook his head. He shoved Jason's belongings into his front pockets and made his way back down the cliff-side.

Jason was grinning, sitting in the grass along the bank and tying his boots.

Mike fished Jason's things from his pockets and tossed them to him. "It's a good thing you jumped. You probably would've fallen with the way your tread looks." He kicked the bottom of Jason's boot.

"Yeah, yeah." Jason still held his smile as he stood and dusted the seat of his pants.

As they made their way around the lake, Mike recalled Billy telling him about what Sami had heard in the forest the day of the storm. That she'd heard something growling, but she hadn't seen the animal behind the anger.

"So, are we all clear then?" Jason broke the silence when they reached the meadow.

Mike sighed. "I don't know."

"Dude, those prints are as old as you are. We're in the clear."

"Just let me check around some more." Mike made his way to the mouth of the trail, just inside the forest, and looked for more tracks within a forty-foot radius. He found nothing.

Jason grew impatient. "There's nothing here, Mike."

Mike stepped back onto the trail. "Billy said Sami heard growling as soon as she entered the forest the day of the storm and that it seemed to follow her. But I can't find anything. If a wolf or some other wild animal had been here, we would've found something, right?"

Jason shrugged. "I don't know, man. It rained pretty frickin' hard that day and all night."

Deep in thought, Mike nodded slowly. *How could she have heard growling without there being tracks close by? Unless...* He looked up into the thickly needled branches of the trees looming over them.

Jason let out a disbelieving breath. "You've got to be kidding me, right? You think the mutant wolf can climb trees?"

Mike threw Jason a warning glare.

Jason's smile faded.

"No, I don't think wolves can climb trees. But a deranged stalker could. And so could a mountain lion or a bear. As a matter of fact, something broke a tree branch across from my house a few weeks ago."

"Branches break all the time," Jason said.

"The branch was green. It was like something heavy was standing on it and broke it. I looked around but didn't see anything or anyone. It could've still been hiding up in the tree somewhere."

"Hmm..." Jason cocked his head to one side and stared at nothing in particular. "I was down by the mailboxes a few weeks ago and heard a branch break in the forest, like something heavy was out there. But there was nothing there." Jason shrugged and threw his hands out to his sides. "And there's nothing here now and hasn't been since the storm. I think whatever it was has moved on."

Mike sighed. "I think you just might be right, *again*."

Jason grinned. "I like it when you say that."

"Don't let it go to your head."

"Too late." Jason lifted his eyebrows while holding his smug grin.

Mike couldn't help smiling at Jason's amusing behavior. "All right, let's go home," he said and headed along the trail.

SAMI AND Billy pulled into the driveway shortly after two. They stepped out of the car and went to the trunk to unload the supplies. Mike and Jason were in the middle of the yard, loading an ice chest onto Jason's quad.

Billy paused at the rear of the car, staring at Mike and Jason. "It's a little early for that, don't you think?"

Sami noticed a bandage on Jason's shin. "What happened?"

"He was complaining instead of watching where he was going," Mike said.

Jason glared at Mike.

"Anyway," Mike continued, "we decided to go up tonight. We scouted the area, and it's all clear. There were just some old tracks that were washed away by the storm."

"You sure they were old?" Billy asked.

Mike raised his brows. "Are you questioning my skills, little brother?"

Billy smiled out of one corner of his mouth. "Tonight sounds cool with me."

Jason looked at Sami. "Please say yes. I already took half the stuff up to the lake and dropped it off."

A surge of excitement brought a smile to her face. "It's fine with me. I just have to run home to get some things together."

"Cool!" Jason grinned and wiped the sweat from his brow with the back of his arm.

"I'll be back in a minute." Sami headed for home. She rushed into the house, tossed her purse on the breakfast bar, and ran upstairs to her room. Deciding to be prepared just in case, she changed into her swimsuit, though she was dead set against swimming after her last encounter with the lake.

She threw on a pair of cutoffs, pulled her white tank top back on, and shimmied her feet into her cross-trainers. She gathered some extra clothes and shoved them into her backpack, along with a few toiletries. On her way down the hall, she snatched a towel from the hall closet and worked it into the backpack. Then, she slung the bag over her shoulder and headed downstairs.

She was just about ready to grab her purse from the breakfast bar when she spotted a plastic container of brownies with a note taped to them, sitting on the other side of her purse.

Samantha,

I heard you were leaving a day early.

I thought I'd make your favorite dessert for you.

Have fun and be careful. I love you.

Mom

Sami's eyes swelled with tears. She had been selfish lately, especially when it came to Steve. Her mother had lost her home, her parents, her husband, and lately, her daughter. With a heavy heart, she grabbed the container of brownies and put it in her backpack. Then, she grabbed the notepad and began writing.

Mom,

I'm sorry for how I've been acting lately.

I'll talk to you in a couple of days.

And thank you for the brownies.

love, Sami

As soon as she returned home, she'd make things right again. She grabbed the backpack, turned the porch light on for her mom, and locked the door before she pulled it closed. She turned the knob, double-checking to make sure it was locked.

Billy met her at the bottom of the porch steps. He grew concerned when he looked into her eyes. "Is everything okay?"

She nodded. "Yeah, I just feel bad for the way I've been treating my mom lately. But I left her a note."

"I'm glad you made peace with her before you left for the weekend."

"Me too." She let out a dismal sigh, wishing she could apologize in person.

"Come on." He took the backpack from her, and they went over to his yard. "Let's see if we can tie this to the quad so we don't have to carry it all the way."

"Here—" Billy handed the backpack to Jason "—make room for this."

Jason slid his arms through the straps, letting the bag rest on his back.

Mike exited his house and locked the front door. "Everything's set."

Jason's quad rumbled to life. "Sami, you can sit on my lap if you don't wanna walk."

Billy took a step towards him with his hand balled in a fist, but Jason sped away before he could reach him.

Sami giggled grabbed Billy's hand. "Come on. Let's go," she said, pulling him toward the trail and following Mike's lead.

When they reached the lake, Jason was sitting in one of the camping chairs surrounding the fire.

He glanced up and raised his beer. "It's about time you ladies showed up."

"Toss me one of those." Mike wiped the sweat from his forehead and plopped on one of the chairs.

Jason tossed Mike a beer.

Billy picked up the tent bag sitting next to the ice chest.

"Do you need help setting it up?" Sami asked.

Billy shook his head. "That's okay. You can sit down and rest. It'll only take a minute." He walked to a flat spot in the grass about seventy feet down the shoreline and began assembling the tent.

She reached into the ice chest, grabbed a bottle of water, and sat next to Jason.

Mike set his beer on the ice chest. He took his shirt off and emptied the pockets of his swim trunks, dropping the items next to his beer.

Sami tried not to stare, but Mike was just as ripped as Billy and Jason—maybe a little more so. *What is it with all the guys around here? Must be something in the water.* She shook her head and focused on Billy. The tent was already erect.

"Why in the hell did you already build a fire, Jason? It's frickin' hot out!"

"Because you can't call it camping without a campfire," Jason replied. "But I'm with you." He discarded his shirt and personal belongings, leaving them on his chair. Then, he and Mike raced each other to the water and dove in.

Billy headed back over to the campfire. "Do you wanna go in?"

Sami wiped the perspiration from her forehead. "I wasn't going to, but *yes!* It is *hot* out today." She stood to undress, but paused, making sure Mike and Jason weren't looking.

Billy grinned. "They swam over to the waterfall. I don't think they're paying any attention to us." He slid his shirt over his head and kicked off his shoes.

She held her breath for a moment and admired his bare chest. The sweat built up in the contours of his muscles and glistened in the sun, defining each cut.

"Do you see something to your liking?" He leaned down and stole a kiss.

"I think it's even hotter out now." She smiled, enjoying his affection.

"It will be as soon as *you* take *your* clothes off." He grinned and pulled her tank top over her head. Next, he unbuttoned her shorts, letting them slip down her legs to her ankles.

She stepped out of her shorts.

With hunger in his eyes, Billy let his gaze roam the length of her nearly naked body. He pulled her close and kissed her again.

Sami welcomed the warmth of his bare chest on hers, as well as the dizziness created from his passionate kiss. "Billy…" she whispered under his lips.

He pulled away. "I'm sorry." He stared at the tent and frowned. "I wish it came with air conditioning."

"Me too." She stuck out her bottom lip.

He sighed. "Come on. Let's go cool off."

"All right."

They went to the shoreline, stopping when their feet hit the freezing water.

An icy jolt shot through her toes. "Oh, it's so cold! You know this isn't really a lake, right? It's a pool of melted snow."

Billy grinned. "You just have to jump in, like this." He dove into its icy depths and resurfaced approximately twenty feet out. "Come on," he coaxed.

"Okay." She took a few deep breaths, trying to mentally prepare for the impending torture. Finally, she ran forward through the shallows and dove into the deep water.

An instant burning engulfed her, followed by painful, rock-hard goose bumps. She broke through the surface, gasping for air. "It's still *freezing*!" she shouted.

Billy laughed and swam to her. He wrapped his arms around her waist. "Maybe this will help." He pulled her tight against his warm body and kissed her quivering lips.

Sudden waves of water pummeled their faces.

"Come on, guys," Jason said, splashing vigorously. "You're gonna to scare the fish away!"

"Yeah," Mike agreed, joining in on the fun. "And you're gonna pollute the lake."

Sami and Billy laughed and splashed them back, engaging in a fierce water battle.

Mike coughed and sputtered. "I've had enough," he said and attempted to swim back toward the waterfall, but Billy followed him with vengeful determination.

Despite the vigorous workout, Sami's teeth began to chatter uncontrollably, and her limbs were so cold she could barely feel them.

Jason chuckled under his breath. "Are you okay, Sami?"

"I-I'm f-fine," she chattered.

Billy gave up on chasing down his brother and swam back toward them.

"I think your girlfriend has had enough swimming for one day," Jason said to Billy. "You better get her back to shore before she drowns."

Billy wrapped his arms around her. "Come on. Let's get you warmed up."

"Naw, leave her in for a few more minutes," Mike suggested. "Then she can hold our beers and keep 'em icy cold."

Mike and Jason started laughing.

"Sh-shut up!" Sami snapped through quivering lips.

"Yeah," Billy said, "or I'll *shut* you up!" He guided her back to shore and helped her out of the water. He looked over his shoulder and slowly bent down to pick up a rock.

Out of the corner of her eye, Sami focused on Mike and Jason. They were watching as she climbed out of the lake.

Billy threw the rock and it *kerplunked* in front of them, splashing their faces.

They laughed, realizing they'd just been caught gawking.

"Dumbasses!" Billy grinned.

Still chuckling, they swam off.

Sami dug into her backpack for her towel and wrapped it around her shoulders. It was warm from being in the sun. She welcomed the heat on her cold wet skin.

"Come here." Billy sat on a chair and pulled her onto his lap. "I'll warm you up faster."

"How are you always so warm?" she asked.

"I'm just hot-blooded, I guess."

She snuggled against his chest and stared across the lake, watching as Mike and Jason wrestled and dunked each other under the water. She snickered.

"Yeah, they're idiots," Billy said.

"So—" she peered over at the only standing tent, wondering how the sleeping arrangements would work "—there's only one tent?"

Billy nodded. "Yeah, Mike and Jason will sleep by the fire in their sleeping bags, and I'll keep you warm in the tent."

She smiled. "I was wondering how that was gonna work out. Did you have it planned that way all along?"

He tried to hide his grin by pressing his lips together. He rubbed the tip of her nose with his as he spoke. "Well, I was hoping. But then, after our first night together, I knew I'd be sharing the tent with you…." His voice trailed off as he planted his hot lips on hers.

She pulled away just far enough to gaze into his eyes. "I can't wait for tonight."

"Oh, come on!" Jason stood over them and shook the water from his hair, raining its iciness on them.

Sami hid under the towel until he was finished.

"Yeah, you guys are gonna ruin my appetite," Mike agreed. "Let's get started on dinner. I'm starving!"

"Me too," Sami agreed.

Jason went to the ice chest to grab everything they would need for hamburgers. Then, they all sat around the fire and ate, teased each other, exchanged memorable stories of their adolescence, and told jokes and horror stories until darkness settled in all around them and the full moon shone brightly in the night sky. Soon after, Billy and Sami retired to the tent to share an anticipated night together in each other's arms.

18

FEELING SOMETHING brush up against her nose, Sami reached up and rubbed it. She felt it again, something tickling the tip of her nose as she tried to sleep. She opened her eyes.

Billy was lying next to her, propped on one elbow and holding a lavender flower in his hand. "Good morning, sleeping beauty."

"Is that for me?" She took the flower and smelled its sweetness.

"No, that's just what I used to wake you up with." He grinned and pulled a beautiful bouquet of wildflowers from behind his back. "*These* are for you."

"Billy, they're beautiful! I've never gotten flowers before."

"You haven't? Aw, poor baby. Never been hiking before..." he said sympathetically and kissed her on the forehead. "Never been camping before..." He kissed the tip of her nose. "Never gotten flowers before..." His lips captured hers.

"Breakfast is ready!" Mike belted from outside the tent.

Billy shook his head, "We're gonna have to do this *alone* next time."

"Yes, we are." She pulled his head back to hers and kissed him again before reluctantly climbing out from the sleeping bag.

Billy handed her the backpack.

She put her bikini back on and chose a pink tank top to wear, sliding it over her head. She snatched her cutoffs from the corner of the tent and pulled them on. Then, she wriggled her feet into her sneakers and ran a brush through her hair.

"I'm just gonna brush my teeth first," she said.

When they stepped out of the tent, the delicious aroma of bacon filled the air. Sami went behind the tent and scrubbed her teeth clean, while Billy waited for her. When she finished, they headed toward the campfire, where Mike and Jason were cooking breakfast.

"Mmm." She smiled at the two of them. "Breakfast smells good!" Her stomach churned, and a wave of nausea rose to the back of her throat. She threw her hands over her mouth and ran back past the tent and up the hill toward the privacy of the trees. As soon as she reached cover, she fell to her knees and vomited.

Billy approached from behind and gathered her hair to hold it out of the way. "Are you all right, Sami?"

She nodded shakily. "I think so. I guess I should've gotten up sooner to eat."

"Well, come eat now. You'll feel better." He helped her to her feet.

"Actually, you go ahead. I'm still feeling kind of sick. I'm just gonna sit here for a minute."

"No, I'll wait with you," he protested, his face full of worry.

She shook her head. "Please, Billy, I just need a minute. You go ahead." She wasn't sure her bout of nausea had passed yet.

He hesitated. "Okay, I'll fix a plate for you. Just call if you need me." He helped her to a nearby log before he headed back.

BILLY KICKED a small rock into the lake as he approached camp.

Mike and Jason were sitting around the fire, eating breakfast. Jason lifted his head and eyed Sami across the way.

"Is she okay?" Jason asked with a worried look.

"Yeah, she'll be okay. She just gets sick when she hasn't eaten anything," Billy replied.

Jason frowned. "Yeah, that's what she said. That really sucks."

"It does," Billy agreed. "But I think all the stress she's been through lately might have something to do with it too."

Jason brows furrowed. "Maybe she has an ulcer?"

Billy thought for a moment but couldn't recall any incidents of her complaining about stomach pain. And she still had a hearty appetite. "Nah, I don't think so."

Mike eyed Billy.

"What?" Billy asked.

Mike paused for a moment before he spoke. "You've been keeping it *covered*, right, little brother?"

Jason's eyes grew big, and his jaw dropped open.

The question caught Billy off guard. A nervous pang filled his chest, but he his brother's lack of faith in him sparked anger. "Yeah! Of *course!*" He scowled.

"But you do realize they're not a hundred percent effective?" Mike added.

Billy grew quiet. He lowered himself onto a chair and stared into the fire, trying to recall if any of the condoms had broken or if there was even a remote chance he'd forgotten to use one. *No, I didn't forget. I know I didn't. Did one break? Shit. I never thought to check. No! This is ridiculous! We were careful! She's not pregnant!*

Jason and Mike were quiet as they stared at Billy.

Billy jumped up, startling them. They steadied their plates of food on their laps to keep them from falling to the ground.

"Dude, she's fine!" Billy belted out. "This has already happened a couple times before we'd even had sex. She just throws up if she doesn't eat. *Okay?* Maybe she does have an ulcer. Or maybe it's just stress or something. Now, enough with the—" He glanced back at Sami, anxious to see her walking toward them. He leaned his head in closer to whisper. "Enough with the *pregnant* crap. And don't mention *any* of this to her."

"Getting sick from putting breakfast off for a couple of hours seems odd to me, but okay." Mike put his hands out in front of him, showing Billy he was finally backing off.

SAMI WALKED back into camp, wearing a sheepish smile. Over the fire, on a large grill, was a pot filled with scrambled eggs, a cast iron skillet full of diced potatoes, and another skillet filled with bacon. Her stomach grumbled with hunger at the sight and smell of the hearty breakfast.

"Sorry about that, guys. I just need something to eat."

"No, it's okay, Sami," Jason said in a caring tone. "We totally understand."

"Here, sit." Billy patted the chair next to him. "I'll fix you a plate. I'll give you some extra potatoes since they're not so greasy." He made her a plate of food and handed it to her, before making one for himself.

"Thank you," Sami said.

Billy winked at her and sat back down.

"Sorry for ruining breakfast, guys," she muttered. She looked at everyone, managing a weak smile.

"You did *not* ruin breakfast," Mike said. He tossed Billy a water bottle. "You just made it more interesting."

Billy caught the bottle and handed it to Sami.

"Well, I'll try to make it *less* interesting tomorrow." She opened the bottle and gulped down half of the water. Then, she dropped the bottle into the cup holder of the chair and popped a potato wedge into her mouth. Chewing slowly, she tested to see if her stomach could fathom food yet. The potatoes tasted delicious and settled just fine. She ate another piece and gazed into the fire, enjoying the hearty meal. She looked up, shocked to see everyone staring at her.

She furrowed her brow and smiled. "I'm okay, guys. Really."

All three men exhaled at the same time as if they had been holding their breaths.

She shook her head and took in another mouthful of potatoes. When she looked up, they were still staring. She stopped chewing, and her hand flew to her mouth.

Billy, Mike, and Jason all jumped to their feet.

Sami laughed, trying to swallow her food between gasps of air so she wouldn't choke. "I'm just kidding, guys!"

With grins on their faces, they all shook their heads and sat back down.

"Good one, Sami." Jason sounded irritated but kept a half-smile.

Mike smirked. "I think she's been hanging around us too much."

"Yeah, I think so." Billy nudged her shoulder with his. "I'm gonna have to keep her to myself more often."

"You were all just staring at me, watching me eat. You were easy targets. I couldn't help it," she teased.

"Now, I *know* you've been hanging around us too much," Mike said.

They all fell silent for a few minutes, each one in their own deep thoughts as they finished eating.

Sami looked up at the sun, now directly overhead. "What time is it?"

Billy checked his watch. "Almost noon."

"Almost noon? You mean I slept until after *eleven*? Wow, I never sleep in this late unless I'm sick. Huh, I hope I'm not coming down with the flu."

Mike shot Billy a wary look and raised his eyebrows.

Billy subtly shook his head at his brother.

Sami was beginning to dislike their secret way of communicating without saying a word to each other. Especially when she was the subject of their silent conversations. Rather than put them on the spot, she decided to ask Billy about it when they had a moment alone.

"Do you feel better now?" Billy asked.

"Yes, I do. Thank you for breakfast, Mike. It was delicious." She smiled.

"Anytime." Mike winked.

Jason frowned. "Hey, I helped."

"Aww, thank you too, Jason," Sami said.

Jason grinned.

"Welp—" she set her plate aside and jumped up "—I guess I'll go for a refreshing swim."

"No!" Mike interjected.

Sami tensed, startled by his sudden outburst. "Why can't I swim?"

Billy crinkled his brow. "Yeah, why can't she swim?"

"The water might be too cold, remember?" Mike urged his brother with a knowing stare. His eyes shifted to Sami's shirt and back to Billy.

There was definitely something fishy going on, and Sami wasn't going to wait for that private moment with Billy to find out what it was. She crossed her arms and narrowed her eyes.

"What's going on, Billy?" she asked.

He looked at Mike and Jason for help, but they stared back at him with blank expressions.

Billy sighed. "I'm sorry, Sami. It's nothing really. It's just…silly."

"What's *silly*?" she demanded.

He shook his head. "It's nothing. Mike just brought up the possibility of you being—" his eyes shifted to Mike and then back to her "—pregnant."

"What?" Sami laughed under her breath, confused as to why the guys would ask. Billy had always used protection, and they had always been careful.

"See, I told you it was silly." Billy motioned to Mike. "He's just jumping to conclusions because you were sick. But you've gotten sick before we even…" He gave a single nod in a knowing gesture.

Even though Billy spared her the humiliation of the words *had sex*, it didn't stop the heat spreading across her cheeks. "No. I'm *not* pregnant." She forced out a small laugh. "You were right, Billy. It *is* silly."

Billy flashed a sheepish smile. "Sorry. We didn't mean to upset you."

Mike stepped forward. "You said yourself that you never sleep this late. And do you always get sick as soon as you wake up in the morning?"

She shifted her feet. "Umm, no. I haven't actually gotten sick *right* after I've woken up. I'm usually… Well, I'm *always* just fine until breakfast. Unless I wait too long to eat, that is. But," she added with enthusiasm, "I did go to bed *late* last night, which is probably why I slept in so late."

Billy's forehead wrinkled. "We actually fell asleep around eleven."

Her enthusiasm dissipated. "What? Eleven? But it seemed so *late*!" The possibility of pregnancy was starting to worry her, but she wasn't about to admit it. Not yet. "Then, I must be getting the flu," she said with assurance.

"How do you feel now?" Jason asked.

Sami wanted to say she still felt sick, which meant the flu. But she didn't. She actually felt great. "Fine, I guess," she replied warily.

"When was your last...*you know*?" Mike asked.

Sami's eyes widened. She hadn't even divulged her menstrual cycle to Billy yet. She surely wasn't ready to announce it to the entire neighborhood of men. "Umm..." Lowering her head to hide her humiliation, she bit her lip while she counted the weeks on her fingertips.

I'm late by almost a whole week? That can't be right.

"No, wait a minute..." She counted again. Sure enough, she was late by almost a whole week. Her heart dropped. She'd never been late before. Not by one day. She lowered her head and sat back down. "I was supposed to start about a week ago."

Billy sat next to her. "But it's normal to be late, right?"

"Not for me," she replied dismally. "I'm always right on time."

His jaw dropped. He took both of her hands in his. "It's okay. We'll find out for sure. It'll be okay. Either way, I love you." He was trying to be brave, but the uncertainty in his eyes proved otherwise.

Another wave of nausea struck. Sami jerked her hands from Billy's grasp and ran up the hill to nearly the same spot as before. She fell to her knees, taking in deep breaths to hold back the sickness, but it didn't work. She vomited over and over, her stomach cramping and throat burning with each heave.

Billy rushed to her side and held her hair back. "Oh, Sami," he said, his voice laden with regret.

She sat back in shock, shaking her head. "What if I *am* pregnant?" she cried. "I *can't* be! What am I gonna do? I'm only *twenty*! What's my mom gonna say? And what about college? I know I'm not going this year, but I am eventually."

He rubbed her back with soothing strokes. "You probably just have a stomach bug," he said, his voice full of hope.

Billy's words didn't faze her train of thought. She suddenly thought of his future. *Is he ready to be a dad yet? Does he even want kids of his own?*

"I'm so sorry, Billy. We should never have—"

"No! It's not your fault. And I'm not sorry I made love to you, Sami." He knelt beside her. "I'll never be sorry. I have *never* felt this way about anyone in my whole life. I didn't even know feelings like this existed until I met you. You stir something deep inside of me. So much that sometimes…sometimes I ache inside just thinking about you. I *love* you. And whether we have a baby *now* or *later*, I will *always* love you."

Sami's heart filled with awe and she threw her arms around his neck. "I love you too, Billy," she cried. "I'm just scared."

He held her tightly against his chest. "I know. I'm scared too. But we'll get through this. We should find out for sure, first, if you are. Then, we'll go from there." He pulled away to face her. Using the bottom of his T-shirt, he wiped the tears from her cheeks. "Okay?"

She nodded. "Okay."

He helped her to her feet, and they headed back to camp.

Jason's forehead wrinkled with worry. "Doing okay, Sami?"

"Yeah," she replied, her voice shaky.

Mike handed her the bottle of water from her chair. "I think we should call it a day and head home."

Sami felt terrible—as if she'd ruined everyone's fun. "No, we don't have to go," she pleaded. "I'll be okay. I might not be, you know. I could just have a stomach bug or something."

"What?" Jason said. "Sami, we can't stay. It's okay. You didn't ruin anything. Besides, even if it is just a stomach bug, you shouldn't be out here in this heat."

"He's right, Sami," Mike agreed. "You don't wanna get dehydrated. We need to get you home, so you can rest and get out of the sun."

She looked at Billy with pleading eyes, but from his knowing expression, he clearly wasn't going to budge.

"We don't have to go just because I *might* be. Anyway…" Her head suddenly felt light as if it were drifting. She shook her head, trying to clear the fuzziness.

"You okay?" Billy asked, his face scrunched with worry.

"Are you gonna hurl again?" Jason asked anxiously.

Their voices echoed faintly, and the world around her started to move, distorting out of place. Off balance, she took a step back. "Umm, Billy," she said shakily and placed a hand on her head, trying to make the dizziness disappear.

She felt as if she were gently floating backward through the air. In slow motion, Billy reached out to her.

"Holy shit! Sami?" Billy wrapped his arms around her.

"Billy?" she whispered, staring at the bright blue sky above her, followed by three very worried faces.

"Sami? Can you hear me?" Mike asked.

"What happened?" she asked, trying to sit up. She eyed the red sleeping bag beneath her. "Why am I on the ground?"

"You fainted." Billy's voice shook.

"What? That's crazy. I've never fainted before." She suddenly recalled the sex lecture her mother had given her a few weeks back and her eyes widened. "Oh no! My mom said she fainted when she was pregnant with me."

Sami was convinced that this could only mean one thing. But she wasn't ready to accept it—not until she knew for sure.

Billy and Jason helped her up from the sleeping bag, each taking an arm.

"Just sit," Billy ordered as he eased her onto the chair. "Don't try to stand yet."

"Here." Mike handed her the bottle of water. "Drink."

With a shaky hand, she took the bottle and eagerly gulped down half of it.

"We should get going," Mike said. "We need to find out for sure. If you're not pregnant then you definitely need medical attention."

Sami knew it was pointless to protest this time. Besides, she was worried too. And exhausted. The urge to pee suddenly hit. "Can I use the bathroom first?"

"Of course," Billy said. "But I'm coming with you."

"Okay, just as long as you don't actually stand behind the bush with me. You have to give me some privacy. I promise I won't faint again."

"All right." Billy took her hand and led her to a group of trees, close to where she had just been.

"I'll be right back." She headed to the cluster of bushes just inside the privacy of the trees.

She unbuttoned her shorts and ducked behind the bushes. As she relieved her bladder, she eyed the surrounding trees, and a strange feeling of being watched overcame her.

Poking her head over the scraggly branches, she caught a glimpse of Billy chucking rocks into the lake. Just past him, in the distance, Mike and Jason were still at camp. Afraid something was out there, she quickly finished and slid her shorts up as she stood. A soft rustling behind a nearby tree caught her attention. Fear crept over her. She held her breath and waited.

A small gray rabbit hopped into view and scurried off.

She let out a relieving breath, feeling silly for being scared over such a helpless creature. Hoping to catch a glimpse of it again, she headed to the tree where she'd last seen the rabbit.

"You okay back there?" Billy shouted.

"Yeah, I'll be right there."

A loud *snap* echoed behind her.

She tensed and spun around.

A humongous wolf-like beast towered over her. The beast narrowed its sinister red eyes and sneered through its pointed snout, revealing sharp fangs drenched with blood and saliva.

A shrill scream tore from Sami's throat. She opened her mouth to scream again, but the beast smashed its hairy clawed hand over her mouth and grabbed her by the waist, squishing her against its solid bulk.

She whimpered and tried to wriggle free, pounding on its chest with her fists, but it was like hitting a brick wall. She bit down as hard as she could on the leathery pad of its palm.

The beast growled and jerked its hand free.

Billy lunged from behind a tree with a large stick and whacked the beast over the head.

Without wavering, the beast roared and knocked him to the ground.

"Billyyy!" Sami shrieked before it crushed its hand to her mouth again, squeezing her cheeks like a vice. Ignoring the sting radiating across her face, Sami punched and kicked the beast in a desperate attempt to break free.

A gunshot blasted through the air, and a ferocious growl echoed through the forest.

Sami stumbled backward and fell to the ground, hitting the side of her forehead on a tree stump. When she looked up, the beast was gone.

"Sami!" Billy rushed to her side, his eyes wide with shock. "Are you okay? Are you hurt anywhere?" he asked with a shaky voice, his eyes frantically roaming her body.

"No!" she yelled with tears streaming down her cheeks, unable to calm her trembling hands. "I'm *not* okay!"

Mike and Jason ran toward them, both armed.

"What in the hell happened?" Mike asked, his eyes wide with horror.

"Shit!" Jason knelt beside Sami and inspected her forehead.

"That thing— Beast— Werewolf! It tried to kill me!" she screamed through heavy sobs.

"Shhh." Billy pulled her into his arms. "It's okay. It's gone now."

"No! It's *not* okay! It *grabbed* me!" she cried. "It had big furry hands and claws! It looked like a monstrous *wolf*. Like a *werewolf*! It covered my mouth, so I couldn't scream! It was gonna *kill* me!" A wave of nausea hit. She swallowed to keep down the sickness.

Mike looked at Jason. "Did you hit it?"

"Yeah, I think so!"

Billy turned to Mike. "I heard a growl! She's right. It looked like a fucking werewolf! It was huge! I hit it upside the head with a stick, but it didn't even flinch. After Jason shot it, it took off like a fucking blur!"

"Which direction did it run off in?" Mike asked.

Billy stood and pointed into the forest. "Over there. But there's no way to catch that thing. It was as fast as a car!"

"I just wanna see if you wounded it!" Mike shouted as he hurried off to find its tracks.

Jason gave Sami hug. "Are you okay?"

The sickness struck full force and she pushed away from him. "No! I'm not!" She crawled a few feet away and vomited.

Billy came to her side and pulled her hair back.

With her gut cramped in knots, she heaved over and over until her stomach was empty. Then, she sat back shakily and wiped away the tears.

"Better?" Billy asked.

She sucked in a deep breath and nodded.

"There's blood!" Mike's voice bellowed from somewhere nearby. "You hit it!"

"Good!" Jason yelled back to him. "Maybe the asshole will run off and die somewhere!"

Mike came back and stood next to Jason. "And maybe not. Maybe it has some kind of freakish power and can heal quickly or some crap like that. If werewolves are possible, then so is anything else."

Billy helped Sami to her feet and a sudden pain jolted through her right ankle.

"Uh." She winced and hunched over.

"Are you hurt?" Billy asked.

"I think I hurt my ankle when I fell." She grimaced, standing on one foot.

"Aw, Sami," Billy whispered. He picked her up and carried her back to where Mike and Jason waited.

"Let's get out of the forest and back over to camp, just in case that thing decides to come back," Mike suggested.

With Sami in Billy's arms, they all headed back to the campfire. Billy set her down on a chair. Kneeling in front of her, he propped her foot on his knee and began untying her shoelace.

"I'll be right back," Mike said. He headed up the slope toward the meadow.

Jason grabbed a napkin from the supply box and a bottle of water from the ice chest. He doused the napkin with water and handed the bottle to Sami. "You need to keep hydrated."

She nodded and gulped down some water.

Jason leaned in close to her face and pressed the wet napkin to the side of her forehead, dabbing gently.

She winced from the sting. When he pulled the napkin away, blood was smeared across it.

"I'm bleeding?" she asked, shocked. "Is it bad?"

"No, it's not bad. Just a scrape." Jason tossed the napkin into the fire and began filling his shorts pockets with the keys and wallets sitting on a nearby boulder. "I'll go get your backpack, Sami," he said and headed toward the tent.

Billy turned her foot from one side to the other as he inspected it. "Yeah, it's a little swollen."

He worked her shoe back onto her foot and sat next to her. Tears filled his eyes, and he shook his head. "I can't believe what just happened," he whispered. "I thought I was gonna lose you." He gave her a hug, squeezing tight before he let go and faced her again. "I love you so much, Sami."

"I love you too," she whispered, glad to be alive, yet still shaken at how close she'd just been to death. The attack pushed its way into her thoughts, and she squished her eyes shut, trying to block the mental image. If Billy hadn't tried to intervene when he had, the beast could've killed her before Jason and Mike had arrived with their guns. She looked at Billy through the blur of tears forming in her eyes. "I'm so glad you were right there with me. What if you weren't? I might not be—"

"Shhh," he hushed and shook his head. "You *are* sitting here right now. Okay? No what-ifs."

Jason returned wearing the backpack and carrying Billy's rifle. "We'll just leave the rest of this stuff for later," he said as he propped the rifle against a chair. "You take Sami back on the quad." He eyed Billy and Sami for a moment. "Are you two gonna be okay?"

Billy shook his head. "Not until we *kill* the bastard."

"Hopefully, it's already dead!" Jason scoffed.

"Thanks, Sheriff." Mike came into view on the hill at the edge of the meadow. He shoved his cell phone into his pocket and made his way down the slope toward them. "Let's get Sami back home. Sheriff Briggs is gonna meet us there before they start the search."

"Sounds good to me." Jason started kicking dirt on the fire.

Billy jumped up and helped. When the flames were extinguished, he snatched his rifle from the chair and slung it over his shoulder.

"All right, let's go," Mike said.

With Sami in Billy's arms, they all headed up the slope, to the meadow, stopping at Jason's off-road vehicle.

Billy set Sami on the back of it and eased in front of her. The engine rumbled to life. "Hold on tight."

Sami wrapped her arms around his waist, and they headed across the meadow and stopped at the mouth of the trail. Billy looked over his shoulder, waiting for Jason and Mike to catch up. They were each carrying their guns—Mike a shotgun and Jason his rifle.

Sami turned her focus back to the path weaving through the darkness of the forest. A wave of fear shot through her. "I don't wanna go in there, Billy!" she shouted over the rumble of the engine. "I don't wanna go back in the forest. What if it's in there, waiting for me? Maybe it's what's been standing outside my bedroom window. It's been *stalking* me! I don't wanna go in there!"

"It's okay," Billy said, his voice soothing. "Mike and Jason are with us. We're all armed. It's the only way back. We *have* to get you home. You're sick and injured. It's not safe here."

"It's not safe in *there*!" she said desperately, pointing to the forest.

"We have to get you home, Sami!" Mike said with a stern voice. "Jason, you take the lead, and I'll take the rear. We'll run." He gave her a reassuring look. "Okay? We've got you covered. We won't let that thing near you. Besides, it's wounded. It's probably long gone or even dead by now."

They were right. She had to get back home to rest. The horrifying ordeal, along with the nausea, had left her feeling mentally and physically depleted.

"Okay," she said, knowing there was no other option.

They proceeded into the forest, following Jason's steady jog. Sami glanced around with caution, no longer able to see the beauty surrounding her. All she saw was impending danger lurking everywhere—behind every bush, tree, and shadow. She tightened her hold around Billy's waist and glanced over her shoulder to make sure Mike was still behind them.

Mike winked, keeping a strong steady stride. A quick blur flashed behind him, and suddenly, the werewolf towered over him.

"Mike! Behind you!" Sami screamed.

Before Mike could turn around, the beast grabbed him by the shoulders and threw him into a nearby tree.

"Shit!" Billy jerked the quad to a stop and jumped off. He yanked Sami from the seat and pushed her behind him.

Eye's wide with fear, Jason raised his rifle and pulled the trigger, but nothing happened. "Shit!" He opened the chamber and inspected it.

"Shoot it, Jason!" Billy yelled, his voice frantic. He took aim and pulled the trigger, sending a piercing blast through the air.

The beast roared and eyed the blood-soaked hole in its arm. Turning its focus back to Billy and Sami, it headed straight for them—each step slow and menacing.

Terrified, Sami covered her ringing ears with trembling hands, anticipating the next blast.

"Shoot it, Jason!" Billy yelled again and took another shot.

Jason raised his rifle and pulled the trigger again. "Dammit!" He lowered the rifle and rechecked the chamber.

Billy shot the beast in the chest again and again, but it didn't stop. "Come on, Jason, shoot the fucker!" he shouted, his voice growing more desperate as the beast grew near.

The werewolf leapt through the air and landed in front of Billy. It hit him across the face, sending him flying backward.

"Billy!" Sami shrieked, watching in horror as Billy smashed against a nearby tree and crumbled to the ground. He rolled onto his side and clutched his chest.

Jason leapt in front of the beast and raised his rifle. He pulled the trigger, sending a bullet right through the middle of its forehead.

Stunned, the werewolf paused. Blood pooled and oozed from the gaping hole. Within seconds, the wound closed and disappeared. The trickle of blood dripped to the corner of its eye, and its lips curled into an ominous sneer as if mocking them.

"What the fuck?" Jason's voice shook.

The werewolf leaned its head down and growled viciously, warming Sami's and Jason's faces with its hot, stale breath. In one swift movement, it backhanded Jason out of the way, sending him tumbling down the trail.

Billy still clutched his chest, coughing. His eyes locked with Sami's and widened. "No!" He rolled onto his hands and knees and pushed himself from the ground.

"Sami!" Jason shouted and scrambled to his feet.

Sami backed up against a tree as the werewolf towered over her. Breathing raggedly, with her heart pounding in her chest, she waited to die.

The beast grabbed her by the arms and threw her over its rock-hard shoulder, handling her as if she were a ragdoll.

"Ugh!" She winced and gritted her teeth, trying to bear the pain radiating through her abdomen.

Billy and Jason raced toward her, their faces wracked with terror.

"Billy!" she yelled.

"Nooo! Sami!" Billy shouted and reached out as he neared her.

"Help me!" she screamed, straining for Billy's hand. Their fingertips touched, and Sami's entire body jerked. Billy was suddenly dozens of feet away, and the surrounding forest melted into a blur.

"Noooo! Billyyyy!" she screeched, no longer able to see him.

The faint sound of his voice screaming her name echoed from somewhere far behind but was soon lost to the whoosh of the forest whizzing past. "Please let me go!" she pleaded hysterically, pounding her fists into the beast's back. "Let me goooo!"

A cloud of confusion consumed her thoughts, and the whirr of the forest faded into darkness.

19

"**S**AMI!" BILLY yelled into the silent forest as he ran. Frantically jumping over fallen logs and bushes, he followed the path of destruction, praying to find her somewhere along the way. "Samiiii!" he bellowed as hopelessness sank in.

"Billy!" Jason caught up to him with Mike right behind, both out of breath.

Billy stopped, lungs burning and chest heaving. "She's gone, Mike! It took her! The fucking thing took her!" Tears filled his eyes. "Why didn't you shoot, Jason? Why in the fuck didn't you shoot!"

"I tried!" He smacked the butt of his rifle with the back of his hand. "My gun jammed! I only got one shot off! I tried. I fucking tried!"

A firm hand on Billy's shoulder turned his attention to his brother. Blood trickled down the right sight of Mike's face from a wound near his temple. But that didn't matter. Not now. All that mattered was finding Sami.

"We'll find her, bro! Don't worry. We'll find her!" Mike said.

"If we're gonna find her, we have to keep going!" Jason said and took off through the forest.

"Come on, Billy. She needs you to be strong. Pull it together and let's go!" Mike ordered.

Billy nodded, finding strength in the shred of hope they would find her.

Mike swatted Billy on the shoulder and took off, following Jason's lead.

"Hold on, Sami. We're coming," Billy whispered and sprinted after his brother.

Billy, Mike, and Jason continued their desperate search. The tracks led into the forest nearly one hundred yards behind Jason's house and ended at the main road.

"Shit!" Billy said, stepping out onto the road. He didn't know which way to go from there. "Now what?"

"Call Sheriff Briggs. Tell him to meet us here instead," Mike said. "I'm gonna check for tracks alongside the road this way..." He pointed with his thumb to the right. "Jason, you head that way...." He motioned with a nod in the other direction.

Mike and Jason departed while Billy called Sheriff Briggs and gave him a brief explanation of Sami's kidnapping. In order to be taken seriously, Billy decided to wait and tell the sheriff face-to-face that a werewolf had attacked Sami, and not a human.

Billy shoved his phone into his pocket and glanced down the road at his brother. Mike looked at him and shook his head.

"Dammit!" Jason's voice bellowed from behind, capturing Billy's attention.

Jason slowed to kick a small rock out of his way. "It's like they've just disappeared." He threw his hands up. "What the hell are we gonna do?"

Billy stood in shock, staring into the forest. All he wanted was Sami. For her to be safe. To hold her in his arms again. But she was gone.

"This has to be a nightmare. It has to be a fucking nightmare!" Billy shook his head in denial. His entire body tensed with anger and heartbreak. "Samiii!" he shouted, standing in the middle of the road, looking around at the surrounding forest, and waiting for a response. The only sound heard was his own voice echoing back at him.

"*Saaamiiiii!*" he screamed louder, but there was still no reply from the woman he loved. He fell to his knees in the middle of the road and cried.

Jason knelt and put an arm around him. "I'm so sorry, Billy. We're gonna get her back. If it's the last thing we do, we'll find her. Don't give up yet! All right, man? Don't give up!"

Mike ran back toward them and crouched in front of Billy. "Don't worry, little brother. We'll find her…. We'll find her."

"What if we find her the same way they found Dad?" Billy said with a shaky voice, squishing his eyes shut to destroy the thought.

"No!" Mike boomed and gripped Billy's shoulder. "If that thing wanted to—" He stopped and clenched his jaw, holding back the forming tears. "If it wanted to kill her, it would've already done it. She's *not* dead!"

Billy nodded, having no other choice than to cling to his brother's words. Gritting his teeth to stay his tears, he wiped his cheeks dry on the sleeve of his T-shirt.

Sirens wailed in the distance. The three of them moved from the middle of the road and waited on the grassy shoulder.

Billy imagined telling the sheriff exactly what had happened, and then, being thrown to the ground and wrestled into handcuffs. He shook his head. "Mike, how in the hell are we gonna get them to believe us?"

Mike let out a heavy sigh. "It'll be tough at first, but they'll find the prints at the lake and the blood it left behind. They'll believe us."

"I hope you're right," Billy said, growing anxious as the sirens grew louder.

Within seconds, they were surrounded by the entire sheriff's department. Sheriff Briggs approached and had them follow him back to his car to take their statements while his deputies roamed the edges of the road, searching for tracks. All three took turns explaining to the sheriff the exact details of the attack.

After Sheriff Briggs finished taking their statements, he shoved his notebook and pen back into his pocket. "That's quite a story."

Billy stepped forward. "I know it sounds crazy, but it's *not* a story!"

The sheriff eyed the three men, his eyes glazed over with suspicion. "If it had been anyone else but you three telling me all this, I would've hauled them off to jail. But I've known you boys all your lives. This werewolf business is a hard pill to swallow, but I do believe something, or *someone*, took Samantha. And my only concern at this point is to find her. You boys come with me. We'll set up the search party at your house."

Within the hour, deputies, dogs, and nearly two dozen local citizens scoured the forest. Soon after, a helicopter joined in. They searched the hills surrounding the road where the tracks ended, at the lake, and in and around the houses. Nightfall came, but aside from the prints and blood at the lake and the broken limbs in the forest behind Jason's house, they didn't find any other sign of Sami or the beast that had taken her.

Seeing their exhaustion, Sheriff Briggs ordered Billy, Jason, and Mike to return home to rest, and promised he would see them soon with an update. In the meantime, he'd have the blood samples analyzed and continue with the search. Wanting to be a part of the action in an area other than around their homes, they all protested, but the sheriff wouldn't take no for an answer. Pissed off and worried, they waited on Sami's front porch for any leads.

SAMI OPENED her eyes. Disoriented, she tried to focus on her surroundings but couldn't see through the darkness. The corners of her mouth ached. She stretched her jaw but the movement cut short, and she quickly realized she'd been gagged.

Panic shot through her.

She tried to sit up from the cold hard floor, but her hands were bound behind her back. Wriggling her wrists to loosen her binding, her fingers brushed against cold metal bars running vertically—like those of a cage. She sucked in a quick breath, suddenly remembering what had happened in the forest.

This can't be real! It can't be! She closed her eyes and shook her head, hoping it was just another nightmare. When she opened her eyes again, nothing had changed. She was still in the dark, bound, gagged, and caged like an animal. Some horrific beast had kidnapped her, and she was going to die. She was sure of it.

Lying down made her feel vulnerable. She used her legs as leverage and shifted her body into an upright position. The jarring sparked a dull ache in her abdomen, and she suddenly recalled being slung over the beast's shoulder. Mentally, physically, and emotionally exhausted, she sat back, rested her head on the bars, and waited to die.

Visions of Billy flooded her thoughts. The first time she'd laid eyes on him. Their first kiss. The first time they'd made love. And the last time she'd seen him in the forest—their fingertips touching before she had been taken away. Now, she would never see Billy again. Or her mom or dad. Or anyone.

Her eyes filled with tears. *They must so worried and devastated. And, after I'm gone, Mom will be all alone.*

Heartbroken and numb, she wondered how she would die. If she would be ripped to shreds, eaten alive, or cooked slowly over an open fire. She shook the horrific thoughts away and started to cry.

A loud creak yanked her from her pity. Across the room, a faint light filtered through the doorway, and a silhouette of a person appeared.

Afraid and trembling, Sami scooted back into the far corner of the large cage.

After a flick of a switch, a bright light came on above her.

"Hello, *Sami!*" Jessica sneered, her white shirt stained with blood.

Sami's breath caught in her throat. *Jessica? Jessica kidnapped me? Why?* She recalled the day in the diner when Jessica had accused Harry of kidnapping her because he'd thought she was a monster. *That's because she* is *a monster! It was* her *in the forest all along! She's the stalker!*

"Surprise!" Jessica winked, and her eyes turned blood-red.

Sami screamed, but the gag turned it into a pathetic whimper. She jerked against the ropes binding her wrists, trying to set herself free. But they were too tight.

"Hmmm, what are we going to do with you, Samantha? You and your *bastard child*!" She seethed in disgust. "The smell a pregnant whore gives off makes me want to puke. I can't stand it. But I guess I'll have to. For nine months anyway. Then I'll kill you!"

Sami stopped struggling and stared at Jessica with a shocked look. *I'm pregnant? No. She's lying. She probably just overheard us talking about it at camp. But…if werewolves exist, then anything is possible.*

Though Sami didn't trust this maniac standing before her, she had a feeling Jessica had spoken the truth. With a sudden need to protect her unborn baby from harm, she curled her legs to her chest to shield her abdomen.

Jessica strutted across the room to the cage and motioned with her forefinger for Sami to come closer.

Afraid, Sami shook her head.

"Come here!" Jessica roared.

Sami tensed, startled by the horrifying boom. Terrified of angering Jessica further, Sami decided to obey her. On shaky knees, she scooted toward the red-eyed woman.

Jessica reached into the cage, grabbed Sami by the arm, and smashed her face up against the steel bars.

"*Uh!*" Sami grimaced from the bone-searing pain.

With an evil grin on her face, Jessica pulled a large hunting knife from behind her back. "Do you recognize this? It was Harry's. When he…" She paused and narrowed her eyes. "Well, *how* he got me into his cage isn't important. Long story short, he locked me up and vowed to kill me. And when he was stupid enough to get too close to the cage, I swiped the knife from his belt to protect myself. Lucky for me, Mike heard my screams for help. But before he came bursting through the door to rescue me—" she held the knife against Sami's cheek "—I vowed to Harry I would kill you with it if it was the last thing I did! And I am!"

Eyes wide with fear, Sami tried to pull away, but Jessica's grip was too tight.

Jessica smirked and shook her head, warning Sami to stay put.

Sami whimpered and tried to wriggle her wrists free from the binding.

In one swift move, Jessica cut the gag from Sami's mouth, nicking her cheek with the knife's tip.

Sami winced.

"Quit your crying! I'm not going to kill you yet! Now, stay still!"

Trembling and fearing she'd feel the sting of the knife sink into her abdomen at any moment, Sami did as ordered.

Jessica reached around and cut the binding from Sami's wrists. "If you scream, I'll kill you now. So, keep your damn mouth shut!"

Sami nodded and rubbed her burning wrists.

Jessica let out an impatient sigh. "Here's the plan, bitch. I'm going to lay low for nine months. Of course, it will be difficult during the full moon when all I feel like doing is going on a killing spree…." She grew quiet as her thoughts seemed to trail off.

"Anyway," she continued with an angry tone, "when the bastard is ripe, I'll cut it from your belly with this knife." Smiling with pleasure, she held it up as if it were a trophy. "Then, I'll tell Jason the baby is mine and his, and we'll live happily ever after." She grinned at the thought, before her face puckered into a scowl. "I was actually supposed to live happily ever after with *Billy*, but then you moved here and screwed everything up!" Jessica reached in and backhanded Sami across the face.

The powerful impact knocked Sami to the floor. She groaned as the sting radiated through her left cheek. Wetness trickled from the corner of her mouth. She wiped it away, blood staining the back of her hand.

Jessica went to the door and picked something up off the floor just outside of it. "Here," she said and she tossed a small paper bag into the cage. "And you better eat it! I want a healthy baby. If you're good and follow my rules, I'll let you out of the cage, and this will be your new room." She waved her hands at the dirty room, obviously used for the storage of boxes and hostages. Then, she turned and walked out, closing the door behind her. The knob jiggled and clicked, and the thudding of footsteps faded.

Sami's eyes burned with tears. She was pregnant with Billy's baby, and Jessica was going to kill her. But she wasn't ready to give up so easily. *No! I can't let that happen. I can't! I'll get away somehow. I'll do as she says and wait for the perfect moment to escape.*

She took a deep breath, trying to calm herself. The wrinkled lunch bag sat at the opposite end of the cage. Food was the furthest thing from her mind, but she knew she had to eat whatever was inside before Jessica returned. She crawled over to the bag and opened it. Reaching in, she wrapped her hand around a bottle of water. She hadn't realized how thirsty she was until then. She immediately gulped down half of it, quenching her parched throat.

She shoved her hand back into the bag and pulled out a smashed peanut butter and jelly sandwich. Forcing it to her lips, she took a bite. The sweetness triggered a wave of nausea, but she held it back and swallowed the muck. When the sandwich was gone, she reached into the bag and pulled out the final item—a severely bruised apple. Not wanting to give Jessica any more reason to snap, she ate the mushy fruit, resisting the urge to gag with every bite.

When she was finished, she leaned against the cold metal bars, keeping her thoughts on those she loved to ease her fear and worry. She recalled happy moments from her childhood, her teenage years, and her new life in Wolf Hill. She imagined how frantic and worried her mother must be, along with Billy, Mike and Jason, and wished there was a way to let them know that she was all right.

The door creaked opened again. Jessica sauntered across the room, wearing a black tank top and cutoffs. Thankfully, there were no blood stains this time, and her eyes were their normal amber color.

"Well, that was easy, wasn't it?" Jessica smiled, took a key from her pocket, and shoved it into the lock on the cage door.

Sami gulped, dreading what was to come.

"There you go," Jessica said in a kind voice as she pulled the door open. "You're free to roam your new room." She reached in and held out her hand.

Sami didn't want to leave the cage. Inside, she felt somewhat safe from Jessica. Now, death could occur at any unsuspecting moment.

With no choice but to obey the unstable beast, Sami placed her hand in Jessica's sweaty palm and stepped out of the cage.

Jessica smiled and backhanded Sami across the cheek.

Sami remained silent, gritting her teeth to bear the sting and not giving Jessica the satisfaction of her cry.

"Stupid bitch! You didn't even see that one coming, did you?" Jessica laughed wickedly. "Oh, and it's too bad about what happened to your mom last night."

Sami held her breath, dreading what she was about to hear.

"She was home when I came looking for you. I really wanted to watch her freak out while I attacked her. But *nooo*. She had to go and keel over from a fucking heart attack instead. What a bitch! Like mother like daughter, *right*?"

"You killed my *mom*?" Sami asked, horrified.

Jessica's eyes lit up. "Not technically. You should've seen the look on her face, though, when I snuck up behind her in her own home... in the safety of her own bedroom. She screamed and screamed." Her eyes glazed over with pleasure. "But there was no one around to help. Then, she clutched her chest and fell to the floor with a loud *thud*! It's no fun killing when the victim doesn't put up a good fight." She shrugged.

"Oh, and I borrowed some clothes while I was there. I hope you don't mind. That's the only downfall of being a werewolf, being stark naked after you morph back into being human. I took your car too. Partly because I've always wanted to drive it, but mostly because it was another one of Harry's prized possessions I just can't wait to destroy. But I'll do that tomorrow. Tonight, there's a full moon, and I just can't seem to control my urge to kill."

She grinned, and her eyes turned red. "If I don't hunt, I'll end up killing you prematurely, and we wouldn't want that to happen. Would we?"

She left the room and slammed the door shut. The knob clicked, and something clattered against the door.

Sami held her breath and waited for the sound of Jessica's footsteps to fade. Then, she sagged onto the cold concrete floor and broke down sobbing. "No, Mom.... Noooooo."

Memories flooded her thoughts. Of her mom hugging her and kissing her on the forehead. She thought of their recent disagreements and how thoughtless she had been to her mom lately.

Did she even see my note? Does she even know I'm sorry and that I love her? Sami shook her head. *Nooo! She can't be gone.... She can't be! First, Grandpa. Now, Mom?*

"Why did we come here, Mom?" Her voice shook. "Why...?"

Sami buried her face in her hands and completely gave in to her sorrow. She sobbed until her heart had nothing left to give, and her mind and body surrendered to exhaustion…

"DON'T GIVE up, Samantha." *Carol stands before her, surrounded by a beautiful white haze. She looks so angelic. So peaceful. "The baby, Samantha. Take care of my grandson." She smiles beautifully. Suddenly, her lips tighten, and she narrows her eyes. "Fight back! Don't give up!" she orders and slowly fades away.*

"Mom!" Sami shouted, opening her eyes. She pushed up from the floor, into a sitting position, bearing through the aches and pains wracking her body. She glanced around the musty, box-cluttered room, realizing she was still where Jessica had left her.

Sami's heart sank. *It was just a dream. Mom's gone. She's really gone.*

She wiped away the tears as they slipped down her cheeks, and she took in an unsteady breath. Dream or not, her mother was right. She had to fight for her baby. For *Billy's* baby. She couldn't just lie there and wait for time to mend her broken heart—if it even could. And she couldn't just wait to die. She had to try to survive, and there was no time to waste.

A cot sat in the corner behind her with an old wooden chair at the foot of it. Sami gripped the seat of the chair and pushed up from the floor. Every muscle in her body ached. Her ankle throbbed. But compared to death, the physical pain was manageable. She looked around, eyeing another door next to the head of the cot. She limped to the door and opened it.

Disappointment set in as she stared at an old, filthy bathroom.

A sulfurous odor engulfed the air like a thick fog. Rust and brown grime lined both the sink jutting from the wall and the claw-foot tub. The once white floor tiles were layered with grime, particles of hair, and clumps of dust. The toilet seat was covered in dirt, and the water in the bowl was a murky brown.

Grimacing with disgust at the foul odor, Sami quickly flipped the lid shut and flushed away the stench. Above the toilet was an octagon-shaped window too small for her to squeeze through.

With a hopeless sigh, she turned and stared at herself in the cracked mirror. The blood on her cheek and the corner of her mouth had dried, and deep bruises had already formed around the wounds. Tears stung her eyes, but she swallowed them back.

She turned the squeaky knob on the faucet and waited for the brown water to stop sputtering. As soon as the water ran clear, she carefully washed away the blood.

A thought occurred to her. She took the dirty towel from the rack and wrapped it around her hand. Taking a deep breath, she smashed her fist into the mirror, shattering it to pieces. She picked up the long shards of broken glass, being mindful of the sharp edges, and hid them under the cot in the other room—hoping they might be useful in her attempt to escape.

She went back into the bathroom, stepped onto the lid of the toilet, and rammed her wrapped fist through the window. A piece of glass clanked to the floor and a burst of fresh air rushed over her face.

Sami stood there for a moment, breathing in the cool air of the night and praying Jessica hadn't heard the destructive clatter. When all remained silent, she finished punching the remaining shards from the pane, glad the rest of the pieces had landed outside. She stepped down from the toilet and picked up the pieces of broken glass from the floor.

"Uh!" She winced as a shard pierced her finger. She tossed the glass into the waste basket before she inspected her cut. Blood oozed from the small wound and dripped down her palm. She turned on the faucet to wash it clean, but another idea came to mind. She shut the bathroom door and wrote *NEED HELP—SAMI* on the back of it, using her finger as the writing vessel and her blood as the ink, hopeful that, if someone came searching for her, they'd notice the broken glass and peer through the window.

She rinsed the wound with water and wrapped it in toilet paper to stop the bleeding. Then, she went into the other room and closed the door behind her. Trying to find anything useful to help her escape, Sami proceeded to search through drawers and the dusty boxes cluttering the room.

BILLY, JASON, and Mike waited anxiously on Sami's front porch as they watched Sheriff Briggs get out of his car and approach them. They all jumped to their feet.

With his gut in knots, Billy braced himself for the worst. *Please let her be alive. Please let her be alive,* he chanted silently and gripped the railing for support.

"I'm sorry, boys. There's no sign of her. But we'll keep searching. Some of my deputies and townsfolk will continue to search through the night. There'll be more reinforcements tomorrow. I suggest you three try to get some rest. Tomorrow's gonna be another long day."

It drove Billy crazy that he couldn't help search beyond their properties. "Why can't we look for Sami?"

Sheriff Briggs eyed the three men. "You all are too emotionally involved. We can't have you making rash decisions."

"That's bullshit!" Mike belted out.

"That's exactly what I'm talking about," Sheriff Briggs said, pointing a warning finger at Mike. "Now, pipe down!"

Mike clenched his jaw, clearly angered.

"What about Carol?" Billy asked. "We've been trying to get a hold of her with no luck. Has anyone contacted her yet?"

Sheriff Briggs sighed. "That's right, you don't know yet because you all were at the lake last night."

Billy didn't like the dismal tone in the sheriff's voice. "We don't know what?"

"Steve Garrison called the station last night. Apparently, he'd come over to pay Carol a visit after she gotten home from work. When he got here, the front door was wide open. He went inside and found Carol lying on her bedroom floor, unconscious."

"What?" Billy belted out. "I can't frickin' believe this! What in the hell is going on around here?"

Jason narrowed his eyes. "Maybe Steve hurt her?"

The sheriff shook his head. "He's been questioned. And we won't know more until the test results are in and she regains consciousness."

"Why didn't you call Sami last night?" Mike asked the sheriff.

"We did call her. Apparently, she'd left her cell phone in her purse, which was lying next to the note she'd left on the kitchen counter. The note didn't say where she was going, so we didn't know where to look."

"Why didn't you contact one of us?" Jason asked with an angry tone.

"We tried that too. Your phones went straight to voicemail," Sheriff Briggs replied dryly.

Jason sighed and rubbed his temples. "That's right, we can only get cell reception in the meadow, but not all the time. I left my phone at home too."

"I had my phone off the whole time." Billy shook his head, frustrated with himself. He glared at Mike. "You had reception this morning. You called the sheriff."

Mike looked at him as if he were crazy. "Are you serious? Sami had just been attacked by a fucking werewolf! Do you think I stopped to check for messages?"

"Calm down, boys," Sheriff Briggs said. "You can visit Carol at the hospital in the morning. I'm sure she'd appreciate it. I know she cares for you all very much. Now, if you'll excuse me…" He headed over to a group of deputies standing in the middle of the road.

With a sudden urge to be alone, Billy went into Sami's house. He turned on the lights and looked around. The room was quiet and still. Hauntingly still. Everyone was gone—Harry, Carol, and Sami. He swallowed the lump in his throat.

Heavy-hearted, he went upstairs and into Sami's room, looking for any signs of her, though he knew it was pointless. Head down, he eased himself onto the bed. Visions of the first time they'd made love forced their way into his thoughts. Her sweet lips, her soft body beneath his, and the love they'd shared—heart, body, and soul.

He gritted his teeth and shook his head, trying to free himself from the mental torture. Her lavender pillow lopped over the edge of the bed. He picked it up and held it to his nose, taking in her sweet scent—the small action nearly pushing him to the breaking point.

He swallowed hard, trying to knock down his weakness. "I'm so sorry, Sami," he whispered, the sting of tears threatening to brim over. "I'm so sorry."

Anger slowly began to take over again. He set the pillow aside and went to the window. Staring out into the darkness, he envisioned the red eyes he'd seen only a few weeks prior. Thoughts of Sami flitted through his mind—of how she'd also seen something with red eyes and standing on two feet, staring at her. He thought further back to when Sami had been chased at Jason's house. Of the basement door with scratches on them. And of Harry. His eyes widened, and the sound of his heart suddenly pounded in his ears as one particular event flashed through his mind.

Harry called Jessica a monster! *A werewolf!*

"No!" Billy whispered in shock. "It can't be true." He bolted back downstairs and out the front door, running smack-dab into Jason.

Jason lost his balance and stumbled toward the steps. "What the—"

Billy grabbed him by the arms and steadied him. "I think I know who did this!" he said, breathing heavily.

Mike jumped to his feet. "What? Who?"

Billy's eyes narrowed with hatred. "Jessica!"

"What?" Mike said, looking at his brother as if he were crazy. "Sure, Jessica's a bitch, but a *werewolf*? It could be anyone. It could be one of the deputies, for all we know."

"But it all makes sense," Billy said. "Come on, let's go tell the sheriff."

Mike grabbed Billy's arm. "Wait a minute. You can't just tell the sheriff you think his niece *kidnapped* Sami and that she's a *werewolf!* He'll lock you up like he did Harry...." Mike's voice trailed off and he lowered his head. "Harry locked Jessica up in his basement,..," he said under his breath as if speaking his thoughts aloud. "No...that's crazy." He shook his head with a disbelieving look in his eyes.

"Jessica?" Jason whispered as he pondered the idea. After a brief silence, he nodded. "I'm with Billy. Jessica showed up at my house right after Sami was being chased that day. Her claws come out when Sami's around. Pun intended."

Mike glanced over his shoulder at Sheriff Briggs. He was still in the middle of the road, talking to one of his deputies. "We can't talk here," Mike whispered. "Let's go inside."

They all went in and huddled in the middle of the living room.

Mike looked at Jason and then Billy. "So, what exactly are we saying? That Jessica is some kind of superhuman *monster*?" He shook his head. "Do you know how crazy that sounds? If we suggest that to anyone, they'll think we've all frickin' lost it, and that *we* did something to Sami."

"I know," Billy said. "But just think. It all makes sense. Even *Harry* thought Jessica was a monster."

"He thought *everyone* was a monster," Mike argued.

"But he only locked *Jessica* up," Billy said, growing irritated with his brother. "He said in the hospital that the werewolves will get us. He must've seen something. She must've tried to do something." He began to pace the living room, trying to make sense of it all. "There are scratch marks on the basement door by something huge. She must have been after Harry, but he stopped her somehow and trapped her in the basement."

"Come on, Mike." Jason chimed in. "You know it makes sense. The huge mutant wolf tracks. The red-eyed monster. The way Jessica's been causing trouble with Sami lately. She's probably getting revenge for what Harry did to her. Jessica probably came after Carol too. Or maybe she came looking for *Sami* last night!" he said angrily.

"Right." Billy rushed down the hall to Carol's room. He flipped the light switch, but nothing happened. He went to the nightstand and jiggled the bulb. He tightened it, and the light came on. "Someone loosened the bulb."

Mike bent down and picked up the flashlight at his feet. "What the hell? There are scratch marks on the floor." He grew quiet as he inspected them. He went back into the living room, eyeing the floor along the way.

Billy and Jason followed him.

"There's some more at the base of the stairs," Mike said, with a bewildered look.

"Werewolf claws," Jason added dryly.

Mike sighed and pinched the bridge of his nose between two fingers. "Fuuuck," he said as if he'd just recalled pertinent information and was silently kicking his own ass for not remembering sooner.

Billy glared at him. "What?"

Mike let out a heavy sigh and his eyes filled with regret. "I think you guys are right. Let's grab our guns from the porch and walk calmly back to the house. Don't let on that we're up to anything."

Billy pursed his lips and sighed impatiently. He knew his brother was hiding something. But Mike wouldn't talk until he was ready, so there was no point in pushing him. At the moment, all that mattered was finding Sami.

They all went outside, gathered the weapons leaning against the corner of the porch railing, and headed next door.

"Where's Sami's car?" Billy asked, realizing it wasn't in the driveway. "Has it been gone all this time? I didn't notice it gone earlier."

Jason shrugged. "I don't know. I don't remember seeing it though." His face scrunched as he thought. "I think."

"I don't know," Mike replied. "But we don't have time to figure it out right now."

When they were safely in the house, they all breathed a sigh of relief.

Mike disappeared down the hallway.

Billy closed his eyes and rubbed his forehead, trying to relieve the tension. The thought of Sami being dead kept trying to demolish the shred of hope he clung to.

Please be alive, Sami. Please be alive. Tears threatened to fall. Determined to stay strong, he clenched his jaw and let anger back into his heart.

Jason slapped Billy in the middle of the back. "She's okay, buddy. I know she is."

Mike emerged from the hallway with a large black duffle bag. He stopped at the gun cabinet and grabbed a box of ammo. He tossed it into the bag along with a shotgun.

Billy and Jason handed him their rifles.

"What good are they gonna do?" Jason asked. "I shot her and the wound healed."

"I don't know," Mike said with an exasperated tone and shoved the rifles into the bag. "Maybe they'll work on her when she's in human form."

"We need to invest in some handguns," Billy said.

"It's next on the list," Mike said. "Now, if the sheriff says anything, we're going to town to visit Carol. We have to assume Sheriff Briggs is in on this, since he's Jessica's uncle."

Billy and Jason nodded.

"All right. Let's do this." Mike headed out the front door.

Billy and Jason followed.

Jason hopped into the back seat of Billy's car and took the bag from Mike.

Mike climbed into the driver's seat and started the car.

Billy opened the passenger door.

"Billy!" Sheriff Briggs shouted from the middle of the road.

"Shit," Billy whispered through gritted teeth.

"You boys aren't going back out there again tonight, are you?" Sheriff Briggs hurried over to him.

"Uh, no." Billy took a deep breath to steady his nerves. "We're gonna visit Carol. See how she's doing."

"Visiting hours are over."

The sheriff's flat tone made Billy feel uneasy. He gulped, hoping his nerves didn't show. "Yeah, we know, but maybe they'll make an exception. We can't just sit here and do nothing. If they find Sami tonight, it'd be nice to tell her that Carol's okay."

Sheriff Briggs studied him for a moment. "I'll see you boys in the morning, then."

"Yep," Billy replied.

The sheriff strutted away.

Billy exhaled as if he'd been holding his breath, trying to calm his thudding heart. He used to respect Sheriff Briggs. Now, the man scared the hell out of him. He hopped into the car and shut the door. "Let's get the fuck out of here!"

Mike backed out of the driveway and headed down the road. When they reached the main road, he turned right, toward town.

Billy grew frustrated. "Dude, what the hell are you doing? You were supposed to make a left, toward the sheriff's house!"

"I know," Mike said, keeping his cool, "but Sheriff Briggs thinks we're going into town, toward the hospital." He made an abrupt U-turn and turned off the headlights. Then, he slowly drove forward, guided only by the moonlight until he passed the road leading to their houses. A safe distance past their road, he turned the headlights back on and sped forward. He didn't slow down until they reached the desolate driveway to Jessica's house.

20

BILLY SMACKED the dashboard in frustration as Mike drove past Jessica's driveway.

"Come on, man! You're really pissing me off with this going-the-wrong-way shit! We don't have time for this!" Billy snapped.

"We have to park down a way on the main road. I don't want Sheriff Briggs to come home and see our car," Mike explained. He drove around the next bend and pulled over on the shoulder. "Look, Billy—" he let out a long breath "—I know all you want is to get Sami back safely. That's what we all want. But we have to be smart about this for Sami's sake."

"I know, I know. It just seems to be taking forever! I can't lose her, Mike! I just wanna hurry before it's too late."

"Don't worry, buddy—" Jason placed a reassuring hand on Billy's shoulder "—it's not too late. Wait a minute. What if we don't find her here? Then, what?"

Mike shook his head. "We'll deal with that bridge when we get there."

They all jumped out of the car. Thankfully, full moon allowed them to see through the darkness without flashlights. They glanced around, looking for any signs of danger. Aside from the adrenaline pounding through their hearts, all remained silent.

Mike grabbed the duffle bag from the back seat and set it on the trunk. He sighed heavily and rubbed a hand across his chin.

Billy knew that sigh. It meant Mike was about to reveal something he knew he should've earlier—like what he had been mentally battling with back at Sami's house.

"You're wasting time," Jason said. "Let me have my rifle."

Mike opened the bag and shoved his hand inside. He paused and let out another heavy breath. "You were right, Jason—" Mike pulled out three hunting knives and handed one each to Billy and Jason "—she was so powerful, bullets didn't stop her."

"Sweet!" Jason's eyes twinkled as the full moon reflected off the blade. "Where'd you get these?"

Mike looked at Billy. "From Harry."

Not wanting to risk his brother putting off his explanation until later, Billy kept his outward demeanor calm. Though, on the inside, he was ready to knock Mike senseless.

Mike studied his brother's expression. "He insisted I take them because they're made of silver. And according to Harry, it's the only way to kill werewolves."

Enraged, Billy clenched his jaw before he met his brother's gaze. "You're fucking *kidding* me! Why didn't you say anything sooner? We could've brought these camping! Maybe the bitch would've been dead by now, and Sami would still be here! Or, better yet, maybe we wouldn't have gone camping at all!"

"Don't you think I haven't been asking myself the same thing all day?" Mike said. "How often do people bring silver knives camping, just in case they happen to run into a fucking werewolf, 'cause the *crazy old man* said to? Anyway, now isn't the time for this shit! Let's go find Sami!"

"Let's go!" Billy shoved his knife into the back of his jeans and stormed off without waiting.

"Come on, man," Jason said as he caught up to him. "None of this is anyone's fault but Jessica's. She's had it out for Sami ever since

Sami moved here."

"Why don't we just shut the fuck up and concentrate on getting Sami back!" Billy snapped.

The sound of the trunk slamming shut caught Billy's and Jason's attention, and they snapped their heads in Mike's direction. Mike jogged up to them, picking up speed as he passed by them. He turned left onto the mile long road leading to the sheriff's house and disappeared around the bend.

"Asshole," Billy muttered before he and Jason sprinted after him. They all ran down the middle of the road in silence.

About halfway to their destination, Billy's lungs began to burn. He ignored the pain and pressed on, keeping his focus on Sami.

Mike stopped a safe distance from the house and bent over, trying to catch his breath.

Jason copied him. "Damn. I thought my driveway was ridiculously long," he said breathlessly.

"Mike, what are we doing?" Billy whispered through ragged breaths. "Let's go find Sami."

"We will. Let's just figure out how we're gonna do this first," Mike whispered back, still panting.

"What?" Jason said in an irritated tone, his breathing heavy. "Let's go in there and search every room and every closet until we find her."

"Just hold on a minute," Mike urged. "We can't rush in half-cocked. You saw how fast she took off with Sami. All you saw was a blur. She could do it again if we're not careful."

"All right then, what in the hell do you suggest we do?" Billy asked, his impatience building.

Mike thought for a moment before he gave out his orders. "It'll be faster if we split up. Billy, you come with me through the front door. I'll take the upstairs while you look downstairs. There's a basement that can only be reached from the inside of the house. If we don't find her, then we'll all meet at the basement door and go down together. Jason, you go around back and come in through the kitchen. That's where the basement door is. Wait there until we work our way through."

"Got it," Jason was more than ready.

"Fine. Let's go," Billy snapped.

They continued on, jogging at a steady pace until they reached the house. The porch was dark, and there didn't appear to be any lights on inside.

With light steps, Billy and Mike ascended the porch steps, remembering to avoid the ones that creaked, while Jason tiptoed his way around back.

Mike paused at the front door and looked at his brother. "Ready?" he whispered.

Deciding it best to put all animosity aside for now, Billy nodded and opened the door. He couldn't see a thing through the pitch-blackness. Using caution, he went in and opened the curtains in the living room, allowing the moonlight to stream through. He glanced at the stairs along the wall next to the doorway and saw Mike creeping up them.

There was nothing out of the ordinary about the quiet living room—it still looked and smelled like a trash can. Using light steps, he made his way to a small door under the stairs. When he opened the door it creaked.

"Shit!" he whispered, looking behind him for any signs of Jessica. When all remained clear, he pulled the thin cord dangling in front of him and the light flicked on. Boxes and spider webs filled the cramped space. He turned the light off and closed the door slowly, avoiding another squeaky disturbance.

Across the hall was another door, slightly ajar. Billy held his breath and pushed the door open. The moon shone brightly through the bare window, highlighting the paper-cluttered desk in front of it. Along the walls were shelves piled with books, and a stack of boxes stood in the far corner. Nothing out of the ordinary, except for another pigsty of a room.

A sudden rustling behind the boxes caught his attention. He gulped and reached for the silver knife. With careful steps, he approached the cardboard tower.

An orange tabby leapt out from behind them, heading straight for his face.

"Shit!" Billy jumped back, batting the cat out of the way with his arm.

The cat hissed and scurried out of the room.

Billy stood dazed, hand over his pounding heart, trying to regain his focus. "What kind of crazy fucking *dog* has a crazy fucking *cat* for a pet?" he whispered through a tight jaw.

Not wanting to leave any hidden corner unchecked, he peered behind the boxes, but there was nothing there. He went to the closet door and slid it open. It was piled high with clothes and other junk. A box shifted and toppled over, sending its contents clattering to the floor.

"Fuck." He held his breath, listening for Jessica's footsteps. When he didn't hear anything, he exhaled and started placing the items back into the box—a couple of notebooks, a stapler, an old heavy book. He stopped and focused in on the book.

Wait, this is a really old book.

He picked it back up and went to the window to get a better look at it. The leather cover was old and worn. There was no title, but the book had an unusual imprinting on the cover—a pattern of intricate swirls surrounding an ancient-looking dagger.

He opened it to a random page and a musty waft blasted his sinuses. Ignoring the stench, he focused on the illustrations of what appeared to be werewolves attacking villagers in a bloody battle.

"What the hell?" he whispered. He flipped through more pages and found another picture of a man stabbing a werewolf with a knife similar to the one he held in his hand. He read aloud part of the script under the picture.

"...thus the blade of silver ended the bloody battle."

"Shit!" he whispered and closed the book. Harry was right. The only way to stop Jessica would be to stab her with the silver knife. "This can't be real."

A loud *thump* echoed from the hallway. Billy set the book down on the desk and made a beeline for the doorway. Peering out, he looked both ways for any signs of evil. Seeing nothing out of the ordinary, he breathed a sigh of relief.

Must've been the cat. He put the book back into the box, shoved the box into the closet, and slid the door shut. Then, he reentered the hallway, making a right toward the kitchen.

MIKE CREPT upstairs, stopping to hold his breath every time one of them squeaked. He glanced over just as Billy opened the living room curtains, allowing moonlight to filter through.

When Mike reached the top of the stairs he peered down the dark hall, listening for any sounds of life. Through the silence, he continued his search, opening every door and looking in every closet and under every bed. But he found nothing aside from the most cluttered bedrooms he'd ever seen.

He moved along, eyeing the door at the end of the hall and wishing he could just skip it. Instead, he opened the door and went inside.

It was another bedroom, just as cluttered as the rest of the house. An unmade bed. A dresser with clothes piled on top. More clothes strewn across the floor. He noticed a glimmer coming from a familiar article of clothing slung over the back of a chair. He held the shirt up—a red tank top decorated with sequins in the shape of a heart.

"Shit. This is Sami's," he whispered and set it back down. The tank top confirmed that Jessica had been in Sami's house.

He spotted a collage of photos above the dresser. Moonlight filtered in through the window, allowing him to recognize Billy's and Jason's faces in the pictures—all of which had hearts drawn around them, though the hearts around Billy's photos had been scribbled over.

Off to the side, separate from the others, a photo of Harry had a red X through it. So did Carol's photo. Mike focused on the photo of himself—a question mark and a heart had been drawn in the bottom corner of it. Alongside his picture was one of Sami, stuck to the wall with several steak knives. One of the knives pierced through Sami's heart, and *bastard child* was written across her abdomen.

"Crazy bitch," he muttered. He left the room and hurried back downstairs, keeping each step quiet. As he neared the last few stairs, a *thud* boomed from the dark corner at the bottom of the staircase. He froze, waiting and listening.

A huge cat shot out from the darkness, heading straight for Mike's face.

He jumped aside, trying to keep his balance.

The cat landed a few steps above him and hissed before darting away.

Mike placed a shaky hand over his pounding heart and clenched his jaw. "I can't believe the crazy fucking dog has a crazy fucking pet cat," he whispered, teeth clenched. He shook his head and continued down the stairs and through the living room, toward the back of the house.

A tall, shadowy figure appeared in the hallway, stopping Mike dead in his tracks. He ducked behind the living room wall and reached for his knife. Peering around the corner, he focused on the large man, recognizing his brother's silhouette. He relaxed and lowered the knife.

"Billy," Mike said in a quiet voice.

Billy whipped out his knife as he spun around, but quickly recoiled. "You scared the shit out of me," he whispered angrily.

"Upstairs is clear," Mike whispered back.

"That was fast. I haven't checked the kitchen yet."

Mike nudged past his brother and took the lead.

JASON CREPT warily around the side of the house, keeping a watchful eye in front of him and behind him. He stopped every few feet to scan the shadowed forest, sure a werewolf would jump out at any moment and eat him. But if he could save Sami first, dying would be worth it.

A loud *crunch* crackled under his shoe. He lifted his foot—shards of glass reflecting the moonlight were scattered in the grass next to a broken window. He pulled his cell phone from his pocket and turned on the flashlight. Then, he knelt and peered inside the dark space.

His eyes quickly scanned the dirty bathroom and flicked up to the red hue on the door. *NEED HELP—SAMI.*

"Sami," he said with relief, glad to have finally found her.

Wait. Is that blood she used to write her name with? He suddenly dreaded *how* he would find her. He shut the flashlight off on his phone and sprang to his feet. *"Please be alive, Sami. Please be alive!"* he chanted as he hurried around back.

He turned the corner and saw Sami's car sitting in the backyard, just outside the back door. "What the hell?" He leaned in through the open driver's window and snatched the keys from the ignition. He shoved them into his pocket, along with his cell phone, and hurried to the kitchen door.

"Shit. Locked," he said quietly. He checked the window next to the door, surprised when it slid open. "That's right, bitch," he whispered with a smug grin. He pulled back the curtain and eyed the kitchen, satisfied he could enter safely when nothing jumped out of the shadows to devour him as a snack.

A small shelf sat directly under the window. As quietly as he could manage, he pushed it aside until he had enough room to climb in. Throwing one leg over the sill, he wriggled his body through the window.

Once inside, he took a deep breath, but immediately gagged at the foul stench blasting his senses. Dirty dishes cluttered the counters and overflowed the sink. A partial package of raw hamburger, infested with buzzing flies, sat on a messy table in the middle of the room.

"Fucking disgusting!" Jason muttered. He swallowed back the urge to vomit, held his breath, and headed straight for the basement door in the left corner. He paused for a moment, wondering whether to stick to the plan and wait for the two angry brothers or to not waste any more time and rescue Sami.

With his heart pounding in his chest and the impulse to gag nagging the back of his throat, he pulled open the basement door, cringing through its loud *creak*. He peered down the dark stairway for any signs of claws, fangs, or red eyes. There were no monsters, but a light filtered from under a door at the bottom of the staircase.

Without another thought, he crept down the steps, freezing every time one of them squeaked.

The door at the top of the stairs creaked closed. Jason froze and held his breath, listening for growling but hearing nothing. One careful step at a time, he proceeded down the steps until he reached the door at the bottom.

A two-by-four barricaded the door. Jason lifted the board and set it aside before turning the knob.

"Of course, locked." He retrieved the knife from the back of his jeans and slid the blade between the door and the doorjamb, trying to work the lock free. It clicked and opened slightly.

"Well, son of a bitch," he whispered. With a smug grin and a firm grip on the knife, he pulled the door open.

SAMI SAT on the cot in the corner, trembling, staring at the ceiling, and listening to the soft thud of footsteps above her.

Oh no. She's back. What do I do? The clomping grew closer and louder with each step.

Maybe she can be killed when she is in her human form? Sami snatched a shard of glass from under the cot and hid it behind her back, praying Jessica wasn't there to kill her this time.

Something brushed up against the door, and the knob jiggled. A few seconds passed before the door finally opened.

Jason stepped in with a relieved look on his face. "Sami!"

"Jason?" Sami cried, wondering if she were dreaming.

"Thank, God!" Jason rushed to her side and pulled her into his arms.

Sami couldn't believe that one minute she had been preparing to die, and the next, she was being rescued. It all seemed surreal. Yet, she felt the warmth of his body, smelled the sweat on his shirt, and heard his heart thudding wildly in his chest. For the first time since the horrific ordeal had taken place, she felt safe. With tears streaming down her cheeks, she wrapped her arms around him, never wanting to let go.

Jason pulled away to look at her. His relieved expression turned into a sorrowful one. "Oh, Sami. What'd she do to you?"

"Just get me out of here" she pleaded, trying to control her sobs. "She said she's gonna kill me...as soon as the baby's born. She's gonna take my baby and tell you that it's hers and yours."

His eyes grew wide. "What? You mean you *are* pregnant?"

"Yeah, Jessica can smell that I am somehow," she answered, slightly humiliated.

"Crazy bitch!" He grabbed Sami's arm and helped her off the cot. "Do you know where she is now?" he asked on the way to the door. Poking his head around the doorway, he peered up the stairs.

"She went hunting," Sami said, limping behind him. "She said if she didn't, she'd have to kill me tonight. She can't control her rage when the moon is full."

"Okay, just stay behind me. Can you walk all right?"

She nodded. "Yeah, my ankle feels a little better than it did earlier."

"I wish I could carry you, Sami, but I'll need to defend you in case she shows up."

"It's okay, Jason." She wiped the tears away with the back of her hand and sniffed. "I'll be okay. I'm just glad you found me."

"Oh, there's something else. If anything happens to me, if she *gets* me, then you take this knife and drive it right through her heart!" He handed her the knife. "It's made of silver. It's the only thing that can kill her. I think."

Sami eyed the shiny blade. "Where'd you get it?"

"It's a long story." He glanced up the stairway again. "Okay, come on," he whispered and slowly ascended the stairs.

Sami clutched the back of his shirt and followed close behind.

Jason reached behind him and wrapped his hand around hers, giving her something other than his shirt to clench. "Don't worry, Sami. We'll get you out of here. I'll die before I let that crazy bitch lay another hand on you."

"Don't say that, Jason. I don't want you to die. Let's just try to live through this. *Please.*"

The thudding of footsteps stopped them dead in their tracks.

"Go back to the room," he whispered.

Squeezing his hand tighter, she did as instructed, pulling him along with her to keep him close.

They went inside the room, and Jason shut the door.

"Is it her?" Sami whispered.

"I don't know. It could be Billy and Mike, but I don't wanna take any chances."

"Billy's here?" she asked, anxious to see him.

"Yes. But we're all here to keep *you* safe. So, don't worry about him and do what I say. Lay back down on the cot. I'll hide over here." He pointed to a stack of boxes next to the door.

"No." She tightened her grip on his hand at the thought of being taken away again. "Please, let me stay with you."

Jason pulled his hand from hers, and his gaze softened. He brushed a loose lock of hair from her cheek and cupped the sides of her face with gentle hands. "I promise you, Sami, with all my heart, you'll be safe. Please trust me."

At that moment, Sami realized Jason still had feelings for her. She could see it in his eyes, hear it in his voice, and feel it in his touch. "I do trust you, Jason," she whispered, feeling awful she could never return the feelings the way he needed her to.

Jason lowered his hands and let out a quick sigh. "If it's her, I'll shoot. When she's distracted with me, you come up behind her with the knife and ram it deep between her shoulder blades as hard as you can. Then run upstairs and don't look back. I'll take care of the rest. Oh, and—" he shoved his hand into his pocket and pulled out a set of keys "—your cars out back. If it comes down to it, you leave us here and save yourself."

Sami's eyes widened and she shook her head.

"You have to—for the baby," Jason whispered in a firm tone and set the keys in her palm. "Billy's car is hidden close by. We'll be fine."

Sami shook her head again. The thought of leaving them to possibly die was unfathomable. Yet, so was the thought of putting her unborn baby in danger.

"Promise me you'll save yourself and the baby," Jason demanded with urgency.

Realizing there was no other choice, she reluctantly nodded. "I promise," she whispered and shoved the keys into her pocket. With fear coursing through her blood as the footsteps grew closer, Sami sat on the cot, while Jason ducked behind the boxes.

The knob turned, the door opened, and Billy stepped into view.

"Billy!" Sami cried.

Jason popped out from behind the boxes. "It's about time!"

Sami jumped up from the cot. The jarring sent a sharp pain through her ankle, and her foot gave out from under her.

Billy caught her and gathered her into his arms. "Sami! I'm so glad you're okay." He hugged her tightly and pulled his head back to face her. His brow furrowed and tears filled his eyes. "What'd that bitch do to you?"

Mike appeared in the doorway. "Come on, we have to get out of here before she gets back."

"Can you walk?" Billy asked Sami.

Sami shook her head and began to cry, partly from her hurt ankle, but mostly from the relief of knowing the horrific trauma she'd just endured was almost over. "No, I hurt it more when I jumped up just now. I'm sorry."

"Shhh," Billy soothed. "It's okay. You're gonna be okay now. I'll carry you." He pulled a knife out from behind his back. "You'll have to hold this and use it if you need to. All right?"

"Wait, I have another one," Mike said. He pulled a knife from his behind his back and handed it to her.

She took the knife and pointed behind her. "Jason, your knife is on the cot."

Billy tucked his knife back into his jeans and scooped Sami into his arms.

Jason snatched his blade from the cot, and they all headed upstairs. Mike led the way, and Jason trailed behind. When they reached the kitchen, there was still no sign of Jessica.

Sami gagged as the smell of death filled the air. She covered her nose and mouth with her shirt.

"Tell me about it!" Jason scowled with disgust.

Mike opened the kitchen door, and they hurried outside, stopping when they focused on Sami's car.

"How'd your car get here?" Billy asked.

"Jessica," Sami said with bitterness. She worked the keys from her pocket and held them out.

Jason snatched them up and opened the rear door for Billy before climbing into the driver's seat.

"Let's get the fuck outta here!" Mike opened the passenger door and jumped in.

Billy helped Sami into the back seat and slid in next to her. He carefully took the knife from her trembling hand and wrapped an arm around her. "I'm so sorry, Sami. I'm sorry I let this happen to you."

Jason shifted the car into reverse and slammed his foot on the gas, kicking up a cloud of dust. Then, he shifted into drive and crushed his foot to the pedal again, sending them speeding down the dark driveway.

"It's not your fault, Billy. You tried to stop her. All of you did. She's just a *monster*!" Sami sucked in an unsteady breath as tears stung her eyes again, but she held them back. "She said I was pregnant. That she could smell it somehow. She was gonna keep me alive for nine months, and then she was gonna cut our baby from my belly with my grandpa's hunting knife."

"What? You *are* pregnant?" Billy's mouth hung open. He reached over and placed his hand over her womb. "You mean, we *really* have a baby in there?"

She nodded, fearing his reaction. "Are you disappointed?"

Billy furrowed his brow. "Of course not, Sami." He leaned down and placed a gentle peck on her lips. "I love you," he whispered with his lips hovering above hers.

"I love you too," she whispered and threw her arms around his neck.

Billy gave her a gentle hug. "I'm afraid I might hurt you." He pulled away to inspect her wounds again, and anger slowly replaced the love in his eyes. "I can't believe she hurt you. I'm gonna kill that bitch!"

Mike glanced at Jason. "Just go straight to the hospital. We'll get Billy's car later. It's safer if we all stay together."

Jason nodded. He slowed at the end of the driveway and, without stopping, made a sharp left, squealing the tires.

With a secure arm around Sami, Billy clutched the back of the front seat. "Hey, slow down a little, will you? We just got her back!"

"Sorry, buddy," Jason stated calmly, "but I'm not taking any chances. I'm not slowing down 'til we reach town. So, I suggest you two buckle up."

Sami fastened her seatbelt and eyed the knife in Billy's hand. "My grandpa's knife looked just like that, but not as shiny. Jessica took it from him. She was gonna use it to cut our baby out of my belly."

Billy sighed and pulled her against his chest.

"We got those from Harry," Mike said as he turned to face her.

The glow of the dashboard lights and the moonlight filtering through the windshield allowed Sami to see Mike clearly.

"He told me it's the only thing that can kill a werewolf," Mike continued. "The one Jessica had wasn't made of silver."

Mike's words stung Sami's heart with betrayal. She pushed away from Billy to look Mike square in the eyes. "What? So, he *wasn't* crazy? All this time? It was all *true*? How long have you known? Why didn't you say anything sooner?"

Mike's eyes filled with remorse. "I didn't believe his werewolf story any more than you did when you visited him in the hospital. But I've known since the day he kidnapped Jessica. I was in the backyard one day when he was heading down his basement steps, carrying a large duffle bag. I asked him if he had a body in the bag, just messing around as usual. He opened it and pulled out a fistful of knives. He said he made them himself. All silver. When he told me it was the only thing that could kill werewolves, I was sure he was drunk.

"He insisted I take the knives to keep safe. I took them out of respect. I was gonna return them the next day when he'd sobered up. I never got a chance to because, later that day, I heard a woman's screams coming from his basement. The rest is history."

Sami's heart grew heavy. She felt awful for her grandpa—spending the last days of his life locked up like a crazy person with no one to believe him. And she felt awful for thinking Mike would put her in harm's way on purpose. She clenched her teeth to keep her chin from quivering. A tear escaped and rolled down her cheek.

"I'm sorry, Mike," she whispered.

Billy glared at his brother. His expression softened when he shifted his gaze back to Sami. "You have nothing to apologize for. All that matters now, is you're safe."

"But what if she comes after me again, Billy? She's out there somewhere," she said, pointing into the darkness. "She wanted *you.* She was obsessed with you until I came into the picture. So, she set her sights on Jason again. She was gonna stay out of sight for nine months, keep our baby, and tell Jason it was hers and that he was the father."

Mike's face puckered with disgust as he looked at Jason. "Please tell me you didn't."

Jason glared at him. "Dude, don't remind me! I'm sick enough about it as it is. It was before she started causing trouble. *And* it was before I knew she was a *dog.*"

"Gross, Jason!" Billy scowled. "So, you just overlooked the shithole she lives in? She probably doesn't even brush her teeth."

"Enough!" Jason snapped. "I didn't overlook anything! She smelled good and was clean when I saw her. And this was the first time I've been in her garbage dump of a home. Just let it go already!" He glanced at Sami through the rear-view mirror. "What else happened, Sami?" he asked, apparently trying to divert the attention away from himself.

Sami's gut knotted as her mom filled her thoughts. "She said that my mom is…" Her chin started to quiver. "That she's *dead.*" She buried her face in Billy's chest and cried.

"What?" Billy lifted her chin to look her in the eyes. "Your mom's not dead, Sami. She's alive. She's in the hospital."

She crinkled her brows together, sniffling. She turned to Mike and Jason for confirmation.

Mike nodded. "She's unconscious, but she's alive."

"What? Jessica told me that she d-died of a heart attack," she said, trying to control her sobs.

"No, Sami." Billy's voice was soothing. "But she has a concussion. She hasn't woken up yet."

"Did she even have a heart attack?" she asked.

"I don't know," Billy replied. "But she's alive."

Overcome with relief, a slight laugh escaped her lips. "Oh, I can't believe she's alive! I was so—" She shook her head. "It doesn't matter. I don't wanna think about it anymore. I just wanna see my mom!"

"That's exactly where we're taking you, Sami," Jason said. He sped even faster down the dark road.

21

THEY ALL breathed a sigh of relief when the lights of the small town came into view.

"Now, hurry up and get to the hospital," Billy said with a worried look on his face.

Sami rested her head on Billy's shoulder. "I'm okay. Just my ankle hurts is all," she said wearily and yawned.

"We don't wanna take any chances," Mike said. "You've been through a lot today, and in your condition, we need to make sure."

A jolt of pain shot deep inside Sami's lower abdomen. It was different from the dull ache she'd felt earlier. This one felt like a menstrual cramp, only more intense. Something was wrong with her baby. She tensed and tightened her hand around Billy's thigh, bracing herself on the seat with the other, silently trying to fight against the pain.

"What is it? What's the matter?" Billy asked, his voice lined with panic. "Sami? Is it your ankle? Is it the baby?"

As quickly as the pain hit, it subsided. She breathed a sigh a relief and smiled. "It's nothing. Just a little cramp."

"Cramp?" Billy looked at his brother. "Isn't that bad, Mike?"

Without giving him time to answer, he turned back to Sami. "Is it gone?"

"Don't worry." Mike turned around and looked at Sami. "We're almost there."

The pain struck again, but this time stronger—as if a muscle deep inside were being ripped in half. Sami moaned and doubled over. "Billy, it hurts!" she cried through clenched teeth.

"Sami?" Billy's voice shook.

"Shit!" Jason belted out. The engine rumbled louder, and the car sped up.

Sami knew she was losing the baby, but the intense pain overshadowed the looming heartbreak.

"Sami, just hold on," Billy said. "We'll be there in a minute. Just hold on." He hit the back of the driver's seat. "Come on, Jason. Get us to the frickin' hospital already!"

"I'm going as fast as I can go! Just hold on, Sami! We're almost there!"

She moaned again, gritting her teeth.

"Okay, we're here!" Mike said.

The car came to a screeching halt in front of the emergency door of the hospital.

Billy jumped out and scooped Sami into his arms.

She clutched her aching abdomen. The pain slowly dulled, giving her hope their baby would live. Exhausted, she relaxed her grip.

The automatic doors opened, and the bright lights consumed them.

WITH MIKE at his side, Billy rushed through the automatic doors and waited for the second set of doors to open. Though he'd just learned moments ago that the woman he loved was carrying his baby, the thought of losing the baby created an unbearable ache in his heart.

The doors opened, and they rushed inside to the front desk.

The woman sitting behind the desk stood. "What's wrong?"

The metal door behind the woman opened, and a nurse wearing

pink scrubs appeared.

"I think she's losing our baby," Billy's voice trembled, and tears filled his eyes. "Please help her."

Sami suddenly jerked and moaned, arching her back, and then went limp.

Fear shot through Billy's veins. "Sami?"

"Oh shit!" Mike said.

The nurse pushed a gurney through the door next to the desk.

"Is she gonna die?" Billy asked. "Please help her. Please don't let her die!" he pleaded desperately with tears rolling down his cheeks.

He draped Sami across the bed and took her motionless hand in his. "She was kidnapped and beaten. Please help her. Don't let her die." His voice quavered.

"You two will have to wait in the waiting room for now," the nurse said. She whisked Sami away through the double doors.

Billy clasped his hands behind his head and watched in horror as other medical staff rushed down the hallway toward Sami before the doors shut, blocking his view. He wanted to go to her. To be by her side. To save her. To save his baby. But he was absolutely powerless.

Jason rushed into the lobby. "Is she okay? What's going on?" he said, trying to catch his breath.

"We don't know," Mike said. "We have to wait out here for now."

Feeling helpless, Billy plodded through the empty waiting room. He slumped onto a chair along the wall and wiped his face dry with the bottom of his T-shirt. With his head down, he stared at the gray specks in the vinyl flooring.

Mike sat next to him.

Jason dropped onto the chair on the other side of Billy.

All three of them sat silently, deep in their own thoughts.

Though Billy had lost his faith in God after his parents' deaths, he couldn't help but pray for Sami and his unborn baby. *Please God...if you're there...please save Sami and our baby. Please don't take them from me like you did my mom and dad. I can't go through that kind of loss again. Take me if you have to, but don't take them.*

A tear rolled down his nose and fell to the floor. With a quick hand, he wiped away the wetness.

Jason lifted his head and cleared his throat, breaking the stillness of the melancholy moment. "I called Sheriff Briggs when I parked the car."

Billy creased his brow and gave Jason a stern look. "How in the hell is that gonna work out? Jessica's his niece. What if he's one too? He probably helped her plan the whole thing."

"The hospital will call him anyway. I gave him a quick rundown, and he believes us. There're deputies at his house right now, investigating. Apparently, he went home sometime after we hauled ass outta there. He saw the broken basement window and Sami's name written in blood on the door."

"What? Sami wrote her name in blood?" Billy's heart wrenched as he imagined what she must've went through—being scared and lonely, beaten and wounded, desperate to find a way to get help. He should've fought harder—found some way to have saved her in the forest. He swallowed hard, trying to keep his tears under control.

"Yeah, that's how I found her. Poor thing." Jason shook his head. "The sheriff claims he had no idea Sami was there or what Jessica was up to. He said he stays in a trailer behind the station most of the time and only stops by the house to check on Jessica every once in a while. But he hadn't been there in over a week."

Mike stood. He walked a couple of paces away before he stepped back toward them. "I think it's all bullshit! I think the sheriff knows what Jessica is. How could he have not suspected her in the first place?"

Jason shrugged. "Maybe he didn't know?"

"How can he not?" Billy snapped.

Jason nodded. "You're probably right. Good thing he didn't come home while we were still there. Who knows how it might've turned out. We all might've been locked up in the basement right now. Or better yet, thrown over a huge fire with sticks shoved up our asses and smothered in barbeque sauce," he said with disgust. "Anyway, Brenda's coming over to take our statements, and she has some information for us."

A nurse entered the waiting room. "She's awake now."

"Thank God!" Billy let out a heavy sigh. "Is she okay?"

"We're still running tests, but you all can go in and sit with her after the doctor has completed his examination. She's been asking for all of you."

Billy stood. "What about the baby?" he asked anxiously.

"Her pain has subsided, but we won't know any more until the doctor is done with his examination and the test results are back. He'll let you know more. I'll come back for you in a few minutes." She pushed back through the double doors and disappeared down the hallway.

The whooshing of the automatic doors caught Billy's attention. Deputy Brenda Cruz entered the waiting room. Though short in stature, she stood tall and proud—her usual meek demeanor taken over by pure confidence. Billy grew wary of her change in behavior.

"Hello, boys," Brenda said in a robust tone. "It's been one hell of a day, hasn't it? Let's go outside and talk."

Billy shot Mike a wary glance, wondering if they could really trust Brenda. She might be leading them right into Jessica's clutches. Then again, what choice did they have? Their only means of protection at the moment was, unfortunately, the sheriff's department.

Mike gave Billy a slight nod, and the three men followed the deputy outside.

Brenda headed over to a bench and propped her foot on it. "Now, tell me exactly what happened. Starting with you, Mike," she said, resting her notepad on her bent knee.

They all took turns explaining the horrific events that had taken place earlier that night. When they finished, she placed the pen back in her pocket and closed her notebook.

Brenda let out a long, heavy breath. "Well, I have some information for you as well. Sheriff Briggs saw what he thought was the wolf and shot it. But it turned out to be Jessica instead. She died from her wounds. We don't know why she was out there. The sheriff thought she might've been sleepwalking. He thought she'd outgrown it, but apparently not. Anyway, there is no sign of her being a *werewolf* or anything like it, and we'd like to keep it that way."

Shocked and confused, Billy opened his mouth to speak but Brenda didn't give him the chance.

"Yes, we know Jessica kidnapped Sami, but this talk of werewolves will get all of you locked up like Harry was or *worse*. The townspeople and the rest of the sheriff's department just thought they were hunting down an enormous, menacing wolf. So, you three and Samantha are just going to accept this for what it is—Jessica kidnapped Samantha out of revenge because she never mentally got over what Harry did to her, and then, she was accidentally shot in the forest. Do you understand? No one is ever going to know about the cutting the baby from her womb part."

"But we know what we saw!" Jason boomed and took a step toward Brenda, glaring down at her.

"Yes, I know," she said calmly. She took a step toward Jason, returning the combative stare. "But do you know how delusional you sound? Do you want to end up like Harry? There is no evidence of any *werewolf*, and there never will be! Do you understand what I'm telling you?" she asked in a warning tone.

Mike put his hand on Jason's shoulder and pulled him back to stand next to him. "He understands, Brenda. And so do we."

Brenda looked at Billy and waited for him to comply.

Billy clenched his jaw. "Right, there are no such things as werewolves," he replied cynically. "Can I go now? I wanna see how Sami's doing."

"Yes," Brenda said. "But you need to make her understand also. I'll be back in the morning to take her statement, and I had better like what I hear. Either way, her statement will be altered accordingly— like yours were."

"What?" Billy snapped. "If you're gonna write down whatever in the hell you want to, then why do you even need to talk to Sami?"

She eyed the three men and sighed. "You know, I'm not the bad guy here. My hands are tied, just like yours. I'm trying to protect you. It'd be easier if you'd cooperate."

"I'll talk to her," Billy said dryly.

"Good. Goodnight, boys. Hope Sami's feeling better." Without another word, Brenda headed to her squad car. She climbed in and sped away.

"I feel like I'm in some freakish horror story!" Billy threw his hands in the air.

"Tell me about it," Jason said.

Mike narrowed his eyes. "I'll tell you what, if the bitch isn't dead, she's gonna wish she was!"

"So, you don't really believe it either?" Billy asked.

"You shot her over and over. Jason shot her between the fucking eyes. It just pissed the bitch off," Mike said.

Jason swiped a hand across his forehead. "The same thing has been going through my mind too. But maybe you *can* kill a werewolf when they're in human form?" He shrugged.

Mike stared at Jason with a blank look. "Do you really think the *sheriff* mistook Jessica for the wolf while she was in *human* form? Or that he even shot her at all?"

Jason shook his head and ran his fingers through his hair. "No."

Billy suddenly felt helpless again. Jessica was powerful. And if her uncle and Brenda were werewolves too, they didn't stand a chance of keeping Sami safe. "Then what in the hell do we do? How do we protect her?"

"We kill Jessica!" Jason said bitterly.

Mike shook his head. "Actually, Brenda was bent on leading us to believe Jessica was dead. I think they want to keep their sick secret an *actual* secret. If she's not really dead, they'll make sure she stays away."

"I hope you're right," Billy said. "Otherwise, Jason's idea is the only other option." He turned around and strode back into the hospital.

Mike and Jason followed.

As soon as they reentered the waiting room, the nurse emerged through the double doors.

"You can see her now. I'll show you where it is."

SAMI'S HEART sank when Billy, Mike, and Jason entered her room, but she forced a slight smile for their sake.

"Sami." Billy's eyes lit up, and he rushed to her bedside. "Are you okay? Do they know anything yet?" He wrapped his hand around hers.

She began to fidget with Billy's forefinger, fighting the urge to cry. "The baby's…gone," she whispered through a frown and a quick sob escaped, followed by more.

"What?" Billy grimaced and tears dripped from his eyes. He pulled her into his arms.

Jason sank into one of the chairs, and Mike in the other. They both lowered their heads and wiped their eyes.

"I'm so sorry, Billy!" she cried against his chest. "I tried to stay safe for our baby. I tried. I did everything she told me to. I'm sorry."

"It's not your fault, Sami. It's not. It was Jessica." Billy held her tighter. "I wish I'd killed the bitch myself!" he snapped.

Confused, she pushed away just enough to look him in the eyes. "What? You mean she's dead?" She sniffed.

"Yeah, she's dead. Sheriff Briggs shot her in the forest near his house. He thought she was a wolf," Billy said.

"What? I can't believe it! You mean it's all over? She'll never hurt me again?"

Billy nodded and his pained look turned into a serious expression. He wiped his face dry on his sleeves and looked at Jason. "Will you close the door?"

Jason shot Billy a knowing look and crossed the room.

"What's going on?" Sami asked warily.

Billy cleared his throat. "There's more…," he said, his voice somber.

She listened carefully while Billy, Mike, and Jason took turns telling her about Brenda's warnings. They explained the importance of keeping the secret and what would happen if they didn't.

Since the day she'd moved to Wolf Hill, Sami had felt there was something more sinister to the creepy town. All along, the nightmares and being afraid of wild animals in the forest, it had all been for good reason. She hadn't been childishly overreacting. Every day she had been on the verge of death, being stalked by a deadly beast, and she'd had no idea. She wondered if there were any more of them out there—whether or not they were truly safe yet.

"Do you think Sheriff Briggs and Brenda are like Jessica?" she asked. "Are *they* werewolves?"

"No," Billy said. "He was just protecting Jessica. He was just protecting her secret."

"Yeah," Mike said. "The sheriff hasn't shown any signs of being like Jessica and neither has Brenda. They've always been good people."

"Yeah, we're sure he was just keeping the fact that his niece was a *dog* a secret," Jason added.

Their reassuring words brought little comfort to ease her fear. Sheriff Briggs's niece was dead, and for some reason, Sami felt at fault. "So, you don't think he'll come after me?"

"What?" Billy said incredulously. "No. Of course not. You didn't do anything wrong. You're a victim in all this, Sami. The sheriff knows that. He doesn't blame you for anything."

"So, I'm just supposed to lie, and if I don't, I'll be locked away like my grandpa was even though it's all true?" She started to cry again as her heart went out to her grandpa.

"I'm sorry, Sami. But please, *please* don't say anything," Billy pleaded. "I can't lose you again. You have to give me your word."

"I promise," she said softly. She reached up and caressed his cheek with the back of her fingers. "I don't wanna lose you again either."

"I thought I'd never see you again," he admitted with a husky voice and gave her a gentle peck on the lips. "I love you so much."

"I love you too, Billy," she said softly. "I'm sorry about our baby."

"Me too," he whispered.

Sami suddenly thought of her mother. "Oh, my mom is okay. The doctor said she's awake, and she's gonna be okay. She's going home tomorrow."

The corners of Billy's lips curled upward slightly, but his eyes still reflected pain. "That's great news."

"Yeah, we were so worried about her," Jason said.

Sami's enthusiasm slowly dissipated. No matter how hard she tried to be happy on the outside, on the inside, she was devastated. She couldn't get past the emptiness inside of her. She wanted her baby back. Billy's baby.

She laid her head on the pillow and placed her hands over her abdomen. Tears filled her eyes. She shut them tight, trying to prevent them from falling, but it didn't help. The tears kept falling, and the grief in her heart kept growing.

"I just wanna be alone now," she whispered with a trembling chin.

Billy frowned, and his eyes glistened with moisture.

Mike left the room.

"Sami, are you sure?" Jason asked with a worried look. "You shouldn't be alone."

Mike reentered the room with a nurse right behind him.

The nurse went to Sami's bedside. "Would you like something to help you sleep now?"

Though Sami had refused the medication earlier, she nodded. She wanted to sleep. She needed to sleep. She felt mentally, physically, and emotionally depleted.

Billy kissed Sami on the forehead. "I'll be back in the morning, okay?"

"What?" Sami cried out. "No. Not *you*, Billy. Please don't leave me," she begged desperately. She looked at the nurse. "Please let him stay."

The nurse nodded as she injected the medicine into the intravenous drip. "As long as you rest."

Billy brushed the hair back from Sami's forehead. "I'll stay, Sami. I just thought you wanted me to leave you alone."

On her way out of the room the nurse looked at Mike and Jason. "I can only let one person stay. You two will have to leave. She'll be discharged in the morning."

Jason nodded. "I know. I'm going." He went to Sami's bedside. "Well, I guess we'll be back tomorrow. I'm so sorry about everything, Sami." Tears filled his eyes. He bent down and pressed his lips to her forehead.

"I know." She sniffled.

Jason let out a dismal sigh. He gave Billy a couple of firm pats on the shoulder and left the room.

Mike stepped to the foot of the bed, his eyes reflecting sadness. "I'll see you two in the morning. Get some rest." He headed out the door.

"Night, bro," Billy called out to him.

Calmness settled throughout Sami's body. "I think the medicine's working."

Billy gave her a soft smile. "Then close your eyes and rest. I promise I won't leave your side all night. I'll be here in the morning when you wake up. Okay? I love you."

"Okay." Sami yawned, feeling safe and loved. Feeling warm and happy. "I love you too," she whispered and closed her eyes.

JASON AND Mike made their way out of the hospital, through the dark parking lot, and to Sami's car. Jason climbed into the driver's seat and stared out the windshield.

Mike sat on the passenger's side, staring at him. "Well? Are we leaving or what?"

"Hell no! We're staying! I'm not leaving here until I know Sheriff Briggs isn't a threat to Sami. At least this way we're close by. Just in case."

"Huhhh," Mike groaned through a heavy sigh. "I don't feel comfortable leaving them all night either. Not until we're sure the danger's gone."

It was quiet for a minute before Mike spoke again. "Santa Cruz sure is sounding good about now."

"What? Santa Cruz?" Jason asked.

"Yeah, that's where Megan moved to. She couldn't stand it here anymore. She and her best friend from high school are rooming together. Billy and I just visited her a few weeks ago. It's nice down there. Different though. I think I'd miss the forest too much."

"Huh, I was wondering where she'd disappeared to. I hadn't given it much thought with everything that's been going on lately."

Jason's lips curled into a cocky grin. He thought back to the last time he'd seen Megan and how hot she had looked. *Especially the way her tight jeans hugged her plush rounded—*

"You better not be thinking what I think you're thinking!" Mike warned.

"What the hell are you talking about?" Jason smirked. "Dude, you need some sleep. You're paranoid."

"I'll give you paranoid. Just close your eyes and fall asleep. I *dare* you!"

"Whatever, dude," Jason let out a devious titter and climbed over the back of the seat. "I get the back seat. Wake me if you hear the sheriff howling."

Mike locked the front doors and leaned the passenger seat back. He shifted against it before settling down.

Jason followed Mike's lead, locking the back doors. "Damn werewolves," he mumbled as he laid back down and closed his eyes.

A loud banging jolted through the silence. Mike and Jason sat up, their wide eyes focusing on Sheriff Briggs standing at the driver's window.

"Dammit!" Jason clutched his chest. "I've had enough frickin' fear for one day," he whispered through gritted teeth.

"Stay inside," Mike whispered. He opened the passenger door and climbed out to face Sheriff Briggs over the roof of the car.

Jason scooted to the window closest to the sheriff and rolled it down halfway. "Sheriff." He gave a quick nod and gulped. Spotting a silver knife on the floorboard, he inconspicuously leaned forward and picked it up, keeping it out of the sheriff's sight.

"Sheriff," Mike greeted, sounding as calm as ever.

"You boys might be more comfortable at home in your own beds, don't you think?" Sheriff Briggs asked.

"We're tired, and we have to be back here first thing in the morning anyway to pick up Billy and Sami," Mike said.

"Yeah." Jason peered up through the window. "We thought we'd kill two birds with one stone, you know?" He clenched his jaw, wishing he could kick himself. *Why in the hell did I have to say the word* kill *in front of a probable werewolf?* He looked up at the sheriff and cleared his throat. "You know, it's easier this way and all."

"So, what brings you here this late, Sheriff?" Mike asked.

Sheriff Briggs eyed Jason, then, Mike. "Just wanted to make sure we were clear on Brenda's instructions. I wouldn't want the whole town going around thinking you all had the same sickness Harry was troubled with."

"Oh, we're clear," Mike said. "But we wanna be sure it all ends here with no further complications. Just in case *you* have the same sickness *Jessica* was troubled with."

Jason gulped, repositioning his hold on the knife.

Sheriff Briggs smirked. "I know what you're thinking, Mike, but don't you worry. I was just sort of Jessica's *guardian*, so to speak. I never meant for any of this to happen. I really thought she was developing more control over her *impairment*. I thought bringing her to an out-of-the-way place like Wolf Hill would've been a good thing for her."

"You mean like relocating a city dog to a farm, so it can roam freely?" Jason said, his voice dripping with sarcasm. He immediately realized his huge mistake. "Sorry, wrong analogy. I'm just tired. It's been a long day." He cleared his throat again.

Mike peered into the backseat and his eyes narrowed in warning.

Jason flashed a sheepish grin at Mike and rolled his window back up in an attempt to lie low for a while.

"Anyway," Sheriff Briggs continued, "is *everyone* clear on all this?"

"Everyone," Mike said, his tone flat.

"Good. And I am truly sorry about everything. But what was I to do? Jessica *is* family, after all." Sheriff Briggs smiled.

"You mean she *was* family," Mike said, his voice lined with suspicion.

"What?" Sheriff Briggs furrowed his brow.

"Oh, shit," Jason whispered.

"It's not important," Mike said. "I just meant I'm sorry you suffered a loss too."

"Oh." Sheriff Briggs gave a slight nod. "You're right. She *was* family."

Jason didn't like the lack of grief in Sheriff Briggs's tone. It meant either the sheriff didn't care that his niece was dead, or that she was still alive.

"Well, I'll let you two get some sleep." Sheriff Briggs tapped on the hood.

Jason jumped at the clunking and clutched his knife even tighter.

"Sheriff," Mike said, ending his part in the conversation.

"I'll be seeing you boys around." Sheriff Briggs headed to his car.

Without moving a muscle, Mike kept an eye on the sheriff until he hopped in his squad car and drove out of sight.

"Bastard gives me the frickin' creeps now!" Mike slid onto the front seat and shut the door.

Jason lay comfortably in the back seat again. "Yeah, you and me both."

"And what the hell, Jason?" Mike boomed.

"What the hell, what?" Jason boomed back.

"You've gotta control that bratty mouth of yours sometimes! I thought for sure we were gonna be *steaks* tonight!" Mike snapped, staring down at him over the seat.

"Yeah, well, it's done and over with. And dude, did you have to say *steaks*? I've been starving all night."

Mike laid back against the reclined seat and rested his arm across his eyes. "See you at *breakfast*. I think I'm gonna have some bacon and eggs in the morning."

Jason grew irritated. "You are such a bitch! That's all right. I was just getting ready to dream about *Megan* anyways."

"Go ahead, then. Fall asleep," Mike warned.

"I think I will!" Jason challenged, closing his eyes.

Finally, all was silent between them.

Jason lay on the back seat, staring up at the roof, wondering whether or not Mike would actually do anything to him if he fell asleep—like write on his face with a permanent marker or cut off a chunk of his hair. He seriously doubted it, but he couldn't be sure. He lay quietly until Mike's steady breathing filled the silence. But even that wasn't enough for him to rest easy. Jason fought through the exhaustion for as long as he could, blinking rapidly to keep his eyes open until Mike's steady snoring reached his ears. Dead tired, he closed his eyes and drifted to sleep.

22

SAMI OPENED her eyes, glad to see Billy smiling down at her.

"Good morning." She smiled and yawned.

A dull ache in her jaw yanked her from her grogginess, reminding her exactly where she was and what had happened. Her heart grew heavy, but she was adamant on being strong.

She pushed the feeling aside. "Didn't you sleep?"

"I slept. I just woke up when the doctor came in. He said you can go as soon as the nurse gets your discharge papers ready."

She noticed Mike and Jason slouched in the chairs along the opposite wall, sleeping peacefully.

Billy smiled halfway. "They snuck in early this morning. I guess it was too cold in the car. I had to beg the nurse to let them stay. You should've seen the look on her face when she came in and saw them passed out."

"They slept in the car?"

"Yeah, they were worried. So how do you feel this morning?" He pulled the back of her hand to his lips and kissed it.

"I feel a little better now that I've rested. *Empty*, but better than I did last night."

He gave her a loving smile. "Good. I'm glad you feel a little better. Are you ready to get dressed? The nurse should be back soon."

"More than ready." She shoved the covers aside and sat up slowly, trying to push through the pain of her tender bruises and aching muscles.

Billy retrieved some clothes from the nearby cabinet and handed them to her. He motioned with his head toward Jason and Mike. "I sent them back to the house a little while ago to get some clean clothes for you. They're actually my clothes. They tried to get into your house, but it was locked."

"That was nice of them."

Billy nodded. "Do you need me to carry you?"

"No. My ankle feels a lot better than it did last night. I'm just a little sore."

She climbed out of bed with Billy's help and limped to the bathroom, closing the door behind her.

The light flickered on, and she stared into the mirror, shocked by her reflection. There were bruises on her forehead, cheeks, and arms. A scrape on the right side of her forehead. And a cut over her left brow, one high on her right cheekbone, and another in the corner of her mouth. She set the clothes on the counter and lifted her gown to just under her breasts. Her ribs were also spotted with hues of black and blue.

The cuts and bruises didn't really matter though. They'd heal soon.

She eyed her abdomen and ran a hand over its flat surface. Though she'd barely realized yesterday that it had been full of life, today it felt empty. Grief filled her heart from the void she now felt. She sighed and let her gown fall loosely about her hips again.

She turned on the faucet and splashed water on her face to wash away the sadness. Today was the start of a new beginning—the first day of her new life in Wolf Hill—free from Jessica's evil manipulation once and for all. And, no matter what it took, she was going to stay strong for her own sake—as well as Billy's.

When she finished changing into the oversized gray sweatpants and navy T-shirt, she forced her lips into a smile and went back into the room.

"They're a little big." She raised her arms out to her sides and let them flop against her hips.

Billy grabbed the drawstring of her pants, pulled it tight, and secured it with a knot. He stepped back and gave her a once-over. "I like you in my clothes." He winked.

She smiled. "They're cozy."

He bent down and picked up her sneakers. "Here you go."

Sami sat on the bed and worked a shoe over each foot.

Mike stirred and stretched, accidentally hitting Jason in the chest.

"What?" Jason jerked and sat up straight while frantically looking around. "Where's my gun?"

"It's still in Billy's car." Mike smirked.

Jason finally grasped his surroundings and narrowed his eyes at Mike. "I know."

Sami snickered, capturing their attention. They both smiled at her.

"You look much better this morning," Jason said. He crossed the room and gave her a gentle hug. "Sorry, I couldn't help it. I'm just glad you're alive and all." He stepped back and shoved his hands in his pockets.

Sami smiled. "Thank you, Jason. That's exactly what I needed."

"Good," Mike said as he crossed the room. He also gave her a hug, but it ended up being more like a quick pat on the back with both hands. "'Cause I can't help it either."

"Come on, guys. She's gonna smell now. Get off my girlfriend," Billy said and raised one corner of his mouth.

"So, now you're ready to admit she's your girlfriend, huh?" Mike teased.

A nurse walked in holding a clipboard. "Well, I'm glad to see you're all feeling better." She smiled and pointed to the form attached to the clipboard. "Just sign here and here, and you're all set. You're free to go.

"Oh—" she set a small paper bag on top of the clipboard "—these are to help you sleep. Just take one before bedtime if you need to. The other medication is in here too. You'll need to follow up with your doctor in a few days. The pain medication administered through your IV will be wearing off soon, if it hasn't started to already. After that, you can take ibuprofen for your pain. The instructions are all in the paperwork."

Sami snatched the bag and tucked it under her arm. Then, she took the clipboard and signed on the yellow highlighted lines before handing it back to the woman.

"Take it easy for the next few days." The nurse patted Sami's arm and left the room.

Sami eased off the bed and looked at the three men towering over her. They were still smiling. She'd never seen them smile so much. They were obviously trying to boost her spirits. She smiled back at them to ease their worries. But, on the inside, she was still crying.

"Ready?" Billy asked.

She nodded. "I wanna see my mom before we go, but she doesn't know about—*you know*." She placed her hands over her abdomen.

Their smiles faded, and they nodded.

"I don't want her to know—*ever*." She eyed them carefully.

"But, Sami," Billy said, "she's your mom. She'll understand."

"No!" Sami said firmly. "I don't want her to know. She'll just worry, and I'll never hear the end of it." She looked at them with pleading eyes. "*Please*. I just wanna try to put all of this behind me."

Billy hugged her. "Don't worry, we won't say anything. Come on." He grabbed her hand. "Let's go see your mom."

Feeling safe with her hand tightly in Billy's, she limped down the deserted hall, around the corner, and into her mother's room. Her mom was propped up in bed, with Steve sitting in the bedside chair.

"Samantha!" Her mother's tired eyes brightened over her pale skin. But she frowned when she focused on Sami's battered face. Tears welled, and she held out her arms.

"Hi, Mom." Sami smiled, trying her hardest to remain strong and not cry. She went to her mother and sank into her arms. The simple action of bending down sent an ache through her abdomen. She bore through the pain with clenched teeth and used the bed as support to push away from her mom's tight grasp.

Carol frowned again. "Sweetheart, your face." She looked down at Sami's legs. "And you're limping? What'd she do to you?"

"It looks worse than it feels." Sami lied to save her mother from further worry.

Carol sighed. "I'm so sorry I moved you here. I talked to your dad, and we think it'd be best if you went back to Monterey. At least for a couple of weeks, to give you a chance to heal. But we're hoping you'll want to stay there."

"What?" Sami was tired of her parents treating her like a child. "I'm not leaving, Mom. Jessica's dead. She can't hurt me anymore."

Her mother nodded. "It's okay. I just thought you'd want to leave after everything that's happened. It was just a thought is all."

"Okay," Sami replied in a wary tone, not expecting her mother to relent so easily.

Carol glanced at everyone before she spoke again. "Well, I'm glad we don't have to worry about that wolf anymore." She shook her head. "I don't remember anything that happened the other night. But, apparently, I left the front door open. The wolf snuck into the house and scared me half to death. I must've hit my head and knocked myself out." She reached up and felt the side of her head and winced. "I am so glad they shot it."

Sami was confused. If her mother was told a wolf had gotten into the house, then she must not know about Jessica being a werewolf or that werewolves even exist. Just to make sure, she reiterated the issue.

"So, it was a *wolf* that got into the house?"

Her mom nodded. "But you don't have to worry about it anymore. Sheriff Briggs said they got it, and they even matched up the prints from before. It was the same wolf you'd seen in the forest."

Steve stood. "Yep. It was in the forest near Sheriff Briggs's place. He said it was the biggest wolf he'd ever seen. That's how the accident happened." His voice deepened. "He was shooting at the wolf, when Jessica got in the way. They think she was sleepwalking." He lowered his head, obviously saddened by Jessica's demise.

Jason stared at Steve as if he wanted to rip his head off. He shook his head. "I gotta get some fresh air. I'll be in the car."

"Wait up," Mike called after Jason. He went after him but stopped in the doorway. "I'm glad you're okay, Carol. I'll see you at home."

"Thank you, Mike." She smiled.

Mike gave a quick nod and continued on his way.

"Well, Mom, I'm gonna go too. I'm getting really hungry," Sami admitted. "I'm so glad the wolf didn't hurt you."

"Me too, sweetheart. I'll see you in a little bit. Here—" Carol handed her some crackers from the bedside tray "—take these. I don't want you to get carsick."

"Thanks, Mom." Sami gave her mom another hug but wished she hadn't once she bent over again. "I'll see you at home." With only a slight limp, she walked out of the room and into the hallway.

The brightly lit hall had been empty on their way to her mother's room. But now, it was full of questioning eyes, all focused on her face. Sami averted her gaze to the floor, trying to ignore the stares. She could hear her mom talking to Billy, but with all the hallway noise, their voices were muffled. After what seemed to be the longest, uncomfortable moment of her life, Billy emerged from the room.

He immediately noticed the unwanted gawking. Making eye contact with one middle-aged man, Billy subtly shook his head. The man quickly looked away and went about his business.

Though she was humiliated about her appearance, Sami felt safe with Billy. He placed a protective arm around her and guided her out of the hospital. As she limped along, she used him as a crutch to ease the pain of her throbbing ankle and aching insides. Thankfully, Jason had pulled her car up to the front curb just outside the automatic doors. Mike was up front with Jason.

Billy opened the back door and she eased onto the seat. After the longest twenty four hours of her life, they were finally on their way home.

Sami dug into the paper bag the nurse had given to her and found some ibuprofen samples. She ripped open two packets and shook three pills onto her palm—enough to equal six hundred milligrams.

"Does anyone have some water?"

Mike handed her a water bottle.

"Thanks." She popped the tablets into her mouth and washed it down with the water.

"Are you in a lot of pain?" Billy asked.

"Some," she replied.

"I'm sorry." He frowned.

"I'll be okay." She smiled to lessen his worry. Then, she opened the package of crackers and took a bite.

"If it's all right with you, Sami—" Jason glanced in the rear-view mirror "—I thought I'd stop at the diner and get everyone some breakfast to go."

"Sure, that sounds good, Jason."

"Good, because I'm starving." He pulled into the parking lot of the diner and parked in front of the door.

Mike climbed out of the car and shut the door.

Jason followed Mike's lead, but before he shut his door, he peered at Sami. "Any special requests?"

"Just some toast," Sami said.

Jason nodded and hurried into the diner.

"Just toast? Are you sure?" Billy asked with a worried look on his face.

"I'm not really that hungry. I think the crackers filled me up."

"Okay." Billy unbuckled his seatbelt and scooted next to Sami. He wrapped an arm around her and sighed. "I have something to talk to you about."

Sami remained silent, dreading what she was about to hear. *Is it about Jessica? Is she still alive? I saw the bullet hole Jason put in her vanish with my own eyes. How could the sheriff's bullet have killed her? Or, maybe Billy had time to reflect on the whole baby scare and thinks we should take a break from each other?*

"Uhhh." Billy gulped. "Your mom talked to me before I left her room. If you wanna get out of town for a while, I'll come with you."

Sami's fears were quickly dissolved with anger. "What? My mom is relentless! I can't believe she'd go behind my back and try to get me to leave town in any way she could. Ugh." She shook her head. "I'm so tired of her treating me like a child."

"She just wants to make sure you're gonna be okay. You know, like taking a vacation from all the stress."

Sami pondered the idea, imagining being on the beach again, enjoying the ocean and the fresh salty breeze with Billy at her side. Her tension lessened, and she let out a sigh.

"I guess it wouldn't be so bad as long as you were with me. But you have to *stay* with me. At my dad's house, I mean. That's the condition," she said.

Billy smiled and gave her a soft peck on the lips. "I wouldn't have it any other way. I just hope your dad doesn't mind."

"If he wants me to visit, then he doesn't have a choice. But I think you'd have to stay in the guest bedroom."

"I guess it's set then. When do you wanna leave?"

She glanced at her reflection in the rear-view mirror and frowned. "Maybe in a week? I'd like to give my face a chance to heal a little first."

"Yeah, we'd have a lot of explaining to do everywhere we went, huh?"

"There'll be a lot of questions around here too. Maybe we could just say I was in a car accident. You know, so I don't have to relive the nightmare over and over. Besides, we're not allowed to tell anyone the truth anyway."

"A car accident it is then."

"But I don't wanna visit any acquaintances while we're there. Just my dad. And maybe I can meet your sister?"

"Anything you want, Sami. I just want you to be happy again," he whispered. He gazed into her eyes and released a heavy breath.

Sami knew she wasn't fooling him. He could see right through the charade masking her pain. And, from the dismal look in his eyes, he was hurting too. They had both suffered a great loss and were heartbroken—all because of Jessica.

Sami let out a long sigh. No matter how much she tried to take the sheriff's word for it, she just couldn't shake the thought of Jessica possibly being alive. "So, do you really think she's dead?"

She didn't give him a chance to speak. "You and Jason both shot her, and the bullet holes just healed. How could Sheriff Briggs's bullet have killed her?"

"Maybe he shot her while she was in human form? Maybe she can die that way?" he replied.

Sami wasn't so sure, but she nodded anyway.

Billy studied her face before his eyes softened. "Sami, after what I saw yesterday, I know anything is possible. *But*, Sheriff Briggs *did* say he killed her. I don't think he'd go around telling everyone his niece had died if she was just gonna show up again. He took care of her somehow. She can't hurt you anymore. Okay?"

His sincerity eased her worries. She nodded again, but this time she meant it. "Okay." She snuggled against his chest.

Billy kissed her on top of the head and rested his chin there.

Feeling safe in his arms, Sami closed her eyes, allowing her body and mind a moment of much-needed rest.

When Mike and Jason returned with the food, they headed home.

Mike handed the bags to Billy over the back of the seat.

"Damn, dude." Billy crinkled his forehead as he took the bags and set them on the seat next to him. "You *are* hungry, aren't you? It looks like you ordered enough food for lunch and dinner too."

Jason glanced into the rear-view mirror. "Well, I know you only wanted some toast, Sami, but Mike and I thought maybe you'd change your mind later. You know, 'cause you're a woman," he replied earnestly.

She smiled and shook her head. Normally, she'd be offended by the sexist remark. But not coming from Jason. He had an innocent charm about him that always seemed to lift her spirits.

"Yeah," Mike added, "we weren't sure what you'd like so we got a little of everything."

"You mean a *lot* of everything," Billy said.

"We should have enough for the entire day," Jason added. "Better to have too much than not enough, right? Besides, I'm starving."

Mike looked at Jason. "I told you that you ordered too much."

"Hey, you were the one going on about steaks and bacon and eggs last night. Dumbass!" Jason glared at him.

Mike smirked.

"You two sound like you're married," Billy teased.

"You better watch it, smartass." Mike raised his eyebrows in warning.

"Yeah, you'll go hungry," Jason added.

Sami snickered at their silly banter, but her smile faded as heaviness filled her heart. "I don't know what I'd do without all of you. I don't think I'd be handling everything as well. You guys are the best friends ever. Thank you for saving me." She swallowed to hold back the tears.

"Aw, Sami," Jason said with a soft tone. "You've brought so much to our empty, misguided lives since you've been here. *You're* the one who saved *us*."

Billy held her close. "He's right. You don't have to thank us. And everything's gonna be better from now on. I promise."

"I'm gonna hold you to that promise," she replied, hoping he was right.

"Well then, Mike promises," Billy teased. "But I'm gonna try my hardest."

"Hey, wait a minute," Mike said. "Don't put all the pressure on me."

"Don't worry, Sami. I've got your back." Jason winked at her in the rear-view mirror.

"Suck-up," Mike said. "Why don't you just shut your pie hole and drive?"

"Yeah, just shut up and drive," Billy agreed.

Jason grinned and sped up.

When they arrived back at Sami's house, they all sat at the kitchen table and ate before they parted ways to shower and rest. Billy stayed with Sami. He insisted on staying until her mom returned home.

Sami didn't object. She didn't even want him to leave when her mother finally did return, but knew he needed to shower and rest too.

"I'll see you in a little while," Billy promised as he stepped outside and pulled the door shut behind him.

Sami gave her mother a hug—which wasn't painful anymore thanks to the medicine. "I'm glad you're okay, Mom."

"I'm glad *you're* okay, sweetheart." Carol's eyes roamed Sami's face and she frowned.

"Stop already. You're gonna give me a complex," Sami grumbled.

"I know. I'm sorry. I'll keep it to myself. So—" Carol sank into the recliner "—did Billy have a chance to talk to you yet?"

Sami eased onto the couch. "Yes, he did."

"And?"

"And he said he'd go with me to Monterey if I changed my mind," she answered casually.

"And?" Her mother persisted with an impatient tone.

"*And* I agreed on one condition—only if Billy gets to stay at Dad's house with me." Sami pretended to inspect her fingernails to avoid seeing the look of shock on her mother's face. Her parents were so overprotective, she'd never been allowed to have a boy visit her in her home—let alone have a grown man stay the night.

"In the guest bedroom," Carol replied.

Sami pursed her lips in an attempt to conceal her grin. All she'd wanted over the past couple of years was for her mother to start treating her like an adult. To let her make her own decisions. And it was finally starting to happen. Slowly, but it was a start.

"Yes, of course, in the guest bedroom."

"I'll call your father later and let him know when to expect you."

"In about a week, after I've had a little time to heal. Oh, and I don't wanna make this a big reunion or anything. So, no visitors. I just wanna see Dad and get away from here for a while."

"I understand, sweetheart. I'll make sure your father keeps quiet about your visit."

"Good, but what about you? I feel bad about leaving you here all alone after everything that's happened, Mom."

"Don't worry about me. I can take care of myself. Besides, Mike and Jason are close by. And I have Steve," she added quietly.

Sami saw the uncertainty in her mother's eyes. But, after all Sami had been through, Steve was the least of her worries now.

"Yeah, I guess you're right. I won't worry then," Sami said.

A subtle smile crossed Carol's face, and she yawned. "I have to lie down and get some rest. My schedule is all turned around now. I'm so exhausted." She rose from the recliner, and her hand went to the side of her head. "And my headache is coming back. I need to take some more medicine."

"Okay, Mom. Feel better."

"Thank you, sweetheart," Carol said on her way down the hall.

Sami stepped out onto the front porch for some fresh air. The cloudless sky was a mesmerizing deep blue today, and a warm, gentle breeze comforted her broken soul. She sat on the cushioned wicker loveseat to enjoy the peaceful day. Gazing dreamily at the trees, she watched them sway gently in the wind.

The hum of a car's engine pulled Sami from her trance. A silver Mercedes convertible with the top up stopped in front of the house, and a woman climbed out.

Sami held her breath, wondering if she should be afraid of the stranger. After her horrific ordeal with Jessica, she didn't know who she could trust anymore.

She studied the woman, whose shoulder-length blonde hair shone brightly in the sunlight. She wore a wispy white blouse with a pair of tight jeans. Eyeing her fancy black heels, Sami knew the stranger wasn't from the area.

"Hello!" The woman beamed with a cheery smile, instantly putting Sami's uneasiness at rest.

Sami remembered her battered appearance and cowered inwardly, wishing she could run into the house to hide her face. Instead, she took a stress-relieving breath and raised a hand to silently say hello.

The woman unsteadily made her way over the patchy grass. She reached the bottom of the porch steps, her blue-eyed gaze appearing unfazed by Sami's appearance.

"My name is Abigail Mercer. I just moved into town, and I'm looking for the Holden residence. I need some work done on the house I just bought."

Sami smiled halfway. "I'm Samantha. Or just Sami. The Holdens live next door. I'll walk you over there."

"Thank you. That's so nice of you, Sami."

Even though the pain in her ankle was barely noticeable, Sami didn't want to take any chances. She eased herself down the steps, using the railing for support. Together, they headed next door.

When they reached the gravel driveway, Abigail stumbled.

"Whoa, I guess I should've worn more comfortable shoes," she said.

Sami extended her arm out to Abigail. "Yeah, I had that same problem when I first moved here."

"Thank you." Abigail grabbed Sami's arm and they continued on.

"Um, Sami, can I ask you something personal?" Abigail asked.

"Sure, I think," Sami replied warily. She couldn't imagine what kind of personal question a mere stranger would be so bold to ask.

They stepped up onto the porch.

"Can I ask what happened to you? I feel like I should be helping *you* across the yard."

Humiliated, Sami's free hand cupped her bruised cheek. "I know. I must look pretty frightening."

The screen door opened, and Billy stepped out. "She was in a car accident," he said smoothly, eyeing the stranger and placing a protective arm around Sami.

"Billy, this is Abigail…." Sami's voice trailed off, and she pressed her lips closed, trying to remember Abigail's last name.

"Mercer." Abigail smiled and extended her hand to Billy. "Abigail Mercer. Most people just call me Abby. Hello, Billy. It's nice to meet you."

Billy hesitated and briefly shook her hand.

Sami put her arm around Billy's waist, feeling the hard bulge of a knife tucked into the back of his jeans.

"I just moved to town, and someone told me you and your brother do excellent remodeling work. So, I was just wondering if I could hire you to fix up my house?" She smiled.

"Oh…well…" Billy sighed and thought for a moment. "I'm going out of town soon, but let me get my brother for you." He pulled the screen door open and stuck his head inside.

"Mike, there's someone here to see you!" he shouted. With his head still in the door, Billy spoke again, his voice quieter. "She says she needs work done on her house."

The door opened wider, and Billy backed out of the way, making room for Mike to exit the house.

Mike's eyes lit up when they settled on Abby. "Hello. I'm Mike." He grinned, reaching his hand out to shake hers.

Abby took his hand and smiled. Her gaze lowered to Mike's arms and shifted to his chest before meeting his stare again.

"Hello, Mike. I'm Abby." She smiled coyly and pulled her hand away.

"So, Billy tells me you need work done on your house?" Mike said.

"Yes, I do. A *lot* of work."

"Well, it'll just be me around for a couple of weeks, but I'm sure that I can handle it," Mike said with confidence.

"Maybe Jason can help you?" Billy said. "I'm sure he's gonna be bugging you every day anyway since Sami won't be around."

Mike nodded. "Yeah, I'm sure he'll help. So, Abby, when and where do you need us to show up?"

"I'm actually staying at the motel in town until the house is completed. Or at least until it's habitable. The sooner the better, I guess. It's the house on Farmington Road."

"Really? The old Williams place, huh? That house *is* gonna need some work. It's been vacant for quite a while." Mike rubbed his chin and thought for a moment. "We can meet you there tomorrow to go over all the details."

"Thank you! That would be great!" She beamed. "Is nine o'clock too early for you?"

"No, that's fine with me," Mike replied.

"I'll see you tomorrow, then. It was nice to meet all of you. Thanks again." She grasped the railing and clomped down the stairs. As she headed across the yard, her heels caught on clumps of grass, and she struggled to balance each wobbly step.

Mike ran over and offered his assistance.

"Oh, why thank you, Mike." She sounded surprised as she took his arm.

Mike walked Abby across the road and opened and shut the car door for her.

Billy smirked. "I think it's finally my turn to harass Mike about the new girl in town."

"It does look like he's drooling a bit, doesn't it?" Sami giggled.

"Yes, he is." Billy wrapped his arms around Sami's waist. "And now, so am I," he said huskily and gave her a gentle kiss.

"Hey, hey, I'm back now," Mike warned.

The corners of Billy's mouth curled upward, and a mischievous spark flashed in his eyes. "You're the one all starry-eyed over the new chick. Even Sami noticed the drool dripping down your chin."

"If you know what's good for you, you'll shut your mouth, little brother!" Mike eyed him, daring him to continue.

Billy strutted to his car and opened and closed the door in a whimsical manner, mocking the show Mike had just put on for Abby.

Sami laughed. She looked at Mike and pushed his arm. "That's exactly what you looked like just now."

"Whatever!" Mike shook his head. As soon as Billy hopped onto the porch, Mike punched him in the arm and went inside.

Billy flashed a smug grin and rubbed his arm. "I guess he didn't like that."

"I guess not." Sami snickered. "But payback's a bitch."

"Yes, it is," Billy agreed, raising his eyebrows. "That's the first time I've ever heard you say anything vulgar, and I like it." He grinned before he planted a delicate kiss on her lips. "Have I ever told you how amazing you are?"

Sami smiled, feeling heat rise to her cheeks. "No, but keep going."

"Well, you are the most *amazing* woman in this entire world, and I love you more than you will ever know."

His tone was playful, yet Sami knew he meant every word.

He leaned down and kissed her again.

"I love you that much too, Billy," Jason said.

They pulled their lips apart and turned their heads.

Jason stood there, grinning.

"Ugh!" Billy's expression fell flat. "Dude, don't you have a home?"

"Yes, but I'm here for dinner. Mike's gonna order pizza. You know, Sami, as long as you're giving out kisses…" Jason puckered his lips.

"You better put those back before you lose 'em!" Billy warned.

"Maybe next time then." Jason shrugged and went into the house, letting the screen door bang shut behind him.

Sami smiled, but it quickly faded with a heavy sigh and an even heavier heart. "It's almost like things are back to normal, yet they aren't." She felt like a bag of mixed emotions. One minute she was laughing, and the next she was ready to cry again.

"I know. It'll be a while before you feel like yourself again. Before we both do. I think getting away will help."

"Yeah, me too." Sami wiped a lost tear from her cheek. "Uh, Billy…I sort of wanted to talk to you about something else."

"About what?" His eyes filled with worry.

She sat on the porch chair and pulled him down next to her.

"Is everything okay?"

"Well, as okay as everything can be for now. But this is about the extra medication the nurse gave me this morning." She bit her lip. "It's not really medicine. It's birth control pills." She stared down at her gray sneakers, afraid of his reaction. He'd been happy when he'd found out they were having a baby. She didn't want to disappoint him by trying to prevent it from happening again. Yet, they were in no position to become parents anytime soon.

"Oh…well, I guess that's a good thing, right?" A long sigh escaped his lips, and he lowered his head. "But I'm sad we lost our baby. A part of me is gone now too. And I wish I could change that, but I guess it wasn't meant to be." Tears swelled in his eyes and he gulped. "So, for now, until we get past this nightmare of a life we've been living and things get back to normal around here, I'm relieved we're being more careful. There's no way I could go through anything like this again so soon." He quickly wiped away a tear.

Tears filled Sami's eyes. She wanted to ease his pain, but she couldn't even heal hers at the moment. She wrapped an arm around his waist. "I'm sorry you're hurting too, Billy."

He shook his head. "I just…I can't lose anyone else in my life." Tears spilled over his lower lashes and rolled down his cheeks. He wrapped his arms around her and buried his face in her neck, releasing his pent-up pain.

Sami tightened her grip on him as his shoulders shook. "I know, Billy…." She cried with him. "I know…."

They held each other for a long moment, tears falling, trying to heal each other's pain with their love.

23

S AMI WENT into her bedroom and shut the door. Though nothing had changed, her room felt emptier now. Or maybe she just felt more alone.

Determined to get a good night's rest, she dressed in her favorite oversized gray T-shirt—a gift from Billy that he didn't know about yet—and her cozy pink pajama pants. She turned off the light and lay down in her bed, staring at the shadows of the trees on the walls. Though she was still wary of what might be lurking in the forest, the darkness of her room didn't scare her anymore.

Sami closed her eyes, intent on getting a good night's rest, but she couldn't stop thinking about the previous day's tragedies. The werewolf. Waking up in a cage. Jessica hitting her. The blood. The silver hunting knife. The fear. The searing pain as her uterus shed itself of the life growing inside of her.

"No!" She sat straight up and snatched the bottle of sleeping pills from the nightstand. She didn't like how groggy she'd felt when she had woken up this morning in the hospital, but she needed a peaceful night's rest.

"I have a better plan," she whispered and set the bottle back on the nightstand. She slid her feet into her gray fuzzy slippers, and tiptoed downstairs. Opening the front door as quietly as possible, she went outside and locked the door behind her.

The cold night air crept up her arms and she shuddered. "Darn it. I should've put on a hoodie," she whispered.

She eyed the forest. Though the full moon was bright, dark shadows loomed everywhere.

Before she could talk herself out of it, she hurried down the steps and across the yard toward Billy's, being careful not to reinjure her ankle. The glow from the window's meant someone was awake. But it didn't matter if they weren't. She was intent on seeing Billy tonight, even if she had to pound on his window to wake him.

She opened the screen door and knocked on the front door, looking behind her for any signs of danger.

The door opened. "Sami? What's wrong?" Billy's eyes grew wide. He grabbed her arm and pulled her inside while scanning the darkness. "What are you doing?" He shut the door and locked it.

She shivered and rubbed the cool skin of her arms. "I couldn't sleep. I had to see you."

"You're freezing." Billy took off his hoodie and wrapped it around her.

"It's so warm." She smiled.

"Come here." He guided her to the front of the couch and sat down. Before she could sit he pulled her into his lap.

She snuggled against him with her legs stretched across the couch.

"I thought you were done going outside by yourself around here at night," he said in a scolding tone.

"I know, but I just needed to see you." She stuck out her bottom.

He smiled and kissed the tip of her nose. "You could've called. I would've come over. I was just sitting here missing you anyway."

"I didn't even think about calling you first. All I kept thinking about was everything that happened yesterday. I couldn't stop. All of these horrifying images kept running through my mind." She sighed and shook her head.

Billy tightened his grasp around her. "I'm sorry. I wish I could make you feel better. Did you take a sleeping pill?"

"No. I don't want to. It just made me feel tired today. But I feel better when I'm with you." She gave him the biggest puppy-dog eyes she could muster. "Can I stay with you tonight? *Please*?"

"Of course, you can. To tell you the truth, I couldn't sleep either. I'm glad you're here. I wanted to call you, but I was afraid you might be sleeping."

"Good. I was afraid I might be bothering you if I came over too late," she admitted.

"What? There's no way you could ever bother me, Sami. I *love* you." He gave her a soft kiss.

She pulled away just far enough to speak, their warm breaths still touching. "I love you too, Billy," she whispered and placed her lips on his again.

After a long, tender kiss, Billy lifted his head and sighed. "Maybe now that we're together, we can finally get some sleep."

"I hope so." She climbed off his lap and stood.

Billy hopped up and guided her down the hall and into his bedroom.

He locked the door and waited until Sami was under the covers before he turned out the light and climbed into bed next to her.

She snuggled against his chest and smiled, feeling content.

Billy kissed her on top of the head. "Good night, Sami."

"Good night, Billy," she whispered.

A LOUD banging jarred Sami from her sleep. Confused, she sat up, flinching from the blinding sunlight. Blocking the beam of light with her hand, she glanced around Billy's bedroom.

"What the hell is he doing?" Billy muttered and sat up.

"Billy!" Mike yelled through the door. "Is Sami in there with you?"

Sami looked at Billy, wide-eyed, afraid of how Mike would react when he saw her. "Is it not okay for me to be here?" she whispered.

Billy pushed the covers aside and climbed out of bed. "Don't worry, it's fine. He's not my dad." He went to the door and opened it. "She's here," he snapped and stepped aside, motioning toward her with a swoop of his hand.

Mike stood in the doorway, wearing a pair of black boxers.

Startled to see him nearly naked, Sami looked down at her fingernails, pretending to inspect them.

Mike breathed a sigh of relief and lifted his cell phone to his ear. "Yes, she's here, Carol."

Sami cringed.

"I will." Mike lowered his phone. He shook his head, his eyes full of warning. "Your mom was worried sick when she woke up this morning and you weren't there. And then *I* was worried that something might've happened to you again."

"Sorry, I guess I should've left a note. I was just too upset to be alone," she admitted.

Mike sighed. "I understand, Sami. I'm just glad you're safe." Without another word, he went down the hallway.

"Well, let's get you home," Billy said and helped her out of bed. He eyed her oversized gray T-shirt. "Hey, I was looking for that shirt. I thought Mike stole it."

Sami bit her lip, hoping he wasn't mad. "You left it at my house the night I spilled milk on it. Thank you for letting me borrow it."

Billy winked. "What's mine is yours. Come on." He led the way out of his house and across the yards, stopping at the bottom of her porch steps. "I don't think I should go in there with you. It might make things worse."

"I think you're right," Sami agreed. She didn't really want him to hear the scolding she was about to suffer anyway. "I'll come over a little later."

"All right." He gave her a reassuring smile and waited until she was in the house before he headed home.

Sami shut the front door and turned around to see her mother standing in the kitchen, wrapped in a fuzzy blue robe. She looked much better today. The color had returned to her cheeks, and the dark circles around her eyes were hardly visible.

"Samantha," Carol said with a look of disappointment. "I was so worried. I thought something happened to you. Or that you wandered off to the lake again or something."

Sami eased her mother's worries with a quick hug. "I couldn't sleep last night, Mom. I just kept thinking about everything, and I didn't wanna take a sleeping pill. So, I went to Billy's. I feel safe when I'm with him."

Dreading the lecture, Sami went to the couch and sat down.

She focused on her mom, who was now standing next to the breakfast bar. If her mother insisted on scolding her like a child, she would just have to set things straight and demand to be treated like an adult.

"Well, you're definitely not a little girl anymore. You're twenty. I know you're responsible." Carol pressed her lips together and shrugged. "Just leave a note next time. Okay, sweetheart? Just so I know you're safe, that's all. Nothing else."

Sami's mouth hung open. "What? You mean you're not mad at me?" An understanding reply from her mother was the last reaction she'd expected. She had been prepared to spar for the next hour, not come to an agreement.

"No, I'm not mad at you. It's time to let my baby grow up. You're an adult now." Her mother's eyes glistened with tears, but a sudden look of determination replaced her sorrow.

"Of course, I still have *household* rules. I don't want to open your bedroom door and find Billy in there with you. But, if it would help you sleep better—especially while I'm at work—I don't mind if he sleeps on the couch or in the guest bedroom. Or, if you need to be at his house, I understand. I know you two love each other and that you need privacy in your relationship."

Grinning, Sami jumped off the couch and hugged her. "Thanks for understanding, Mom. I promise I'll leave a note next time."

"Okay. I'll keep my promise, if you keep yours. And be careful with your ankle. You're going to reinjure it."

"Okay." Sami headed upstairs. "I'm gonna go get ready for my day."

"Good idea. Me too," Carol said.

After her shower, Sami took more ibuprofen to keep the aches away. Then, she went to her bedroom and dressed, deciding to wear Billy's favorite outfit in hopes to lift his spirits—her light blue skirt and white tank top. Staring in the mirror, she frowned at the bruises on her arms and face. She snatched her light-weight hoodie from the hook on the back of her door and put it on.

"Much better." She held her chin high and headed downstairs. Her smile faded when she saw Brenda sitting at the breakfast bar, talking to her mother. She stopped in the middle of the stairs.

What's she doing here? Is she gonna arrest me? Kill me?

"Hello, Samantha." Brenda stood to greet her.

Trying to keep a cool exterior, Sami finished descending the steps and gave Brenda a quick nod. "Hello." She looked at her mom. "Well, I'm going over to Billy's, Mom."

"Actually," Brenda said, "I'm here to get your statement on what happened the other day. I was advised to give you a day to recuperate. How are you feeling?"

"Better."

"Good. I'm glad to hear that. Let's go outside, and you can tell me what happened."

Carol gave an encouraging nod.

Sami followed Brenda out onto the porch and sat on the top step next to her.

"Okay," Brenda said, pulling a small notebook from her back pocket. "Tell me what happened first."

Taking in a deep breath, Sami forced herself to relive the tragedy. "Well, we were at the lake, and that's where I was…*taken*," she replied carefully. Afraid of reporting the wrong information and putting all their lives at risk, she waited for Brenda to guide her into the next answer.

"And what, or *who*, was it that took you?" Brenda asked.

Sami remained quiet, unsure of how to answer. She glanced over at Billy's house and saw him, Mike, and Jason standing on the front porch with their arms crossed, glaring in her direction. Their presence gave her the courage to continue.

"Jessica. Jessica took me," she replied.

"You saw her?"

"Yes," Sami replied diligently, remembering to keep quiet about which form she saw her in.

"How did she kidnap you?"

"I'm not sure—maybe she had help. I fainted, and then, I woke up in a cage…in Jessica's basement." Sami shook her head, trying to clear the mental image.

"I'm sorry this is hard for you. We'll be done in a minute." Brenda gave a reassuring smile before she continued. "How'd you get the bruises?"

Sami couldn't wait for the test to be over. She glanced over at Billy again, longing for his comfort. He uncrossed his arms, took a step forward, and gripped the porch railing. It looked as if he were ready to hop over it and sprint toward her. Sami turned her attention back to Brenda.

"Jessica hit me a few times, knocking me to the floor. And she smashed my face against the bars of the cage. She said she was gonna kill me. That she wanted my—"

A jolt of fear shot through Sami's chest at her near slipup. She eyed Brenda, wondering if she was a werewolf too. Sami imagined giving the wrong answer and Brenda turning into a killer beast. She shook the thought away and continued.

"She wanted Billy, and I messed everything all up."

Brenda nodded her approval. "Okay, keep going."

"I broke the window in the bathroom hoping someone would notice and look through it. I accidentally cut my finger—" she held up her bandaged finger "—so I wrote my name with blood on the back of the bathroom door so that whoever looked in the window would see it. And it worked. Jason found me because of it. Billy and Mike found me also. They took me to the hospital."

"Where was Jessica during the last part?" Brenda narrowed her eyes in warning.

Afraid, Sami looked back at Billy, wishing he'd come over and help her through the questions. Scowling, Billy hit the railing with the palm of his hand and shook his head. Jason ran a hand through his hair and began to pace the porch. Mike continued to stare in their direction, his expression stone cold and his arms crossed.

Brenda let out an impatient breath and looked over at the three men. "They were informed to stay put until we're done. So, are you going to give me your full attention now?"

Not wanting to ire Brenda further, Sami nodded.

"Good girl," Brenda said flatly. "Now, where was Jessica when they found you?"

"She left before they got there. I don't know where she went. She didn't say."

Brenda looked pleased. "Well, now, that wasn't so hard, was it?"

Sami bit her lip and shook her head. "But—" she leaned in closer to Brenda so that her mother couldn't hear "—my mom doesn't know about the baby part. And I don't want her to."

Brenda nodded. "I haven't given her any details. Since you're a grown woman, it's up to you what you share with her."

"Thanks."

"Okay, that's all." Brenda stood and smiled. "You take care now. Tell your mom I said bye." She strutted to her squad car, hopped in, and drove away.

Sami jumped up and headed across the yard toward Billy's house, but he was already at her driveway. She threw herself into his arms and breathed a sigh of relief.

"Are you okay?" Billy asked, sounding relieved.

"Yeah, I think so. It was so creepy talking to her."

"I know. We had to talk to her the other night at the hospital. She was pretty threatening. She even warned us this morning to stay away while she talked to you. She's definitely not the same Brenda I used to know. But at least it's over now." He hugged her again.

"Are you okay, Sami?" Jason asked as he approached. "That bitch wouldn't let us near you until she was done."

"I will be once I can put all of this behind me," Sami said.

Mike came up behind Billy and put his hand on his shoulder. "Are you two gonna be all right? Jason and I have to meet with Abby."

"Yeah, we're good," Billy said.

"Okay, you ready?" Mike looked at Jason.

"I'm more ready to kick some ass," Jason said.

Mike swatted him in the middle of the back. "Maybe we can get started today, and you can work off the anger."

"Maybe," Jason said. He and Mike headed to the yellow car parked in front of Billy's house.

A wave of nausea churned Sami's gut. She put her hands over her queasy stomach and hesitated.

"Sami, didn't you eat?" Billy scolded.

"No, Brenda sort of sidetracked me."

"Come on." He grabbed her hand, led her across the yard, and into his house.

Sami sat at the dining table, while Billy went to the kitchen.

"Lucky for you, Mike made biscuits and gravy this morning."

Sami's mouth watered at the thought. "Ohhh, that sounds so good. I wonder why I keep feeling sick."

"So, this isn't normal for you?" Billy asked as he prepared her a plate.

She shook her head. "Getting car sick is normal for me, but getting randomly sick isn't. It started recently, since I moved here. Maybe it's all the stress I've been through?"

"It could be. Have you seen a doctor for it?"

"No."

"Maybe it's time to go in and get checked."

"I will when we get back from our trip."

"Good. Here you go, milady." He winked and set the meal before her, along with a fork and a napkin.

"Thank you, kind sir." She snickered and eagerly dug into the savory food. She watched Billy wash the dishes as she ate, her mind on their upcoming trip to Monterey. A week was too long to wait. She wanted to go now—to get away from the horrifying thoughts and the constant fear of what might be hiding in the shadows.

"Billy, I was wondering…"

"What were you wondering?" He glanced up from washing a pot and flashed a warm smile.

"I'm ready to leave sooner, if that's all right with you?" She held her breath and waited, hoping he'd say yes.

Billy raised his eyebrows. "Sure. That's fine with me. What changed your mind?"

"Brenda. And not being able to sleep." She shook her head. "All I see when I close my eyes is Jessica. And I keep waiting for red eyes to appear in the forest. I need to get away, with you, to try to forget for a little while."

"Okay, let's leave today."

"Today? Really?"

"Yes, today." Billy grinned. "Now, hurry up and finish your breakfast so we can go tell your mom."

"Yay! I'm so excited!" She shoveled the rest of the food into her mouth, and they hurried next door to tell her mother the good news.

Sami burst through the front door just as her mother exited the kitchen.

Her mother's eyes widened and she clutched her chest. "Sami, you scared me!"

"Sorry, Mom." Sami giggled. "I'm just excited. We've decided to leave today."

"I think that's a great idea!" Carol smiled. "Your dad won't be there for a few days though, he's on a business trip. I'll call him and let him know you're coming now. He sure is going to be happy to see you."

"So, you don't think he'll be mad that Billy and I will be there alone for a couple of days?"

"Don't worry about that. I'll talk to him," she said.

Billy gave Sami's hand a gentle squeeze. "I'm gonna go home and pack. I'll be back in a few minutes."

"Okay." Sami walked him out to the front porch. "Let's see who can pack the fastest."

Billy grinned. "You're on!" He bolted down the steps and ran across the yard.

She went inside and headed upstairs to gather her things. Within ten minutes, her suitcase was packed, and she hurried back downstairs to wait for Billy. To her surprise and disappointment, Billy was sitting on the couch.

"Uh! That's not fair. How did you get back here so fast?" she asked.

"Magic," he taunted, raising one corner of his mouth.

Carol came out of her room with money in her hand.

"No, Mom. I don't need any more money. I still have more than enough left from what you and Dad gave me."

"Well, it's not for you. It's for Billy," Carol said as approached him.

"What?" Billy said with a surprised look and stood from the couch.

"No, I don't need any money, Carol. Really. I've got it covered."

"Please, take it!" she insisted, holding the money in front of him. "It's for gas." When he didn't take the money, she shoved it into his shirt pocket and patted it closed. "Your car is a gas guzzler," she teased. "And Samantha is my daughter. I'm going to help, and you're going to let me."

Billy nodded his defeat. "Thank you."

"Well, you two had better get going." She gave Sami a hug. "You feel better, sweetheart, and call me when you get there."

"Don't worry, Mom. I will, and I will." Sami smiled and gave her mother a big squeeze before pulling away.

Carol hugged Billy. "You take care of my daughter."

"I will," he assured and patted her back. Then, he picked up Sami's suitcase and headed outside.

Sami followed him across the yards and to his car. She climbed into the passenger seat and waved to her mother. "Bye, Mom," she shouted.

Carol waved from the porch.

Billy put Sami's suitcase in the trunk and hopped behind the wheel. The engine roared to life and they headed down the road.

"What about Mike and Jason?" Sami asked.

Billy turned right at the stop sign. "We're headed there now. I called Mike and told him to meet us at the mouth of Farmington Road."

"Oh, where Abby lives?"

"Yeah, it's on our way," he said.

Within a minute, Billy slowed down.

Mike and Jason were waiting on the left shoulder of the road, leaning against Jason's car.

"That was fast," Sami said. "Her house is close."

"Yep. I'm sure Mike's happy about that." Billy parked next to Jason's car and climbed out.

Wearing a big smile, Jason hurried around the front of Billy's car and opened Sami's door.

"Thanks, Jason." She got out and gave him a big hug.

"I sure am gonna miss you," he said, his tone genuine.

"Yeah, I'll miss you too." She frowned.

"Well, little brother." Mike hugged Billy with one arm and swatted him on the back. "I'll see you in a couple of weeks."

"Yep. Try not to give Jason too hard a time in my place." Billy stepped away from his brother and gave Jason gave the same manly half-hug.

With a soft smile on his face, Mike approached Sami and hugged her, handling her as if she were fragile. "You get better. And take care of my little brother."

"I will." Sami smiled.

"So, Mike—" Billy gave a quick nod toward Jason "—are you sure you can handle the remodel with only Jason here to help?"

"Gee, thanks for the support," Jason said dryly.

"You take Sami away from here and have some fun for once, Billy. You both need it. Of course, I'm sure Jason's work doesn't compare to yours." Mike smirked.

"Screw you guys!" Jason said.

"I'm sure you do great work, Jason," Sami said, taking his side.

"Thank you, Sami," Jason said with a smug grin. "It's nice to know that I have one friend around here who appreciates me."

"Lucky for you," Billy teased. "Well, we should hit the road. I wanna make it as far as we can before we hit traffic."

"Okay." Sami nodded, more than ready to leave Wolf Hill far behind.

Jason opened the passenger door again.

"You're such a gentleman, Jason," Sami said as she climbed in.

Jason shut the door and pushed the lock down. "Roll up your window."

She smiled at his caring gesture. "Oh, and will you two check in on my mom for me? I'm sure Steve will be there most of the time, but just in case."

"We will," Mike and Jason said in unison as they peered through her window.

Billy slid onto the driver's seat and started the engine.

"Hey, don't forget to bring me back some souvenirs," Jason said. "Oh, and maybe a hot California chick too." He flashed a charming grin and raised his eyebrows.

"We'll see what we can do, Jason. As long as she's cheap," Billy teased.

They all laughed.

A heaviness filled Sami's heart. "I know it's only for a little while, but I'm really gonna miss you guys."

"We'll miss you too, Sami. And don't worry about your mom, we'll look after her," Mike said. He tapped the hood of the car and he and Jason took a step back.

"I'll call you when we get there, bro." Billy stepped on the gas pedal and the car rolled forward.

Sami peered out the back window.

Jason and Mike were smiling and waving.

She smiled back at them and waved until they faded into the distance.

"Are you sure you wanna leave?" Billy glanced over at her.

"Yeah, are you?"

He let out a low throaty chuckle. "Of course! I get to spend some time with you alone. *Finally.*"

"Good, because I was looking forward to that too." She smiled.

They continued to drive at a steady speed, only slowing when they reached town. As soon as they were out of town limits, Billy sped up again, welcoming the open road.

Sami gazed out the window, mesmerized by the lush green forest as it passed by.

A sudden streak of red appeared next to a tree.

Sami sucked in a fearful breath. "What the…?" She turned her head, straining to focus on the same spot as they drove away, but there was nothing there.

"What is it?" Billy asked anxiously, slowing to scan the forest.

"I thought I saw something red, kind of like eyes. Did you see anything?"

"No, I didn't see anything." He glanced in the rear-view mirror and back to Sami, his eyes full of worry.

She stuck her head out the window and studied the forest behind them, seeing nothing out of the ordinary. She turned back to Billy and shrugged. "I guess it was nothing. It was probably just red flowers or the leaves of a red plant." She gave him a reassuring smile. "I didn't see any fur or anything. Just a glimpse of red."

Billy crinkled his forehead. "Are you sure? Maybe it was a wolf, uh, werewolf. I don't think I'll ever get used to saying that." He shook his head.

"No, I'm sure it wasn't, Billy. It's daylight out. I would've seen it. I'm sure it was just my mind playing tricks on me."

He let out a heavy breath and stepped on the gas. "You scared me there for a minute."

"I'm sorry." She stuck out her bottom lip.

"Don't be sorry." He smiled and wrapped his hand around hers.

She smiled back at him, enjoying his loving touch and anticipating their time ahead.

Back in the forest, a menacing growl erupted as a werewolf stepped out from behind the trunk of a large pine. Standing on the side of the road, its eyes blazed red with fury as it watched Billy and Sami drive out of sight.

THE STORY CONTINUES

AN OBSESSED WEREWOLF WILL DO ANYTHING TO SATISFY ITS CRAVING.

Not convinced the danger is gone, Sami and Billy dread returning to Wolf Hill. They just can't shake the feeling another werewolf is out there, waiting for its chance to strike, especially as Sami's nightmares become more frequent and disturbing. When she runs into a stranger in the middle of the forest, Sami's deepest fears resurface, compelling the three men in her life to do what it takes to protect her. But when one of them is bitten and another disappears without a trace, Sami puts her own life in danger to discover the truth—a decision that turns her nightmares into a reality.

Moonlit Shadows Bitten is available on amazon.com,
or you can find it by visiting my website **www.shawnagautier.com**.

THANKS FOR READING!

I hope you enjoyed *Moonlit Shadows Taken*, book one of the Moonlit Shadows Series. I'd love to hear your feedback. You can leave a review on Amazon.

Thank you!

ABOUT THE AUTHOR

SHAWNA GAUTIER lives in Northern California with her husband, daughter, and two sons. She loves being outdoors, and some of her activities include camping, dirt-bike riding, and going to the beach.

So far, Shawna has written the Moonlit Shadows Series, a four-book YA/adult paranormal fantasy series, and Under the Midnight Stars, an adult contemporary romance.

Please visit Shawna's website to learn more about her books, upcoming new releases, and to sign up for her newsletter·

WWW.SHAWNAGAUTIER.COM

Made in the USA
Monee, IL
25 February 2021

61291440R00194